A YUMCHA STUDIOS GRAPHIC NOVEL

VOLUME 1

ENTER THE DUMPLING

Created and Written by

COLIN GOH & YEN YEN WOO

Illustrated by

SOO LEE

Colored by

LAUREN BAKER

This volume contains Dim Sum Warriors
episodes 1 through 6 in their entirety

Story by
Colin Goh & Yen Yen Woo

Illustrations by
Soo Lee

Colors by
Lauren Baker

Lettering by Colin Goh

Cover Illustration by
Colin Goh (pencils), Soo Lee (inks)
& Lauren Baker (colors)

Edited by
Yen Yen Woo & Colin Goh

Published by
Yen Yen Woo

First published by Yumcha Studios LLC through the
Dim Sum Warriors App on the App Store

Published by
YUMCHA STUDIOS
3625 Main Street
Suite 2B
Flushing, NY 11354

ISBN-10: 0988189909
ISBN-13: 978-0-9881899-0-4
Printed in Singapore: 1st printing, October 2012

Table of Contents

What happens when you mix delicious Chinese delicacies (点心 dim sum, or dianxin) with sensational Chinese martial arts adventures (武侠 wuxia)?

YOU GET THE DIAN XIN XIA OR DIM SUM WARRIORS, OF COURSE!

About Dim Sum

The Chinese words 点心 ('dian xin' in Mandarin, and 'dim sum' in Cantonese) literally mean 'a little bit of heart', and refer to a meal consisting mostly of small servings of delicately-crafted morsels, typically accompanied by pots of steaming tea. For more about the long history of dim sum and the different kinds available, visit www.DimSumWarriors.com

SOME OF OUR FLAVOURFUL FIGHTERS

Character

叉烧包太子
PRINCE ROASTPORK BAO
Steamed bun filled with roast pork
Mandarin: Chā Shāo Bāo
Cantonese: Cha Siu Bao

虾饺
XIAJIAO
Steamed shrimp dumpling
Mandarin: Xiā Jiǎo
Cantonese: Har Gau

烧卖
SHAOMAI
Steamed pork and shrimp dumpling
Mandarin: Shāo Mài
Cantonese: Siu Mai

MEET MORE DIM SUM WARRIORS AT WWW.DIMSUMWARRIORS.COM

For all our perfect little dumplings

Creators & Writers
Colin GOH
& Yen Yen WOO

Pencil & Ink Artwork
Soo LEE

Colors
Lauren BAKER

Thumbnails
Colin GOH

Cover Art
Colin GOH, Soo LEE
& Lauren BAKER

Letters
Colin GOH

Graphic Design
Rory MYERS

Art Assistants
James FLORES
& Dion SANDY

Martial Arts Consultant
Suo LIU

Editors
Yen Yen WOO
& Colin GOH

Publisher
Yen Yen WOO

Printer
Tien Wah Press

Inspiration
Kai Kai

Inspiration's Nanny
(without whom this or any work would be impossible)
Min LI

Very Special Thanks To:
Our families, Julian Kwek, Desmond Wee, Sharmila Nair, Shee Tse Koon, Teo Hiang Long, Steven Lo, Jason Lou, Ferry Djongianto, Edmund Baey, Eddie Ng, Daniel Long, Chade-Meng Tan, Simon Siah, Lieng Seng Wee, Judy Lee, Min Min Jiang, Rob Salkowitz, Nick Sousanis, Calvin Reid and all our supporters and friends for believing in the project and everything we do. Thanks too to all the digital pioneers who're paving the way for us in this exciting new era of publishing.

MORE DIM SUM WARRIORS AT WWW.DIMSUMWARRIORS.COM

CHAPTER 1

ENTER THE DUMPLING

WELCOME TO DIM SUM CITY! Proud capital of the great Xiaochi Empire!
INNERSTRENGTH
内劲
ENERGY DRINK
歡迎
INNERSTRENGTH
内劲
ENERGY DRINK
茶

Founded twelve centuries ago when General Meaty Bao united the many squabbling tribes of the Xiaochi Sub-Continent, the Empire is now undergoing a period of unprecedented prosperity and peace, thanks to the leadership of EMPEROR REDBEAN BAO and EMPRESS CUSTARD BAO...
包
包
包
Archival footage of the parade celebrating the birth of Crown Prince Roastpork 'Porky' Bao
- courtesy of Dim Sum News Network

...as well as the legendary DIM SUM WARRIORS, who have valiantly defended the Empire for generations.
The Dim Sum Warriors! Their bravery and skill have inspired millions worldwide, while the mere mention of their names causes enemies to quiver like tofu!

The martial monks of the BOILED KUNG TEMPLE, set high atop Mount Baotang!
The fast-kicking furies who form the BAKED KUNG SISTERHOOD!
The once-great SCHOOL OF STEAM KUNG...
And perhaps the finest of them all...

The fabulous, fantastical, phenomenal
FRIED KUNG ACADEMY!
Winners of the Imperial Dim Sum Olympics nine years in a row!
Voted 'Coolest Kung Fu School' by the Dim Sum City Times and 'The Empire's Hottest Heroes' by Playdough Magazine!
Better Woks and Kitchens
YUM
PLAYDOUGH
What is the secret of their success?

Haaa!
Yaaah!
Waaah!
Aiyeeeah!
AAAAHHHH!
INNERSTRENGTH
内劲
They drink InnerStrength - a powerful taste for those with a taste for power! This Dim Sum City Tourism Board holo-short is sponsored by InnerStrength - the new power drink!
Farm fresh vegetables! Plucked from the soil just this morning!
Shawls! Colorful shawls! Like Grandma used to knit!
Saucy Sisters' Sauces! 100% organic! Spice up your life!
"Once great"? "Finest of them all"? Give me a break!

And what's the big idea covering the School of Steam Kung behind all that mist?
Um, Miss? I'm still here... are you still selling this?
Oh! Sorry! That commercial always annoys me... What was I saying? Oh right, Master Phoenix Claw's Handy Dandy Handi-Wipes clean grease and grime in a single swipe...
Whatever. Your little thingamajig is way overpriced!
Lady Malaigao's Softy-Wofty Spongey-Wongies do pretty much the same thing and they're five for three bucks. Plus, her customer service and retail display are so much better!
"Customer service?" "Retail display?!"

Then!
Why!
Don't!
THWACK!
THWACK!
THWACK!
Aiyah!
THWACK!
You go buy it from her!!!
How trashy can some people get?
Um, Xiajiao? Sis?
That's the third Handi-Wipe you've broken from thwacking somebody today. We have to make up for them, and sales are very slow, which means You-Know-Who is going to do you-know-what to us. *Again.*
-Sigh!- Okay, Shaomai. Hand me a new one...

Okay, now where to find the next suc... I mean, *customer*?
Well, he-llo there!
H'otp'ot Raids On Rise
Excuse me, sir, but can I interest you in Master Phoenix Claw's Handy Dandy Handi-Wipes?
Wipes grease and grime in a single swipe? Um, sir? Yoo-hoo...
KZAAAAK!!!
AIYO!!!
Huh? W-what?

Wow! I'm so sorry! I must have forgotten to deactivate my force field! I'll do it right away!
Ugh... *force field*? Who wears a force field to the street market? Who do you think you are? The Emperor?
Um, a-are you hurt? Can I do anything to help?
A-actually, yes...
Oh! Please don't cry! Wh-what do you want me to do?
Well, how about buying a set of Master Phoenix Claw's Handy Dandy Handi-Wipes?

Grimy windows? A single swipe restores the shine!
SQUEAKY SQUEAK!
Mud on your vaportrolley? The Handi-Wipe soaks it up with our patented polymetasuckolytic technology!
SHLOOORP!
Got the weight of the world on your shoulders? It makes a great massage implement!
THWACKA THWACKA THWACK!
Okay, stop right there! Nice try!
You really had me going for a while with your little act!
"Act"?!
I didn't fake getting zapped by some paranoid doofus's force field, alright?
Sure you didn't! They warned me there would be people like you in the market!
People like *me*? Well, this is your lucky day, Tubby!
I'm going to personally demonstrate a special use of Master Phoenix Claw's Handy Dandy Handi-Wipes just for you!

It's a fantastic SELF-DEFENSE WEAPON!!!
THWACK!
OWWW!!!
Good for multiple assaults!
Whoa, whoa, whoa, Xiajiao! That's enough thwacking for one day!
Whooo...
Why is...
...every-thing...
...spinning?
Hey, you okay? Sorry about my sister...
Aw, Shaomai! I didn't thwack him *that* hard! Besides, he has a force field!

No! I...
I turned
it off,
a-and
uh...
Unh... it's just
that n-n-nobody's
ever t-touched
me...
...before.
Wow,
seriously?
That's kind
of... sad.
But
that doesn't
mean you can
stare at me in
that weird way!
Cut it out!
THWACK!
Xiajiao!!!
What's it with
you and thwacking
people for the slightest
reason? Um, hey... are
you alright? Let me
help you up!

Just. Back. OFF!
KZAAK!!!
Aiyo!
Shaomai!

Just what are you con artists up to? Hitting me, making me see things...
Hey! You started this by zapping me with your fancy force field!

We're just doing everything we can to earn a few bucks to be able to eat...

...you know, after a whole day of standing in the hot sun trying to persuade skeptical folks to buy chicken-feet-shaped sponges!
Xiajiao, just forget it... leave it be.

You're right, Shaomai! We'll never be understood by fat rich kids who can afford force fields anyway.

Well, maybe this will help balance the scales a little.
SHING!
W-what... *Holy Hot Sauce!* This coin...
It's an imperial sovereign! They're incredibly rare and valuable! How...
Hey!
Don't think you can buy us off so easi... Huh? Where did he go?
Who *is* that guy?
Socks! Soooocks!
Genuine certified pre-owned vaportrolleys!
Souvenirs! Novelties! Party tricks!
Homemade jewelry!
Fortunes told!
Holo-games! Newest releases!

O fragrant citizens of Dim Sum City! Do not blink - behold!
From the barren air, I conjure a flame! Let it burn! Let it burn!
But with a whisper from the ancient tongue of my H'otp'ot ancestors...
HOOMBALABALAHOOM!
From the blaze, I bring you a bloom! From the fire, a flower!
Ooh!
Aah!
Wow!

If you enjoyed the show, please throw some-thing into the pot, Sir! So I can go to school, Sir! Thank you!
Oh! That...
CLINK!
This... um...
I want to learn how to do that trick with the flower.

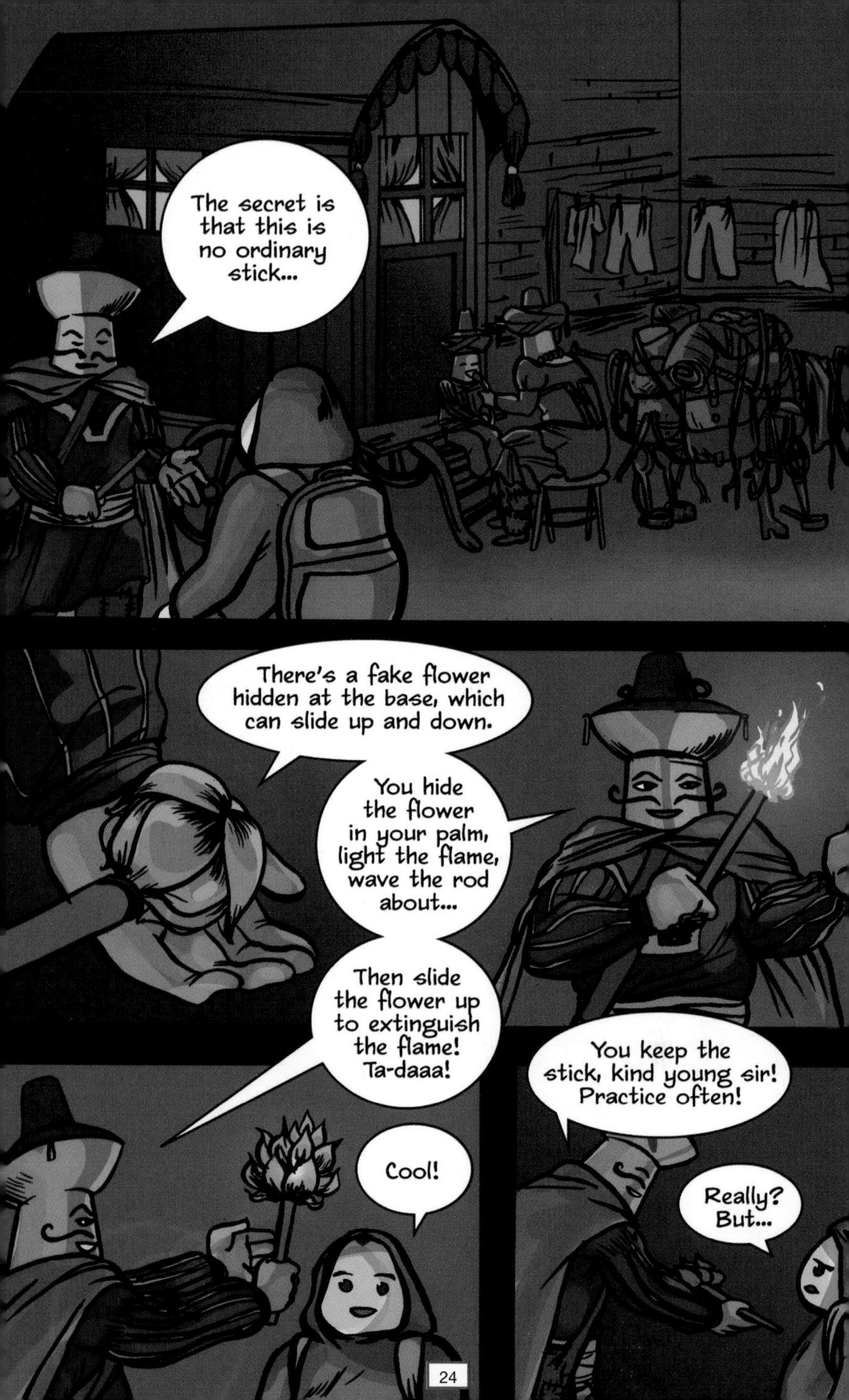
The secret is that this is no ordinary stick...
There's a fake flower hidden at the base, which can slide up and down.
You hide the flower in your palm, light the flame, wave the rod about...
Then slide the flower up to extinguish the flame! Ta-daaa!
Cool!
You keep the stick, kind young sir! Practice often!
Really? But...

...Thank you!
No, thank *you*, young master. I can make another trick stick, but with your coin, we can feed ourselves for three weeks.
We can even afford repairs for our poor old Na'ara here!
And what do you hope to achieve by mastering this trick, young sir? Toimpress a young lady, perhaps? Heh!
Oh no, nothing like that! Heh heh!
Oh! What a sudden, strong wind! A storm must be brewing.
Hm, what is that red light shining on your head, my wife?
Look! What's that?
Oh, no, no, no...

Attention, H'otp'ot scum! Stand away from **Crown Prince Roastpork Bao** or we'll cut you down where you stand!
The Fried Kung Academy?!
Imperial snipers?!!
Crown Prince Roastpork Bao?
...not this again!
TO BE CONTINUED...

CHAPTER 2

FEAST OF FURY

dedicated with awe to Jack Kirby

H'otp'ot scum, release **Crown Prince Roastpork Bao** or the Empire's premier Dim Sum Warriors - the **Fried Kung Academy** - will make you pay!
No! Wait! You don't understand! They didn't...

Aah! Papa! Mama!

My child! Don't hurt my child!

-Uff!-

Filthy terrorists! How dare you sully the Crown Prince's dragon-like physique?

"Dragon-like physique"? STOP!!!

Let them go immediately! That's an Imperial Command!

Your Royal Highness, are you alright? Did they hurt you?

Master Taro Ball.

When your father said you'd gone missing again, I immediately volunteered the services of my A-team.
Of course you did. It's the fourth time you've done it too.
Hey! Didn't you hear me? I ordered your thugs to let them go!
Your Highness, we will let them go. But we need to question them first.
They're innocent! They didn't do anything!
We'll let the Imperial Inquisitors decide that. But please, we must hurry back to the Palace. It's your mother's birthday, and we're already late.
Birthday? ...Oops.

...I'm terribly sorry.
I told them you've done nothing wrong. No harm will come to you - I promise!
Bow when the Crown Prince addresses you!
Hey, Xiajiao, give me a hand with this trash bag, won't y... Oops.
What're *you* looking at?!
Shoo, peasants! This is an Imperial matter. It does not concern you!

It's not my place to say it, Your Highness, but to vanish on this of all days, not to mention wasting valuable police time and the state's money...
I didn't call the police! Cough! Cough!
I was in no cough danger!
Your Highness is perhaps too innocent...
Those were H'otp'ots! Haven't you been following the holo-news? H'otp'ot terror raids have been growing in frequency and daring!
They weren't terrorists! They're an ordinary family!

An ordinary family that stands to profit from a handsome ransom... EEYAH!!!
⥼KzzzzK!⥽ Ah, Taro Ball! Found you at last!
Yeow! Who the...?!
Your holo-phone ⥼KZZZK⥽ must be nearly exploding from my calls! There's a change of plans...
Rrrr! Lousy holo-phone!
When the strikeforce enters the Palace, I need your men to go to Plan Delta 9 instead of ⥼Kzzzzk!⥽
Always picking up other people's calls! Hhh!
FSSH
How could it be another person's call? The dude clearly called you by name!
Heh! These holo-phone marketers get craftier all the time!

Imperial Palace: this is Steamforce Two commencing descent. Codename: Sonofabun is aboard. Prepare reception.
Steamforce Two, this is Imperial Palace. You're cleared for landing. Welcome home, your Highness.
All hail the arrival of Crown Prince Porky Bao! A thousand years! A thousand years!
SSSSSS
SHWASHWASHWA
A thousand, thousand years!
Ffffff Whatever, dudes.
SHWASHWASHWA

Announcing the late arrival of His Royal Highness, Crown Prince Porky Bao!
TARANTARAAAA!
Can we *please* hire taller trumpeters?
MURMURMURMURMURMURMURMURMURMURMUR
Fine! Please... Just carry on as if I never stepped into the ballroom. Or existed.

WHOOF!!!
Oh.
Hi, Dad.
Roastpork
Bao,
I had to lie
to your mother.
Told her you
were late
because you
were doing
homework.
Sorry.
Taro Ball
told me everything.
Consorting with
H'otp'ots? When will
you stop playing
the fool?
Roastpork, you're
going to inherit the
throne someday!

Yeah, well, nobody ever asked *me* if I wanted to be Emperor.
What's that?
Nothing.
Good!
And you wonder why I keep running away.
Let... the... stress... pass... through... my... toes!!!
You've done that for so many years. Has it ever worked?
We'll discuss that later. You should hurry and go wish your mother a happy birthday.
Oh yeah, that.

Um,
I actually have
a present for
her too.
You...
remembered
to get her a
present?!
Porky
Pooples!!!
包
Hey, Mom...
Happy Birthday.

Daddy told me you were being a hardworking little dumpling-wumpling! Were you, my Porky Pooples?
Heh... Mom, I've a gift for you...
Porky Pooples has a birthday prezzie for his Mumsy-wumsy? Oh Porky Poopikins!
Yep... I have it here in my robe...
TA-DAAA!!! Behold, from the barren air, I produce a flame! See it burn, see it burn!
Ooh! You can do magic!
But watch as my fingers waggle an ancient spell, and I whisper the magic words...

Hoombalabala... uh, why is everyone looking at me like that?
Oh.
Yeeeow!!! Excuse me! Sorry! Out of my way!
KA-SPLOSH!!!

FSSSSSSSSSSSSSS
Um, anyway... this was supposed to turn into a flower and...
...happy birthday, Mom..
Let... the... tension... pass... through... my... toes!
TARAN-TARAAAAAAAA!!!
Oh!
Who...

Announcing: **Lady Mango Pudding!**
Sorry I'm late, Your Majesties... but I had to pick up the Empress' present!
Lady Mango Pudding, it's been only days since we last met. How did you become so fu...firm?
I had some secret help... from what I'm now giving to the Empress...
...InnerStrength!
Inner strength?
No, no... "InnerStrength": you have to say it together. It's the health drink everyone is taking nowadays! Drink it and it tackles all your ~ahem~ problem areas...
It's like magic! I've always been lardy... but after just one week of drinking InnerStrength, with no diet or exercise blah blah blah blahblah

What the... Hey! It's you! Aren't you the peddlers from the market?

⇒Munch munch⇐ Well, if it isn't Prince Fancy Force Field himself.

Xiajiao!!! Forgive us, Your Highness! Don't execute us! We didn't know who you were!

Yeah, well... I guess the whole point of my civilian disguise was to hide my true identity. So what're you doing here anyway?

I'm Xiajiao, and this is my little brother Shaomai...

Our *shifu*, Master Phoenix Claw, had to attend in his capacity as the Head of the *School of Steam Kung*. We're here with him.

What? *You're* Dim Sum Warriors?

We're training to be... though I don't know when we'll actually start training!

Aw, Xiajiao, don't be so negative all the time!

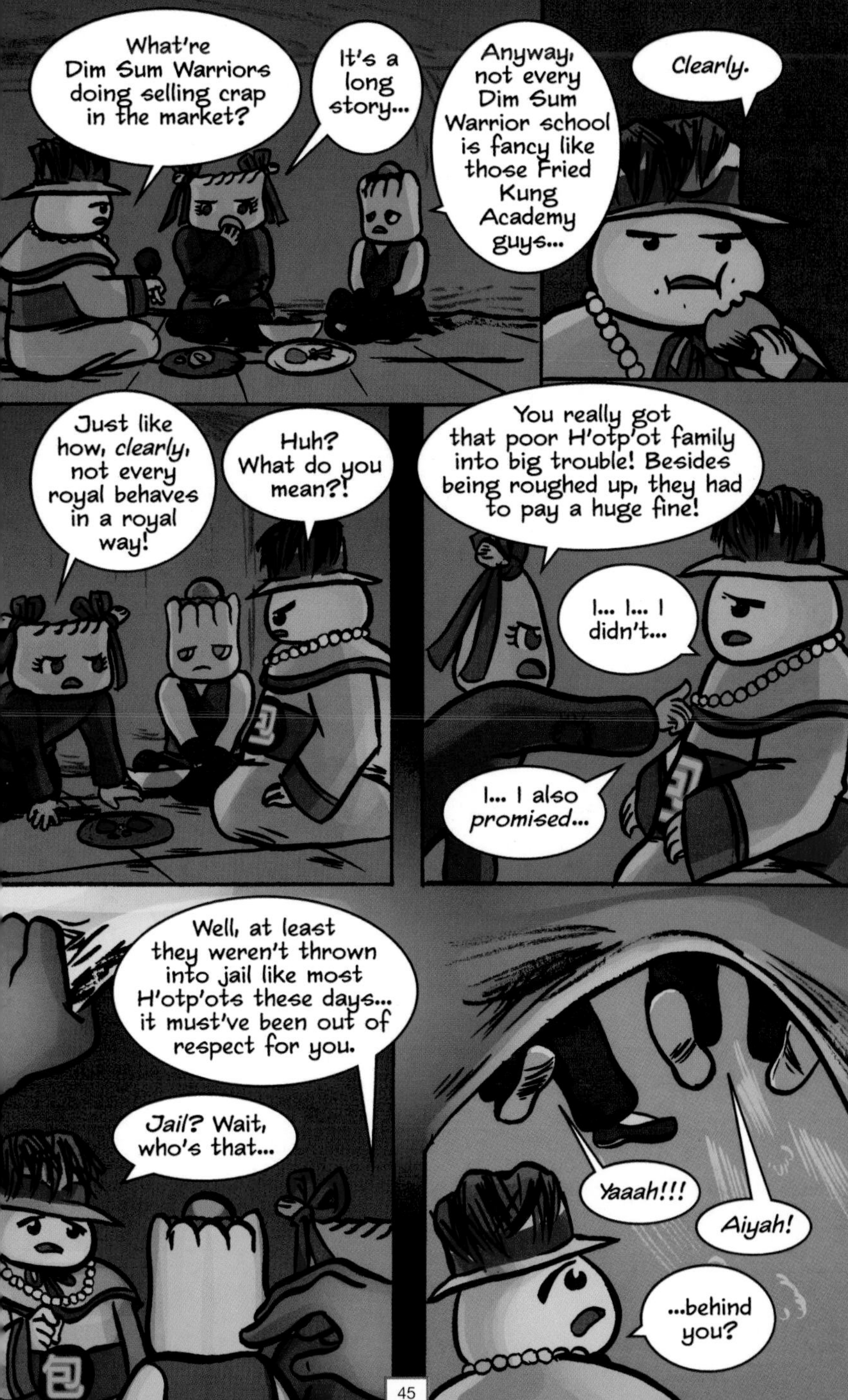
What're Dim Sum Warriors doing selling crap in the market?
It's a long story...
Anyway, not every Dim Sum Warrior school is fancy like those Fried Kung Academy guys...
Clearly.
Just like how, clearly, not every royal behaves in a royal way!
Huh? What do you mean?!
You really got that poor H'otp'ot family into big trouble! Besides being roughed up, they had to pay a huge fine!
I... I... I didn't...
I... I also promised...
Well, at least they weren't thrown into jail like most H'otp'ots these days... it must've been out of respect for you.
Jail? Wait, who's that...
Yaaah!!!
Aiyah!
...behind you?

What's going on...
You pair of greedy, lazy lackeys! How dare you leave the cart unattended while you come here and stuff your faces!
Sorry, Master Phoenix Claw! We were working all morning and just got really hungry and...
...Uh.
I keep telling you: hunger is the best way to train minds! Now your punishment is extra latrine duty... Oh!
Your Highness! I am Master Phoenix Claw, the...
Principal of the School of Steam Kung, I know. Please don't punish your disciples.
It was I who invited them to eat.

Your highness is too kind. These urchins need to build discipline and character.
Give them a break this time.
It's my mother's birthday. Don't spoil the mood.
Your humble servant wouldn't dare!
Um...
Your Highness... Get behind me!
BA-DOOM
-Cough! Cough!- Prince Roastpork Bao, are you alright?
Xiajiao... you saved me?
Your imperial majesties, ladies and gentlemen and other oppressors: kindly get down on the floor...
Who's that?

You are all now hostages of the...
H'OTP'OT REPUBLICAN ARMY!
TO BE CONTINUED...

CHAPTER 3
H'OT P'OT
HIJACK

Emperor Redbean Bao and Empress Custard Bao: for oppressing the proud people of the H'otp'ot nomadic tribes...
You will now be hostages of the *H'otp'ot Republican Army*!
Protect the Emperor and Empress!
Dad? Mom?

Ah, the Imperial Guards - loyal enforcers of tyranny! Our quarrel is not with you lackeys...
Your employers, on the other hand, are a cancer we intend to excise!
WHIZZEOWHIZZEOWHIZZEOWHIZZZING!
Aiya!
Aiyo!
Now, your malignant majesties... if my Windfire Wheel could slice through steel like it was sludge...
...imagine what it might do to flab?

Brother, I've already fettered the lackeys.
Excellent! Now to wrap up this party!
Beanikins!
Be brave, Sweetie-Poo!
Ah, but this is no ordinary party, terrorist...
Ah, there you are! I was wondering when you would show yourselves...
...not when there are senior Dim Sum Warriors in attendance!
MASTER CONGEE
Abbot of the Boiled Kung Temple
MISTRESS BOLUO BUN
Headmistress of the Baked Kung Sisterhood

Holy Hot Sauce!
Xiajiao, we're looking at real Dim Sum Warriors!
Soooo cool, Shaomai!
Wait a second! Master Phoenix Claw, you're a Dim Sum Warrior too! How come you're not joining them and protecting my parents?
Shhh, Prince Roastpork Bao!
I am serving as their secret backup...
...discerning the optimum time to strike through the covert technique of 'Observation Kung'!
Otherwise known as 'Cowering Tortoise Hidden Turtle'.
Xiajiao, be more respectful!
Oh, we were completely prepared to have to deal with the much vaunted Dim Sum Warriors...
We already knew that our weapons wouldn't stand a chance against your fighting skills...

That's why we're aiming at all the other namby pamby guests instead. No matter how fast you are, you can't possibly save everyone in this ballroom.
Scum! We...
Master Congee, Mistress Boluo Bun... stand down.
Majesty?
I won't have innocent blood spilled for me.

Your Majesty is so noble...
But when it comes to spilling innocent H'otp'ot blood, you don't even bat an eyelid!
I have ordered H'otp'ots to be detained, but never executed. What are you *really* here for?
Uh...
If this was really about justice or revenge, you'd have blown us all to pieces by now. Let me guess: you're after some ransom money, right?
Oh no. We want something much more valuable...

...your reputation! Let me activate my ladlecams. I think the whole empire will be very interested to watch this awe-inspiring scene!
"Their great leader, protector and tax collector, his invincible army, and even the legendary Dim Sum Warriors, all laid low by a trio of lowly H'otp'ot nomads!"

This is getting out of hand! Master Phoenix Claw, perhaps it's finally time for you to intervene?
Nay, Your Highness... My finely-honed intuition tells me I should wait a little longer...
You're the head of the School of Steam Kung! How can you cower like this?
Ah, to the untrained eye, this might appear to be cowering, when in reality...
C'mon, Master Phoenix Claw! We've never seen your combat skills! This is a great teachable moment!
Get in there, Phoenix Claw! That's an imperial order!
Sigh!

Salutations, O audacious H'otp'ot!
Who...
What're you saying...
Oh no! Not him!
I was lying there, safe amongst the other hostages, when I said to myself: Master Phoenix Claw (for that is my name), you should be standing with these bold souls instead!
Hey, this guy wasn't in the plan. Should I kil...
We still haven't got the signal. Hold off!
Ahem! I was meaning to say...
Chicken Foot! You're out of your league! Get back!

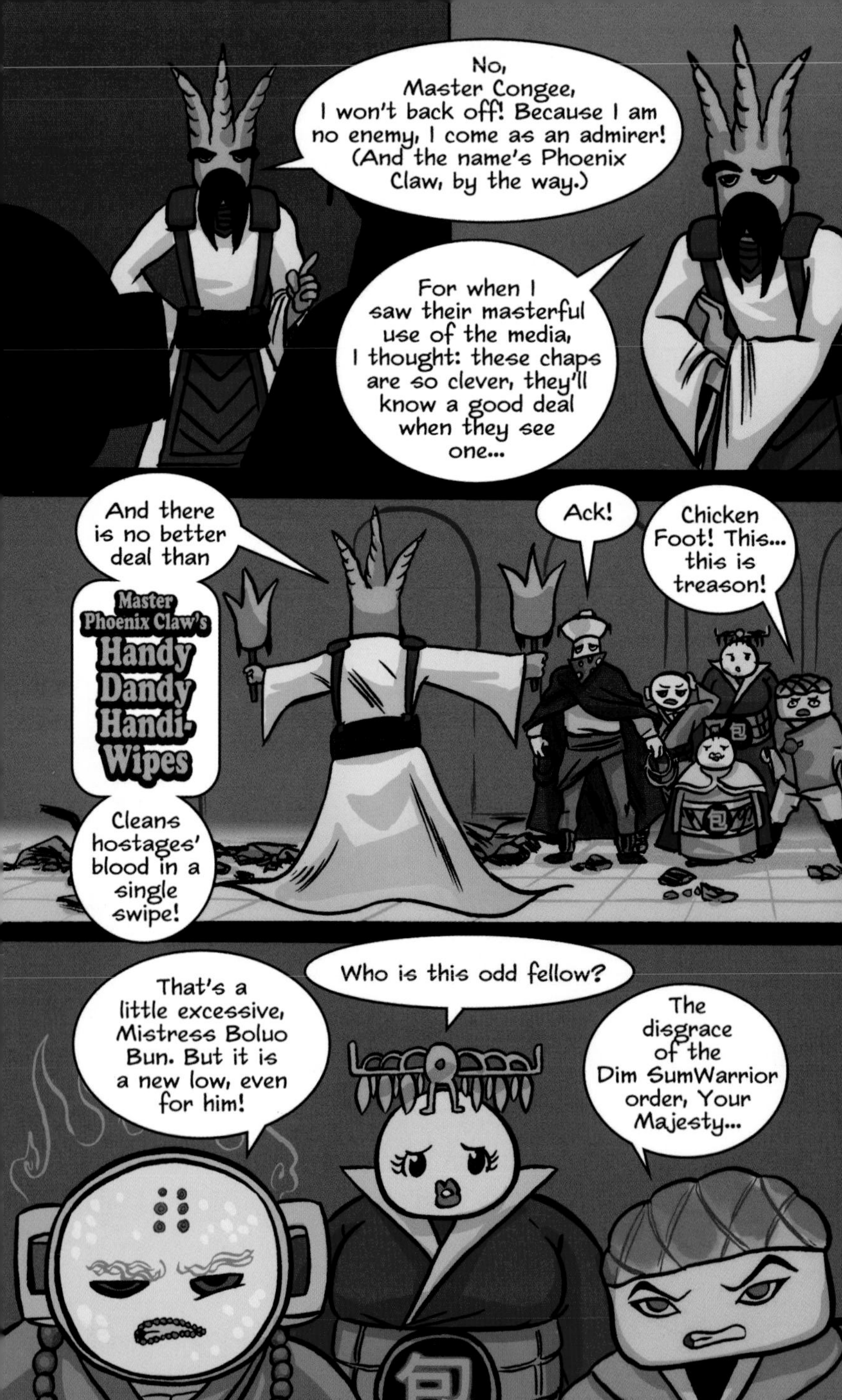
No, Master Congee, I won't back off! Because I am no enemy, I come as an admirer! (And the name's Phoenix Claw, by the way.)
For when I saw their masterful use of the media, I thought: these chaps are so clever, they'll know a good deal when they see one...
And there is no better deal than
Master Phoenix Claw's Handy Dandy Handi-Wipes
Cleans hostages' blood in a single swipe!
Ack!
Chicken Foot! This... this is treason!
Who is this odd fellow?
That's a little excessive, Mistress Boluo Bun. But it is a new low, even for him!
The disgrace of the Dim SumWarrior order, Your Majesty...

AIYO!
Enough! What are you trying to pull here?
-Unf!- You're the one doing the -agh- pulling here, actually...
-Sigh!- We should've known it would end up like this...
Honestly, H'otp'ot, -hnnnh!- I assure you I have no intention of interfering with your affairs...
...Crown Prince Roastpork Bao over there made me do it!
Oh poo.

You have nothing to fear from us, Your Highness. I hear you are a sympathizer to the H'otp'ot cause.
How'd you know...
It's true; I did hang out with a H'otp'ot family. But they're nothing like you creeps.
Porky, stay out of this! You don't...
No, Dad. I *know* bad things are being done to the H'otp'ots.
But terrorizing people like this won't solve the problem.
If you let everyone go safely, I make a personal promise to help your people!
...Where are you? What are you waiting for?

What? Did you say something?
Hurry! This is going waaay off-script! Sonofabun is turning this around!
He'ff talking to fomeone on hif wrift-communi-cator!
Hey! I asked you a question!
We're almost there! Sorry for the delay but You-Know-Who ate some bad beans and had to...
Ah! I hear you coming alrea..
Heads up, H'otp'ot!!!
Mmm! Mmmfff!
YEEEOWW!!! My moustache!
AAAGH!!!

POTSTICKER!
SPRING ROLL!
Let the Empire's premier Dim Sum Warriors teach you a lesson!
THE FRIED KUNG ACADEMY!
CHILI PEPPER!
M-my beautiful moustache! It took me 8 years to grow it!
Your Majesties! Are you alright? It's a good thing my team came just in time to rescue all of you, as well as my ≈heh≈ two fellow Dim Sum Warrior Masters!
Taro Ball... on time and on message as usual.

Um, I don't think it's quite safe to resume the party just yet...
-Unf!-
Let me go!
This Mark-IV
Thermo-Cannon...
...is
primed.
SHKOW

Cough! Cough! Xiajiao, you alright?
Cough! I'm fine, and so's everyone. Looks like the explosion was mostly noise and smoke!
Taro Ball, you really should teach your disciples to think before they start thumping!
Wait! Where's my Porky Pooples?
Nyah, nyah, nyah...
Your precious dumpling is right here, Your Majesties. The bomb's smoke enabled us not just to regroup, but also snag a much more valuable bargaining chip...
Now, you will let us depart here unharmed. No fancy moves! If you try anything funny, Fatty here gets a hole in the head.
"Fatty?"

Nooo!
I beg of you!
Let my Porky
Pooples go!
He's only
little!
Mom,
d-don't...
Beanikins! Hurry!
Get
down
on your
knees with
me and
save our
precious
baby
boy!!!
I...
The ruler of
the Xiaochi Empire
kneels before no
one, and for no
reason.
Beanikins!
He's
our only
child!!!
Roastpork,
when you become
Emperor yourself
someday, you will
understand.
Ha!
But he
may have
no head
left to wear
the crown
if...
what's
this?

YAAAAHHHH!!!
W-what...
Are those... noodles?!
Holy Hot Sauce!
Porky!!!

AIYO!!!
Quick! Secure the H'otp'ots! And don't let them slip away from you again!
Oh, Porky Pooples! Smooch! Smooch! Thank heaven you're safe!
Mooom!!!
Roast-pork, are you...
I'm fine, Dad. Thanks for your concern.
Smoochie smoochie smooch!
Majesty, we can't let our guard down yet. We don't know where these noodles came from, or...
Relax, Master Congee...

...I only use my noodles for good!
便
Who is that?!
Hmm... Why does this guy look so familiar?
EEEK!!! It's him! It's really him!
It's
COLONEL QUICKYNOODLE
NEXT ISSUE:
Just Who Is Colonel Quickynoodle?

CHAPTER 4

THE RIDDLE OF THE NOODLE

Eeeeeee! It's him! It's really him! It's
COLONEL QUICKYNOODLE!
Emperor Redbean Bao, Empress Custard Bao, this is the man I was telling you about just before the H'otp'ots attacked us! Colonel Quickynoodle is: (A) the genius behind InnerStrength, the amazing new health drink; (B) Moolah Magazine's Entrepreneur of the Year; and (C) Dim Sum City Weekly's Eligible Bachelor of the Week!

Oh, he's so awesome!
Majesties, I fear Lady Mango Pudding's hyperbole is completely substantiated.
Ahem! Additionally, the Colonel is the Fried Kung Academy's most generous patron!
To be able to support Master Taro Ball and the Empire's foremost Dim Sum Warrior school is my honor.
Colonel, by rescuing the Prince from those terrorists, you have done the Empire a great service!
Your Majesty is too kind! I merely did my duty as a loyal subject.
Hey, Xiajiao, should we check on Prince Porky? He's looking a bit odd...
He's probably in shock, Shaomai. He was just held hostage, after all...

Um, Your Highness, you okay?
That noodle-headed dude...
...Why is he so familiar?
...Oh!
That was the guy who called Taro Ball back in the Vaportrolley... the one he pretended not to know. But why...
Roastpork! What are you doing mumbling over there? Hurry over and thank Colonel Quickynoodle for saving your life from those H'otp'ots!

Um, yes... thank you so much!
It was my privilege, Highness. I only regret that you had to make my acquaintance under such trying circumstances.
Actually, I learned of you earlier on the Vaportrolley, when Taro Ball tried to dodge your call by frying his holo-phone!
What?!
Ack!
Uh, Majesties, with great respect, I think the Prince's brain has been somewhat addled by his ordeal. There was no such incident...
Brain addled?!! Taro Ball, you lying scum...

GASP!
An imperial rebuke!
This is the first time in history that the honor of a Dim Sum Warrior has been denigrated by a member of the Royal Family! And broadcast in front of millions!
I've only ever showed concern for the welfare and security of the Empire, and yet I've now dragged the Fried Kung Academy into disgrace!
I... but... I meant...
Whisper, whisper
Truly, this will bring about the downfall of our centuries-old institution!

I'mtrulysorry Itakebackeverything IsaidaboutyouTaroBall andbythewaythankyou verymuchColonel Quickynoodle
Oh! Prince Roastpork Bao!
To be able to apologize publicly shows your graciousness!
To have conceded the Royal Family's fallibilty before the screens of every corner of the Empire is truly a magnanimous gesture!
I am touched - touched! - to have been part of this epoch in the Bao Dynasty's long and illustrious rule and I accept Your Highness's apology with all my heart!

THWACK!
Good, that's sorted! Now we can get back to more cheerful matters - like resuming my birthday party!
Oww!!!
Colonel Quickynoodle, you simply must demonstrate your acclaimed merchandise for our guests and us. Let us adjourn to the Throne Room. Courtiers, fresh munchies for all, please!
Hooray!!!
Certainly, Your Majesty!
Owww...
Uh, Dad? I really wasn't lying! There really is something fishy ab...
Enough, Roastpork! You've done enough damage to our Dynastic name for one day!
You need to open your eyes and learn that there's a larger world out there than just what's between your ears!

Prince Porky? Are you feeling okay? That was pretty rough...
Oh, it's you two. Stayed around to see insults added to my injuries, huh?
C'mon, be fair! We just wanted to tell you that we know what it's like for people to always misunderstand you...
Yeah, you're not the only one who's...
Huh. Just a few hours ago in the market, when we first met, you said I'd never understand you, but now you understand me?
Please, I don't need your pity. Thanks for the sentiment, but I grew up in this toxic environment all my life...
...It's not like I'm going to cry over it or whatever. Anyway, you're welcome to join everyone in the Throne Room. There'll be more food.

Prince Porky's putting up a brave front, but I know he's really hurting inside...
We should help him...
Help? How? Maybe he just needs some time to be alone...
No way, Xiajiao!
It's times like these that people need friends the most!
I'm not sure he regards us as friends...
Then we just have to show him that we are!
B-but, Shaomai, he's the Prince and we're just...
Lowly dumplings! There you are!
Aiyo!
Aiyah!

Master Phoenix Claw!
Uh, what's with the fan?
Half his moustache got ripped off by the H'otp'ot terrorist, remember?
=Ahem!= Before I am embarrassed any further, let us hurry and depart the palace.
Um... but we can't! Prince Porky, he... he ordered us to follow him to the Throne Room!
What?! Really?
Yeah! He asked us to, uh, taste his food for him, because, like, the palace kitchen's X.O. rice cakes can be deadly and...
Scamps! Do you expect me to belie...
CHICKEN FOOT.
Eh?

The name is Master Phoenix Claw, you... Oh! It's you, Mistress Boluo Bun.
Spare me the pretension, Chicken Foot. We've known each other since we were children. Anyway, I merely came to say that although we've had our differences, I thought your attempt to distract the H'otp'ots was very brave.
Inelegant to the point of stupidity, but brave nonetheless. There's hope for you yet.
Thank you... I think.
Now, aren't you joining the rest of us in the Throne Room? You're the Master of the School of Steam Kung after all... at least what's left of it.
Sigh! I guess...
Hey! Save some X.O. rice cakes for me!

Your Majesties, Lords, Ladies and fellow subjects, I am truly honored to have your attention on this most august of evenings...

...As honored, I'm sure, as that peon over there is about to feel!
Eh? Who? Me?
Yes! And what's your name?
I... I'm Beancurd Roll. Steward, third class, banquet department.
Oh, old Beancurd Roll, look at your weak arms, wobbly legs, crooked spine... a testament to a life of bending over in subservience! I bet you couldn't even defeat a little girl in combat!
Little girl?
Munch! Munch!
Yes... like this one!
Mmfff! What the...?!
Xiajiao!!!

Oww!
What's this
about?
Come,
little girl. You can
knock this frail old
waiter over. You're a
Dim Sum Warrior,
aren't you?
A Dim Sum
Warrior?!
What're you
saying...
You're one of
Master Phoenix Claw's
disciples, right? Show
us your skill!
Oho!
She's from
the School of
Steam Kung.
Phew!
For a moment
there, I thought she was a
real Dim Sum Warrior, like
those Fried Kung Academy
fellows!
WHAT-DID-
YOU-SAY?!
THWACK!
Aiyaaah!

Steady, old timer... I'll fix you up... with just a teensy weensy drop of InnerStrength!
Ouchie ouchie ouch...
BLOOP!
Gulp!
Urk!
Don't blink, citizens, see what InnerStrength has given Old Beancurd Roll... greater height, strength, and, dare I say it? Even his youth back!
I... feel... FANTASTIC!
Uh-oh...

Come on, you little speck! Let's play again!
KRAKK!
Aiyah!!!
Sir! Please don't hurt my sister!
Oho... so you're related, are you?
Shaomai!
FWUMP!
Then let me organize a little family reunion for you!
Aghhh!!!
Yaaahhh!

Ooh...
Care to try InnerStrength for yourselves, Majesties?
Um...
Ow Ow Ow...
I've shown all of you what it can do...
Stop this!
To peddle a drink, you'd hurt old folks and kids? You're a real sicko!
R-roastpork?
You're up to something, I know it!
Even if other folks can't see it!
Again, Roastpork? This is the last time I'll let you insult me and my guests! When will you learn...
But, Dad...
Ahem! Your Majesty, if I may... it's not the Prince's fault.
It's not?

It's this environment. It's not good for a boy growing into a man. Young men need structure, need discipline...
...need exercise...
They need all this to channel their energy. If Your Majesties will allow an ex-military man to make a suggestion...
What suggestion?
Shut up, Roastpork. Please proceed, Colonel.
Enrol the Prince in the Fried Kung Academy.

Huh? What?
Oh!
Interesting... no member of royalty has been a Dim Sum Warrior for many, many years. But there was a time...
Why the Fried Kung Academy? You and Taro Ball are in cahoots, aren't you?
Shush, Roastpork! But he has a point, Quickynoodle. It's a delicate matter. The Palace can't be seen to favor a particular school...
Your Majesty, that's easily resolved...
Hold a public tournament! Let the four Dim Sum Warrior schools compete in battle for the privilege of enrolling the Prince.
GASP!
I'll cover all the costs. And all ticket sales will go towards the treasury.
Most intriguing.

Wait a minute! Don't I get any say?
NO! No, you do not! I'm your father, I'm the Emperor and I have decided! You're going to Dim Sum Warrior school, and that's final!
I see.
Prince Porky, is there anything we...
Like what? My entire life has been decided for me.
And if you know what's good for you, stay away. I seem to bring bad luck to everyone around me.
Holy Hot Sauce! Xiajiao...
Oh, don't worry, Shaomai. He's the Prince. How bad could things really get for him?
Next Issue THINGS GET REALLY, REALLY BAD

CHAPTER 5
DIM SUM WARRIOR
SMACKDOWN

Good evening, Dim Sum City! This is ***Lady Egg Tart*** reporting to you live from the Imperial Stadium. People are forming seemingly endless lines that snake beyond the stadium gates, waiting to witness the event of the century...
Welcome to the inaugural ***DIM SUM WARRIOR SMACKDOWN!***

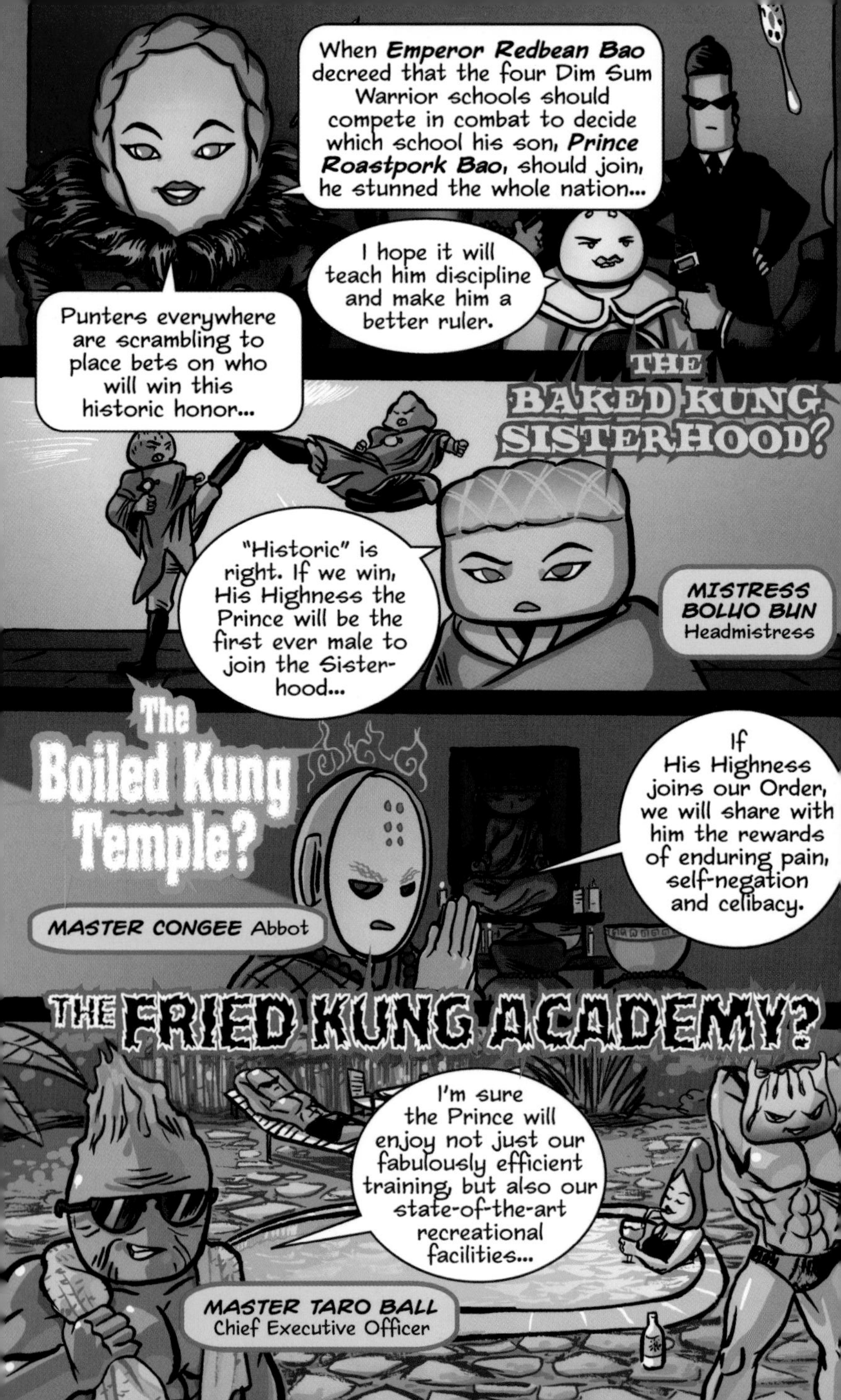
When Emperor Redbean Bao decreed that the four Dim Sum Warrior schools should compete in combat to decide which school his son, Prince Roastpork Bao, should join, he stunned the whole nation...
I hope it will teach him discipline and make him a better ruler.
Punters everywhere are scrambling to place bets on who will win this historic honor...
THE BAKED KUNG SISTERHOOD?
"Historic" is right. If we win, His Highness the Prince will be the first ever male to join the Sister-hood...
MISTRESS BOLUO BUN Headmistress
The Boiled Kung Temple?
If His Highness joins our Order, we will share with him the rewards of enduring pain, self-negation and celibacy.
MASTER CONGEE Abbot
THE FRIED KUNG ACADEMY?
I'm sure the Prince will enjoy not just our fabulously efficient training, but also our state-of-the-art recreational facilities...
MASTER TARO BALL Chief Executive Officer

But there is one Dim Sum Warrior school that has, in fact, produced several Emperors in the past: the School of Steam Kung.
蒸
Unfortunately, ever since the mysterious disappearance of its principal, Master Xiaolong Bao ten years ago, this venerable institution has not been able to recover its former status...
However, its current principal, Master Phoenix Claw, assures everyone that the School of Steam Kung is merely undergoing a "rebranding exercise".
So the School of Steam Kung will be competing for the enrollment of Prince Porky as well?
Well, I can confirm that my disciples will definitely be at the Stadium...

INNERSTRENGTH
内劲
We now return to the Imperial Stadium, where Empress Custard Bao and Emperor Redbean Bao have already arrived. In the procession is the Man of the Moment himself: Prince Roastpork Bao. Prince Porky must be very excited!
Prince Porky, you must be very excited.
INNERSTRENGTH
内劲
I'm thrilled to bits.
This is a very grand event, Colonel Quickynoodle. Thank you for sponsoring it.
Don't mention it, Your Majesty. To be part of this historic occasion is my honor.
To be able to plaster ads for that snake oil of yours everywhere must be pretty satisfying for you too.
Your Highness is referring to my health elixir, *InnerStrength*? I wouldn't dream of using this event to make money.
In fact, I'm giving every spectator a ***free sample***!

"The Masters of the four Dim Sum Warrior schools are now gathered at the Stadium's main gate to welcome the Emperor, Empress and Prince."
Ten thousand years! Ten thousand years! Ten thousand, ten thousand years!
Masters, we wish you the very best today. We trust we need not emphasize the personal importance of this event.
Your Majesty, our representatives will all strive to earn the enrollment of His Highness, the Crown Prince.
And the Fried Kung Academy is so sure we'll win that we've even set aside a brand new Vapor-trolley DSX, just for Your Highness! Sure beats a free Handi-Wipe as a gift, eh?
Master Phoenix Claw, are Xiajiao and Shaomai really going to participate in the competition?
Your Highness, they're already hard at work...

SOUVENIRS!
Get your official Dim Sum Smackdown merchandise right here! Pennants, t-shirts, mugs! Support your favorite school!
Buy any souvenir, and get a free sample of Master Phoenix Claw's Handy Dandy Handi-Wipes!
Xiajiao! Shaomai! Why are you not warming up like the other contestants?
Oh! Mistress Boluo Bun! Um, Master Phoenix Claw said selling stuff on a humid summer day beats any kind of exercise at warming us up.
He calls it "Retail Kung".
Anyway, it's not like we can win this contest...
Also, do you really think the Emperor would allow the Prince to be in a dump like the School of Steam Kung?

Porky Pooples, are you alright?
Just feeling a little weird, Mom...
Well, obviously! It's your big day, so of course you're excited!
My big day?
I'm not sure this day has anything to do with me...
Master Taro Ball, the bookmakers have the Fried Kung Academy as the favorite to win today. But many people are criticizing your representatives, saying their drinking Inner-Strength gives them an unfair advantage. What's your response?
Heh heh! Well, Colonel Quickynoodle's wonderful beverage product augments strength, but not skill. That's all thanks to our rigorous training blah blah blah...

Roastpork, we know this must be unnerving for you, but someday, you'll thank me for doing all of this.
Yeah, gee, thanks a lot, Dad.
Why? Why are you always giving me attitude? Do you think I'm being unfair to you?
Well, *other people's* kids...
You are *not* other people's kids! Do you think your grandfather gave *me* a choice and asked me if I wanted to run this madhouse of an empire?!
So you want me to be happy about not having any choice?!
This is an honor! You *should* be happy!
Happy like *you*?
Let... the stress... pass... through... my... toes!
Beanikins, watch your blood pressure...

Your Majesties the Emperor and Empress, Your Highness the Prince, Lords, Ladies and Gentlemen, please take your seats. Let us introduce today's contestants...
This isn't over, Roastpork! You hear?
From the Baked Kung Sisterhood: PORK PUFF and ALMOND CREAMBUN
Representing the Boiled Kung Temple: SOYBEAN CUSTARD
And from the world-famous Fried Kung Academy: POTSTICKER and CHILI PEPPER
Finally, from the School of Steam Kung...

Um, School of Steam Kung... Yoo-hoo? Anyone there?
Here!
⇒Puff!⇐ Why do they make these contest platforms so high? ⇒Wheeze!⇐
⇒Gasp!⇐
Once again, from the School of Steam Kung: ***XIAJIAO*** and ***SHAOMAI***
C'mon, little brother! I've got you! ⇒Unf!⇐
Uh, Xiajiao... that's not my hand you're pulling, it's...
...my belt!
Oops.
BWAH-HA-HA-HA-HA-HA!
Well done, Chicken Foot, for upholding Dim Sum Warrior standards!

The goal of the tournament is simple...
MURMURMURMURMURMURMURMURMURMUR
...rescue the dummy!
Hey! Wait a second...
Was that dummy purposely made to look like m... never mind.
♪
Contestants must race to be the first to place the dummy on the throne at the opposite end of the ring...
The winning team will earn the privilege of enrolling Prince Roastpork Bao as a disciple!

Dim Sum Warriors, do your schools proud! Ready, get set...
⊰Heh!⊱ You know what? You guys go first...
...GO!!!
Yaaah!
Haaaa!
Raaah!
ZZZZIIIIPPPPP!
ZWOOOSSHHH!

Yow!
Yeep!
Ah!
ZA-SHING!
ZEOWZEOWZEOW
After all, a true Dim Sum Warrior needs not just strength and speed, but also the ability to keep a cool head regardless...
Ha ha! We should not have expected our task to be so easy...
...of conditions. EEYAHH!!!

Wow, Xiajiao! Look at Brother Soybean Custard, dodging all those spikes with such grace!
Um, Shaomai, I think we'd better do some dodging ourselves, unless you fancy becoming a kebab...
Ulp!
FWAAASH!
Tsk. Don't panic. Our Broiler Kung will vaporize the spikes.
Th- thank you!
Your kung fu is so deficient, and you still got dragged into this kind of contest. How awful!
Aw, but I like having them around! They're really useful for distracting soft-hearted morons! Heh heh!

Got you, you little...
ZWOOOOSH!
Wha...
Churls who seek to benefit from the suffering of children do not deserve victory.
Ooh, aren't we high and mighty. You need to be brought down to earth, Soy Boy!
You lot are a disgrace to us Dim Sum Warriors... eh?
BTKOK!
You sappy monks just don't get it: being a warrior involves warring... and to win a war, there's no issue about what's fair or not!
Unghh!

In the name of the Great Kiln, Potsticker, have you no sense of honor?
We can discuss that topic, Almond Creambun...
How about later, over cocktails at our victory party?
YEEAAGH! What's this?
SSSSHING

KA-CHAK!
Gaaakk!
Holy Hot Sauce, Xiajiao!
POIT! POIT!
We... we've got the dummy!
Just go, little bro! Maybe today's the day we salvage the name of the School of Steam Kung!
I can't believe this...
FA-ZOOSH!
WAAAH!!!

Ah-ah, little dumpling. No taking what belongs to your superiors!
Tell you what, this time I'll let you off the hook...
...or on the hook, as the case may be.
Hang in there, Shaomai!
I'm hanging! I'm hanging!
Hnnh! I'll pull you down!
...Um, part of you anyway.
Ack!

And now, little dummy, for your tush to meet the throne!
FLOOMPH!
Sorry to step in, Chili Pepper, but it's time I put my best foot forward. Though, honestly, I'd rather be kicking *your* butt!
Aiyah!
Well done, Sister Almond Creambun! Now we may all return to competing honorably.
Whoops! Sorry! Sorry! I didn't mean to grab it!
SWIZZISH!
Oh!
Ah!

I-I'll definitely give the dummy back to you, but I don't know how to...
FWOMP!
...stop! OWWW!!!
Glad to be of help. Let me also relieve you of this burdensome doll...
Ow, ow, ow... Potsticker, please put me down.
As you wish!
AIYEEEE!!!
VVVOOSH!
SHAOMAI!!!
TO BE CONTINUED!

CHAPTER 6
YOU WIN SOME, YOU DIM SUM

This is Lady Egg Tart 'live' at the Imperial Stadium, where there's been a fierce contest between the 4 Dim Sum Warrior schools for the honor to enrol Prince Roastpork Bao and... oh!
SOYBEAN CUSTARD, Boiled Kung Temple
PORK PUFF & ALMOND CREAMBUN, Baked Kung Sisterhood
CHILI PEPPER, Fried Kung Academy
SHAOMAI, School of Steam Kung
AIYEEE!
"The Fried Kung Academy's Potsticker has just hurled the School of Steam Kung's Shaomai right intothe audience!"
Shaomai! Noooo!

"Up in the Royal Family's Box, ***Prince Porky Bao*** himself is looking very agitated about this unorthodox move..."
Somebody stop this! Please!
Unh...
Wh- wha...?!
Gasp!
Have no fear, young dumpling! You're in the good hands, or should I say, good *hair*, of
COLONEL QUICKYNOODLE

Now I'm going to let you down. You've done some letting down yourself too - mainly, of your school.
Th-thank you... I think.
Little bro, are you okay?
This is outrageous, Master Taro Ball! What are your goons playing at? Shaomai could have been hurt!
Porky! You have no idea what...
Heh...
Um, actually, Beanikins, I did think it was indeed a tad unsporting...
Really?
You tell him, Mom!
Empress Bao, I concur. Thankfully, this situation can be resolved quite easily...

Ack!
Potsticker, you're disqualified! **Spring Roll!** Into the ring, on the double!
Yes, sir, Colonel Quickynoodle, sir!
You too, Shaomai!
Sigh! Yes, Master Phoenix Claw...
If you ask me, they should've just disqualified the whole Fried Kung team!
Enough, Roastpork. Let the contest resume.
"Contestants! Due to the penalty..."
"...the competition will be reset and the Dummy returned to the starting position...."

"In the meantime, you may recuperate, while we bring on the intermission show...
"LORD LONGAN PUDDING AND HIS FLEET-FOOTED FRUITY FOLK DANCERS!"
...sponsored by *InnerStrength*, the powerful drink for those with a taste for power!
Ouch!

It was really rough out there! I don't know if we can survive the next round.
Silly dumplings!
Master Phoenix Claw!
You're just not using the right techniques. Have I never taught you 'Sneaky Shifty Dodgy Kung'?
Um, but how will that help us win the competiton?
WIN? Are you crazy? No one expects you to win! You just do what you can to stay out of everyone's way and try not to get killed!
Listen to your Master.

Who? Ack! Prince Roastpork Bao!
Chicken Foot's combination of pragmatism and cowardice has enabled him to maintain his position all these years.
A thousand years! A thousand years! A thousand, thousand years!
Shaomai, Xiajiao, I appreciate the great personal risk you're both taking for my benefit...
...so I'm offering to have you honorably disqualified from this farce of a contest.
Thank you, Your Highness, but... no way!
WHAT?!
Of course we can't win. But we don't know when we'll ever get the chance to be like real Dim Sum Warriors, and even fight alongside them! That's always been our dream!
Sure, we might face danger, but hey, attaining your dream's never been an easy thing, right?

Well, alright... but you must be careful.
We will... I'll take getting bruises over selling crappy merchandise in the market anytime!
All competing Dim Sum Warriors, please return to the arena for Round 2!
Phoenix Claw, you're unworthy of your disciples, you know that?
They're calling us! We should go, little bro!
Right behind you, sis!
If it pleases Your Highness to say so...
Welcome back, Majesties, Highnesses, Lords, Ladies and Gentlemen to the Dim Sum Smackdown! Once again, we have our competitors from the four Dim Sum Warrior schools in place...
...and their objective remains: to place the dummy in the throne!
Again with the dummy nonsense!

Warriors:
on your marks,
get set...
GO!!!
Wait...
why aren't
the Fried Kung
team racing
with us?
Racing?
Oh darling
Almond
Creambun...
...Racing would
imply we somehow
regard *you* as
competition.
FWOOSH!
Huh? Why's
Chili Pepper landing
there, when the
dummy's *behind*
her?

SIZZLE!
Oh, I'll get to him in good time...
...I just thought I'd deal with the *other* dummies in front of me first.
SLASH!
Aieee!
Argh!
Aiyah!
Spicy Eyes Pepper Spray Kung!
=Cough!= Eyes... stinging!
Good work, Chili Pepper!
=Wheeze!=
Watching these crybabies almost brings tears to *my* eyes. Heh!
=Aah!=
C-can't see!

=Cough!= I see... if this contest is to be played with mystical techniques as well...
Then it's time I showed my hand too!
THRUMMM
=Uff!=
RAPID RISING PHYLLO DOUGH KUNG!
KSPLATCK!
Woo...
Unh... I s-still can't see. Xiajiao, are you okay?
Yeah, =cough!= I'm fine, little brother. Don't worry about me.
GASP!

Xiajiao!
Don't take another step forw...
AIYEEEE!!!
Force field...
Roast-pork? What are you...
包
VREEEEE
...ENGAGE LAUNCH MODE!
包
Porky Pooples?
The wretched boy has modified his force field again!

Oooff!!!
VOOOM
Hang tight, Xiajiao...
Prince Porky?! You're saving me?
Um, it might be a little premature to say that...
...since I haven't figured out how to land yet.
VABAROOM!

This is Lady Egg Tart on the scene, to bring you live coverage of an historical moment in an already historical event! The Crown Prince has personally intervened to rescue a commoner!
Unh... my eyes don't hurt anymore... but I keep seeing these flashes and lights...
"Commoner"?
Xiajiao? Sis? What was all that noise? Are you okay? If so...
...I sure could use a hand here.
Be still, little one. I am vaporizing the pepper from all your eyes.
Oh! Thank you, Brother Soybean Custard!
So you can all see again, eh?

Then feast your eyes on *this*!
No! They have the dummy!
Oh yes...
You can say that once again, the Fried Kung Academy has the upper hand...
...which we're now unclenching! Haw haw!

Turbo Convection Air Stream Kung!
FWOOOOOOOOSH
What?
Why so surprised, Chili Pepper?
You were already generating so much hot air, I figured another stream wouldn't be amiss.
Huh! That's chea... something we would've done too.
But so what if you've got the dummy? You still have to go through us to plant it on the throne!
"Through you"?

We'll pound you through till you're crustier than the bottom of a burnt pot!
Your Highness, we'd best return to the Royal Box.
Shush. Xiajiao, are you alright?
Better. My eyes don't sting anymore.
Prince Porky?
What?
Thanks again for the save. I know the School of Steam Kung is too crap to win, but... I'd have been honored to have you as a schoolmate.
Thanks. That means more than you can know.

KRAK
RAAGH! Back off, you pesky pastry!
You Fried Kung clowns can't win by skill...
...so you resort to brute violence, obstruction and tricker... what are you doing?
HRRRH!!!
Resorting to brute violence, obstruction and trickery, at the same time!
AGH!
FWAAAM!!!!

WAH-
HOO!!!
Spring Roll has placed the dummy on the throne!
The Fried Kung Academy has won the Dim Sum Warrior Smackdown!
Majesties, according to the rules, whoever plants the dummy's bottom in the throne wins. The Fried Kung's methods were unorthodox, but legal.
Congratulations, Master Taro Ball.
My pleasure, Colonel Quicky-noodle. I now look forward to fulfilling the next phase of our enterprise...

Ahem!
Empress Custard Bao, Emperor Redbean Bao, I am absolutely delighted at this outcome!
The Crown Prince will have the finest training and care at the Fried Kung Academy. Perhaps he would now care to pack his...
...bags?
Porky Pooples?
Roastpork! W-where are you?
Sound the alarm! PRINCE PORKY BAO HAS GONE MISSING!
End Volume One: TO BE CONTINUED!

COLIN GOH & YEN YEN WOO,
WRITERS & PRODUCERS

Colin and Yen Yen are the creators and writers of Dim Sum Warriors.

Together, they are also international award-winning filmmakers. Their feature film 'Singapore Dreaming' (2006) won the Montblanc New Screenwriters Award at the San Sebastian International Film Festival, the Audience Award for Narrative Feature at the Asian American International Film Festival in New York, and the Best Asian/Middle Eastern Film Award at the Tokyo International Film Festival. The film has since been sold to multiple territories worldwide, and has also been screened at the Brooklyn Museum of Art and the Smithsonian Institution.

They also founded TalkingCock.com, an award-winning satirical website about their home country of Singapore, which has been featured by the BBC, the Economist and Wired, amongst many other international media. The website also spawned the bestselling Coxford Singlish Dictionary, a lexicon of vernacular Singapore English which the Times of London has pronounced 'invaluable'.

Colin graduated from the Faculty of Laws in University College London and obtained his Masters from Columbia University's School of Law, where he was named a Harlan Fiske Stone Scholar. At 17, he became the very first Singaporean to write and draw a daily comic strip for the Singaporean newspapers, which he continued to do for over 20 years, even while practising as a commercial litigator. His cartoons have also been published in England, the USA, Japan and Malaysia. He now writes for many publications, including The Straits Times, 8Days and Esquire.

Yen Yen received her doctorate from Teachers College, Columbia University in New York, where she was awarded the prestigious Spencer Research Fellowship. She is now an Associate Professor at the College of Education and Information Sciences at Long Island University, C.W. Post, teaching courses in Curriculum Development, Social Foundations of Education, and Research for Teachers. She has also worked as an educational consultant for UNICEF to help the Education Ministry in Afghanistan design their new curriculum, as well as an instructional designer with a leading education software and animation company in Singapore. Her work has been published in journals such as Educational Researcher, Discourse, and the Asia-Pacific Journal of Education.

Colin and Yen Yen now live in the bustling town of Flushing in New York City, together with their daughter.

OO LEE, *ARTIST*

The winner of the Art Spiegelman Alumni Award during her time at the High School of Art and Design, Soo is a graduate of the School of Visual Art in New York. Dim Sum Warriors is her first published comic. She lives in Flushing, Queens with two dogs and a cat.

UREN BAKER, *COLORIST*

Lauren Baker is a graduate of the School of Visual Art in New York. Besides Dim Sum Warriors, she is working on her own graphic novel, Aquapunk, which is available to read at Aquapunk.net. She also dabbles in printmaking, constructed languages, worldbuilding, astronomy and mysticism. She currently lives in California with her cat, Lucky.

YUMCHA STUDIOS LLC

We're a New York-based multimedia company that's combining everything we've learned in the disciplines of comics, filmmaking, education, martial arts and interactive content—and also parenting!—to bring you exciting and meaningful cross-cultural stories for all ages. Dim Sum Warriors is our inaugural project. Join us on our journey!

A Teatime Chat with Yumcha Studios Founders YEN YEN WOO & COLIN GOH

What was your inspiration for Dim Sum Warriors?

Yen Yen: I guess we wanted to create something really special for our daughter, and Dim Sum Warriors just seemed to hit so many of the right notes... like our love for kung fu movies and Chinese food. It helps living in Flushing, where you get the best dim sum on America's East Coast!

Colin: Dim Sum Warriors also combines the visual and storytelling styles we've both been developing over the course of our filmmaking, as well as my personal passion for comic books. I've been cartooning professionally for over 20 years, but this will be my very first comic book series. So to me, Dim Sum Warriors is the fulfillment of a very, very old dream. I mean, a major part of my wanting to move to New York was that this was the home of Spider-Man...

Yen Yen: We also wanted our American-born daughter to be aware of her Chinese heritage, and learn both English and Chinese. But there's a real dearth of well-conceived materials to support bilingual learning. So we decided to translate the comic into both English and Chinese. When the iPad came out, we saw an opportunity to do something really special. So we created an app which incorporates features that support language learning, and also enrich the reading experience.

Colin: In high school, I also learned Japanese through reading manga, armed with three dictionaries. So doing a comic that helps teach a language makes complete sense to me. I can't think of a better bequest to our daughter. Dim Sum Warriors is a labor of love, it represents her hodgepodge heritage, and it might actually be useful!

Who are your favorite characters an what do they represent?

Yen Yen: I think our protagonist, Princ Porky Bao, is like so many sheltered k in our modern world. He's not bad, bu his privilege handicaps his ability to se how his actions affect others. He also chafes at his parents' aspirations for h to become the Emperor someday. But his friendship with Xiajiao and Shaoma and their adventures together take him beyond his comfort zone and allows him to learn and change. I think Porky is a very real character. For a steamed bun anyway.

Colin: My favorite character is probab Master Phoenix Claw, who's basically a cheap con artist, but who's unexpectedly burdened with a very bi responsibility, and he has to somehow reconcile his sense of duty with his m venal impulses.

Yen Yen: There's also Xiajiao and Sha mai, who're brother and sister. They're polar opposites in terms of character and temperament, but are very protec tive of each other. They also have a de sense of justice. That's something I ho our daughter will learn—to work with others for greater justice.

How did you do the translation in Dim Sum Warriors?

Colin: The translation process is actu quite painstaking. We don't just plonk all the text into Google Translate and hit a button, then do some tweaking. I Dim Sum Warriors, you won't find thos unintentionally hilarious translations you get in the subtitles of many Chinese movies!

Yen Yen: For literary translations, you need to honor the grammar, humor an expression of both languages as far as possible. We tend to write in English first, which we send to our translator, Chee Keng Lee, who's an amazing translator, one of the best in the world He's actually translated Shakespeare into Chinese! He's a professor who eaches at both the Nanyang echnological University in Singapore s well as the Shanghai Theatre cademy. Dim Sum Warriors must be e first comic to have two professors n the team.

olin: Once we get Chee Keng's anslations, there's a back and forth etween the three of us as well as the rtists who do the voiceovers on the pp, to refine the text and expression in oth languages so that there's as close match as possible, not just in terms of eaning, but tone as well.

en Yen: So for instance, certain umorous possibilities aren't evident ntil we see the Chinese translation, and hen we change the English to match, nd vice versa. We work very hard n the translations. It also helps that hee Keng, Colin and I are all bilingual urselves and can see the possibilities in oth languages.

Vhat does Dim Sum Warriors mean to ou as the parents of a bilingual child?

olin: Plenty! Presently, our 2½ year old aughter speaks English and Mandarin, nd thanks to being in Flushing, knows few words in Cantonese, Korean and ven Spanish. Well, that's thanks more o Dora the Explorer...

en Yen: We believe the more languages ne knows, the better. It helps us avigate differences, and to understand hat people with different contexts from urselves is a given, not an abnormality.

olin: We both grew up in multilingual nd multicultural environments in our ome country of Singapore, which is mix of Chinese, Malay, Indian and ther ethnic groups. Singapore is not s ethnically or linguistically diverse as lew York City, but I think we share the ame realization that New Yorkers have ome to—that there's a huge payoff if ou just get over your differences—be ney cultural or linguistic—rather than ying to shoehorn everybody into the ame mould.

Yen Yen: Across the US, there are now dual languages learning environments in different school districts—where it is not simply about learning a second language, but to value more than one language and culture equally. And you'll see that sentiment reflected in the characters and storyline of Dim Sum Warriors too.

What do you hope to achieve with Dim Sum Warriors?

Yen Yen: We just hope people will like the story and its crazy characters. In some ways, we hope that all our titles—Dim Sum Warriors, the upcoming Kung Fu Guide to Romance—all express the anarchic energy of the postmodern Chinese diaspora, which is very much evident in Flushing, Queens.

Colin: The new generation of Chinese émigrés has a very different attitude from previous generations because of the growing economic strength and influence of China. It's also why we set Dim Sum Warriors in a chaotic science fiction universe rather than some hoary chop socky past.

Yen Yen: We also hope readers can learn Chinese and English through a fun context. As Colin said, he learned Japanese when he was in high school mostly through reading manga.

Colin: And American comics were also a great help to me in improving my English. We hope our Dim Sum Warriors app will make things a lot easier for those who want to learn to read or write more Chinese or English. I certainly think our app is a great way for learners to get used to the sound and text of either language in an unthreatening and entertaining way. I really wish I had something like it growing up!

Yen Yen: And last but not least, if they haven't already, we hope our readers will learn to love dim sum like we do!

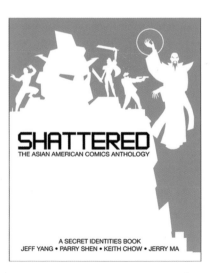

Readers' Favorite 2017
Silver Medal Winner

An Unexpected Afterlife

The Dry Bones Society
Book I

DAN SOFER

First edition: March 2017

ISBN: 0-9863932-3-1
ISBN-13: 978-0-9863932-3-5

www.dansofer.com

Cover Design: Damonza Book Cover Design

In loving memory of

Winston Earl Miller

CHAPTER 1

Moshe Karlin emerged from a deep and dreamless sleep with a premonition of impending doom. The world seemed out of place. The dawn chorus of summer birds filled his ears, but louder than usual, as though an entire flock had perched on the windowsill above his bed. The mattress pressed against his back, hard and coarse. A chill breeze tickled the hair on his bare chest.

Bare chest?

His eyelids snapped open. The endless blue velvet canopy of heaven stretched overhead, and as he gazed, a star winked out. His heart thumped in his rib cage. He was not in his bed. Or his bedroom. Or even his house.

He craned his neck forward. He lay on his back in a stony field, as naked as the day he was born.

His head slumped to the ground.

Moshe Karlin, you are in deep trouble.

Galit would kill him when he got home. That is, if she ever found out.

As his bold plan for sneaking home unnoticed grew flesh and sinew, the crackle of a loudspeaker jarred his thoughts, and a nasal voice boomed: *Allahu akba-a-ar! Allahu akba-a-ar!*

Moshe heard the East Jerusalem *muezzin* most mornings but always from a safe distance. This morning, however, the blaring call to morning prayers seemed to issue from only a stone's throw away.

Correction. You are in very *deep trouble.*

He rolled onto his side and scrambled to his feet, covering his privates with his hands. The field was perched on a hilltop. In the valley below, streetlights still burned and the Dome of the Rock glowed golden behind the ancient walls of Jerusalem's Old City.

A low rock wall snaked along the edge of the field and around the gnarled trunk of a large olive tree. Above the wall, rows of rounded headstones poked at the sky like accusatory fingers.

Moshe knew the cemetery well. His parents' twin graves lay a short walk away. He hadn't visited them lately but he was in no state to do so now.

How in God's name had he spent the night—naked—in the Mount of Olives Cemetery?

Hayya alas sala-a-ah! Hayya alal fala-a-ah!

A ball of searing pain burst behind his right eyeball. He fell to one knee and released a hand from modesty duty to massage his temple.

Of course! His birthday party last night. He had sipped a glass of Recanati Merlot as he discussed his business plans with Galit's grandmother. He had looked about for Galit and then… a black interplanetary void. He had never drunk to blackout before, not even in his single days, but that would explain the headache. It might also help explain his current predicament.

The *muezzin* call ended.

He glanced at his wrist and swore under his breath. His watch—his dear father's Rolex, the heirloom from his grandfather—was gone. Moshe took it off only to shower. One person alone would dare take his watch. One person alone would abandon him overnight and buck naked in an East Jerusalem graveyard. Moshe would deal with him later. For now, he had to get home.

He hobbled in the twilight toward the access road—rough

and lacking shoulders—that bordered the field. Sharp stones bit into the tender soles of his feet. The headache spread to his left eye and throbbed with his every step.

With luck, he'd avoid early-bird terrorists. With more luck, he'd slip under the covers before Galit got up to dress Talya for kindergarten.

He quickened his pace. A truck whooshed along a hidden street far below. Thankfully, the access road had no streetlights. As the road fell, walls of stone rose on either side.

Through a breach in the wall, he spied a yard with a clothesline. He reached through the hole and, with some effort, snagged the edge of a bedsheet. After brushing dirt and leaves from his goosefleshed body, he fashioned the sheet into a crude toga. His new attire would still draw stares but the sheet was dry and covered the important bits. He lacked only a laurel wreath to complete his Roman emperor costume. Pity it wasn't Purim today. He would have blended right in.

The road meandered around stone houses with dark windows and emptied into a two-lane thoroughfare. Sidewalks. Streetlamps. Civilization. He flagged down a white taxi and climbed into the back seat.

"Shimshon five," he said.

The driver, a young Israeli in a leather jacket, started the meter, and the car pulled off.

Moshe inhaled the sweet scent of new leather. He had worked with taxis all his life but he had not hired one in years. The upholstery felt soft and smooth through the thin sheet.

Eyes watched him in the rearview mirror and they crinkled at the edges. "Wild party, huh?"

Details of the previous night surfaced in Moshe's bruised brain. "My fortieth birthday," he said. "My wife threw a party at the Botanical Gardens."

He regretted the words the moment they left his mouth. Karlin & Son ran the largest taxi dispatch service in Jerusalem and he did not need this story circulating among the city's cabbies.

The driver, however, did not seem to recognize his voice. Newbie. Of course—who else drew the graveyard shift?

The eyes in the mirror narrowed. "Botanical Gardens?" he said. "That's the other side of town."

Newbie or not, he knew the lay of the land. The Italian restaurant at the Botanical Gardens overlooked a large pond in western Jerusalem. Moshe had sipped his merlot and told Savta Sarah of his plans to extend Karlin & Son from Jerusalem to Tel Aviv. They already controlled the shuttle routes to Ben Gurion Airport. He had looked around for Galit. He had wanted to raise a toast in her honor. They had hardly spoken with each other all day and, with his recent work schedule, they had spent little quality time together. He had wanted to tell her how much she meant to him. Where was she? And then… another gaping abyss in his memory.

"Avi," he said. He spat the word like a curse.

"Who?"

"My friend." The word "friend" dripped with sarcasm. "He's always trying to drag me to nightclubs like the old days. Last night, I guess he succeeded."

Moshe massaged his temples with his fingers. He needed an Acamol.

The driver laughed. "With a friend like that, who needs enemies, right?"

After a short, annoyed pause, Moshe laughed as well. In the safety and comfort of the backseat, on his way to his warm home, the stunt seemed harmless enough. Hilarious. A juicy story for the grandkids. *Did I tell you the one about my fortieth birthday? Now that was a bash to remember. Or not!*

The road rounded the high crenellated walls of the Old City, hugged Mount Zion, and dipped through the Hinnom Valley.

Avi, you crazy bastard. They say you can choose your friends—but that wasn't always true. Moshe could never shake off Avi, practical jokes and all. Too much history. And Moshe had given him a job at Karlin & Son. They ran the business together.

You overaged rascal. The time had come for the eternal bachelor to settle down. A wife. Kids. He'd have a word with him later in the office, if he even showed up after last night. He was probably hung over too. Ha!

The trickle of cars thickened on the triple lanes of Hebron Road. God turned His great dimmer switch in the sky and the heavens brightened.

Forty years old. How time flew by! He didn't feel forty. The Israel Defense Forces had released him from reserve duty, all the same. He had many reasons to be grateful: a loving—if stormy—wife; a delightful little girl; a booming business and a beautiful house; and a best friend who moved mountains to create an unforgettable fortieth birthday surprise. Perhaps *unforgettable* was not quite the right word.

The cab turned into the suburbia of the German Colony, past the sleepy storefronts, apartment buildings, and houses in white Jerusalem stone.

He'd sneak another hour of sleep before heading to the office. He'd drive to Tel Aviv and nudge his list of cab operators and independent drivers to sign on the dotted line. *First, we take Jerusalem*, he thought, channeling Leonard Cohen's baritone, *then, we take Tel Aviv.*

An invisible hand moved him, pushing him harder and farther. After Tel Aviv, he'd spread north to Haifa, and south to Beersheba. Within a few years, he would conquer the entire country, one cab at a time.

A dark cloud settled over his mind. What then? Was that to be his sole "dent in the universe"?

He yawned and shook the dreary thought from his head. The hangover—or an on-schedule midlife crisis—had hijacked his brain. A national dispatch network would be a fine achievement. His father, of blessed memory, would be proud.

The car pulled up beside Moshe's duplex on Shimshon Street. The driver stopped the meter and printed a receipt.

Moshe reached for the wallet in his back pocket and got a handful of buttocks. No wallet. No underwear either. He decided to keep that information to himself.

"Wait here a moment," he said. "I left my wallet at home."

He skipped up three steps of cold stone and slid the spare key from beneath a potted plant. A row of purple cyclamens caught his eye. When did Galit get those? Takeaways from the Botanical Gardens?

He unlocked the door, tiptoed inside, and padded down the hall. In a drawer of the telephone table, he found a fifty-shekel note among the memo pads, pens, and car keys. He handed the driver the money through the open car window, told him to keep the change, and hurried back indoors. All he needed was an insomniac neighbor to spot him wearing a borrowed sheet. People loved to talk.

He closed the door behind him with a soft click. Silence in the dim entrance hall. *So far, so good.* He climbed the staircase tile by chilly marble tile, then eased down the handle of their bedroom door and slipped inside.

Shutters down and door closed, the room sank in Egyptian darkness. He inched over the cool parquet toward the sound of soft breathing until his leg touched the hard edge of the bed frame.

He let the sheet slip from his shoulders to the floor and kicked the pile under the bed. Never mind pajamas—the creak of a closet door might wake her. He lowered his rump to the soft bedsheets, transferring his weight ounce by ounce. Not a single spring squeaked. The mattress upgrade had proved to be a good investment.

He leaned back, slipped his legs beneath the covers, and rested his head on the pillow.

Mission accomplished!

He exhaled a lungful of pent, anxious breath and shifted further onto the bed. The surface of the mattress sank. Galit must have rolled onto his half of the bed. He turned toward her. The warmth of her body radiated through her pajama shirt. He pressed his shins against her hairy legs.

Hairy legs?

A reflex fired in his brain stem. With a primordial cry—

wooo-aa-ahh!—a mixture of terror and revulsion, as though he had snuggled up to a large cockroach, he sprang out of bed.

CHAPTER 2

Moshe stood barefoot in the darkness of his bedroom. His entire body quaked.

"What's that noise?" said Galit's voice, thick with sleep.

Before Moshe could answer, a man said, "Who's there?"

There was a loud click. Yellow light flooded the room and seared a horrifying image in his brain. Two figures lay in his bed: Galit and another man.

Moshe froze, his eyelids shuttering in the bright light. The two sleepers gawked at him. Their eyes moved from his face to his nether regions. Moshe didn't care about that—he had other things on his mind right now.

The man brushed a fringe of oily hair from his face.

"Avi?" Moshe said. Shock gave way to disbelief. Then rage shoved them both aside. He stood over them, a lone accusatory presence. "What the hell are you doing here?" he roared, as though he hadn't figured it out for himself.

His ex–best friend blinked at him as though Moshe had just stepped off the ramp of a steaming spaceship. He didn't grab his clothes and flee out the window. He didn't beg for his life or claim that this was "not what you think." Instead, he slunk out of bed and reached a quivering hand toward him. When his fingers touched Moshe's forearm, he recoiled. "Dear Lord!" he gasped.

Moshe turned to his cheating wife. "Galit, how could you?"

She sat in bed, silky black hair falling over her shoulder, her eyes large and white, her mouth open. She didn't cry. She didn't beg for forgiveness.

That deep, dark pit opened beneath Moshe's feet again. Something was wrong with the scene. Something *besides* the fact that he had caught his best friend in bed with his wife—in *his* bed and on the day after his birthday. The entire scene felt wrong, like an Escher sketch where the floor had become the ceiling and he could not tell which way was up. Why did he, the only non-adulterer in the room, feel out of place?

He did not ponder the situation for long. Galit screamed—a loud, high-pitched banshee shriek—and the two men cringed. When her lungs emptied, she sucked in air and screamed again.

Avi rose to his full height, a full head shorter than Moshe. "Get out!" he shouted.

"What? Me?" The bastard sure had *chutzpah*! "*You* get out!"

Galit bounced on the bed, screaming her head off. She wore the Minnie Mouse pajama shirt he had bought her for her birthday. She ran to the far corner of the room and clawed at the walls, like a hamster trying to escape her cage.

Avi swiped at him with a black shoe. "Get out! Get out!"

Moshe almost fell over backwards. Avi charged forward, opened the door, and herded him out of the room and down the corridor.

Moshe glanced around for a suitable weapon and found none. The heel of the shoe pummeled his head and arms. "Hey! Stop that!"

Avi halted the barrage to put a finger on his lips. "Keep it down, or you'll wake Talya."

"What?" Waking Talya was the least of their problems.

Avi came at him again with the shoe, and Moshe retreated down the stairs. "Out! Out!"

"This is my house! *You* get out!"

Avi grunted as he thrust and swiped. "Get out now or I call the cops."

"Call the cops!" Moshe staggered into the entrance hall. "This is *my* house, and that is *my* wife." Did he even recognize him? "It's me, Avi. Moshe Karlin."

Avi paused to catch his breath. He shook his head. He stared at Moshe with wild eyes. "That's impossible."

"Oh yeah? Why?"

"Because Moshe Karlin is dead."

"Excuse me?" He might as well have slapped Moshe. That had to be the lamest excuse in the history of cheating friends.

"Dead and buried. Two years ago."

"*What?*"

Avi swung the shoe again.

It was the shock of those words. Or the conviction with which Avi delivered them. Either way, Moshe found himself outside his front door. He slipped on the steps and sprawled on the cold hard stone.

"Wait!" he cried. But the door slammed shut and bolts shifted into place.

CHAPTER 3

For the second time that morning, Moshe stood alone and naked in a public space. He banged on the front door with his fist. "Hey!" He banged some more. He pressed the buzzer. He pressed it again. A car engine started nearby. Soon, the neighbors would pass by on their way to work.

Overhead, a window slid open. Avi poked his head out, a portable phone in his hand. "Go away," he hissed, "or I'll call the cops."

"Some clothes would be nice."

The face disappeared. Then a pair of jeans and a T-shirt rained from the sky, and the window slid shut. Moshe pulled them on. Avi's jeans barely closed over his waist and the hem of the legs reached his shins. No underwear. No shoes or socks. He shook his fist at the window.

Seeing Galit and Avi in his bed had been traumatic enough, but to be thrown out of his own home! He charged at the door and bruised his shoulder. He kicked it and stubbed a toe. He pressed the buzzer again.

He paced the welcome mat. *Call the cops. See if I care. Dead, my foot!* Dead people didn't come knocking on a person's front door. *Moshe Karlin is alive and well, thank you very much.*

He sat down on the top step.

And then he understood.

The bedroom scene, like the cemetery, was part of one big, extended joke. A very bad joke. Not funny at all. Avi was always pressing people's buttons, and a fortieth birthday had provided him with an irresistible opportunity to push all of Moshe's buttons and then some.

How had he convinced Galit to play along? Phenomenal job, he had to admit. He had fallen for it. Freaked out. The cemetery routine was probably her idea. Maybe now he'd agree to see that darned cardiologist.

Moshe drew a long, deep breath and stretched his neck. Soon they'd open the door and bring out a cake to the tune of "Happy Birthday." No rush. He'd wait outside until they decided he had suffered enough.

A bearded man in a black suit jacket and fedora hastened along the street—Rabbi Yosef Lev, his phylactery bag under his arm, on his way to morning prayers.

Perfect.

Moshe had last seen the rabbi at the synagogue down the street on the Day of Atonement. This morning, he was muttering a prayer as he walked. He glanced at Moshe, nodded a greeting, and continued on his way. Moshe had managed to dress with only seconds to spare.

Suddenly, the rabbi stopped in his tracks. He turned slowly and peered at Moshe. His mouth dropped open. His face turned deathly white.

"Morning, Rabbi." Moshe chuckled and pointed at the door. "Locked out. Silly me. Nothing to worry about. All under control."

"Moshe?" the rabbi muttered. He seemed to be thinking aloud, not speaking to an actual person. He grabbed his thigh with his free hand and gave it a hard squeeze. Then he slapped his face and rubbed his eyes. "Moshe *Karlin*? God save us."

"Rabbi, are you OK?"

The rabbi cackled, a man teetering at the edge of sanity. "Sure," he said. "Besides for seeing ghosts. Otherwise, thank God, I'm fine." He gave another nervous laugh.

Moshe rolled his eyes. Not the rabbi as well. "OK," he said, loud enough for Galit and Avi to hear through the upper window. "The joke is over. It wasn't funny anyway. As you can see, Rabbi, I am not dead."

"You certainly are. I officiated at your funeral. I visited the house of mourning."

Moshe got up, walked over to the wide-eyed rabbi, grasped his bony shoulder, and shook his cold, limp hand. "See? When was the last time you shook hands with a ghost?"

The rabbi swallowed hard, and for a moment, Moshe thought he was going to collapse. Then an expression of wonder animated his face and understanding blossomed in his eyes. "Ribono Shel Olam!" Master of the World! "You're alive!"

Moshe's weird sensors fired again. A shiver slithered down his back like a snake over a fresh grave.

The rabbi's face fell from joy into sudden doubt. "Or am I hallucinating? Come with me. Please. I must show you to Rocheleh."

So that's the plan, is it? The party had moved to the rabbi's house. He had to hand it to Avi—Moshe would never have expected that. Galit and Avi must have ducked out the back door and beat him to the rabbi's house. Moshe looked up and down the street and sighed. "OK."

He followed the frantic rabbi, who turned back every few steps to make sure his guest had not evaporated into thin air. Moshe winced as his tender feet stepped on stray stones and cracks on the sidewalk.

A small single-level house of old stone sat at the end of the street near the grassy tracks of a defunct railway line. The rabbi knocked on the door, jiggled a key in the lock, and stepped inside.

Moshe had never visited the rabbi's home. Pictures of bearded rabbis hung on the walls of a small, tidy living room. There were no balloons. No birthday cake. No signs of people hiding behind the worn couches, or the bookcase—its shelves droopy with holy books—or beneath the dinner table of scratched, dark wood.

At a counter bordering the kitchen, a woman looked up from her newspaper and coffee. She wore a stern expression.

"What have you forgotten now?"

Moshe had never met the rabbi's wife. The kerchief on her head covered every strand of hair.

"Rocheleh, do you remember Moshe Karlin?"

The rabbanit sniffed at her husband's guest and his bare feet, unimpressed.

"Hi," Moshe said. He pointed in the general direction of his house. "I got locked out."

"Isn't he dead?"

Here we go again.

The rabbi smiled. "So he's not in my imagination! It's a miracle!"

Moshe felt his patience run out. "Rabbi, I think I would know if I had died."

The rabbanit put down her mug and ignored him. "If you're home, you can get the boys ready for school."

The demand seemed to jog the rabbi's memory. "I have to open the shul." He turned to Moshe. "I'll be right back. Please wait here. Make yourself at home. Help yourself to some coffee. Breakfast. Is there anything you need?"

Moshe clenched his fists. He wanted to shout "I am not dead!" but he held back for the sake of the rabbi and his wife. He didn't have time for this. He needed his car keys and his own clothes to get to work, but he could not get into his house. He resigned himself to a late start. He might as well accept the rabbi's offer. He said, "I could do with a shower."

Rabbi Yosef led him down a corridor, through a main bedroom with two single beds and peeling wallpaper, and into a pokey bathroom. He handed him an old but clean towel and a new bar of soap, and hurried off.

The bathroom sink and counter were a mess of creams and makeup, hairbrushes and dental equipment. The wall tiles had chipped and the scent of damp rot hung in the air. But a shower was a shower.

Moshe locked the door, stripped, and stepped into the shower closet. Pipes groaned in the walls and then a jet of hot water burst from the showerhead. He massaged his scalp, shoulders, and back. *That's better.* He worked up a lather with the soap and wiped the patina of dirt from his feet and legs.

How long would the prank go on? Rest assured, Moshe would return the favor in double measure. Avi's birthday fell in December. Plenty of time to prepare. An alien landing, a terrorist kidnapping. Leave him outside and naked overnight. In winter. That would cure him of practical jokes.

Moshe soaped his arms and chest, and his hands worked their way down his body.

When his fingers slid over his belly, he screamed.

CHAPTER 4

The Prophet sat at a small, round table outside Café Aroma. He typed away on his laptop and ignored the stares of the waitress.

He enjoyed his daily coffee on Emek Refaim. The outing allowed him to get some work done and mingle among the common people without attracting too much attention. He savored the colors and whispers of their clothing, the scent of food and perfume, the snatches of conversation in a hodgepodge of languages and accents, as tourists and locals drank their coffee and bustled along the strip of trendy stores and restaurants. He had to keep up with the changing times, and in the last few centuries, the times had changed at a breakneck pace.

Women were one of few constants, their unwanted attentions an occupational hazard. The present hazard—a waitress with a blond ponytail and intelligent green eyes—leaned against the wall at the edge of his peripheral vision and watched him like a hawk as he emptied the small silver pot of hot milk into his cup. Waitresses left their telephone numbers on his receipts and napkins. The bolder ones sat down at his table and struck up conversation. When that happened, he moved on.

What drew them to him? The shock of untamed black

hair? The persecuted expression? Or his refusal to make eye contact? Humanity desired what it could not have. Experience had taught him that only too well.

This waitress rocked on the balls of her feet. Was she a scribbler or a sitter? She launched from her perch and tended to an elderly couple that had settled at another table.

He lifted the empty silver pot. Waving the waitress over for a refill would only invite conversation, so he took the easy way out. He tilted the pot and flexed the muscle in the center of his brain. Hot milk poured into the cup. He tilted the pot a second time and espresso flowed. He sipped his coffee. *Perfect.*

The scent of fruity perfume reached him before she did.

"How on earth did you do that?" asked the waitress, sitting down across from him. A broad, incredulous smile split her face and revealed perfect white teeth. Her large green eyes threatened to swallow him whole.

Pity. He had liked the coffee and the view. Jerusalem had only so many coffee shops at a convenient distance from his apartment.

"Do what?"

"That trick with the milk pot."

Busted. He kept a straight face. "What trick?"

She rolled her eyes. "I've been watching you. Sometimes milk comes out, sometimes coffee. Always steaming hot."

Time for a change of subject. He said, "Like those bottles of black and white liqueur?"

Her eyes narrowed and confusion wrinkled her pretty brow. "Sheridan's?" She glanced over her shoulder. "Am I on candid camera?" She seemed delighted at the prospect.

"Yes." He closed the laptop. "You're on candid camera."

He shoved the laptop into his shoulder bag and applied his charming smile. "Do you like magic tricks? Why don't you leave me your number, and we can talk at leisure?" He winked and dropped a fifty-shekel note on the table.

A flush washed over her face. "I'll get your bill." She got up and rushed indoors to the cash register.

He slung his bag on his shoulder and walked off. Let her believe in magic tricks. In her memory, he'd be the cute big tipper who got away. Humanity believed what it wanted to believe. Never the truth.

As he crossed the road, he felt a familiar tingle in his core. A breeze ruffled his hair and the world froze. Café patrons paused mid-bite. Shoppers and dog-walkers struck stiff poses like wax models. An Egged bus halted in mute mid-motion. The wind swirled and rose, became a turbulent storm cloud that wrapped around him, and then fell silent. And in the silence, the Thin Voice spoke. Without words. Without language. With absolute clarity.

In an instant, the Prophet knew what he must do. The where, the how, the why. He would obey. He always obeyed. Against his better judgment.

Then the world thawed. Mouths chewed, legs walked, and vehicles zoomed, none the wiser.

He reached the curb and sped off on foot. The Day had arrived. He had better move fast.

CHAPTER 5

"Heart attack?" The question burst from Moshe's mouth like an accusation. He sat on the low couch in the rabbi's living room, his arms folded over his chest, his feet in velvet slippers one size too small.

Rabbi Yosef nodded and lowered his eyes. He sat on an old wooden chair from the dining table set. He reminded Moshe of the visitors at the house of mourning after his father had passed and, years later, his mother.

At this *shiva* house, however, Moshe filled the roles of both bereaved and deceased.

The rabbi nodded. "You collapsed at the Botanical Gardens. The paramedics were unable to revive you."

Moshe had suspected that much. Heart attack. Without warning. Like his father and grandfather. He should have seen that coming, but he'd been too busy to bother with doctors.

After his shower, he had drifted through the house, alone with his thoughts. The rabbanit had taken the boys to school and continued to her own teaching job. He paced the living room like an angry tiger, from the overloaded bookcase to the sagging couches to the kitchen counter and back. The framed rabbis on the walls watched him without expression as the ball of hot magma grew in his chest.

He could try to explain away the morning's events, but he could not account for the signs on his body or the date of the newspaper on the kitchen counter. Just over two years had passed with Moshe dead to the world.

When God's representative returned home from morning prayers, the volcano erupted.

"It's not fair!" Tears flooded his eyes and seeped into his nasal cavity.

Rabbi Yosef handed him a tissue and studied the floor.

Moshe blew his nose. "Dead at forty. No sons to say *Kaddish* or carry on the family name." He shuddered. What would his father have thought of that? "We moved into our house only a year ago. I was about to expand my business. I left so much undone."

The rabbi nodded, then brightened. "But you're alive now. You can pick up where you left off."

Moshe emitted a short, bitter laugh. "Tell that to my wife. You should have seen her face this morning." A sudden doubt drained his sense of humor. "We're still married, aren't we?"

The rabbi shifted on his seat. "Marriage ends with divorce or death, so the moment you died…" He let Moshe draw the conclusion. "But," he added, "you can remarry."

Moshe spared the rabbi the gory details of finding Avi and Galit in his bed. That ship had sailed. Of all the men in the world, why Avi? Had she not married Moshe first, he would have seriously doubted her taste in men.

"Galit inherited everything?"

Another nod. Moshe constructed a mental syllogism. His worldly possessions now belonged to Galit; Galit belonged to Avi. That bastard had taken over his life. The joke was on Moshe, all right, and it ran far deeper and darker than he had thought.

"Moshe?"

"Yes?"

"If you don't mind me asking…"

"Go ahead, Rabbi."

"What was it like?"

Moshe gave him a confused look.

The rabbi said, "The World of Souls."

"World of Souls?"

The rabbi's cheeks reddened above his beard. "You know—after the tunnel and bright light."

Moshe racked his memory. He had been talking to Savta Sarah at the Botanical Gardens, wineglass in hand. He had looked about for Galit. And then… he had woken up on the Mount of Olives to the sound of the *muezzin*.

He shook his head. "I don't remember anything. No tunnels or lights either."

"Did you meet God?"

"Not that I can recall."

"Deceased relatives?"

"Nope."

"Angels? Cherubs?"

"None."

The rabbi seemed disappointed. Moshe had died and lost everything, including any memory of the Hereafter. And yet, here he sat, alive again, in the rabbi's living room. "Rabbi," he said. "How can this be?"

The rabbi rediscovered his enthusiasm. "It's a miracle!"

"Yes, you said that. But how? Has this happened before?"

"Not in three thousand years."

Now the rabbi had his attention. "So people *have* come back from the dead?" That did not sound like a very Jewish idea.

The rabbi walked over to the shelf and returned with a small, thick, and well-thumbed volume. He opened the Hebrew Bible halfway and flipped the pages. "Elijah the Prophet revived the son of a widow in Zarephath. His successor, Elisha, resurrected the son of a rich benefactor in Shunem." He read from the book: "'Elisha lay on top of the boy, placed his mouth on his, his eyes on his eyes, his hands on his hands, and the boy's body became warm.'"

"I don't know," said Moshe. The passage sounded suspiciously like CPR, but he kept his doubts about the Biblical story to himself. "I was dead for two years. There wasn't much left to resuscitate."

"Unless," the rabbi said, "you didn't decompose! There are stories about saintly rabbis—"

Moshe raised his hand, cutting the rabbi's argument short. "Then how do you explain this?" He lifted his shirt.

The rabbi's eyes narrowed with alarm and then widened with surprise. He squinted at Moshe's exposed belly. "*Ribono Shel Olam!* You have no navel." The rabbi jabbed a finger at the spot. "But that means…"

"Exactly. I wasn't revived. My body was… regenerated."

The rabbi's face lit up with that now familiar ecstatic expression. "I've got it!"

"Don't tell me," Moshe said. "It's a miracle."

"Better than that!"

"What could be better than a miracle?"

"A prophecy!" He fanned the pages of the Bible again, bouncing on the couch in excitement. "Isaiah, chapter twenty-six: 'Your dead will live, their corpses rise. Awake and sing praise, you that dwell in the dust, for your dew is the dew of light…'"

A shudder ran down Moshe's spine. The verse described a zombie apocalypse. Was he in the lead role? He had no desire to eat brains. He couldn't even stomach a Jerusalem mixed grill.

The rabbi turned more pages. "Ezekiel thirty-seven. The prophet had a vision—a valley full of dry bones. Human bones. The Spirit of God assembled the bones into skeletons, wrapped them in sinew, flesh, and skin, and breathed life into them."

That was more like it. "What happened to them?"

"There are two opinions in the Talmud. They either lived forever or died of natural causes."

Moshe preferred the first option. "You mean the rabbis don't know?"

Rabbi Yosef shrugged. The unresolved debate over that

critical detail didn't seem to bother him.

"But if they lived regular lives, what was the point?"

"You could ask the same question," the rabbi said, stroking his beard, "about life in general."

Moshe waited for Rabbi Yosef to answer the question of questions, but he didn't. "The vision of dry bones," he continued, "was a symbolic message for Ezekiel's generation, the Jewish exiles in Babylon: don't lose hope; soon you will return to the land of Israel and revive your independent state, just as God revived the dry bones. But on another level the prophecy predicts an actual resurrection of the dead."

The rabbi found a passage toward the end of the tome. "Daniel, chapter twelve. 'And many of those that sleep in the dirt will wake, some for eternal life, others for eternal shame.'" More turning of pages. "'And you, find your end and rest; but you will rise for your destiny at the End of Days.'" He closed the book.

"The End of Days?" Moshe asked. It sounded like a Hollywood blockbuster, not an event in the here-and-now.

The rabbi's smile widened. "The Messianic Era. We believe that the End of Days will see the Resurrection of the Dead, the return of Elijah the Prophet, and the revelation of the Messiah-King, son of David. The Messiah will gather the exiles from the Diaspora and rebuild the Temple in Jerusalem. He'll restore the Kingdom of Israel to its former glory and bring peace and justice to the land."

"Peace?" Moshe asked. "In the Middle East? Good luck to him."

The rabbi was undeterred. "The order of the events is unclear. The Ingathering has begun already. Jews have poured into the State of Israel from across the globe: holocaust survivors from Europe; entire communities fleeing persecution in Arab countries; airlifts of Jews from Morocco and Ethiopia. Every day planeloads of Jews from around the world land at Ben Gurion Airport." The rabbi sighed at the thrill of it all. "When these signs come to pass, the Messiah will usher in the World to Come."

"Wait a moment," Moshe said. "I thought that the World to Come is the Afterlife, the—what did you call it—the World of Souls?"

The rabbi produced a sheepish grin. "The rabbis argue that one too." Moshe should have guessed. "Maimonides says you're right—the World to Come is the Spirit World after death. But according to Nachmanides, the World to Come refers to life after the dead have risen in the Messianic Era, when the world will reach perfection."

Moshe's head spun with resurrections, messiahs, and Worlds-to-Come. His credulity choked on the cocktail of conflicting beliefs. The rabbis really needed to get their act together. None of it made any sense, and none of it was helping him get his life back.

The volcano of bile erupted again in his gut. He hated Avi. He hated ancient prophecies and the valley of dry bones. And he sure as hell hated the Resurrection.

He jumped to his feet and threw his hands in the air. "I don't get it," he said, louder than he had intended. He stomped around the room again. "I've lost everything. God could have saved my life if He had wanted to. Why bring me back now—just to satisfy some stupid old prophecy?"

Rabbi Yosef stared at the floor and said nothing.

Red-hot lava bubbled in Moshe's belly. "No, sir," he said, to Rabbi Yosef or God, he couldn't say. "I'll have none of this."

He leaned against the wall and sucked in long drafts of air.

"Rabbi," he said, when his voice had calmed. "May I use your phone?"

CHAPTER 6

Moshe dialed his home phone number by heart and paced the rabbi's living room as he waited for the call to connect.

Galit had quit her receptionist job to stay home with the baby. When Talya started kindergarten, they had forgone the meager second salary. On a Tuesday morning, Galit should be at home.

The phone rang twice. Galit answered. "Alo?"

He fought the urge to talk to her, to beg her to kick Avi out and take him back. Instead, he hung up. She was home, that was all he needed to know. On the phone, she could easily cut short the conversation; he stood the best chance of tugging at her heartstrings face-to-face. He would need all the help he could get. He'd be asking a lot of her—he'd be asking her to turn back time.

The rabbi's living room lacked mirrors, so Moshe patted the hair of his reflection in the tin Blessing for the Home hung on the wall beside the framed pictures of bearded rabbis. Still wearing the velvet slippers, he made for the door.

"Shall I come with?" said Rabbi Yosef.

Moshe considered the earnest rabbi. A familiar religious figure at his side might help convince Galit that he was not a ghost.

"Yes. Thank you, Rabbi."

The trees along Shimshon Street murmured in the breeze and made the morning sunbeams dance over the cracks in the sidewalk. The cars that usually choked the street had moved to the parking garages of office buildings across the city. An alley cat sunbathed on the green lid of a municipal garbage bin and watched them pass.

Every human being is a network of desires and fears. This was a truth that Moshe knew well, and he had plugged into those wants and needs to clinch deals with new customers. To independent cabbies—hard-working men with mortgages and mouths to feed—he sold a steady stream of patrons; to the managers of taxi fleets he peddled the freedom to focus on growing their business. Nothing beat the rush of a handshake at the end of a long negotiation. This was how Karlin & Son had conquered Jerusalem and this was how Moshe would reclaim his old life.

A white Kia Sportage lazed at the curb outside number five. "That's her car," Moshe told the rabbi. "Bought it for her last year—no, make that three years ago."

The venetian blinds blocked his view, but he knew every detail of what lay beyond the windows. He and Galit had selected everything together at factory outlets in the Talpiot industrial zone, deliberating over floor tiles and faucets, and taking turns to run after Talya when she climbed into a bathtub or danced on a plate of Italian marble tiling.

He remembered the day that Talya had burst into the world. At 3 AM, he had sped down Herzog Boulevard to rush Galit to the labor ward at the Shaare Zedek Medical Center. That experience, like the night they had first met—now there was a story!—bound Moshe and Galit forever. Even death could not part them, he felt it deep inside.

Moshe and the rabbi climbed the three steps to the front door of the house. Moshe's house. Their house.

He'd break the ice with two choice words, the very first words he had spoken to her.

If romantic nostalgia didn't melt her defenses, he'd drop the gloves and use guilt. Every little girl needed her father—

her real father. Galit could not deny Talya that.

With a plan and a backup, Moshe rubbed his palms together and pressed the buzzer with a trembling finger. He needed this too much. He had to gain some mental distance. He was just a salesman; his product—a family healed after being torn by tragedy. He only hoped that she had calmed down since the morning. Hell hath no fury like Galit in a sour mood. Worst case scenario, he could take cover behind the rabbi.

He listened for her footfalls. He waited for the light in the peephole to darken.

He envisioned success. Galit would rush into his arms. She'd welcome him back into her home and her life. In fact, he convinced himself, it was her overpowering love for Moshe that had driven her to marry his best friend—that even made sense! But loyal consumers always prefer the original brand to cheap imitations.

Still no movement in the house.

Until today, Moshe had encountered religion mostly at major life-cycle events: circumcision; bar mitzvah; marriage; death. He visited the neighborhood synagogue once a year, on the Day of Atonement. He had never given much thought to God's existence. If he had harbored doubts before, now he had none. God alone was responsible for Moshe's new lease on life. He worked in mysterious ways—even the rabbis had no clue—but He was no figment of the imagination. And now, for the first time in both his lives, Moshe mouthed a silent prayer.

Oh, God. Please help me. Make things the way they were before.

He made a mental list of the good deeds he would do in return. He'd join the rabbi at synagogue every morning and strap on phylacteries. He'd write fat checks to the city's soup kitchens. And, for Heaven's sake, he'd see a cardiologist.

Moshe had learned his lesson. He had internalized the moral of the story. God had given him a second chance and this time he would do better.

If You can resurrect the dead, surely You can do this?

He pressed the buzzer again.

Come on, Galit. Give me a break.

The handle rattled.

Thank you, God!

The door opened but a security chain held fast. Through the crack, a little girl peered up at him, her dark eyes framed by thick black glasses.

It took him a moment to make the connection. "Talya?"

His precious four-year-old with the bushy crown of black curls had transformed into a young lady with satin locks that fell over her shoulders. He wanted to kneel on the floor and hug her.

Her solemn expression and tight mouth told him not to dare. "*Ima* says she's not home."

Moshe beamed at the adorable little girl. His girl.

"Talya, it's me. Your *aba*." Did she remember him? Galit had taken her to kindergarten each morning, and she was usually asleep by the time he got home from work.

Talya bit her lip. "*Aba*'s at work," she said.

The thought of Avi as her father winded him. *She doesn't know me. My little Talya doesn't know me.*

Her eyes flitted to the rabbi and her mouth twitched. "I have to go now."

Moshe put his foot forward and the closing door bit through the slipper and into his foot. "Ow!"

Talya's eyes widened and her hands shot to her mouth. *Great. Now you've frightened her.* "It's OK," he said. *Stay calm. Don't panic.* "I know *Ima* is home," he whispered. "I really need to speak to her. Please. It's super important."

Talya's lips squirmed while she mulled it over. She glanced over her shoulder. "*Ima* doesn't want to speak to you," she whispered. "You have to go away."

He removed his bruised foot from the door as a gesture of good will. They were on the same side now.

"You can open the door. It's OK. Please. I'll give you candy."

Her eyes sparkled.

Bingo! He had said the magic word.

"What candy?"

Galit's voice carried from upstairs. "Talya, close the door and come here."

He was close. So close. Choose the right words and he'd mend his broken world.

"What candy do you like?"

The sparkle in her eye vanished. Her real *aba* would have known the answer.

"I have to go now," his daughter said, as she shut the door. "I'm not supposed to talk to strangers."

CHAPTER 7

Moshe woke in the dark with a start. In his nightmare, he had died and lost everything he held dear. *Just a dream, a horrible, unbearable dream.* What a relief. Anxiety drained away from his chest and he breathed at ease.

He sat up and banged his forehead. Something very hard had impeded his movement and forced him down onto the stiff pillow. He caressed the fresh bruise on his head. His eyes adjusted to the dark. He lay on the lower level of a bunk bed. Wooden boards pressed against his back through the thin mattress. His legs stretched beyond the bed frame and his bare feet hovered in the air. The bed smelled of grimy feet and pee. On the pillow case, Superman punched a fist in the air.

Oh, no.

He lingered in limbo, unable to move after his nap. This was no dream. He had nothing, was nothing. God had not answered his prayers. Why on Earth had Galit shut him out? They had been a team. Together they were going to conquer the world. Didn't she at least want to see him again?

The door creaked open and sent a shard of yellow light into the room. The silhouette of a little boy peered around the door. A large skullcap sat on a thick tangle of hair.

"Hey," Moshe said and raised a forearm. The feat spent

his energy.

"Are you dead?" the boy asked.

Moshe wished he were. He said, "What do you think?"

The boy mulled the question over. "Do dead people talk?"

"Probably not."

That seemed to satisfy the boy, and he walked off. "*Aba*," he said, from the corridor, "the dead man woke up."

Rabbi Yosef appeared at the door. "Sorry about that. You OK?"

Moshe pondered the question. Was he OK? He was lucky to be alive, but he felt anything but lucky.

"Hungry?" the rabbi said. "Dinner is served."

Moshe said nothing. He had lived the modern suburban dream: the ideal family; the ideal career; the ideal home. That perfect life floated in his mind. Magical. Complete. And unobtainable.

He stared at the beams of the upper bunk bed. Dark swirls in the grain of the wood eyed him in the gloom, unseeing. The rings testified to long years of sun and wind. Good years, as a living tree. Now, only hardened struts remained. Dead wood.

"You can stay with us as long as you want."

The offer touched the tiny corner of Moshe's heart that could still feel anything. The rabbi had a small house and many mouths to feed without Moshe's dead weight. But he could not muster the strength to accept. He did not belong in the rabbi's home. He didn't belong anywhere. In the cosmic game of musical chairs, Moshe remained without a seat.

"I'm better off dead."

Rabbi Yosef sat down on the edge of the bed and placed a warm hand on his shoulder. "Don't say that."

"My parents are gone. I'm an only child. My daughter thinks I'm a stranger. My wife won't even talk to me."

"People react differently to death," the rabbi said. "And to life. She might be angry at you."

"Angry? I didn't choose to die."

"Emotions don't always make sense. You left her and that

hurt. She had to move on, and now the sight of you brings it all back."

Moshe had not looked at his death that way. He could see Galit getting angry at that. She owned the quickest temper in the Middle East. And she had moved on. Avi was the man in her life now, and Talya's new father. The eternal bachelor had finally settled down—into Moshe's shoes. There was no room left for him.

"Besides," the rabbi continued, "the sight of you must have scared her half to death. I almost had a heart attack when I bumped into you."

The rabbi had finally succeeded in making him laugh.

"Give her time," he said. "Where there is life, there is hope."

"Rabbi, I'm beyond hope."

"I wouldn't be so sure of that," he said. "I know something that can help. We'll do that tomorrow morning. But tonight," he added, "you must eat."

CHAPTER 8

The Prophet heaved two bulging plastic bags onto the marble countertop in his kitchen that afternoon. He untied one bag, widened the opening, and a mound of glistening green olives stared back at him. His order of five kilos of Nabali had elicited a double take from the stall owner at the Machaneh Yehuda market, but he had shoveled the choice fruit from a large vat all the same.

The Prophet sat on a designer stool beside the kitchen island, and dropped a well-formed and unblemished specimen into the funnel of the specialized stainless steel press he had rigged to the countertop. He turned the long arm of the crank, and a single drop of buttery liquid dripped into a glass beaker. He released the crank, extracted the bruised olive, and repeated the process with the next.

By the time daylight faded through the large windows, an inch of golden-green virgin oil had settled at the bottom of the beaker.

Why do I bother? A bottle of extra-virgin from the corner mini-market would suit his purposes too. But tradition was tradition, and the rich, bitter juice of the local species reminded him of the sacred oils of his youth.

Battered olives littered the island countertop. The sight would have appalled his interior decorator, who had decked the kitchen in dark panels of wenge, chrome, and the best marble money could buy. He had settled into the penthouse only a few months ago. Soon he'd have to leave it all behind.

He extracted the beaker from the press and poured the contents into a small glass vial, which he sealed with a cork, wrapped in a thick cloth, and slipped into his shoulder bag alongside the hollowed-out ram's horn that he had set aside for the occasion.

He dismantled the press, cleared the discarded olives into a large garbage bag, and wiped the counter. His work done, he retired to the adjacent living room with a tall glass of Shiraz.

He stood at the large French windows and sipped the fruity wine. The setting sun painted the Jerusalem skyline orange. Below, cars and buses crawled along Jaffa Road like scarab beetles, their engines and horns a soft murmur. The city appeared calm, blissfully unaware that tomorrow the world it knew would end.

If everything went according to plan. In his experience, nothing to do with humanity ever did. In all likelihood, the oil would remain in the vial, the *shofar* would never touch his lips, and his toil would be in vain. *Again.*

For all their industry and technology, humankind remained a horde of shortsighted brutes. They erred; they paid the price. Every time. Without fail.

But the Boss was a romantic, and He called the shots.

Darkness settled over the city. "Here's to tomorrow," he said, and drained the glass. Tomorrow, humanity would get another chance.

CHAPTER 9

The rabbi's old Subaru had seen kinder days. The door creaked when Moshe, wearing the same ill-fitting jeans and T-shirt as the day before, yanked it open Wednesday morning. Springs in the passenger seat groaned under his weight. The interior smelled of dust. He fastened the seat belt and fed the strap back into the retractor hole. The mouth of a cassette player gaped on the dashboard. Moshe had not seen one of those in decades. The jalopy was an accident waiting to happen.

His palms left wet patches on the armrest. He prayed that the car would fail to start. An earthquake or tidal wave would do nicely too. Anything to force the rabbi to cancel the excursion. Their destination was the one place on the planet Moshe wanted to avoid at all costs.

Rabbi Yosef turned to him and held out a thin roll of bank notes.

"I can't."

"Please," the rabbi said, and dropped the money on Moshe's lap. "You'll need some money to get back on your feet."

The rabbi was right. Moshe examined the worn bills. Two hundred shekels: a lot of money for the rabbi. He had probably not consulted with the rabbanit before parting with their grocery money.

Back on your feet. The smiling rabbi made it sound possible.

"I'll pay you back," he said.

Rabbi Yosef turned the key. The engine turned over, coughed twice, and started. God had sided with the rabbi.

The cassette player kicked into action as they pulled off. To Moshe's surprise, he recognized the song. He had expected the wail of violin and clarinet—the traditional klezmer music of Eastern European Jewry—or the festive Chasidic wedding ditties he stumbled upon when scanning through radio frequencies. Instead, the air filled with synthesizers and an '80s dance beat that shouted teenage rebellion. A girl sang.

"'Girls Just Want to Have Fun'?" Moshe said. "You listen to Cyndi Lauper?"

The rabbi's cheeks turned pink. "Cyndi is the best," he said. "A great soul."

There was more to Rabbi Yosef than Moshe had imagined.

The rabbi seemed to feel obliged to explain. "I wasn't always religious," he said.

Moshe found it hard to imagine the bearded rabbi with the constant smile and unbeatable optimism as a secular Israeli, but he didn't press him for details. He didn't have to.

"I spent a year in India after the army. I suppose I was searching even then. At university, I lost my way. Cigarettes. Alcohol. Girls. You name it." The rabbi's cheeks went from pink to tomato red. "One day, the campus rabbi invited me to a Shabbat meal at his home, and the rest, as they say, is history."

The sun climbed in the sky. The morning traffic choked the back roads of Baka but eased up as they turned onto Hebron Road toward the Old City. Throughout the country, millions of people rushed about their daily lives and worried about their everyday concerns. Moshe envied them.

They passed the Old City and his stomach knotted. *Are you ready for this?* That morning, his body had answered a loud and unequivocal "no," but the rabbi had been adamant.

The road dipped into a valley, and then they climbed the winding access road that Moshe had descended, on foot and naked, exactly one day ago—the narrow, walled road to the Mount of Olives Cemetery.

The rabbi parked in the small lot of gravel at the top and they got out. The car hissed. Unseen parts creaked as they cooled beneath the hood.

Moshe pointed to the empty field, walled on three sides. "That's where I woke up yesterday."

The rabbi studied the lot in solemn silence, then said, "You ready?"

Moshe swallowed hard. The rabbi patted his shoulder and led the way, past the field and along a path of long, flat stones.

"This is Jerusalem's oldest cemetery," he said. He seemed to be talking for Moshe's benefit, to distract him from what lay ahead. "Jews have buried their dead here for three thousand years, since the time of King David."

With every step, Moshe's feet grew heavier. He had followed that path many times before. The rabbi walked down the aisle between the long rows of tombstones. Crumbled edges and cracks. The ravages of time and vandals. Tufts of wild grass rose between the stepping-stones and wavered in the mountain breeze. In daylight, above the silent rise and fall of the Jerusalem hills, the graveyard radiated serenity.

Rabbi Yosef pointed. "Nachmanides is buried down there. Bartenura, too. And a host of other famous rabbis."

He turned left and stepped between the graves. He halted before a line of gray headstones in polished granite. The etched names and dates stood out in white lettering beneath a patina of dust and the occasional spatter of bird droppings. Moshe passed the graves of his grandfather and his grandmother, then his father and mother, of blessed memory. His mother's stone was shinier and cleaner than the others. He placed a white pebble on each grave.

Moshe had not visited enough. Did the dead care? Did they even know when a relative paid their respects? Moshe had no recollection, and yet there he stood, living proof that the spirit survived death.

"It is a great merit to be buried here," the rabbi said. "They ran out of space years ago."

"My great-grandfather bought plots in bulk and divided them up between his children. Turned out to be a good investment."

He remembered his father's funeral in every detail. The sight of the body on the stretcher, wrapped in a white shroud, had startled him even as a young man.

"Only soldiers are buried in coffins," the officiating rabbi had explained.

The somber bearded men of the *Chevra Kaddisha* lowered the body into the gaping hole. They sealed the space with rough slabs of concrete, climbed out, and took turns shoveling dirt.

Why had God resurrected him and not his dear mother or his father, or any of the thousands of righteous men and women around them?

Rabbi Yosef touched his shoulder again, not to comfort him for his parents, but to give him courage for the next and final stop, and stepped aside.

Moshe stood before the next grave in the row.

Moshe Karlin. Mourned by his wife and daughter. May his soul be bound in the Bundle of Life.

A pile of white pebbles lay at the corner of the slab. The wind whispered in his ear and caressed his face.

One step forward, and six below, lay his corpse. What remained of a man after two years in the earth? Or twenty? Or two hundred?

A tremor spread from his legs through his body. He sank to his knees at the foot of his grave.

"I'm dead." There—he had said the words. His breath came in halting gasps. Then he broke down and bawled into his hands.

Moshe Karlin had died. Nothing would change that fact. But if Moshe Karlin was dead and buried, who was he?

He stared at his tombstone, tears trickling down his cheeks.

A tissue materialized in front of his face. He thanked the rabbi and blew his nose. He drew three long, deep breaths. He leaned back, his hands in the dirt, and stretched his legs at the foot of his grave. He looked up at the rabbi. "Yet, I'm alive," he said, in wonder.

He held out his hand and the rabbi helped him to his feet. He brushed the dirt from his jeans. His vision cleared. "Look." He pointed at the horizontal slab. "Over there."

A small, round hole lay opened in the earth at the corner of the grave, like the mouth of a mole tunnel.

They stepped forward to get a better look, when the crunch of gravel behind them cut their investigation short. They spun around. A pale figure flitted between the graves and cowered behind a tombstone. A woman. She reminded him of the fairies in storybooks for young girls: large eyes, a hint of a nose, and a head of short matted hair so blond it seemed white. She lacked only a pair of fairy wings. And clothes.

She peered at them over the headstone, her eyes flitting between the bearded rabbi and his teary companion, her brow a battleground of need and confusion.

"Please," she said in Hebrew, her accent heavy with Russian. "Help me!"

Moshe and Rabbi Yosef exchanged a meaningful glance. He too had noticed the key detail, and drawn the same conclusion.

During her split-second dash between the grave markers, Moshe had glimpsed milky skin dusted with flecks of dirt. One arm pressed over her breasts, the other thrust over her lap, and, between the two, a clear patch of milky skin. No dirt. No freckles. Not even a belly button.

CHAPTER 10

In a parking garage beneath Jaffa Road, the Prophet pulled on a black leather jacket and a pair of matching riding gloves. The winged Harley Davidson emblem gleamed in the cool fluorescent light on the matte black chassis of the Sportster Iron 883.

He kicked his leg over the decal of a fiery chariot on the rear fender and settled on the leather seat. He squeezed the clutch, lifted the shift lever to neutral with his boot, and thumbed the starter. The V-twin engine growled to life.

He clicked the remote, and the gate of the private parking bay rolled upward. He eased back on the throttle and launched up the ramp and onto the street.

Air blew through his hair. He didn't bother with a helmet. He never stopped or slowed—the traffic lights of downtown Jerusalem knew better than to get in his way—and soon he tore along open road toward East Jerusalem.

Jonah, man, I feel your pain. He would have preferred to stay in bed. The Redemption had loomed so many times that he had lost count. Why would today be any different?

And yet…

And yet a small thrill of anticipation quickened in his chest.

He reached the Mount of Olives and gunned along the

walled access road like a bullet through the barrel of a rifle. An old white car hugged the perimeter wall at the top of the hill. Two men emerged from the cemetery: a brown-bearded man in a hat and shirtsleeves, and a clean-shaven companion in jeans and a T-shirt. They glanced toward the Harley's rumble. *There you are. Right on schedule.*

A third figure appeared behind them. The woman wore a man's suit jacket over her shoulders and, it seemed, nothing else. The bearded man held the car door open for her. *Hello? What do we have here?* The Thin Voice had not mentioned the girl.

He pulled back on the throttle and the bike hurtled forward. He would career around, spinning the wheels and spraying pebbles, and stop at their feet. Humanity loved dramatic entrances.

As he crested the hill, however, a horn blared—very loud and very close. Too close. The world became the flat metal front of a large truck, and the driver opened his mouth to scream.

Bam! He flew forward. His head connected with the windshield. Bones crunched. Glass shattered. He floated in the air, an astronaut in zero gravity. Then planet Earth rose up and slammed into his back.

Pale blue sky filled his world. He tried to think. He tried to move.

A face replaced the sky. The bearded mouth moved but the words fluttered away. He felt a wetness at his back. His backpack. *Oh, no, the oil!* Clean-Shaven joined Brown Beard, his face as pale as a ghost.

He tried to move his lips. Say the words. Deliver his message. He must!

Brown Beard spoke into a mobile phone and the men moved out of his field of vision.

Far above, a cloud hovered in the blue morning sky, a hand with one long accusatory finger aimed at him.

His head tingled. Weariness washed over him. He closed his eyes and knew no more.

CHAPTER 11

The fairy-woman nursed a cup of steaming tea on the couch in the rabbi's living room. She had borrowed a potato-sack gown from the rabbanit's wardrobe and her hair stuck to her forehead in damp, blond leaves.

Twenty-four hours ago, Moshe had sat on the same spot on the couch. The young woman was coping well—her hands didn't even shake—despite the two extra complications. The first had involved a motor accident.

The leather-jacketed biker had passed out while they waited for an ambulance. The truck driver, an old Sephardic man, emerged from the truck without a scratch on his body, but a large gash in his conscience. He wrung his hands and muttered prayers as the paramedics shifted the biker onto a stretcher and into the ambulance.

When Moshe and Rabbi Yosef finally came around to questioning the fairy-woman, after providing her with two Acamol tablets for her head along with a shower and fresh clothing, they discovered the second complication.

"Let's try again," Rabbi Yosef said. He sat opposite on a wooden chair and clasped his hands. "What is your name?"

Her large eyes searched the bookcase at the end of the living room for answers. She shook her head.

"Where do you live?"

Another shake.

"Do you remember anyone? Anything?"

They had hoped that a hot shower and drink would jog her memory. The poor thing had started life over in every way: no clothes; no memory; not even a name. One creature walked the earth more miserable than Moshe, but the discovery gave him no comfort.

The woman on the couch sipped her tea and glanced from Rabbi Yosef to Moshe and back, with surprising calm and detached curiosity.

She doesn't even know she's been dead! With no memory, how could she?

Moshe and the rabbi exchanged an uneasy glance. *Do we tell her?* The rabbi frowned and gave his head a mild shake. He was right: rather let her figure it out herself.

Moshe had experience with lost people, usually in the form of customers who needed a taxi but had no clue where they were. "Do you remember any landmarks?" he said. "Street names?"

Another shake of the head. She sat there, erect and proud, and took another long sip.

"You can stay here while we figure it out," the rabbi said.

"And I'll help too," Moshe said. "Many thousands of Russian Jews moved to Israel after the iron curtain fell. That trail should lead to who you are, or at least to some people who know you."

"Thank you," she said.

"Until then what should we call you?"

"*Chava*?" the rabbi suggested. Chava was the Hebrew name for Eve.

"Hmm," said Moshe, his voice a moan of uncertainty. "A bit old-fashioned. How about Eva?" That sounded more Russian.

Her big blue eyes searched the walls. Then her face beamed.

"Or Irina," she said. "Yes. I like Irina."

The rabbi grinned. "Irina it is." He glanced at his wristwatch. "I have to teach a class now. I'll be back in a few hours. Moshe, can you help her with lunch?"

"Sure."

Moshe had learned the ropes. The Lev family divided their kitchen into meat and dairy halves, each with separate sets of plates, cutlery, cooking ware, and even a separate sink. He chopped tomatoes, cucumbers, and red peppers, and served the salad with slices of toast, a block of white salted butter, and a tub of five percent cottage cheese. He scrambled the three remaining eggs in the box, thus exhausting his entire cooking repertoire.

Moshe and Irina munched away at their Israeli brunch. She polished off her fifth slice of toast and cheese, and then stared at the fridge, her eyes distant.

"I'm dead, aren't I?" she said.

Moshe almost choked on a cucumber.

She tapped her slim stomach. "I'm pretty sure I should have a belly button. And if some mad scientist had cloned me, I would have woken up in a laboratory, not a graveyard." She was no dumb blond. She gazed at him with defiance, daring him to deny the evidence. There was no point.

"We thought you had enough to deal with already," he said, by way of apology. "Yes, you died. But you're very much alive now." Her shoulders relaxed and she let out a deep breath. Her speculations were over, no matter how bizarre the conclusion.

"We're the same, you and I," he continued. At least she would not feel alone. "I woke up in the cemetery yesterday. I died two years ago."

"So you remember your life?"

"I don't remember dying or anything in between, but yes, I remember my life before. I had a hard time accepting that I had died."

She let the idea sink in. "How did this happen?"

Moshe washed down his scrambled eggs with a tumbler of tap water. "Rabbi Yosef thinks it's the fulfillment of a prophecy. The Resurrection of the Dead." He decided to skip the

Valley of Dry Bones, the Messianic Era, and the World-to-Come. Too much information. Had she been religious in her former life? She looked at home in the rabbanit's gown even without the head covering.

"So no one is looking for me?" She studied his eyes.

He shook his head. "Don't worry. We'll figure it out." She had the kind of face he'd expect to see on billboards for Fox Clothing, although she sure didn't eat like a supermodel.

"How do you know that?"

"Sooner or later your memory will return. And if it doesn't, someone is bound to remember you. You're not easy to forget."

She smiled and avoided his eyes. An awkward moment passed in silence.

"Were you born here?"

"Born and bred. Seventeen generations in Jerusalem, on my great-grandmother's side."

"So you must have a lot of family here." He knew what she was thinking: you, at least, have a place to go.

"Yes and no. None of them are on speaking terms. Some old feud. Nobody even remembers how it started."

"Oh." Another silence. "Do you have a family of your own?"

"A wife and a little girl."

She smiled. "You're lucky."

"I don't know about that. My wife locked me out and my daughter doesn't remember me. You have a clean slate," he told her, his inner salesman taking over. "A fresh start. All I can think about is what I lost."

Irina considered his words. "If you know what you lost," she said, "you can get it back."

Moshe laughed. "Easier said than done."

"Why?"

"My best friend took over my life: my wife, my business."

"A best friend might understand."

"Not Avi. He's a real ugly Israeli."

Her eyebrows arched. The Russian immigrant had not encountered the term. *Lucky you, Irina.*

How could he explain without causing the new immigrant to lose faith in society?

"Most Israelis are decent and caring people," he said, transforming at once into a spokesperson for the Jewish Agency. "Hard workers with family values who help old ladies cross the street." He cleared his throat. "There is, however, a small but loud group of people that gives the rest a bad name. They push in line. Run you off the road. Trash their hotel rooms and steal anything not nailed to the floor. Real scumbags."

Irina did not seem too bothered. "There are scumbags all over the world," she said.

"True," he conceded. "But Avi won't give a centimeter without a fight." He threw up his hands in preemptive surrender.

She nodded in sympathy but didn't cut him any slack. "Some things," she said, "are worth fighting for."

CHAPTER 12

Gastric juices sloshed in Moshe's stomach as he boarded Egged bus number seven on Emek Refaim.

The driver took his twenty-shekel note and handed back thirteen in coins. Ticket prices had risen in the decade since Moshe had used public transportation last. He'd have to do more walking to stretch his budget.

The commuters didn't give the man in jeans and slippers a second look as he found a seat next to an old lady with pale round cheeks and a halo of white hair. The bus rose and fell, roared and sighed, as gears changed and they charged along King George Street.

By his count, he had been away only two days, but he missed Karlin & Son already—the frantic buzz of telephones, the brusque exchanges on CB radio, the large mounted television screen with the numbers of waiting calls and routed customers.

He missed his team: Arkadi and his crude Russian jokes; Sivan's no-nonsense practicality and feminine touch; mild-mannered Pini with his large white *kippah*, kosher sandwiches, and the unintelligible Moroccan Arabic he had suckled at his mother's breast. And, of course, Mathew's Wisconsin accent and frequent tantrums.

They were more than employees; they were friends.

Among the four of them, they spoke five languages—Pini could get by in French too. Mathew and Moshe handled the English speakers. Sivan understood crap in any language and answered in kind.

The bus turned left and climbed Jaffa Road.

Soon he'd arrive at his destination. How would the team react to his return? His plan: get inside and spark a rebellion. None of them liked Avi much, especially Mathew, and Sivan swatted Avi's constant advances and innuendos like flies. Galit had inherited the ship, but Moshe was still the only rightful navigator. A mutiny would force her to parley with the pirate captain.

A sudden doubt stirred the acidic juices in his belly. In two years, the workload must have skyrocketed, the headcount doubled to keep up with demand in Tel Aviv. He'd need a majority of the team on board if he was to challenge Avi. If they had pushed northward to Haifa as well...

"Don't worry," said the devil on his shoulder. "Avi won't even let you through the door, never mind start a mutiny."

Moshe thumbed the button on the handrail and got off at the next stop.

Clal Center loomed on Jaffa Road, a hulking gray ghost. In the seventies, shoppers had flocked to the tiered corridors of Jerusalem's first indoor shopping center and filled the consumer stores.

By the turn of the millennium, most businesses had migrated to shinier office buildings far from the crammed city center, and foot traffic along the tired corridors petered out.

Moshe walked through the open door of the defunct shopping center and passed an abandoned security desk. Not even terrorists bothered with the faded building. The jingle of the coins in his pocket echoed off the blackened windows of stores, many of which served as storage warehouses for stalls at the nearby Machaneh Yehuda street market. Everything changes, and faster than one expects.

Moshe had renewed the rental contract every three years, for the low price and the sense of continuity. His father had inaugurated the offices, and many of his happiest childhood memories haunted the corridors.

The elevator—graffiti etched in the panels, the last working fluorescent flickering—groaned all the way to the third floor.

Moshe walked down the corridor to the door of frosted glass. He touched the proud silver lettering: Karlin & Son. His first love. His firstborn.

His finger hovered over the buzzer. The ominous silence behind the door unnerved him. Did Avi know he was on his way? Had he preempted the visit and cleared the place?

He pressed the buzzer.

He shifted on his feet. His heart thumped in his chest. His mouth went dry.

He buzzed again.

Still no movement behind the glass.

Moshe slapped his forehead. *Of course!* Karlin & Son must have relocated. By now, the call center would fill an entire floor in the Malcha Technology Park. Avi had lobbied for fancier premises even before their expansion. He must have pushed ahead as soon as the cash had started flowing.

Moshe needed a computer and an Internet connection. He'd settle for a telephone book, if Bezeq still printed them. He made for the elevator, when a door handle squeaked.

He turned around. Avi stood in the doorway. Moshe's chest tightened at the sight of him. His muscles braced for fight or flight.

Avi brushed his long, greasy fringe from his eyes. "Moshe," he said, spreading his arms wide. He stepped forward and wrapped Moshe a tight hug.

The warm welcome dumbfounded Moshe. Avi held him out at arms' length and looked him over. "I missed you, pal. C'mon in."

Moshe followed him inside. The cubicles stood empty, the headsets on the keyboards, the screens dark. *Where is everyone?*

"Coffee?" Avi said. "One sugar and a splash of three percent, right?"

"Sure. Thanks."

Moshe breathed in the familiar scent of the carpet while ceramic jars of coffee and sugar tinkled in the kitchenette.

The mounted LCD television was a silent black square between framed black-and-white photographs. A man wearing an impeccable suit and tie stood outside the stenciled door of Karlin & Son. A square watch glinted on his wrist. His hands rested on the shoulders of a young boy with combed hair. In the next photo, the man sat at a desk and held a bulky radio receiver to his ear.

Hot water poured from the water fountain, or "the bubbler" as Mathew used to say.

The imposing façade of a house in Jerusalem stone filled the third photograph. Two men stood on the street corner. The bearded man in the shiny dark suit and top hat stuck his chest out, the tail of his coat brushing the cobblestones. An Arab in a baggy gown and white headdress touched his arm and grinned beneath the bushy mustache and bulbous nose.

The ghostly quiet of the cubicles gnawed on his nerves.

Avi emerged from the kitchenette. "Here you go."

Moshe accepted the mug of coffee. "Thanks." He sipped it. If Avi was trying to kill him, he had used a tasteless and odorless poison. "You kept the photos."

"Are you kidding me, my brother?" Avi said. He called everyone his brother or his uncle, a habit that now annoyed Moshe. "What is Karlin & Son without the Karlins?" He pointed to the first photo. "That's you with your dad at the opening of the office, right?"

"Uh-huh."

"And there he is again with the first two-way radiotelephone system. Hard to believe we used to route cabs without computers, hey brother?"

Avi had been present at neither of those events. What he knew, he had learned from Moshe. He had called him "brother" twice in as many minutes. What was he plotting?

"What's with the Arab dude?"

"The man in coattails is my grandfather, also Moshe

Karlin. That was his house in the Old City."

"Pssh. You have a home in the Old City? Must be worth a fortune."

"It would be if we still had it. His parents—my great-grandparents—had to flee that home in 'twenty-nine. They returned when the violence settled, but lost it again in 'forty-eight." Moshe didn't have to explain the dates. As every Israeli knew, Arab mobs massacred Jews throughout the country in 1929, and in 1948 Arab armies invaded the nascent Jewish State. They expelled Jews from the Old City of Jerusalem and blew up synagogues.

"Our old neighborhood," Moshe continued, "is now in the Arab Quarter. The guy in the *kaffiyeh* was my grandfather's neighbor."

Avi, invader of Moshe's life, shook his head at the invaders of the past. "Let's have a seat."

They settled at the kitchen counter. A veil of steam rose between them. Moshe felt like a stranger in his own office. Which of them was the trespasser?

Avi said, "You scared the crap out of me yesterday."

"I was pretty surprised myself."

Avi studied Moshe's eyes. "You don't remember, do you?"

"Remember what?"

"Dying."

"I remember the party. Then I woke up on the Mount of Olives."

Avi leaned back on the kitchen chair. "So why did you come back? To haunt me?" He gave a nervous laugh. "Ghosts don't drink coffee, do they?"

Moshe put himself in Avi's shoes. How would he react if a dead friend showed up on his doorstep? He shrugged. "I'm alive. That's all I know."

"So you didn't see Heaven or whatever?"

"Nothing."

"God?"

"Nope."

Moshe sipped his coffee. He was getting used to this sort

of conversation. Whatever he had expected of his confrontation with Avi, it had not involved chitchat over coffee like old friends.

He could hold out no longer. "Where is everyone?"

Avi put his coffee down on the counter. "I let them go."

Had his ears heard correctly? "You did what? Why?"

"Business has gone downhill. Fast."

"But we were about to expand."

Avi placed his iPhone on the counter. "And then this came along. Some kid made an app for ordering taxis and our drivers jumped ship. *We don't need you and your monthly fees. Customers go direct.*"

Coffee spilled over Moshe's fingers. "Ow!" He put the cup down.

"How many did we lose?"

"A trickle at first. Then the dam wall burst."

"But they still need the radios, don't they?" Karlin & Son provided custom dual-frequency handsets and CB radios to drivers free of charge. It was a major selling point.

"Obsolete," Avi said. "Now all a cabbie needs is a smartphone and a data plan."

Moshe thought of the cab he had flagged down that first morning at the Mount of Olives. The young driver had not recognized his voice. He had probably never heard of Karlin & Son.

"There's cash for a few more months," Avi continued, "but without a miracle, I'll have to close the doors for good."

Avi might as well have floored him with a five-kilo sledgehammer. Moshe had died all over again. Karlin & Son—his purpose in life, not to mention the decades of devotion—poof! The flame of three generations sputtered out. On his shift. Or right after. He had known that technology would be the next step, but this—he had not seen this coming. He had not evolved Karlin & Son in time. He had failed.

Or had he?

"Did you reach out to this—what is the company called?"

"Ridez. With a zee."

Moshe groaned. A company with a typo for a name had torpedoed Karlin & Son. "Have you reached out to them?"

"Why would I do that?"

Moshe wanted to cry. "To make a deal! They want to grow fast; we have the clientele. We can partner up."

Avi's face went pale. The strategy, apparently, had never occurred to him. His jaw clenched. "It's too late for that. They don't need us."

A dozen different pitches for cooperative ventures flashed in Moshe's mind, but during the last two critical years, he had not stood at the helm. Avi had.

Avi pulled a bunch of paper towels from the dispenser and dumped them on the spilled coffee. His face twisted with sudden rage. "They've always hated us," he said.

"Who has?"

"The drivers. They were dying to give us the finger. All but a few loyals and not enough to pay the rent."

Moshe stared at the mess of coffee and soaked paper towels on the counter. He had failed his father and his grandfather.

Avi's rage passed as quickly as it had arisen. He patted Moshe on the shoulder. "I'm sorry," he said. "Never thought you'd live to see the end of Karlin & Son, hey, brother, never mind to rise from the dead?"

Moshe gaped like a fish, unable to speak.

Avi got to his feet. "I've got something for you that will cheer you up." He strode to the corner office—Moshe's old office.

What could possibly cheer him up? A note from Galit? Or better yet—his wife and daughter in person. Were they waiting for him in the office?

Avi returned with a white plastic bag. He pulled out a folded beige sheet. "This must be yours."

Another parting prank from Avi? Galit had laundered the sheet. Moshe made a mental note to return it to the clothesline on the Mount of Olives.

"I thought you'd want this too." Avi handed him a square

silver rectangle on a black strap of battered leather. "It was your father's, right?"

Moshe caressed the heavy angled frame and weathered strap of the Rolex. He never thought he would see it again. "My grandfather's. Made in 'forty-eight."

"So it's real?" Avi seemed surprised. Would he have parted with it had he known it was valuable?

Moshe strapped his family heirloom to his wrist before Avi could change his mind. "This watch," Moshe explained, "was the last purchase he made before the war took everything. He once said that he would never sell the watch. It was a reminder that…" He trailed off.

He remembered that day in every detail. The thick square of silver had felt unbearably heavy in the hands of the young Moshe, but sunlight had glinted off the glass face like fairy dust, and he had accepted the challenge. Now, the added weight of the timepiece made his arm feel whole again.

A Karlin never quits. His father's words rang in his ears and a chill spread down his spine.

"Reminder of what?" Avi said.

"Of the life he wanted to regain." His vision blurred and he blinked back the tears. "Thank you."

"And then there's this." Avi held out a blue identity book. Moshe opened it. The card within displayed Moshe's mug shot and official details. Across the card and in large black letters, a rubber stamp had printed the word "deceased."

The surreal sensation Moshe had experienced at his own grave swept over him again. He pocketed the booklet.

Avi watched him closely. The watch was a peace offering, the identity card a veiled threat: *Moshe Karlin is dead. Move along, pal.*

Moshe held his gaze. He wanted more than his father's watch. Much more. How much was Avi willing to give? If the tables had turned, if Avi had come knocking on his door, would he have stepped aside?

Moshe folded his arms over his chest. "So," he said, addressing the elephant in the room, "how is Galit?"

Avi stretched his arms and inflated his chest. "You know Galit. A new malady every day. Every sore throat is strep. Every mosquito bite a cancer. No shortage of drama." He chuckled. "Last week she threw a plate at my head, shattered all over the kitchen floor."

"She can do that." Moshe laughed. Another tear crept into the corner of his eye. He missed her tantrums.

"Piece of work, isn't she? Tell me, my brother, how did you ever get her to calm down?"

Moshe adjusted the strap on his wrist. The drama had never bothered him much. In a perverse way, he had enjoyed the challenge. "Humor," he said. "Make her laugh."

Avi nodded. They were old friends joking around about shared experiences, only this shared experience happened to be Moshe's wife.

"Avi, I just—"

Avi raised his hands as if to deflect a blow. "Listen," he said. "This has been *very* difficult for us all. Especially Galit. And I understand you wanting to jump back into her life, really I do. I'm your best friend, remember? I miss you too. You think I want to keep little Talya from her dad?"

Moshe's lips parted. Avi had opened a door. He had argued Moshe's side. "If I could just speak to her for a few minutes—"

Avi shook his head and hugged his chest. "Do you have any idea what this has done to her? Seeing you, out of the blue, after two years in the ground? Give her time. A month, at least. Let her get used to the idea that you're alive, and then, slowly, we'll work something out."

The display of maturity and compassion humbled Moshe into silence. He wanted to hug Avi. He had misjudged his old friend, slandered him to Irina. Avi, the eternal playboy and ugly Israeli, had changed. Moshe owed him an apology. Tears welled up in his eyes again. "I don't know what to say."

"Don't mention it." Avi stood. Their meeting was over. He put an arm around Moshe's shoulders and escorted him to the door.

"Call me in two months?"

"You said one month."

Avi pointed a finger pistol at Moshe and winked. "One month it is," he said, and he shut the door.

CHAPTER 13

By the time Moshe reached the rabbi's home, the sunlight was fading fast. He had danced along the back alleys and streets of Jerusalem on his way back and taken far more time than necessary.

Irina answered the door in her potato sack of a gown. "I was worried about you," she said. "Are you OK?"

"More than OK. I'm getting my life back!"

Her face glowed. "That's wonderful!"

"Where's the rabbi?"

"They're bathing the kids. Might take a while."

"Let's go."

She gave a cautious smile, as though suspecting that he had lost his mind. "Go where?"

"Out for dinner. We're celebrating."

He led her across the defunct train tracks, overgrown with grass, toward Emek Refaim and told her about his visit to Karlin & Son. The girl in the formless gown and the man in the house slippers won amused glances from passersby, freshly showered and dressed for dinner dates. Moshe would have to speak with Rabbi Yosef about expanding their wardrobe.

They stopped at Pizza Sababa on Emek Refaim, ordered slices, and sat at one of two wobbly square tables. Not a fancy meal, but within budget, and it felt good to get out of the rabbanit's hair—and fridge—for a change.

In a month, he'd be back in Galit's life.

He asked Irina how her day had gone. She had spent the morning at the Mount of Olives Cemetery with Rabbi Yosef, searching for another disturbed grave and hoping that the names on the tombstones would jolt her memory, to no avail.

Irina gobbled a strand of melted cheese that dangled from her slice of mushroom pizza. "How did you and Galit meet?"

Moshe took a sip from his bottle of Coke. "Avi dragged me to Hangar 17, a nightclub in Talpiot. I remember that night as if it was yesterday. Fake smoke. Disco ball suspended from the rafters. Seventies music. They played that Bee Gees song from Saturday Night Fever. 'Somebody help me. I'm going nowhere.'"

"'Staying Alive'!" Irina said.

"Yes! Wait a minute—how do you know that?"

Irina seemed just as surprised and delighted as he was. Her fairy eyes widened like those of a little girl. "I don't know. I know all sorts of useless things, just nothing about me. Go on, maybe I'll remember more."

"I saw her from across the room," he said. The moment had frozen in time: the shiny jeans that hugged her hips; the frills on her shirt that drew his eye from her neckline to the generous orbs below; her long, dark hair that fell over her shoulders; large eyes; red lips. "When our eyes met and she smiled I felt an electric current rip through my body."

"Like a fairy tale," Irina said, enthralled.

Moshe continued, "I walked up to her, through the crowd. A dozen pickup lines came to mind but I felt as though we already knew each other, so I just said, 'You're late.'"

Irina's mouth dropped open. "You didn't."

"Crazy, right? She didn't bat an eyelid. She said, 'I got here as fast as I could.'"

Irina giggled. "Are you making this up?"

"Then Avi arrived with our beers. I swept them from his hands with a 'thanks' and gave one to Galit. I found us a nice, quiet spot and we talked. We danced. We went for a stroll and landed up at the Tayelet." Irina shook her head, so he explained. "The Haas Promenade. South of the Old City. Great view. We sat on the wall of the promenade, side by side, our feet dangling over the edge. We stared at the huge walls of the Old City as they glowed in golden spotlight, and we talked until morning. 'So what do you want out of life, Moshe Karlin?' she asked me. 'To conquer the world,' I said. She just laughed. 'And how are you going to do that?' 'One day at a time,' I said. 'One day at a time.' It became a running joke. 'Time to conquer the world,' we'd say after breakfast and head out to work."

Moshe took another bite of pizza. That last morning, the day of his birthday party and the day he had died, there had been no playful banter at the breakfast table. He had dined alone and hurried off to the office. He had not made much of that then but now that solitary last breakfast seemed like a sign. An omen.

"That's very special," Irina said. Her eyes glazed over. "I hope I find a love like that."

"Maybe you already have," he said. "And he's waiting for you to come home."

They chewed their pizza in silence. He had tried to encourage her but his words had only made her sad.

A month. Thirty days seemed unbearably long. And what exactly had Avi promised him after that month? Galit had moved on. Would she turn back the clock two years, or would he remain a ghostly spectator at the sidelines of her life forever?

Avi had been right about one thing: Moshe had never thought he'd live to see the end of Karlin & Son. It still seemed unreal. Had he lived, he probably would have been powerless to stop that. The rosy image of his perfect former life lost its shine.

Even if, by some miracle, Avi stepped aside, how would Moshe provide for his wife and daughter? Like his grandfather, he'd have to start over from nothing. He had never prepared for that possibility. His urge to celebrate now seemed grossly premature if not outright delusional.

"Are you OK?" Irina asked.

"It's not going to be easy," Moshe confessed. "Karlin & Son was the only job I've ever known. I didn't go to university. Why bother? A thriving family business waited for me. Now that's gone. I don't know how I'll survive."

"Don't worry," she said. "I'll help you."

Moshe had to laugh. She didn't even know who she was, but she was ready to solve all his problems. Memory loss had its perks.

"What?" Her lower eyelids twitched. Was he making fun of her?

"Nothing." He raised his bottle of Coke. "To friends."

The brave fairy-woman answered his toast and their bottles met in mid-air with an optimistic clink. "To friends."

Moshe would need all the friends he could get.

Then, as he swallowed the last of his drink, he remembered. He had a friend. An old friend. A friend with unrestricted access to Galit. How had he not thought of her before?

CHAPTER 14

Irina had never seen the inside of a police station. Not as far as she could remember. In other words, not in the past twenty-four hours.

She could count the clues to her former life on the fingers of one hand: late twenties; Russian; speaks Hebrew; and no sign of childbirth. The last fact meant nothing—her brand new body provided little evidence. Cancer and Car Accident topped her list of probable causes of death, but she preferred not to think about her demise.

Instead, she filled the blank pages of her past with fantasies. As a wealthy heiress—a modern-day princess—she flitted across the globe to exotic getaways and dodged the advances of celebrities and moguls. Then she fell into the powerful embrace of her tall husband and doted on her brood of laughing children. The contradictions in her alternate pasts didn't bother her in the least; she got to live the best of all possible worlds.

As she followed Moshe, however, into the low building of Jerusalem stone and beneath the legend that read "Israel Police," other possible worlds loomed in her mind and her stomach tightened. Did she have a criminal record? Would the officers arrest her on sight and lock her away for crimes she didn't remember? Would she even know whether she was guilty? Her fate lay at the mercy of other people's memories. She was glad to have Moshe at her side.

A police officer at the entrance waved a metal detector baton over their clothes. Her jeans had frayed at the hems and the T-shirt showed bleach stains from too many laundry cycles, but they beat the rabbanit's shapeless gowns. That morning, Rabbi Yosef had escorted them to Tal Chaim, where she and Moshe selected old clothes from cardboard donation boxes and clothes hangers in a basement. The rabbi paid a few shekels for each item and they promised to pay him back as soon as they could. Then Rabbi Yosef hurried off to work and they set out for the station.

Irina studied the eyes of passersby for a glimmer of recognition: commuters on the bus; old ladies towing wheeled trolleys; loiterers dragging on cigarettes. Did they know her? Would they open a window on her former life? Most women ignored her. Not the men. One middle-aged man locked eyes with her so long that she stopped to ask him whether he knew her. "No, honey," he said and winked. "But I'd like to." Moshe had placed a protective hand on her shoulder and they moved on. Men stared. She'd have to get used to that.

The police officer waved them in. Two women with blue uniforms and dark ponytails sat behind an information counter. They looked like identical twins. Twins with very different temperaments. One sat upright and typed away at a hidden computer terminal. The other glanced at them, her eyelids droopy with boredom. "Yes?"

"My friend has lost her memory," Moshe said. "We were hoping you could help us find out who she is."

My friend. His voice was clear and confident, his words polite. Even with the bus driver.

"Lost person inquiries are down the hall, room 113 or on the telephone service."

Moshe glanced at Irina. "I'm not sure that will help. We don't think she's missing."

The other policewoman stopped typing and perked up. "If you don't know who she is, how do you know she's not missing, ah?"

Moshe did not say, "Because until yesterday she was dead." That would earn them a referral to a psychiatric ward.

Bored Cop turned to Irina. "Identity card?"

"She doesn't have one."

"*Your* identity card?" she countered.

No Nobel Prize for Bored Cop this year but she got points for determination. Moshe produced the card jacket of blue plastic. Bored Cop studied the contents.

A barrel-chested policeman with coffee-colored skin strutted behind the counter. His eyes lingered on Irina for a split second and her stomach clenched again. He continued down the corridor. The tension dissipated. *Was that disappointment or relief?*

Bored Cop elbowed Perky Cop. "Says here that he's dead." She handed the blue card jacket to her colleague. Perky studied the document and then Moshe.

"That's a mistake," Moshe said, with a good-natured chuckle. "Obviously."

Perky tapped at a hidden keyboard and stared at the hidden screen.

"Moshe Karlin?"

"Yes."

"Moshe Karlin died two years ago. So how can this be your ID, ah?"

Their search for Irina's identity had turned them into identity theft suspects.

"I told you, there was a mistake. Can I have that back?"

"Everything in order?" Barrel-Chested Cop leaned a large, hairy hand on the counter. A handgun poked out of the holster on his belt. His mouth drew a tight, short line. His skin reddened about his cheeks. Irina's stomach tightened again.

"My friend has lost her memory," Moshe repeated.

Perky handed Barrel-Chest the ID and pointed. "And he's dead." The silver plate above the badge on his chest read "Golan."

"I'll take it from here," he said. "This way."

Irina and Moshe exchanged a nervous look. Were they in trouble or was this a lucky break? They followed Golan down the corridor of closed doors. He opened one and stepped into an office. The sign at the door read *Detective Alon Golan. Homicide.*

Irina felt her throat dry.

A desk dominated the room. He pointed to two empty chairs, then closed the door and perched on the edge of the desk.

"Memory loss?" he said.

Irina nodded.

He clasped his fingers and turned to Moshe. "How do you know each other?"

"We met yesterday. I'm just trying to help."

Golan studied them, his eyes large, dark, and expressionless. "Are you sure you don't remember anything? People? Places?"

Irina shook her head.

Golan nodded. "I'll see what I can do."

"Thank you," she said. He stepped behind the desk and poked thick fingers at a keyboard.

She breathed, finally at ease. Moshe gave her a reassuring smile. *Lucky break, it is.*

Thick fingers drummed the desk as Golan waited.

Irina held her breath. This is it. Princess or pauper. Mother or maid. Which will it be? Her hand reached for Moshe's and he gave hers a squeeze.

Golan leaned toward the screen. "There are no missing person reports for your description."

Irina felt her shoulders slump.

He clasped his hands over the desk. "We can test your fingerprints. Not all citizens are in the database but it's worth a shot. Is that OK?"

"Yes, of course."

"Follow me."

He led them to another room, where a policewoman with

half-moon spectacles and a mane of thinning red hair asked Irina to press the thumb and four fingers of each hand onto an electronic pad. The woman clicked a mouse and glanced at a screen. Officer Golan leaned against the wall and folded his arms.

Irina tried to keep her breath even. Convicts had fingerprints on file for sure. If they found a match, would that make her a criminal?

The policewoman tutted, peering at Golan over her glasses. "She's not in the system."

Irina released pent-up air from her lungs. Back to square one.

Golan thanked the policewoman and led them out. In the corridor, he took a photo of Moshe's identity card on his mobile phone and returned the blue book. "I'll be in touch if anything comes up," Golan said. "Contact me if you need anything." He handed them each a business card.

They thanked him and left the station, down the steps to street level in the Talpiot industrial zone.

"Disappointed?" Moshe asked.

"I suppose. For a moment there, I almost wished I were a felon. Any identity is better than none."

He laughed. "We can put your photo on fliers and pin them up around the city."

She remembered the leers of the men on the street. "Maybe later," she said. "If nothing else comes up."

Moshe nodded. He understood. Her new friend glanced down the street and a sadness fell over his features.

"She'll come around," Irina said. He looked up, surprised that she had read his thoughts. "If she has a brain in her skull, she'll beg you to come home." That made him grin.

Home. A short word. Simple. Warm. And yet so elusive. Home was all she wanted.

He gave her a quizzical look. "Do you mind if we make a detour on the way back?"

"Not at all. My busy schedule just freed up." Moshe had given her a few hours of his time; she'd be happy to return the favor.

He asked, "Are you hungry?"

"Very." She had started the day with a single bowl of Telma cornflakes in the rabbi's kitchen.

"Good," he said. "You'll need a healthy appetite."

CHAPTER 15

"Today," Rabbi Yosef said, "we will learn something new."

Excited noises rippled down the neat rows of desks, and smiles bubbled on the expectant faces of twenty boys. The second graders loved the spice he sprinkled into his classes: stories of villagers in India who carried pails of water from the communal hand pump; the laws of physics that keep airplanes afloat in thin air.

The enrollment requirements at Daas Torah Primary excluded children who had a television at home, and although their parents instructed their children in matters of Jewish custom, they offered little insight into the mundane world beyond the four cubits of *Halakha.* And what normal young boy wouldn't welcome a break from the intricate laws of the blessings recited before consuming food and drink.

Rabbi Yosef stood before the class, his back to the whiteboard. Once he opened the can, the worms of curiosity would not return without a struggle. But how could he remain silent? First Moshe, then Irina. An isolated incident had developed into a pattern. At night, awake in his bed, he could think of little else.

Before class that morning, he had driven to the Mount of Olives and stalked between the rows of the dead. The heavy slabs over the graves, once the final seals of fate, were actually revolving doors. He peered behind headstones and the trunks of the olive trees. His failure to discover new arrivals did not dampen his spirits. Both Moshe and Irina had awoken from death in the early morning. The miracle obeyed rules, as did Nature, and the mounting discoveries bounced inside him like bubbles in a well-shaken bottle of champagne. If he didn't share the good tidings soon, he'd explode.

The expectant smiles widened with anticipation. A new healing sun rose on the horizon. Warm rays of change sped toward them. Today, a pair of protective glasses would serve his students better than a debate entitled, "Bananas, fruit or vegetable?"

"Who knows the song '*Ani Maamin*'?"

The first two words of the familiar song got the boys singing.

"I believe with perfect faith in the coming of the Messiah. And even though he may tarry, nonetheless, I wait every day for his coming."

"Very good. That is number twelve of Maimonides' thirteen principles of faith. The last principle is this." He read from a prayer book. "'I believe with perfect faith that there will be a revival of the dead at the time willed by the Creator, blessed be His name and exalted be His mention for eternity.'"

The boys stared in silence. Talk of the Resurrection required wrapping their minds around death, a concept far removed from their youthful world.

"In other words," he continued, "at some time in the future, God will give life to people who have died."

He swapped the prayer book for a Bible, but before he could turn to Ezekiel's Valley of Dry Bones, a little hand shot into the air.

"Yes, Menachem?"

"Will Grandpa Isaac come back to life too?"

"I'm sure he will."

A smile washed over Menachem's face. He'd see his grandpa again. Then he looked concerned. "Will he be back today?"

"Probably not today. God alone knows when. But," he added, "it might be sooner than we think."

"But," the boy said, his concern deepening, "my sisters have already moved into his room."

He had a good point. The resurrected would need a place to stay. Rabbi Yosef would not be able to host them all. Clothing too. The basement outlet for secondhand clothing at Tal Chaim would not meet future demand.

Rabbi Yosef improvised, "We'll all help him as best we can."

Menachem raised his hand again. "Will Grandpa still have his wheelchair?"

Rabbi Yosef had scoured the volumes of Talmud and Midrash in his library for details on the awaited resurrection, following cross-references, and hunting down more obscure sources on the Internet. "No," he said. "He will rise in full health. Although, according to one opinion, the blind and lame will rise with their disability so that the Messiah can heal them."

The little boy's smile threatened to split his face.

Another hand waved in the air. "Will Tuli come back too?"

A murmur of muffled laughter.

"Who is Tuli?" The rabbi had met Yankel's father at the parent-teacher evening, but he was sure that neither his mother nor his siblings went by that name.

"I found him on the street and gave him milk but Ima said he's dirty and that cats belong outside. The next day, Ima said he died."

"Oh." The seven-year-olds revealed far more about home life than any parent imagined. "Sorry," he said, with a sympathetic frown. "The resurrection is only for people."

Another hand. Then three more. Class had become a news conference. He pointed to a questioner.

"And the goyim? Will they come back as well?"

Yosef had hoped to avoid that one. "Only Jews," he said. "And only in Israel," he added, preempting the follow-on.

"According to some Midrashic sources," he added to appease his conscience. Few details of the End were unanimous.

"My *zeidi* is buried in America," said a distraught little Yankel. "Won't he come back to life?"

"Don't worry," Yosef said. He was *really* hoping to avoid that one. "God will provide tunnels." He swallowed hard. "The dead will roll through the tunnels to the Land of Israel and then come back to life. Next question!"

Another hand. "Uncle Dudi married Auntie Avigayil after Auntie Ora died. If Auntie Ora comes back, will Uncle Dudi have two wives?"

The kids giggled. For every answer, three more hands rose. No hope of squeezing the worms back in the can now. He did his best to answer or parry the rest before the bell chimed.

"We will have a lot of questions in those days," he said. "But Elijah the Prophet will return in time to answer them all."

Thankfully, the second graders had not raised the topic of reincarnation—whether a soul would be resurrected in a separate body for each previous incarnation—or class would never have ended.

In the staff room, he ate his packed lunch: a tuna sandwich and an apple. He could do with Elijah's wisdom now. The Resurrection weighed large and heavy on the shoulders of a simple schoolteacher with modest beginnings. The World to Come called for the Messiah, for rabbis of the greatest stature and purest lineage.

He paused mid-bite. *You silly man. What did you think you were trying to do?* He abandoned his sandwich and reached for his phone. He searched for the number—the number he dialed in his darkest moments, the number he had not used in over four years. He reached the end of his contacts list and tuna churned in his stomach. Had he erased the number by accident? Had he failed to transfer the details from his old phone?

Then the precious ten digits displayed on the screen and

Yosef breathed again. God had sent Moshe and Irina his way for a reason. Even a humble teacher could serve as a stepping-stone on the path to the Final Redemption. For he, unworthy Yosef, knew just the man to usher in the Messianic Era.

CHAPTER 16

Noga stared at the mystery patient in room 419C of the Shaare Zedek Medical Center. Slings hung from the ceiling and suspended the plastic casts on his left arm and right leg. A tuft of thick, jet-black hair fell over the white bandage that wrapped his forehead. Stubble peppered the solid jawline above the spongy neck brace. The name on the clipboard at the foot of the bed read *Ploni Almoni*. John Doe. Under the covers he slept, his handsome face a picture of serenity.

She shouldn't stare. She shouldn't even be in his room. Noga had wandered the wards, as she did, wearing a white cloak—although, being neither doctor nor nurse, she had no right to either activity—when she noticed the leg cast on the bed through the open door. On a hunch, she ventured inside and now her eyes would not budge from him.

"Cute, isn't he?" said a voice behind her. She spun around. Eliana smirked. The Russian senior nurse with the beefy forearms and dirty mind moved about the ward with surprising stealth.

"I was just..." Noga began in her defense. What exactly was she doing?

"Feast your eyes. He won't mind." Eliana stripped the sheets from the bed on the other side of the partition curtain.

"What happened?"

"Motorcycle accident. Out cold since he arrived yesterday morning. Dr. Stern operated on him most of the day."

A biker. Noga's interest surged.

"Will he be OK?"

Eliana bobbed her head from side to side. "Time will tell."

Noga looked him over. The nurse was right: he was cute.

"I wouldn't get my hopes up if I were you," said Eliana, reading her mind.

"Why not?" Eliana had tried and failed to set her up with any number of doctors. Why stop now?

Eliana placed her hands on her hips, the stance of a protective mother. "If by some miracle he survives, he'll probably have brain damage. Which might actually be an improvement," she added with a sour grin. "The fool wasn't even wearing a helmet."

"Oh."

Eliana bustled out of the room to her next task.

That explained a lot. Noga had terrible luck with men. Scumbags flew to her like fruit bats to overripe mangos. Her extreme bashfulness around men did not help. The result: still single at twenty-eight.

An ECG blipped on a stand. She moved to the head of the bed and placed her transparent folder of forms on the bedside table. She stood over him. His breath came deep and even. *What a waste.*

He lay there. Nameless. Helpless. Alone in the world. Like her.

She put out her hand and—fingers trembling—she touched his shoulder. His skin felt warm through the hospital gown. *What am I doing?* She moved her hand to his forehead and stroked the shock of black hair.

There was a sudden movement, and she gasped. Fingers tightened around her wrist. He stared up at her, an urgent plea in his dark brown eyes. And a fire.

He spoke, the words flowing with a mad intensity. Noga didn't wait for him to finish. She wrenched her arm free and fled the room.

CHAPTER 17

Moshe knocked on the door of the second-floor apartment. The sound bounced off the lumpy wall plaster in the dingy stairwell. Was he doing the right thing?

The visit could be dangerous. Not for him or Irina, but for their hostess. The surprise that waited outside her front door might succeed where Hitler had failed.

The apartment building in Jerusalem's Katamon neighborhood had no elevator. The hall light flickered out, so he pressed the light button again.

In the 1950s, the State of Israel had built the long, unimaginative apartment blocks to house the waves of Jews who had fled Arab countries in North Africa and the Middle East with little more than the clothes on their backs. These *shikunim* returned maximum living units for minimum investment. At the time, the refugees must have felt lucky to trade their shanties in the absorption towns for a solid roof over their heads. Two generations later, however, the cement monstrosities still marred large swaths of prime Jerusalem property, even as realty prices skyrocketed.

He used the buzzer. He shifted on his feet, which itched inside the scuffed sneakers from the Tal Chaim secondhand store.

Behind the door came the sound of shuffling feet. The

lock rattled and a hunched old woman stared up at Moshe. Her eyes filled the thick lenses of her glasses. She froze. Had an aneurysm paralyzed her? The visit was a terrible mistake.

Then Savta Sarah reached out both arms. "Moshe!" she gushed. An ecstatic smile split her wrinkled face from ear to ear. She pulled his head down, kissed both his cheeks in Hungarian fashion, and beckoned him inside.

Had she forgotten that he was dead? He returned Irina's surprised glance and shrugged. The familiar homey scents of carpet, wood polish, and old lady hung in the air of the square living room. He closed the door behind them.

"This is for you." He held out his offering: a small plastic doll in a ballroom gown.

The old woman's eyes lit up like those of a little girl. She turned the doll over and played with the limbs. "Beautiful!" She shuffled to the vitrine of shiny wood that covered one wall of the pokey room and contained books and ceramic dishes, and she positioned the doll on a shelf beside a dozen other dolls. "Thank you, Moshe. You always thought of me."

Thought. Her use of the past tense jarred him. She had not forgotten his passing, and the idea of a ghostly visitation didn't seem to bother her.

"Sit! Sit!" she implored.

She waved them to a small square table of worn plywood. The hard surfaces of the steel-framed chairs pressed against his back and bottom. Savta Sarah set two large and flowery dinner plates before them, and disappeared into the kitchen.

They sat at the table. A clock ticked over the background music of busy kitchen sounds.

A large black-and-white family portrait dominated the adjacent wall. Six children orbited two seated parents. Pins held the mother's hair in a tight bun. The frilled edges of a laced bodice peeked out the neck of her coat. The husband looked respectable with his trimmed beard and heavy frock coat. Four daughters—with prim white dresses and braided hair—stood behind their parents, and two little boys—trousers, wooly coats, and red cheeks—stood at attention on either side.

Irina followed his gaze. "Is that her family?"

"Savta Sarah is second from the right. Dark curls."

"All in Jerusalem?"

"All dead. Murdered in the Holocaust. Only Savta Sarah survived. When the Russians liberated Auschwitz, she moved to Palestine. Married. Gave birth to Galit's mom and uncle. That's them as kids." He pointed to the framed photo of a little boy and girl on a cracked sidewalk, one of many smaller color photographs that surrounded the portrait. "The rest are grandchildren and great-grandchildren." He did the math. "Four grandchildren. A bunch of great-grandchildren too."

The photos of her descendants circled the black-and-white portrait with defiance. *Take that, Hitler.*

"Wow," Irina said. "What a large family."

"We didn't see them much. Galit's uncle moved to America after the Six Day War. Her parents followed soon after we got married."

"Why?"

"They were convinced that, any day, our Arab neighbors would wipe Israel off the map. You can liberate Jews from a concentration camp, but a little shard of Auschwitz still lodges in their heart. The hearts of their children and grandchildren too."

Irina didn't probe further. Instead, she pointed at another framed photograph. "There you are," she said. She had found the close-up from the wedding. Galit leaned her head on his chest. White dress. Big smiles. Love sparkling in their eyes.

Savta Sarah reappeared and unloaded a stack of tinfoil trays onto the table. She shoveled mounds of food onto their plates: steaming white rice; meatballs in tomato gravy; sticky triangles of baked chicken with potato and sweet potato. The savory smells made his stomach growl. Their octogenarian hostess returned to the kitchen.

"Wow," Irina said, her mouth full. "This is delicious!"

"Pace yourself," he said. "She's only getting started."

On cue, Savta reappeared bearing fresh trays: cabbage

stuffed with minced meat and rice; ox tongue boiled soft as butter; beef goulash; *nokedli*, the Hungarian dumplings of oddly shaped egg noodle; and wobbly squares of beef jelly. Hungarians, it seems, had never heard of cholesterol.

"How did she know we were on our way?"

Moshe chewed a juicy meatball. "She didn't. She used to run a catering business and never learned to cook for less than a hundred people. She didn't stop when she retired. The cooking keeps her going."

Savta Sarah pulled up a chair and watched them eat. "Have some more stuffed cabbage, Moshe. It's your favorite. You've hardly eaten a thing. Is it any good?"

"Excellent!" Moshe and Irina said as one.

Savta Sarah didn't seem to hear them. "The meat didn't come out well today." She clucked. "The chicken burned on the stove."

"Not at all," Irina said. "Aren't you going to eat?"

"I ate earlier."

Moshe had never seen Savta Sarah eat. A sad, distant look clouded her eyes. *Here we go.*

"We had a lovely home," she said. "In Poton," she added for Irina's sake, "a village near Dunaszerdahely in Hungary. Or Czechoslovakia. We moved countries every other year without even moving house." The bags under her eyes seemed to sag lower. "One day, the Germans took my father. We never saw him again. There was no money. I was fourteen. What could I do? I went to the city and bought fabric to sell at home. That was how we survived. Then the Germans came for us too."

She shook her head at bygone years. "I was the worst of the children. The troublemaker. My sisters were angels. Why did God take them and leave me?"

Moshe had heard the stories countless times and for once he understood how she felt. He wiped his mouth on a paper napkin. "Savta, you do know that I died, don't you?"

"Of course." She leaned forward, conspiratorial. "And now you're back! Edith told me." Savta had named her daughter after her dear mother. Galit had told her mother, who, in turn, had told her mother, Savta Sarah. The news of his return had crossed the Atlantic twice. He interpreted that as a good omen.

"I told her to go back to you," Savta continued. She reached over and pinched his cheek. "Moshe is like me," she told Irina. "*Businessman*." She had used the one and only English word she seemed to know. "I was so glad when Galit married you." Her face darkened. "And so sad when you passed."

"Galit won't speak to me," he said.

"You must make her listen," Sarah said. "Before she marries that no-good friend of yours."

His mind did a double take. "Before she… what?"

"You don't know? The wedding is in two weeks."

He steadied himself on the table. "They're not married?"

"No." She tutted. "He moved into her home without even a ring."

Moshe reeled with the sudden discovery: Galit and Avi were not married. Moshe had assumed too much. He didn't know whether to jump for joy or to punch the wall. *Avi, you lying bastard!*

"I have to speak to Galit."

"Not dressed like that, you won't." Savta eyed his worn shoes under the table.

"I have no choice. She inherited everything. I have only a hundred shekels to my name."

Savta got to her feet. "That will do," she said. "I'll show you."

CHAPTER 18

Yosef waited in the foyer of Frumin House in downtown Jerusalem and hoped that he would not sound crazy.

The stately block of rounded Jerusalem stone stood three stories tall over King George Street in the center of town. Once home to the Knesset—the legislative branch of the Israeli government—the structure now housed the Rabbinical Court.

Beyond the security fences and guards, the foyer teemed with rabbis and their clients, who awaited hearings on matters of marriage, divorce, and religious conversion. Yosef felt out of place among the sure-footed, bustling masses. When the great doors of the main courtroom swung open, he glimpsed rows of wooden seats and white pillars, and heard snatches of arguments and pronouncements.

The doors swung open again and a tall, straight-backed rabbi in a black bowler and impeccable suit emerged between the doors, a briefcase of black leather in his hand. He scanned the rushing crowd and, when his eyes fell on Yosef, he smiled.

"Reb Yosef," he said, gripping Yosef's hand, his perfect ivory teeth gleaming. "Good to see you again, my friend."

Although Rabbi Emden soared leagues above the poor teacher and neighborhood rabbi, he always addressed his former student as a colleague. "Coffee?"

Rabbi Emden treated him to a Nescafe from a vending machine. The rabbi placed his briefcase on a vacant bench and they sat side by side.

After an exchange of pleasantries, Yosef got to the point.

"A man in my congregation passed away two years ago," he said. "A few days ago I bumped into him on our street, alive and well."

The older rabbi studied Yosef for a while. Would he dismiss the story out of hand? Did he think his old pupil had lost his mind?

"Are you sure of this?"

"I officiated at the funeral. I saw the body. It's him. He's been staying at our house since I found him. He eats and sleeps. Remembers nothing since he died. And one more thing." Yosef leaned in close and whispered. "He has no navel."

Rabbi Emden seemed to understand immediately. "The grave?"

"I checked the next day. Undisturbed, except for a small hole in the ground at the corner of the cover stone. And we found a woman."

"Also resurrected?"

"Yes, and with severe memory loss."

Rabbi Emden's eyes moved as he processed the data and matched the facts with the sea of Jewish learning stored in his great mind. A high-profile rabbi would have to think twice before diving into speculations of the Resurrection.

"This is big," he said eventually. "Very big."

Yosef sucked in air. He had known that his mentor would not let him down.

"We need to tell the world," Yosef said. "To announce the miracle. What a Sanctification of God's Name this will be! We must prepare for the others that will come."

Rabbi Emden rested a reasonable hand on his shoulder. "Slow down, Yosef. Two resurrected Jews do not the Resurrection make. Now, start again. From the beginning. Tell me all you have learned. We must prepare our case."

"Our case?"

"Yes, my friend." His wise eyes glittered. "We must present your findings to the Great Council."

CHAPTER 19

The Prophet opened his eyes. He lay on a bed in a strange room. Clear liquid dripped into a thin plastic tube from a pouch on a metal stand above him. Electric sockets and mounted equipment lined the headboard behind. A framed print of Van Gogh's *Sunflowers* hung on the shiny green wall.

A machine emitted rhythmic beeps. Outside the room, busy feet hurried and voices spoke in hushed tones. A telephone rang.

He knew about hospitals from TV, but had never had cause to visit one. How had he gotten there? Images flashed before his eyes. The rock walls of the Mount of Olives. Two men and a white car. The blare of a truck horn. Glass shattering. Bones crunching. *His* bones.

That's impossible!

He turned his head. Blue sky filled an open window of steamed glass.

He must get out. He must complete his mission. He moved, and pain flared in his head. His left arm and right leg swayed heavily in slings. The thick casts locked his joints in position.

"Good morning," said a man's voice. The man at the foot of the bed wore a white cloak and gave him an appraising glance. "Or rather," he added, "good afternoon." The doctor drew near and flashed a light in his eyes. He asked him to watch his finger as he moved it back and forth. Patches of gray hair covered his temples and worry lines furrowed his cheeks. The identification card clipped to the pocket of the gown read Dr. Yariv Stern. He pocketed the flashlight and trained his grim, penetrating stare on his patient.

How much does he know? The Prophet swallowed hard. "How long have I been here?"

"A day."

"When can I go home?"

Dr. Stern gave a short laugh. "Your skull is fractured. Your leg is broken in two places. You have a shattered left arm and three broken ribs. You're lucky to be alive. We weren't sure you'd wake up. You'll be here for some time." He drew a breath. "Now tell me: What's your name?"

Panic seized the Prophet. He racked his memory. Who was he? What year was this? *Remember!*

"Eli," he said. "Eli Katz." *Yes, that was it!* Relief washed over him.

Dr. Stern repeated the name. He mulled over the information like a wine connoisseur swishing a new vintage in his mouth. Pale blue eyes searched his face. "Are you sure?" he said.

The dread returned. *Does he know?* Eli managed a slight nod of his head.

"That's strange. Earlier you claimed to be Elijah the Prophet from the village of Tishbe in Gilad."

Oh, God, no! He feigned surprise. "Did I?"

"Yes indeed. You were quite adamant."

Eli managed a nervous laugh. "Must have been a fever dream."

"You also said that the End of Days is nigh and that you had an urgent mission to fulfill. A mission from God."

Oh, crap! Never tell anyone. The Golden Rule. The only thing standing between him and the stake or, these days, the insane asylum. He had broken the Golden Rule for the first time in two millennia. *Quick! Think of something!* He said, "Could it be the drugs?"

The doctor pursed his lips. "You're not on painkillers, if that's what you mean. You were comatose. I can prescribe some if you like."

"Yes, please." He had never taken medication, not even vitamins. He had never had the need, but now he was eager to start. By the time the pills arrived, he would be gone, but the request would get the doctor out of the room. A few seconds alone. That was all he needed.

The doctor walked to the foot of the bed, picked up a clipboard, and scribbled with a pen. "Your medical aid?"

"Don't have any. I'll pay direct."

The doctor's eyebrows lifted. "That'll be very expensive."

"I'll take care of it."

"Would you like me to contact anyone? Relatives? Friends?"

"No." Then he added, "Maybe later," to allay suspicion.

The doctor put down the clipboard. "I'll stop by later," he said. "Mr. Eli Katz."

When his footfalls faded, Eli closed his eyes. "God, please. Heal me, please." He flexed the muscle in the center of his brain. He pictured the bones mending, torn flesh and sinew regenerating throughout his battered body.

He held his breath. *Sit up!* He willed his limbs to move, his neck to lift from the pillow. The suspended leg trembled. *That's it!*

Pain burst in his skull and tore along his spine like a bolt of lightning. His head slumped back on the pillow. He breathed in short, fast spurts. The beep of the heart monitor accelerated. The room began to spin and fade to white. Sweat trickled down his brow and stung his eye. He blinked back the pain.

This can't be happening!

Tak-tak-tak.

The sound of tapping on glass came from the end of the room. He turned his head. A large black bird hopped on the windowsill. The bird tossed its head from side to side and studied him with bulging black eyes. A strip of torn meat dangled from the sharp beak.

A crow. A cruel bird. And an old friend. The Boss had a flair for poetic justice.

The bird gulped down the morsel. *Caw! Caw!*

Eli groaned. “OK,” he said aloud. “I get the message. Now, please, get me out of here.”

The bird shook its head, and, with a final, loud caw, flew off.

CHAPTER 20

A bell jingled as Moshe and Irina left the throng of pedestrians on Jaffa Street and followed Savta Sarah into the shop.

The old lady made a beeline for the till. She had dressed in a beige blouse and skirt for the occasion and donned a matching round hat with faux flowers.

Moshe fell back. He folded his arms over his chest. "This will be embarrassing," he whispered.

Irina scanned the display shelves of men's shoes. "Why?"

"You'll see."

Savta Sarah adjusted the strap of her handbag on her shoulder and placed a hand on the counter, which came to her chin. "Good afternoon, sir," she said with the well-oiled voice of an attendant to the Queen of England. "My grandson-in-law requires a pair of your finest shoes."

The man behind the counter looked as though he had just rolled out of bed. He pulled at his crumpled T-shirt and straightened his toupee. He peered at the little old lady, and a cunning smile cracked his pockmarked face, the smile of a Tyrannosaurus rex scenting a wounded herbivore. "Today is my lucky day," the smile seemed to say. Unbeknownst to him, a grandmother-sized asteroid hurtled toward the planet at dinosaur-extinction speed.

With a generous sweep of a hairy arm, he indicated the

display shelves and haphazard piles of shoeboxes. "Madam, we have the widest selection of the best quality footwear in the country. What type of shoe does your grandson desire?" He had adopted the old lady's genteel speech in a display of showmanship that jarred with his shabby outer appearance. The street show had begun.

All eyes turned to Moshe and so he pointed to a pair of brown loafers.

"An excellent choice," he said, in his Savile Row voice, and he hurried to the storage room behind the counter.

Moshe sat down on the low padded shoe bench and liberated his sore feet from the worn sneakers.

Two weeks. Avi had always had an eye for Galit—who didn't?—but he had been his best friend. Friends didn't deceive friends. They didn't steal their wives. The treachery made Moshe's blood boil.

"You're in luck," said the shoe salesman.

He carried a shoebox in two hands as though presenting the Crown Jewels. He pulled the new shoes from their wrapping of crinkly paper and applied them to his customer's limp feet, giving Moshe an unparalleled view of the misaligned toupee.

Galit's refusal to speak to him now made perfect sense. Avi had deceived Moshe with his one-month waiting period, and he had probably deceived her as well. Moshe had been a bad dream, a ghost, a hallucination, or—better yet—an undead zombie from a cheap horror flick. It was a wonder she hadn't fled the continent.

Moshe felt a tap on his shoulder. "If Sir will stand up and take a few steps?" The salesman's glance said: be a good boy and please the old lady.

Moshe clambered to his feet. He paced the shop under Savta's eagle eye. "They fit well," he said.

The salesman beamed. "First time! Madam, you came to the right establishment. Shall I dispose of the old shoes?" He lifted the grimy sneakers by the laces like a dead rat.

Moshe nodded. He slumped back on the bench. A pair of

new shoes would not shatter Avi's lies, nor would they grant him an audience with Galit.

Irina sat down beside him. "Are you OK?"

His shoulders rose and fell with despair. "Avi loved to tell me about his nightclubs and one-night stands. 'You married too soon. You're missing out.' Now he's stolen my wife. I thought he was my friend. The lowlife."

Irina nodded. "There's something I don't understand," she said. "How did someone like Avi become your best friend?"

Moshe took that as a compliment. "That's simple," he said. "Years ago, he saved my life."

Savta Sarah plopped her handbag on the counter and fished out her wallet.

Moshe said, "Here it comes."

The salesman pecked at the cash register. "That will be six hundred shekels," he said. "Credit card or cash?"

Savta Sarah threw a single bank note onto the counter. "Fifty shekels!" she declared.

The man's mouth fell open. "Lady," he said, the polish slipping from his voice. "These are imported shoes. Real leather. And this is the start of the season. You know what? You're a fine, respectable woman. I'll give them to you for five hundred."

Savta folded her arms over her bosom and lifted her nose in the air. "Fifty!"

"You have got to be kidding me." The polish evaporated. "Four hundred," he said. "You won't get that price anywhere. Believe me."

"Fifty!"

"Lady, this isn't the Machaneh Yehuda market." The man looked to Moshe for help. Moshe shrugged. "Three hundred. Final offer. That's the rock-bottom discount we offer at the end of the season but I'll give it to you now."

Savta Sarah slapped the counter. "Fifty shekels!"

The man turned purple. Veins pulsated at his temple. "Where are you from, lady?" he yelled. "The jungle?"

"Yes!" she cried. "The jungle!"

His mouth opened and closed like a fish. Moshe knew what he was thinking: women liked to talk, especially about bad shopping experiences, and this nice old lady probably knew many, many potential customers. "Great God! Two hundred and fifty."

Savta Sarah mulled over the offer. She threw another note on the table. "Seventy shekels."

"Are you trying to starve me? I won't make a profit. Fine! Two hundred shekels. Just get out of my store."

"Seventy!"

The man pulled at his hair and the toupee came away in his hand. He didn't seem to notice.

Moshe hid his face in his hands. He couldn't bear to watch. Poor guy. And poor Savta Sarah. She had learned to survive on a prayer and sheer force of will. Old habits die hard. He could learn from her tenacity; maybe then he'd win back Galit.

Two hours and four stores later, they sat at a bus stop. Moshe wore his new shoes, beige trousers, and a designer collared shirt. Irina looked beautiful in her new summer dress and fashionable pumps. Savta Sarah had parted with five hundred shekels in total. The storeowners had probably taken the rest of the day off.

"Thank you, Savta," Moshe said. Irina thanked her too. Savta Sarah had refused to take his hundred shekels.

"I could have got him down further," she said, wistfully, of the last salesman. "But I felt sorry for him."

The sun crept toward the horizon. In a few hours, working men and women would crowd the streets on their way home. Moshe had woken up that morning hoping to build a bridge to his estranged wife. By lunchtime, he had lost a best friend, but gained two weeks in which to win back his wife. The stakes had soared while the odds of success plummeted.

Once, when he had forgotten their anniversary, Galit had thrown kitchen plates at his head. He longed for her to hurl plates at him now. He could work with an angry Galit, a Galit who still cared, but not with this brick wall. A new set of clothes would not make a dent.

Savta said, "At least now you'll be dressed properly when you see Galit."

"But Savta, she won't speak to me. She wouldn't even come to the door. And if Avi answers—"

Savta Sarah patted his arm. "Don't worry, Moshe," she said. "Tomorrow is Friday and I happen to know exactly where she'll be and when. I can promise you this: you will speak to her and Avi won't be able to stop you."

"You're the greatest!" He lifted her hat and planted a kiss on her forehead. A private meeting with Galit—an open miracle!

"And this time," she added, and her red lipsticked lips curled into a devilish grin, "she will not get away."

CHAPTER 21

"Hey. It's me."

"I told you never to call me on this number."

"We need to speak. It's urgent."

"I'm ending the call."

"I saw the girl. Hello? You there?"

"What girl?"

"*The* girl."

"You're mistaken."

"It's her, all right. She says she lost her memory. Doesn't remember a thing. Not even her name. She goes by Irina. She showed up with a man, a Moshe Karlin. And get this: his ID says he's supposed to be dead. Hello? Hello?"

"It's not her. Forget about them."

"But if she talks, we're screwed. I thought you said you'd taken care of her. What if—"

"Calm down. Stop worrying and keep your mouth shut. It's not her."

"How can you be so sure?"

"Trust me. I know."

CHAPTER 22

Friday morning, Moshe walked down Emek Refaim, his heart galloping in his chest. The huge bouquet of roses on his arm won smiles from the women who bustled along the sidewalk with fresh *challah* loaves and other Shabbat groceries.

Thorns pricked his palms through the cellophane and made him loosen his grip on the flower stems. The roses had gobbled what remained of his cash and although Moshe was not a gambling man, today he had gone all in.

He paused outside a storefront of tall glass windows. Two large words hung above the store: Zohar Raphael. Moshe had heard the name but he had never met the legend. He peered at the long row of women seated inside. The whir of a blow dryer resonated on the street. No sign of Galit. Had Savta Sarah miscalculated?

Moshe rehearsed his two-pronged plan, patted his hair in the reflection, drew a deep breath, and pushed the glass door inward.

The pungent smells of dye and singed hair assaulted his nostrils, the thunder of the blow dryer his ears. A line of women faced the wall mirrors, their heads buried in round plastic orbs, their hair wrapped in foil, like abducted humans in an alien laboratory. A longer line of women sat reading Cosmopolitan and Oprah magazines on the chairs and couches along the opposite wall. Between the rows of women, a skeletal girl with rings under her eyes swept severed hairs around the floor with a broom.

The blow dryer fell silent.

"Ooh," crooned the man who held the blower. "Some lucky girl is in for a big surprise." Zohar seemed to slouch even while standing. A strip of skin peeked from between the low waistline of his tight jeans and the hem of the faded T-shirt.

He looked Moshe up and down and smirked. "Can I help you, honey?"

No one had ever sized up Moshe that way—or called him "honey" for that matter—and he was not enjoying the experience. The woman in the seat before Zohar stared at her reflection like a well-trained poodle with long blond curls. She didn't seem to mind the interruption.

Moshe scanned the rows of women. "I'm looking for…"

Before he could complete the sentence, a slender form strolled toward him down the aisle of the salon. A towel wrapped her hair like a pink turban. Her shapely hips gyrated to a familiar rhythm, but when she caught sight of Moshe, she froze. Her eyes narrowed and flitted to the exit, as though she wanted to sprint past him and escape. After a moment's hesitation, her mouth tightened. She plopped onto one of the padded hairdressing chairs and trained her eyes on the mirror.

Savta Sarah, you are a genius! Galit was not prepared to lose her appointment, even if it meant facing Moshe's ghost.

Moshe made for her chair and stared at her in the mirror. As beautiful as ever, turban and all. Words lodged in his throat. Her reflection stared at her feet.

"Looks like our Galit has an admirer," said Zohar. "Shiri, get a vase for those heavenly flowers."

The skeletal assistant dropped the broom and took the roses from Moshe. He had hoped for a moment of privacy but that was not going to happen. *Remember the plan. Right!*

He said, "You're late." With those two words, the first he had ever spoken to her, he hoped to conjure their fondest shared memories.

"Oh, no," said a meek voice behind him, an old lady in the waiting line. "She was here before I got here, oh, two hours ago."

"Two hours?" Moshe could not hide his disbelief. He had never waited more than ten minutes for a haircut.

The blond poodle spoke up. "I waited three." She nodded with pride. "Last week I waited four hours." A murmur of commiseration ran along the line of waiting women.

Zohar raked her hair with his fingers. "That's the price of art, honey," he said.

Of all the women in the salon, only Galit seemed not to have heard him. This was not going the way he had planned. "Galit," he said. "It's me, Moshe."

"Well, well, well," Zohar said. "If it isn't Mr. Karlin, back from the grave." He rolled his eyes.

Moshe didn't know what surprised him more: Zohar's knowledge of his return or the sarcasm in his voice. He ignored both.

"Hangar 17?" he said. "The night we first met?"

Had she made the connection?

Zohar snorted. "Might as well give up now. You won't get a word out of her."

Moshe gave him a warning look that said, "Stay out of this."

Zohar didn't take the hint. "And I don't blame her," he added. He shot an imaginary bullet at Moshe with the blow dryer, and blew smoke from the barrel.

What was he on about? *Stay focused.*

"Galit," he said, desperation crawling into his voice. "We've been through so much together. Aren't you glad to see me again?"

Her head stayed down; her mouth tightened further.

Zohar snorted again. "Typical," he said. "Men think they can run off and have fun, and when they come home everything will be just fine."

Moshe could ignore him no longer. "What are you talking

about?"

Zohar hooted. "I know all about you, Moshe Karlin. I know your type. The girls keep no secrets from me, right, girls?" The rows of women sang a chorus of agreement.

Zohar removed the plastic gown from the blond with a flourish. "See you next week, dear. Regards to that no-good husband of yours. And do me a favor—throw out that blouse. You look a hundred years older in that *shmata*. Excuse me." He bumped Moshe aside with his hips, pulled the towel from Galit's head, and placed his hands on her damp hair like a mind reader.

"Look at those ends! You need a cut, darling. And highlights. Shiri, get the color ready."

Galit seethed on her seat. She had eyes only for the hairdresser. Moshe could use that to his advantage.

"What did she tell you?"

Zohar combed a length of her hair and chopped at the ends with a pair of scissors.

"You're like poor Etti's husband." He tutted. "Business trips to America for weeks at a time. Years on end. As it turns out, he was very busy indeed. Married another girl. Had children with her too! Etti was devastated when she found out."

Moshe could not believe his ears. "But that's not me! I didn't run off. I died!"

Zohar rolled his eyes again. "Oh, please! Have you no shame? To fake your own death—funeral and all!"

"What? No! I didn't fake anything. That's ridiculous."

"Less ridiculous than rising from the dead? Did you honestly expect her to believe that?" Zohar threw up his hands and tossed the implements onto the wheeled trolley of rollers and hairpins. "This is too much for me! I need a smoke." He sashayed out the door.

Moshe looked around at the flock of cowed women. "He hasn't finished her hair." On the sidewalk, Zohar lit a cigarette and stared at the sky.

"Oh, he does that all the time," said the meek old lady in

waiting. "He can go off like that for a half hour."

"He's an artist," said another. Heads nodded in awe.

Moshe sighed. Some things he would never understand.

Galit sat in the chair, her hands clenching the armrests. A trapped animal.

"I didn't leave you, Galit. I died. I know this is hard to believe—I don't understand it either—but I've been given a second chance. *We've* been given a second chance." He had to prove it to her. "I have to show you something," he said. He lifted his shirt. Behind him, voices gasped. "See. No belly button. This is a new body."

Her eyes flitted to his stomach. Her mouth twitched. Her barriers were crumbling.

The door whooshed open. "You still here?" said Zohar, trailing a cloud of smoke.

"Please," Moshe said. His time was running out. "Things will be just the way they were before."

"Ha!" said Zohar. "And things weren't exactly wonderful then."

"Yes, they were!" Moshe fought the urge to throttle the hairdresser right in front of his worshippers.

"OK, Mr. Right. When was the last time you brought her flowers?"

The question caught him unprepared. He had not been big on flowers. The stores only opened after he set out for work, and closed before he left the office. Galit had never seemed to mind.

"Um," he said.

"Exactly," said the hairdresser. "Avi buys her flowers every week."

Moshe disliked Zohar more with each passing second.

"And," the hairdresser continued, "he's better in bed."

Giggles behind him. Moshe did not need to hear that. The very thought of Avi in bed with Galit made him want to puke.

Zohar waved the scissors in the air and resumed chopping at her hair. "Living with you wasn't easy, you know. Working late every night. Never paying attention. It's a wonder she didn't throw you out sooner."

Was it true? Was life with him so bad?

"I'll do better," he said. "I'll change."

"Ha! How many times have you heard that, girls?"

The women in waiting muttered their agreement. Zohar was their God; his every word, their Holy Scripture.

Time for Plan B.

Moshe said, "What about Talya? She needs a father in her life—her real father."

Zohar stopped chopping. "Look what you've done. You've made her cry."

He gripped Moshe by the shoulders, scissors still in hand, and shoved him toward the door.

"Please," Moshe said. "Give us a chance. Don't marry him!"

Zohar pushed him onto the sidewalk and closed the door behind him. "You're not welcome here," he said. "If you care about her at all, you'll leave her alone."

CHAPTER 23

Sunbeams poured through the leaves above and warmed the patches of dirt and wild grass in the courtyard. Birds squawked in the trees. The sounds and smells of Rocheleh's Shabbat cooking drifted through an open window.

Yosef sat in the center of the yard on a low stool of hard plastic designed for a child. He dipped the horsehair brush in the circular tin of polish and spread thick black paste along the side of a leather Sabbath shoe.

He loved Friday mornings. After dropping the boys at school and shopping for groceries at the store, he continued his preparations at leisure. The air tingled with an almost palpable tranquility streaked with eager anticipation. Each passing second brought the Sabbath sanctity closer.

This particular Friday morning, his anticipation skyrocketed, as he sensed the approach not only of the weekly Sabbath, but the final and long-awaited Day of Complete Sabbath. The Messianic Age.

He tilted his hand inside the shoe and polished the other side.

And yet…

After morning prayers, he had stopped by the Mount of Olives. Again, he patrolled the rows of tombstones. Again, he searched the perimeter of trees and bushes. Again, he found nothing.

Two resurrected Jews do not the Resurrection make.

Rabbi Emden's words echoed in his ears and unsettled his Shabbat eve peace of mind. Two days had passed since the discovery of Irina, yet the count of resurrected Jews remained the same.

Have faith, Yosef.

God worked at His own pace and by His own rules. Human impatience would not dictate the course of history. The world had waited two thousand years. The world could wait a little longer. One thing was clear—the Final Redemption had begun. He found no other way to read the facts.

He placed the blackened shoe on the square of old newspaper, then replaced the lid of the tin with a loud click.

A sudden thought vaulted Yosef to his feet, and he rushed indoors to his bedroom. He opened the closet door and ran his fingers over the nylon plastic cover among the suspended shirts and dresses.

The Redemption could arrive any day and without warning, the Sages of Blessed Memory taught, and one should forever be ready to greet the Messiah at a moment's notice. And so, the day after his wedding, Yosef had dry-cleaned his suit and hung it in his closet, awaiting the call of the ram's horn over the hills of Jerusalem. Four children and two homes later, the suit remained in the plastic cover.

Yosef lifted the suit from the rack and slipped the trousers from the hanger. He kicked off his shoes and wriggled out of his weekday slacks. The suit trousers rose over his shins and thighs, but the metal clasps refused to meet over his waist. Yosef shook his head at his own stupidity. He'd need to visit the tailor on Sunday morning. A small delay in the Redemption would not be a bad thing, after all.

"Yossi," said Rocheleh. She stood in the open doorway, a stained apron over her house gown. She had caught him, literally, with his trousers down. "What are you doing?"

"Just trying on my old suit."

She shook her head at his silly antics and got to business.

"It's been four days, Yossi. We have four children to feed. Five, counting you. And now your two houseguests too. We can't go on like this."

"You're right," he said. Their teaching salaries barely covered their own basic needs, and the added load in cooking and laundry fell to her. Good thing he had not discovered more resurrected Jews!

His poor Rocheleh. Born and raised in the ultra-Orthodox community, she had never dreamed that she would marry the once-secular Yosef. The real catches—the Torah prodigies and sons of the Charedi aristocracy—had married her girlfriends whose families had deeper pockets. Rocheleh, however, had collected dust on the shelf until her age had convinced her to settle for a lesser man. Her fortune was about to change.

"Rabbi Emden called this morning," he said. "We're going to meet the Great Council on Sunday evening."

"*The* Great Council?" Her eyebrows lifted on a gust of awe mixed with suspicion.

"Yes! When they find out about Moshe and Irina, they'll want to visit them in person."

Rocheleh brushed a rogue strand of hair beneath her kerchief. "Here, in our house?" The corners of her lips curled into a smile. Her eyes explored the wall, already preparing a menu of delicacies to serve the leading rabbis of the generation—and their wives—in her home.

"Yes! What great merit we have had to have discovered and honored them first in our home."

The smile dropped. He had overdone it. "Sunday they'll be gone?"

"Add a few days to make arrangements. Tuesday, tops."

Rocheleh grunted, cast a parting contemptuous glance at his bare legs, and returned to her pre-Sabbath tasks.

Yosef dressed and returned the suit to the closet.

In every generation, the Sages taught, a Messiah is born. He waits in anonymity and longs for the Redemption, when the time will come for him to reveal his true nature. Coming to think of it, the Messiah must surely be one of the great Torah authorities of the Great Council.

Oh, no!

Yosef grabbed the suit and ran to Emek Refaim. If he hurried, he'd reach the tailor before closing time. If he begged, his suit might be ready on Sunday. If Yosef had the merit to greet the Messiah, he would not do so shabbily dressed.

CHAPTER 24

Noga hesitated outside room 419C in the Shaare Zedek Medical Center.

You have nothing to fear. According to Eliana, the cute mystery patient had woken from his coma. He had a name, and his behavior was as sane as that of the other patients. But Noga remembered the crazy dark eyes and the pink lines his fingers had left on her wrist, and her pulse raced as though she was about to enter a lion's cage.

She should probably stay away, but she could not resist the call. The attraction went beyond his looks or even curiosity about his sudden recovery. He had a name but no family or friends. No visitors. He remained a lonely island in a sea of indifference. *We have a lot in common.* She wasn't exactly hitting on him, either. She was just doing her job.

She drew a deep breath, clutched the transparent folder of papers to her breast like a shield, and stepped over the threshold.

The leg in the cast hung from the sling, the other lay beneath the blanket. As she rounded the divider curtain, more of his body came into view. *Be asleep!* But the fairy godmothers ignored her wish. Mr. Eli Katz lay in bed, his eyes fixed on the blank television screen in the corner.

She cleared her throat. "How are you feeling today, Mr.

Katz?"

His head rolled on the pillow. The mop of jet-black hair fell over the bandage on his forehead. His dark eyes considered her. Then the head returned to the blank screen. If he remembered her from yesterday, he hid it well.

"Trapped," he said.

Not a man of words. She would have to do the talking. She didn't do small talk, although her job forced her to speak with strangers of all sorts. For some causes—and some people—she was willing to make the effort.

She got to the point. "I'm conducting a study," she said. "Genetic research. We're—"

"I'm not good with blood," he said, interrupting her without even making eye contact.

A full sentence. Progress. She rushed ahead with the good news. "No need for that," she said. "The lab already has samples."

That got his attention. "The lab has *what*?"

She felt her cheeks redden under the gaze of those deep, dark eyes. "Samples. Of your blood. When you arrived, they had to run tests before surgery. It's standard."

He ran his uninjured hand through his hair as though she had just informed him that his mother had died. What was his problem?

She took advantage of the silence to plow on with her sales pitch. "We're tracing a particular gene—"

He raised his hand for her to stop. "I'm not interested. Just… just leave me alone, OK?"

Her cheeks burned again but with an entirely different emotion. "As you wish," she snapped. She had liked him better comatose.

She turned to leave, but stopped at the curtain to deliver a parting shot. "You're going to be here a long time, Mr. Katz," she said. "You might want to make some friends."

CHAPTER 25

Moshe and Irina followed Rabbi Yosef down Shimshon Street. The setting sun bathed the low stone buildings and leafy trees of Baka in gold. The rabbi's sons ran ahead in black trousers and white collared shirts, their curled side locks swinging at their ears. Their footfalls reverberated off the homes and apartment buildings of the quiet suburban street. In a window, twin Shabbat candles burned on silver candlesticks. The smells of freshly baked bread and chicken soup wafted in the gentle breeze. Cars straddled the sidewalk as their owners relaxed at home after a tiring week.

Moshe and Irina fell a little behind.

"How did it go?" she asked. She looked particularly fairy-like in the green dress from Tal Chaim and the rabbanit's makeup—a fairy on her way to a palatial ball. In the rush of Shabbat preparations, he had not had time to update her.

"Good, at first," he said. The hot shower and fresh clothes had raised his spirits. Then details of the encounter rose in his memory. "Terrible, actually," he added.

Irina chuckled. "Good and terrible?"

"I finally got to see her and speak to her," he explained. "But she didn't say a word. She's furious. She thinks that I faked my death and that I've been leading a double life. Oh, and that I was a terrible husband."

He had reeled from the revelation for a full hour after Zohar Raphael had thrown him out of the hair salon.

"I find that hard to believe," she said.

"Which part—the double life or the bad husband?" At least he still had his sense of humor.

"Either."

They passed his old home. The blinds remained down, the door shut. Slivers of light at the edges hinted at the warmth of his old life, the warmth he would probably never know again.

"I thought we were doing well," he said. "We were a team. We were going to conquer the world together. But toward the end, I suppose I ran too far ahead. I didn't even notice that she had fallen behind."

Irina said, "But you've stopped running now. Maybe she just needs time to catch up. Don't give up, Moshe."

He smiled. "'A Karlin never quits,'" he said. "That's what my father used to say."

"Those are good words to live by."

They strolled along in silence. It felt good to have her support—a pair of objective eyes to keep him sane. And thank God for Shabbat. He sorely needed a break from the strain of his new life.

They turned a corner. Rabbi Yosef held open the metal gate of a low-walled courtyard and ushered them inside.

The Emek Refaim Synagogue on Yael Street—a humble oblong of rough stone blocks—reminded Moshe of the Western Wall in the heart of Jerusalem's Old City.

In the late 1800s, German Templers journeyed to the Holy Land to promote the rebuilding of the Temple and to await the Second Coming. The former Protestants bought large swaths of land in Haifa, Jaffa, and Jerusalem's Refaim Valley, where they tilled the holy soil and invented the Jaffa orange.

New suburbs mushroomed around their German Colony in Jerusalem—Katamon, Talbieh, and Baka—and housed wealthy Arabs.

During World War II, however, the British deported the

German settlers. Only their cemeteries and the stone homesteads with arched doorways and metal shutters remained as reminders of their presence.

Then, in 1949, Jewish immigrants established the Emek Refaim synagogue in one of the old stone structures of Baka, abandoned during the War of Independence. And so, by yet another ironic twist of history, the pious Germans had helped build not a Temple for a resurrected Jesus Christ but a synagogue for holocaust survivors—and now, two newly resurrected Jews.

The rabbi directed Irina to the door of the women's section. Inside the synagogue, he handed Moshe a velvet *kippah* and a prayer book, and seated him at a pew of dark, carved wood and navy blue velvet upholstery.

The rabbi took his seat at the front, facing the congregation, and recited the Song of Songs, in a traditional singsong.

Never in his life had Moshe been the first to arrive at synagogue. Old men wearing their Sabbath finery trickled inside and filled the pews. Moshe caught snatches of conversations in German, Hungarian, French, Persian, and English.

According to a bronze plaque on the wall, the furnishings had once belonged to a synagogue in the small town of Busseto in northern Italy. Moshe studied the elaborate carvings of the Holy Ark, the banisters of the raised dais, and the pews.

In this renovated Jerusalem ruin, beneath a canopy of Arabian arches, European Jewish refugees rested on furniture rescued from an extinct Italian Jewish community.

Emek Refaim—*the Valley of Giants.* Or *Valley of Ghosts*—for what was this nation if not a heap of disenfranchised souls, a valley of dry bones drawn together from the four corners of the Earth, after enduring every catastrophe, and surviving every prophecy of doom? In the middle sat Moshe, the biggest ghost of all.

The singsong ended. Rabbi Yosef nodded at a bony old man in a blue suit, who hobbled to the central podium, wrapped a fringed *talit* over his shoulders, and led the afternoon prayers.

The congregation rose for the silent Standing Prayer. Moshe placed his prayer book on the stand and turned the pages. The first of nineteen blessings invoked the patriarchs: Abraham, Isaac, and Jacob. The second made the hair on the back of his neck stand on end.

You are eternally powerful, Lord; You are the Resurrector of the Dead, and redeem abundantly.

You sustain life with loving kindness, revive the dead with great mercy; you support the fallen, heal the sick, release the fettered, and are steadfast to those that sleep in the dust.

Who is like You, Master of Powers, and who even resembles You? The King Who kills and revives, and nurtures redemption.

And dependable You are to give life to the dead.

Blessed are You, Resurrector of the Dead.

Moshe had read the blessing countless times, but he did not recall the focus on resurrection. The living pay little attention to the dead.

Jews uttered this prayer three times a day as their ancestors had over the centuries. As a vulnerable minority, and the target of entrenched prejudice and blind hatred in many countries, the specter of sudden death haunted their every step. The return to Jerusalem and a national homeland on their holy ground must have seemed as impossible and incredible as Ezekiel's dry old bones standing up and breathing again. And yet it was that unreasonable hope that had kept them going.

His thoughts drifted to the words of the Israeli anthem.

Od lo avda tikvatenu / Our hope is not yet lost

Hatikva bat shnot alpayim / The hope of two thousand years

Lihyot am chofshi be'artzenu / To be a free nation in our land.

The synagogue windows darkened. The congregation welcomed the Sabbath Bride with song. Their voices rose and fell, then rose again. On the Sabbath day, Jews in synagogues around the world sang these same words and notes. Moshe hummed along and found a measure of comfort.

He too hoped to revive the past. That past, however, had

lost its rosy hue. He had spent little time with his daughter. He had steered Karlin & Son toward the sharp rocks of disaster. He had neglected his wife. Did that old life deserve revival?

His wrist itched beneath the heavy watch.

Now that he knew his shortcomings, he knew what to fix. To win back Galit, he would need to change. Spend more time with her. Work less. That part shouldn't be a problem. With Karlin & Son diving toward bankruptcy, he'd soon have plenty of free time.

You have two weeks.

Two weeks until the wedding. Two weeks to reinvent himself. To prove to her that he deserved a second chance.

The prayers concluded. Rabbi Yosef approached the podium and announced the prayer times for the next day. The congregants poured out the doors and into the courtyard.

Irina emerged from the women's entrance, green sleeves reaching beyond her elbows. She and Moshe exchanged Sabbath greetings in the yellow streetlight. The sweet scent of the rabbanit's deodorant clung to her.

They waited for the rabbi, who shook hands with the line of exiting congregants, some of whom gave Moshe strange looks and whispered to each other. The rabbi's children dived between the men and women, darted out of the courtyard, and down the street like a flock of young sparrows.

Irina looked at home in the modest garb, and again he wondered whether religion had played a role in her forgotten former life. She looked equally comfortable in jeans and T-shirts. Without memory, we could be anyone. Without memory, we are all the same.

There was a movement in the corner of his eye. He turned, but not fast enough. A freight train slammed into his jaw and threw him off his feet. He sprawled on the dusty cobblestones. Women cried out. Shoes shuffled behind him. He rolled over. A man lunged at him, held back only by the rabbi, who stood between them with outstretched hands.

Avi straightened his shirt. A fire glowed in his eyes.

"Come near her again," he said, "and you'll regret it."

Irina crouched over Moshe and touched his shoulder. The few remaining congregants watched from a safe distance.

Moshe tasted blood in his mouth and touched his bruised lip. "She's still my wife," he said.

"No she isn't. You died, remember? Now it's my turn."

"*Your turn.* What is she—the village bicycle? You're a thief."

Avi jabbed a finger at him in the air. "Just stay away from her, unless you think you'll come back from the dead twice." He nodded at the rabbi and skulked away.

Moshe knew a threat when he heard one. "So now you're a thief *and* a murderer?"

"Murderer?" Avi said and laughed as he disappeared into the night. "Can't murder a dead man."

CHAPTER 26

Moshe washed dust from his hands and blood from his face in the rabbi's bathroom. His hands trembled. Avi had a point. In the eyes of the State, Moshe Karlin no longer existed. What charges would a prosecutor file against his murderer—desecration of a corpse? Would the police even make an arrest? The law provided no protection for the deceased Moshe Karlin.

He added Death Threat to his growing list of challenges and returned to the living room. Uriel, the rabbi's oldest son, read a book on the sofa. Simcha and Ari played with soccer cards on the carpet. Little Yehuda pushed a toy car along the edge of a shelf and made it fly in the air.

"Boys," Rabbi Yosef said. "Let's start."

His children dropped what they were doing and took their seats at the dinner table. Moshe had never encountered such obedient kids. They had helped with the Sabbath preparations without complaint. They had dusted the furniture, washed the floors, set the dinner table with a white tablecloth and white faux china.

The rabbi and his wife sat at either end of the dinner table. Moshe made for the empty chair between the rabbi and Irina. Uriel, Yehuda, and Simcha eyed him from across the table and over the two polished candlesticks that held burning tea lights.

Rabbi Yosef led the singing of two songs. The first welcomed the Sabbath angels, and the second praised the industrious mother of the household. The rabbi stood and called on each of his sons to approach him for a whispered blessing sealed with a kiss on the forehead.

Friday nights in the Karlin residence had involved TV dinners and weekend newspapers. In the rabbi's home, however, time seemed to have stopped, and an otherworldly calm replaced the flurry of pre-Shabbat activity.

A warm glow spread over Irina's face. She must have been thinking the same thing.

Blessings completed, Rabbi Yosef raised a silver goblet that brimmed with red wine and he recited the Sabbath *Kiddush* prayer. He poured the wine into plastic shot glasses and passed them down the table. Moshe downed his in one gulp. *Grape juice.* He could do with something stronger.

They filed into the kitchen to wash their hands using a double-handled jug. A tall tin urn hissed on the counter. On a hot tray perched over the gas stove, a large pot of soup and a pile of tinfoil trays bubbled. The rabbi had set timers in wall sockets around the house to turn lights and fans on and off as desired, for the *Shabbat* rules prohibited the use of electric switches on the holy day.

They returned to their seats at the table. Rabbi Yosef removed the velvet cover from the twin plaited loaves of bread, recited the blessing—*Who brings forth bread from the earth*—and broke off clumps of bread, dipped them in salt, and tossed them across the table to his guests and family.

"Welcome," he said as he sliced the rest of the loaf with a silver bread knife. "It's not every week we have such honored guests."

A chair leg creaked as the rabbanit stood and made for the kitchen.

"Thank you for taking us in," Irina said. "This"—she indicated the Sabbath table—"is lovely."

Moshe agreed. The bread was warm and sweet. A spirit of

contentment filled the home. Even the rabbi's wife seemed to have softened.

The rabbi leaned back, a king on his throne. "Shabbat," he said. "Me'en Olam Habah." A taste of the World to Come. The rabbi must have been referring to the World of Souls, for Moshe's bodily afterlife had been anything but relaxing.

The rabbanit placed steaming bowls of watery chicken soup before them.

Yehuda, the boy who had asked him whether he was dead that first day, ogled him as he ate. "What happened to your mouth?"

"Yehuda!" the rabbanit chided.

"It's OK," Moshe said. The soup tasted heavenly but the salt stung his torn lip. "A man hit me outside synagogue."

The boy's eyes widened. "Did you hit him back?"

"No."

"Oh." He seemed disappointed.

Not now, Moshe thought. *And not with fists in the street.*

Rabbi Yosef cleared his throat. "Moshe, Irina. I almost forgot. I have good news. Rabbi Emden, a close friend and a great man, has arranged for us to meet with the Great Council on Sunday night."

Irina looked to Moshe for an explanation but he had none. "The Great Council?"

"The Council of Great Torah Sages. The leading Torah authorities of our generation. Rabbi Alter. Rabbi Teitelbaum. Rabbi Auerbach."

"I have Rabbi Auerbach!" cried Simcha. He pulled a wad of crumpled soccer cards from his trouser pocket and fanned through them. He held up a card. Instead of a soccer superstar, the laminated surface framed the stern face of a bearded rabbi.

"Hey, give that back," Ari said from between Irina and the rabbanit.

"No, I won it fair and square!"

"Enough!" said the rabbanit. She had seated Ari and Simcha across the table from each other for a reason.

Irina glanced at Moshe, her eyes conveying a mix of delight and concern. "Should I go as well?" she asked the rabbi.

The beard twitched. Heavy-duty rabbis avoided interacting with women, but Rabbi Yosef had enough tact not to say so. "Just Moshe for now."

"And these rabbis," Irina asked, "they'll be able to explain what happened to us?"

"Yes, and more. The sages of the Great Council head famous yeshivas. They have connections to charitable institutions…"

The rabbi faltered and lowered his eyes to his bowl of soup.

"In other words," the rabbanit said, "they will find you a new home."

They slurped their soup in silence. Her last sentence had killed the conversation.

Moshe didn't blame her. Moshe and Irina could not sponge off them forever. But he had hoped to stay close to Galit a little longer, long enough that he would not need another home.

The bookish Uriel interpreted the lull in conversation as an invitation to ask questions.

"Moshe, what do you do?"

Moshe's soup spoon hovered in the air. He had no answer for that most trivial of questions for an able-bodied adult man. Karlin & Son was not just a job—he *was* Karlin & Son. At forty-two, Moshe found himself penniless, jobless, and in the throes of an identity crisis.

He felt his brow moisten with sweat. "I'm still figuring that out," he said.

Confusion dumbfounded the boys as they struggled with a new mental box: a grown man with no profession.

Rabbi Yosef came to his rescue. "Life is a journey," he said. "We might start out in one direction, and later try another until we find our true path."

Moshe would settle for a regular paycheck.

The rabbi turned to his guests. "Rabbi Nachman of

Breslov said that the entire world is a very narrow bridge. And what is the main thing?" His voice rose in a school-teacher tone of expectation.

"Have no fear at all!" the boys responded, like good students. The rabbi winked at Moshe and then he and his sons broke into song.

Kol ha'olam kooloh / The whole world is

Gesher tzar me'od / A very narrow bridge.

They accompanied the slow, calming melody with well-rehearsed hand gestures. The pace picked up for the chorus.

Ve'ha'ikar / And the main thing

Lo le'fached klal / Is to have no fear at all.

By the end of the song, youthful smiles had returned to the table. The rabbanit placed tinfoil trays of browned chicken, potatoes, and steaming white rice on the table.

"Rabbi Nachman lived two centuries ago," Rabbi Yosef said. "He taught that we are forbidden to lose hope. No matter what we did in the past, today—every day—we start our lives anew."

Moshe piled food onto his plate. The chicken drumstick fell apart under his knife. *Start our lives anew.* Again, the rabbi made it sound easy, as easy as putting one foot ahead of the other and not looking down.

There came a loud knocking at the door.

Moshe's heart skipped a beat. He pictured Avi outside the door with a large club. Irina gripped his arm.

Rabbi Yosef stood and approached the door. He peered through the peephole. Moshe held his breath. *Don't open it, Rabbi. Don't do it.*

The rabbi, however, did not obey Moshe's thoughts. He turned a baffled expression to the table, and pulled the handle.

A woman stood on the doorstep. Short. Olive skin. Young. Her dress dusted the ground. The shawl on her head covered most of her mousy brown hair. She scanned the room behind the rabbi with the large dark eyes of a frightened deer.

"Rabbi Yosef?" she said. Her Hebrew had a guttural edge, the unmistakable accent of a tongue more at home in Arabic. "I'm sorry to disturb you." She looked over her shoulder at the dark street. "Please. May I come in?" she said. "I need your help."

CHAPTER 27

From his bed, Eli heard the chant of a man's voice down the hall. The Friday night *Kiddush* blessing. The nurse had dimmed the lights in his room. The weekday hospital sounds in the hallways had subsided as staff and visitors returned home for the holy day.

That morning, the Russian nurse had detached the sensors of the heart monitor from his chest but he remained immobile and helpless. The Thin Voice, silent. His powers, fled. He was starting to miss the crows.

A terrifying thought whispered in his ear. *You will never heal. Your fate is that of the mortals now.*

The chant ended and a motley chorus answered *Amen.* Eli added a prayer of his own. *Don't abandon me! Don't deny me your Holy Spirit!* Somewhere in the hospital, vials of his blood awaited the scrutiny of modern medicine. The results would raise questions. Questions would lead to further tests and yet more questions. He had to get out now, while he still could.

He inhaled three deep breaths and closed his eyes. He focused on the muscle in his head. *Flex!* A tingling sensation crept down his spine and along his limbs.

Yes!

He commanded his shattered leg to heal.

He wriggled his toes. He lifted his leg from the sling.

Yes! Yes!

Now, to the side—

Pain erupted in his bones. The leg fell limp and swung in the sling.

This can't be. Tears welled in his eyes. He had a job to do. The destiny of the entire world weighed on his shoulders. After waiting long centuries, to be trapped just when—

Something moved. At the edge of the divider curtain, a hand floated in thin air. A white-gloved hand, palm out.

Eli blinked. *Have I gone mad?* The glove hovered like the Divine hand at Belshazzar's feast. This hand, however, did not write riddles on the wall. Instead, it extended into the room and grew a forearm—a naked, hairy forearm. A second hand joined the first. The two gloved hands shifted sideways, one by one, feeling their way along an invisible wall. A head appeared above the hands. Wild orange hair. Large white frown painted over the mouth. Large red ball of a nose.

The clown jumped into Eli's private space with a flourish and a bow.

"Get lost," Eli said.

The clown waggled a finger at him and placed his hands on his hips.

"Scat!"

The clown seemed to consider his advice, then thumbed his nose, stuck out his tongue, and pranced back to the safety of the curtain.

"And don't come back."

He waited for the fool to return. He didn't. *Good!* He hated clowns. He hated humanity. He hated hospitals.

He sighed. Hate would not free him. The girl in the white cloak was right. He needed friends. How did one make friends? He was out of practice.

The large Russian nurse charged into the room and glanced at the clipboard that dangled at the foot of his bed.

"Shabbat shalom, Mr. Katz. Would you like to hear *Kiddush*?"

"Did you see… a clown?"

She gave him a quizzical look. "A clown? Afraid not." She placed his nightly painkillers and a plastic cup of water on the bedside stand, and she replaced the drainage container at the end of the catheter.

Had he dreamed the mime act? This was no time to lose his mind. He needed all his wits about him.

A plan condensed in his mind. The plan involved risk and deception, and a small sacrifice, but what was the alternative?

"Drink up," said the nurse. She towered over him, hands akimbo.

He read the name on her tag. "Eliana," he said. "Can you do me a favor?"

CHAPTER 28

Yosef held the door open for the Arab girl. He had a bad feeling about this. The sleeves of the dress fell past her hands. He studied her body for signs of a machete or an explosive belt. Arabs worked at the shops on Bethlehem Road and Emek Refaim but they did not wander around his neighborhood at night, certainly not a young, lone woman.

She stepped inside, barefoot.

"The woman at Tal Chaim said that you help people like me," she said.

People like me. His intestines tied in a knot. *She couldn't possibly mean… No, that was impossible.*

Her eyes moved to the hot food on the table. The aromas filled his nostrils as they surely did hers. His heart went out to her.

"Please," he said. He indicated the chair of his youngest son. "Sit there. Yehuda, move over and sit with me." Yehuda jumped off the chair and made for the head of the table.

"Rocheleh," he added, "please fetch a bowl of soup for our guest." She glared at him for a second, then did as he asked.

Abraham, the first Jew, had welcomed desert wanderers and idol worshippers into his tent. His wife, Sarah, prepared the delicacies and Abraham served the guests himself. Should

Yosef Lev do any less? Was this not an opportunity to teach his children the *mitzvah* of hospitality?

The girl took her place at the table and thanked Rocheleh for the bowl of soup.

Yosef returned to his seat and placed Yehuda on his lap. The uneasy sense of déjà vu returned and unsettled his Sabbath peace. He had seen this film before. Twice. But this third showing made no sense!

The girl mopped up the remnant of her soup with a slice of challah bread and wolfed it down.

"What is your name?"

She looked at her host, and the hunted look returned to her eyes. "Samira," she said in a low voice, as though the mention of her name might bring misfortune.

"Are you in trouble?"

She lowered her eyes to the table and nodded. She closed her eyes as though the memory was too difficult to bear. "They might be looking for me."

"Who?"

She shook her head.

"Who, Samira? Who is looking for you?"

She opened her eyes and stared, unseeing.

"My father. Or my brother."

"No one knows you are here, Samira. It's OK." His words seemed to comfort the girl.

He relaxed on his chair too. The girl had run away from home. An ordinary domestic dispute. He would hand her over to social services as soon as Shabbat ended. She was not a resurrectee. Of course not. A resurrected Arab? That was impossible.

"They must not find me," she said.

"Your family?"

"My father."

What could make her shudder so at the mention of her father? "Why not, Samira?"

"Because," she said, choking on the words, "the last time we met, he killed me."

CHAPTER 29

Saturday night, Moshe plunged his hands into the soapy water of the kitchen sink. He pulled a plate from the pile of meat dishes and scoured the surface with a sponge. Irina worked beside him at the dairy sink.

It felt good to be busy after the long summer day of rest. Moshe had never kept the Sabbath in all its restrictions—he had not even known how extensive they were. No computer. No phones. No cars. No cooking. No preparations for after the Sabbath day.

He had slept on the couch Friday night as Irina and Samira had taken over the boys' room. When he awoke Saturday morning, the rabbi had already left for synagogue. After Avi's attack the previous night, Moshe had preferred not to stroll past his old house alone.

He spent the morning lounging in the living room. He studied the rabbis on the wall. Maimonides struck a regal pose in his turban and clerical gown, his tidy beard and mustache. The Chofetz Chayim gazed through shuttered eyelids beneath a simple Polish cap, his prolific white beard tucked into a heavy black coat.

Moshe perused the rabbi's library. He read from the Bible for the first time since childhood. Abraham's journey to the Promised Land. Isaac's devotion to the land despite conflict and famine. Jacob's return after a forced exile. Joshua's conquest of Canaan. David's united kingdom. Solomon's golden temple in Jerusalem.

The calamitous destruction. The exile to Babylon.

During two thousand years of national dormancy, like disembodied souls, the Israelite nation turned inward. The exiles found comfort in their Torah and its prophecies of dry bones.

"Son of Man," God asked Ezekiel. "Can these bones live?" Moshe felt as though God was speaking to him as well. "They say 'Our bones have dried, our hope is lost; we are done for.'" But God had not lost hope. "I will raise you from your graves, My nation, and I will bring you to the Land of Israel."

Among the many religious works on the shelves, Moshe found a biography of the early Prime Ministers of the State of Israel. Ben Gurion. Levi Eshkol. Menachem Begin. They invoked the heroes of the Bible as they burst back onto the pages of history. The returning Jews no longer resembled the shepherd prophets and glorious monarchs of the past, but the same ancient spirit animated their new collective body.

Moshe placed a clean dish on the drying rack and scrubbed the next. Down the corridor, bathwater splashed and little feet pounded on the floors, as the rabbi and his wife prepared the boys for bed. Occasionally, the rabbanit raised her voice at the rabbi. Moshe could not hear her words but he guessed their meaning.

"We need to find a new place to stay," he said. "I'm not sure we'll like the accommodations the Great Council will provide, if they do."

Irina squirted dish soap on a blue sponge. "Where can we go?"

By "we," she meant the three of them. A Russian, an Israeli, and an Arab—it sounded like the start of a bad joke, but circumstances had bound their fates together. With Irina's forgotten life and Samira's murderous family, the task of finding a new home would fall to Moshe.

"I'll call in a few favors."

He cleaned out the sink and dried his hands. The rabbi marched into the living room and pulled a book from the shelves.

"Rabbi, may I use your phone?"

The rabbi turned and smiled. "Sure."

The title on the spine of the book read Deeds of Our Sages. Bedtime stories about righteous rabbis. Rabbi Yosef deserved to feature there too.

"And the laptop?"

"Of course, I'll get it right away."

Moshe opened the computer—a bulky ASUS with duct tape holding the disc drive in place—on the dinner table and jotted down telephone numbers from the Bezeq online telephone directory. He dialed the first number into the rabbi's home telephone and pressed the receiver to his ear.

He had interviewed many prospective employees over the years but he had never sat on the other side of the table. He was not enjoying the experience.

The number rang, then switched to an answering service.

"Sivan," Moshe said, after the tone, "it's Moshe Karlin. I've got a lot of explaining to do." He left the rabbi's home phone as his contact number.

One down, two to go. Arkadi was not listed. That left Mathew and Pini. If his former employees had a spare bedroom, he was sure they'd help him. He would have done the same for them in an instant. Pini had a large family of his own to feed, so Moshe tried Mathew next.

After two rings, he picked up.

"Holy crapola!" Mathew said in English. Moshe breathed a sigh of relief. Finally, a figure from his old life who was willing to speak to him. "I heard rumors but I didn't believe them. You've got to come by my place."

The walk to the end of Palmach Street took ten minutes. Moshe and Irina stared at an old soot-stained apartment block. Samira, who had spent most of the day cowering in her room, had opted for an early night. Moshe had dropped

Mathew home after many a long shift at Karlin & Son, but he had never ventured inside. They climbed the three flights to apartment number six.

The door opened before he could knock. Mathew slouched on the threshold wearing shorts and a T-shirt. Stubble on his chin. Lanky hair. Unemployment had taken its toll.

"Moshe Karlin," he said. "Back from the dead." His mouth hung open, and he nodded his head. He was always nodding his head. He wrapped Moshe in a bony hug. He glanced at Irina. "Who's your friend?"

Moshe made the introductions.

"Come on in. Soda or beer?"

He made for the refrigerator in the corner of the living room. No, not the living room. The entire apartment. An unmade bed lined one wall beneath the window and faced a lopsided closet, a mounted flat-screen television, and a framed print of a castle atop an immense rock that floated in thin air above the crashing waves of a seashore. A white plastic chair and a wheeled coffee table filled the little living space that remained.

There was no spare couch for Moshe in the American immigrant's studio apartment, never mind Irina and Samira. With no family in Israel, and no safety net, Mathew was as alone and defenseless as they. Without his job at Karlin & Son, how far was he from landing on the street?

Mathew handed out Carlsbergs in green bottles of frosted glass. He spread the sheet over the bed, indicated for them to sit, and pulled up the white plastic chair. He asked the usual questions about Moshe's death, return, and Heaven. The answers rolled off Moshe's tongue.

Moshe said, "I'm sorry about your job."

"Don't be. Getting fired was the best thing that could have happened to me."

"It was?" Moshe sipped his beer to hide his disappointment.

"Avi is an asshole. He didn't come up to your ankles, man,

and I'm not just saying that." He gave a bitter laugh. "That jerk got under my skin from day one, even before he became the big boss." He took a swig of beer. "But besides that, getting fired opened my mind. I signed up for unemployment and took a course in technical writing. I start my first job next week. I'll earn double what I used to and work fixed office hours."

"That's great," Moshe said. "Good for you."

"You should try it."

"Try what?" Moshe's English was workable but not on a level for technical writing.

"Unemployment." Mathew nodded his head with enthusiasm. "Go to the Ministry of Employment. Fill out a form. Check in once a week. You don't even have to look a human being in the eye—just use the self-service terminal. You worked hard all those years, right? Might as well get something back. Until you find your feet."

Unemployment benefits. The thought had never occurred to Moshe. Mathew had a valid point. Irina nodded her support for the motion too. Moshe had kept careful books. He had paid his social security levies to Bituach Leumi every month. The Ministry might even find him a job. He had never spent so long without the buzz of an all-consuming project, and the days of inactivity gnawed on his nerves. Why not?

"Thanks, Mathew," he said. "I'll try that."

"You're welcome." He nodded his head some more. The immigrant had lived in a large box for years, lost his job—but not his optimism—and still came out smiling. Life in Wisconsin must be pretty tough.

"Mathew," he said, curiosity bubbling up through the beer, "do you ever regret moving to Israel?"

Mathew blinked at him and then searched for his answer on the blank wall.

"Nope," he said. He took another long gulp of beer. "But sometimes," he added, "I regret that some of the other people moved here."

CHAPTER 30

Avi ducked as a dinner plate hurtled overhead and shattered against the wall of the living room. Shards of china and plaster rained on his head.

Galit reached for another plate. "You lied to me!"

He spread his hands like a lion-tamer in the corner of a cage. "Calm down. Please."

She had spent the day crying in their bedroom. When she emerged Saturday night, Avi thought that she had settled down. He was wrong.

"You said he faked his death," she said.

Avi dodged another plate and stepped closer. Eventually she'd run out of ammunition. He hoped to reach her before then. They had no money for a new dinner service, but now was probably not the best time to tell her about the financial crisis at Karlin & Son.

This was Moshe's fault. Everything was Moshe's fault. Not for the first time, Avi wished that he had never met Moshe Karlin. He sure as hell wished he had never saved his neck. Moshe had stolen Galit from him once before—he was not going to steal her again.

"I was wrong," he lied. "I made a mistake. What made more sense—that he came back from the grave?"

Moshe's death had been a windfall. Finally, Avi had gotten

the girl and inherited a business—the head start that life had never offered him.

But Moshe couldn't let him enjoy it, could he? He had to return from the dead and ruin his life. Again.

Another plate spun through the air. This time, he ducked too late. The plate glanced off his temple and crashed on the marble tiles. He touched his wound and his fingers returned red and wet.

Humor, Moshe had said. *Make her laugh.* Avi saw nothing to laugh about, so he said, "Just listen to me for a second, will you?"

Galit allowed the ceasefire, her chest heaving. He didn't blame her for freaking out. The sight of Moshe in their bedroom had made him almost pee his pajamas. But the apparition had neither torn him limb from limb, nor cursed him for his sins. The ghost had not remembered dying. He didn't even know that he was supposed to be dead.

When Moshe moved to throw him out, Avi chose fight over flight. This time he would not step aside.

"You're right," he said. "He died. But that doesn't change who he is. It doesn't change what he did to you."

Galit loosened her grip on the plate. Avi stepped closer. He understood how she felt. He felt it too. The terror. The anger. The fear. *Aim those emotions at Moshe.*

"Can't you see what he's doing?" he said. "He's trying to confuse you. To make you forget."

One more step forward and he wrapped his arms around her. She shuddered in his embrace as she sobbed. "It's him. It's really him."

"I know," he said. "But I won't let him hurt you again."

Avi's knuckles were still raw from decking Moshe the previous night. In two weeks, Avi would marry Galit and—dead or alive—Moshe wouldn't matter anymore. Two weeks was a long time to keep Moshe at bay.

"But God brought him back..." she said.

"Shh." He rocked her in his arms. She was asking questions again. He feared those questions the most. He had to act fast—fast and smart—to remove Moshe from the scene for good.

And now he knew how.

"He won't bother you again," he said. He kissed her head and smiled. Moshe would never see it coming.

CHAPTER 31

Noga curled up on an oversized beanbag and tried to get the dark eyes of Eli Katz out of her head.

The television stood blank and silent in the living room of her rental off Ussishkin Street in Nachlaot. She took a sip from her mug of coffee.

Why can't I meet a normal guy?

When she was eighteen years old, her body had shed the extra pounds of adolescence. Her podgy face and bloated limbs became slim and slender, and all of a sudden, the cocky boys who had ignored her for years vied for her attention. She saw right through them and she despised their advances. Then loathing had turned to fear: that one day an exceptionally sly brute would penetrate her defenses, conquer her heart, and make her his trophy wife. Would he care about the girl behind the pretty face?

She built walls of suspicion around her, relying on well-meaning friends and coworkers at the hospital for a supply of random single men.

The term "blind dates" did not do them justice. She preferred to think of them as "blind, deaf, and dumb dates" as the slew of doctors, computer geeks, and academics fell into three classes: men who saw only themselves; men who didn't listen to a word she said; and men blessed with the conversation skills of a dead fish.

Noga preferred the company of her library. Books provided hours of entertainment. You could shut them if they bored you. And you never had to wait for them to call.

As she approached thirty, fewer invitations came her way. Which did she prefer—the torrent of disappointments or the deathly silence?

The click-clack of high heels on hard floor tiles announced that Sharona had entered the living room. The young student's denim skirt barely covered her behind and the neckline of her Guess tank top dipped toward her navel. New Yorkers had different ideas about fashion.

"Going out with girlfriends," she announced in English. "See you later!" Noga had asked her flatmate always to let her know where she was going in case she went missing. Yes, she had turned into a crazy old aunt.

Noticing Noga sprawled on the beanbag, Sharona gave her a sad, puppy-dog face. "Aw. Do you wanna come along?"

Poor old maid mopes at home alone on a Saturday night. Let me save her.

"Thanks, but I've got work to do," Noga lied.

Sharona's eyes brightened. "I can help with your makeup."

She was always offering Noga a makeover. "With the right clothes and hair," she had once told her, "you'll be stunning."

Thanks a lot.

Sharona wasn't the brightest crystal in the chandelier. She studied International Relations at Hebrew U and her fieldwork seemed to involve visiting every mall and coffee shop in the capital. She took pride in the fact that her parents had named her after a pop song in the late seventies.

At the end of the year, Sharona would pack her bags and return home to Manhattan, and Noga would find a replacement, as she did every year.

"You have a good time," Noga said. Sharona didn't need her aging Israeli flatmate to spoil her night on the town.

Sharona gave her one last pained look and marched out the door in a cloud of powdery perfume.

Her young flatmate meant no harm. She might even be right. *Crawl out of your shell. Maybe then you'll meet a normal guy.*

Like Eli Katz.

She almost sprayed Nescafe over her legs as she laughed. What a waste of time that had been. Her curiosity about the mystery patient had grown into sympathy for a lonely and tormented invalid. When he grabbed her arm, however, a dormant emotion stirred inside her. The sensation went beyond his magnetic gaze, boyish locks, or manly jaw, although she could not deny those. She had felt a sense of belonging—that he had claimed her, that she had come home.

She had been willing to write off the delusional outburst to brain trauma and drugs. Yesterday, however, the illusion had shattered into tiny jagged shards: Eli Katz was a first-rate jerk. *Then why am I still thinking about him?*

Noga's phone jingled.

"Hi, Sarit."

"We're going out tonight."

"No, thank you."

"I'm not accepting 'no' for an answer."

Sarit, her old classmate from Hebrew U, never ran out of bubbly optimism. It drove Noga insane.

"What are we doing this time?"

"Folk dancing at Binyanei Ha'uma."

"Folk dancing? What are we—seventy years old?"

"Hey, be grateful. The other option was a sing-along. I'm sure there'll be lots of single guys there tonight."

"Yeah. Seventy-year-old singles. Who like folk dancing. Besides, I just met someone at work."

"Really? A doctor?"

Noga had planted the half-truth to avoid death by folk dancing, but she regretted her words already.

"No, a patient."

"Is he married?"

"No, he's not married."

"I thought you worked with couples from IVF."

"Mostly. This guy is in a different ward."

"Which ward?"

"Neurology. Motorbike accident."

"So he's brain dead? Sounds like a match made in heaven."

"Very funny. He's mentally sound, I'll have you know, except..." She trailed off.

"Except what?"

Noga had already said more than she had planned to, but the rest was too good to omit. "Well, sometimes he thinks he's Elijah the Prophet."

Laughter on the line. "Shut! Up!"

"No kidding."

"Well, at least you actually spoke to him. That's a step forward for you. Now, about tonight—"

"I told you, I'm not interested."

"Forget about yourself for a minute. *I* need you, remember? You're the bait."

"What am I—a worm?"

"A diamond. You attract the big fish. I reel them in. We're a team."

"You're crazier than the guy at the hospital."

"Fine, stay home and be miserable."

"I will. Warm regards to the granddads."

"Yeah, same to Elijah. Who knows, maybe he's legit."

Noga ended the call. At least Sarit made her smile, even if it was at her own expense.

She drained her coffee and got up. She stepped under a hot shower and combed the knots from her hair. Then she poured herself a tall glass of Shiraz, turned on her Logitech UE Boom wireless speaker, and returned to the living room. She hit play on her phone and leaned back on the beanbag.

The lazy jazz musings of a piano and bass guitar mellowed the atmosphere, and the soothing, husky voice of Norah Jones sang "The Nearness of You." Noga swirled the red wine in the glass, breathed in the fruity scent, and took a sip. The dark eyes of Eli Katz bored into her. His fingers tightened on her skin.

She opened her laptop on the coffee table and searched the Internet. According to Wikipedia, the biblical Elijah—zealous prophet and miracle-worker—had championed the cause of God in the northern kingdom of Israel and fought against the worship of Baal. He poured oil from empty vessels, called down fire from the heavens, and even raised the dead, until a whirlwind had whisked him away to heaven on a chariot of fire.

As such, he never died, and he continued to pop up throughout Jewish history: he rebuked the sages of the Talmud, imparted esoteric wisdom to saintly rabbis in the Middle Ages, and—to this day—paid surreptitious visits to Passover meals and circumcision ceremonies around the globe. Elijah was a busy man.

Two details stood out. Legend identified Elijah with the biblical Phineas—grandson of Aaron, the brother of Moses and the first High Priest. This factoid crowned Elijah as both prophet and priest, and dovetailed nicely with her own research project.

Secondly, Jewish tradition tapped Elijah the Prophet as harbinger of the Messiah, and predicted his return to the stage of history ahead of the "great and terrible Day of the Lord." At that time, Elijah would create peace within families and restore the Ten Lost Tribes of Israel.

She remembered Eli Katz's deranged speech about the End of Days. He had spoken with such urgency and conviction. Her anger at his rudeness evaporated, leaving a silt of pity. Poor creature. Confined to a hospital room. Broken. Depressed. Alone. Once again, she found her own face reflected in his dark eyes.

She closed her laptop and took another long sip.

Too bad, she thought. Time to move on.

CHAPTER 32

Eight o'clock Sunday morning, Irina and Moshe walked through Safra Square, an expansive plaza of checkered gray stone in downtown Jerusalem. The large government buildings on every side made Irina feel very small.

Samira had remained at the rabbi's house, fearful of bumping into family members who worked at the government institutions. What had the Arab girl done to enrage her family so? Irina had not dared to ask. She could not hide at the rabbi's home much longer. None of them could. Tonight, Moshe and the rabbi were to appear before the Great Council, which would probably split them up. This might be her last day with Moshe.

Moshe greeted the guard at the door of the Ministry of Employment. The elderly man raised his fluffy eyebrows and returned the greeting. Moshe always had a kind word for waiters, janitors, and security guards—the invisible people that others ignored. Irina noticed that. Moshe was a gentleman.

He plucked a ticker tape number from a dispenser at the entrance to a large waiting hall and found two empty bucket seats of hard plastic. They watched a digital display. Each time the number changed, a computerized voice instructed the bearer to approach a numbered counter. Twenty turns to go. Irina didn't mind. She savored her last hours with Moshe, one of her few friends in her new life and the one she trusted most.

A dark cloud hovered over him this morning. His wife had refused his advances and flowers. Her loss. If she didn't recognize a good man when she saw one, then she didn't deserve him. In addition, his treasured family business had failed—the main reason for their excursion to the Ministry of Employment. She wished she could ease his pain.

"You never told me the rest of the story," she said. This might be her last chance to find out.

Moshe looked up. "Which story?"

"How Avi saved your life."

"Oh." He folded his arms over his chest. "We were on reserve duty together in the South Hebron Mountains. Eight-hour shifts securing the roads between Jewish villages. There were four of us in the pillbox—that's a cement watchtower surrounded by concrete blocks and barbed wire—in the cold."

Irina pictured him in an olive uniform, a rifle slung over his shoulder like the soldiers she saw on the streets and buses.

"Avi had something to say about everyone," he continued. "Especially Nimrod, a rich kid from North Tel Aviv. Nimrod said his wife complained all the time, so Avi said..." Moshe trailed off.

"Said what?"

His cheeks reddened. "Well, he said: 'Women always moan; you get to choose the reason,' implying that Nimrod didn't, well, you know…"

"I get it," she said. This Avi was not a gentleman.

"Avi loved to get under his skin. One afternoon, Nimrod came down to the yard and handed out cigarettes. His wife was pregnant. 'Boy or girl?' Avi asked. When Nimrod said 'girl,' Avi laughed. 'The Arabs have a saying,' he said: 'What you put in is what you get out.'"

Irina took a few seconds to figure out that one. "Oh, my."

Moshe continued. "Yep. Nimrod didn't let that one go.

He lunged at Avi and I had to keep them apart. Then Avi tackled me to the ground, and the world exploded. Machine gun fire. The ricochet of bullets. A terrorist had walked right in. Avi rolled over and returned fire. The terrorist got away. Nimrod wasn't so lucky. He never saw his daughter. If Avi hadn't pulled me down, I would have joined him."

"Wow." She had assumed that Moshe had served in the Israel Defense Forces, but never imagined what he had gone through in uniform.

A loud noise startled her, and she grabbed Moshe's arm.

He looked over his shoulder. "It's OK," he said. "Someone dropped a book. Half the room had a heart attack."

Irina released his arm. "I'm sorry."

"Don't be," he said. "Anyway," he continued his story, "Avi was out of work, so I offered him a job. And so our lives became entwined."

The automated voice announced their number and directed them to counter number four, where they found a desk and another two bucket chairs.

"ID?" their attendant asked without looking up from the screen. The well-preserved woman had dyed her long hair black. She squinted at a computer monitor over reading glasses that clung to the tip of her nose. Her nametag read Dafna Siman-Tov.

Moshe recited his nine-digit identification number, and the lady pecked at the keyboard with two fingers.

She clucked and shook her head.

"Stupid computer. They put in a new system yesterday. Rinat?" she called. A younger woman in a white blouse arrived and peered over her shoulder.

"Says here he's dead."

Rinat pointed at the screen with long, pink manicured nails. "Click Override. I'll approve it. Must be another glitch."

Irina and Moshe exchanged glances and hid their smiles. They might actually make progress here.

Dafna moved the mouse, gave it a click, and her face brightened.

"Right, Moshe Karlin." She glanced at him now that he officially existed in the system. "How long have you been unemployed?"

"A week."

"First time here?"

"Yes."

"Last job?"

"I ran my own business."

"We're fresh out of CEO positions, sweetie. You'll have to fill in the survey." She squinted at the screen and jabbed at the keyboard. "Do you have any degrees?"

"I didn't go to university."

Click. Click. "Skills?"

"Uh, management?"

She shook her head. "No Management here. Typing?"

"No."

"Brick laying?"

"Nope."

"Agricultural work?"

"Never got around to it."

"Sanitation?"

"Not if I can help it."

Poor Moshe. His humor plastered over his embarrassment. Work meant so much to a man's ego.

Click. Click. Dafna frowned. "Nothing," she said.

"Nothing?"

"There's telemarketing and call center work, but you need to be a student. Oh, wait, what's this?" She squinted at the screen again.

Irina held her breath. *Give him something. Anything.*

"Public office."

"Pardon?"

Dafna turned the screen around. "See for yourself. Mayor. Member of Parliament. Prime Minister."

Irina laughed. Was this a joke?

Moshe laughed too. "Prime Minister?"

"That's what it says. They're the only jobs that don't require skills or education."

Irina read the screen. Dafna wasn't joking.

"So do I just sign up?"

"No, it's a self-employment recommendation. You have to join a party, or create one. Politicians do it all the time. Hard to keep track. Next elections are in three months, so you better get started. Your unemployment payments start in a few days. Check in every week at the self-service computers on the first floor."

"Every week?"

"If you're still unemployed. I'll need your bank details and pay slips for the last six months."

"I… I don't have them with me."

The clerk's shoulders sagged. *Silly man*, they seemed to say. *Didn't do your homework, did you?* She folded her hands on the desk. "Then you'll have to come back and reregister. What about your wife?"

"Oh no," Irina said. "We're not married."

"She's a friend," Moshe said.

"Just friends," Irina added. Her cheeks felt hot.

"Are you unemployed too?"

"Yes."

"ID?"

"I don't remember. I don't have my identity book."

"Name?"

Moshe said, "We'll come back another time."

They crossed Safra Square toward Jaffa Street and a line of tall palm trees. The late morning sun reflected white off the public buildings of Jerusalem stone. People flowed around them. People with skills and jobs. Hawkers offered them hot bagels and bottled water. Moshe's shoulders slumped as he walked.

"I'm sorry," Irina said.

"It's OK. We had little chance of getting anywhere."

"What do we do now?"

"Odd jobs, I suppose. Wait tables." Moshe stared at something behind her.

She turned around. A man stood in the middle of the square, an island in the stream of pedestrians. A sign with large black letters hung from straps on his shoulders: "Honest Work. Honest Pay."

"Jobs!" the man cried, first in Hebrew, then Russian. "Money! No documents required."

A passerby took a slip of paper from his hands. Moshe and Irina walked over and took one too. No company name or logo. No marketing copy. Just an address in Talpiot.

"What is this?" he asked.

"Shto?" the man said. What?

Irina took over in Russian. "What jobs?"

He shrugged. "I just hand out the fliers, miss."

She translated for Moshe, who was still staring at the address.

"Sounds good," he said.

"Yes. Too good."

Moshe shrugged. "What do we have to lose?"

CHAPTER 33

Yosef stared at his sandwich on the staff room table. He had not touched his lunch. In a few hours, he would stand before the Great Council of Torah Sages bearing the best possible tidings, but a drop of doubt muddied his excitement.

In his mind's eye, Samira stood on his doorstep in a makeshift hijab, desperation in her eyes. None of the ancient sources had mentioned resurrected gentiles; some had explicitly limited the miracle to Jews. How was this possible?

He glanced at his wristwatch. Half an hour until his next class. He had debated whether to call Rabbi Emden Saturday night, and decided not to bother the busy rabbi. Yosef must have misread the sources. As the meeting drew closer, however, he changed his mind. Best to update the good rabbi before they stood before the leading sages of the generation. No surprises.

He dialed the number on his phone. The call cut to an answering service. He didn't leave a message. *Stop worrying, Yosef.* The Great Council would know what to do, no matter what.

"May I have a word with you, Rabbi Yosef?" said a calm, crisp voice.

Yosef looked up. Rabbanit Leah Schiff, the principal of Daas Torah Primary, stood over him. He pocketed the phone with a sudden sense of guilt, as though she had caught him cheating. Rabbanit Schiff had that effect on him.

"Of course." He followed his employer to her office. He did not close the door. Jewish law forbade seclusion with a married woman.

Rabbanit Schiff sat down behind her desk, her back ramrod-straight. Her fingertips formed a steeple as she considered Rabbi Yosef with unblinking eyes. With her symmetrical *sheitel* of short, dark hair, she reminded him of the humanoid robots from the science fiction movies of his youth. The rabbanit ran a tight ship and always smiled. On occasion, the smile had moved unfortunate teachers to tears. Today she aimed her smile at Yosef.

"Rabbi Yosef," she said, choosing each word with care. "Do you know why parents choose our school?"

Yosef knew better than to reply.

"Purity," she said. "Parents entrust their children's pure minds to our pure environment where we teach them pure Torah." She let the weight of her words sink in. Her gaze dropped to the edge of the table. "I have ignored your little adventures beyond the approved syllabus in the past. Harmless tidbits for a child's wandering mind. But now we have received complaints."

"Complaints?" Yosef squeezed the seat of his chair.

The unblinking eyes trained on his. "Last week, children in your class returned home with questions about their dead grandparents. Disturbing questions. Our job is to fill their minds with knowledge, not questions."

"But the Talmud is filled with questions."

"Yes, Rabbi Yosef. Questions that arrive with ready answers. The questions you have raised only lead to more questions. They are… dangerous." She straightened the row of pens on her desk. "There are enough distractions in the outside world. We don't want to unsettle their pure minds. Do you understand?"

Yosef blinked. He needed the job. If one school blacklisted him, word would spread, and he would need a new career.

"Yes," he said. "Of course. No more talk of the Resurrection. My apologies."

Her smile widened. "Thank you, Rabbi Lev. That will be all."

He got to his feet and left the office. Never mind. Tonight the sages of the Great Council would hear all and, within minutes, the religious world would know the joyous truth: the long-awaited Redemption had begun! Then the Resurrection would be on everyone's lips.

CHAPTER 34

The sudden screech of tires on asphalt made Irina grab Moshe's arm again. All eyes turned to the white car that had halted before the bus shelter on Jaffa Street where they sat. The man in the passenger seat lurched forward and whipped back in his seat. The smell of burning rubber wafted in the air. On the roof of the car, the word "taxi" was displayed in a yellow half-moon.

Hearing no crunch of fenders, the startled pedestrians continued on their way, but Irina's relief was short-lived. The driver's door opened, and a short, dark-skinned man of middle age walked around the car and marched toward her.

Moshe stood and the man stopped inches from him. "Moshe Karlin," he said, "is that you?" His voice had a rough, raspy edge.

The old man didn't wait for an answer. He threw his arms around Moshe and hugged his chest. Moshe gave Irina a helpless, bemused look.

The driver held Moshe at arms' length and inspected him like a long-lost lover. "Great God! Moshe Karlin. I thought you were dead."

"Hey! Driver!" the passenger yelled out the window. "The meter is running."

The cabbie didn't seem to hear. "I heard rumors but I

didn't dare believe them. How can this be?"

"God alone knows," Moshe said.

"Fantastic! Wonderful news!"

He seemed to notice Irina for the first time.

"This is Irina. Irina, meet Rafi. A very dear friend."

"A friend?" Rafi seemed insulted. "More like family. I've known Moshe since he was in his mother's womb."

The passenger got out of the cab, slammed the door, and flagged down another taxi.

Rafi wiped a tear from his crinkly eye. "I didn't hear you on the radio. Are you back at work?"

Moshe's smile faded at the mention of his company. "It's complicated."

"Of course," Rafi said, as though not keen to pry. "And Galit? She must be overjoyed to see you."

"I'm afraid that's complicated as well."

"I see." Rafi seemed genuinely distressed at his friend's plight. "I can imagine. After, what, two years? Where are you heading? Let me give you a ride. Let's talk in the air conditioning."

They got inside and the taxi pulled off.

Irina had the back seat to herself. The soft upholstery was a welcome change after the hard plastic chairs of the Ministry of Employment.

Rafi caught her eye in the rearview mirror. "Let me tell you about the Karlins," he said with pride. "Moshe's father, David, got me into this business. I was a young soldier when the Yom Kippur War hit. The Egyptians crossed the Suez Canal and marched across Sinai. Syrian tanks rolled through the Golan. Iraq and Jordan joined the assault. Their leaders talked of driving us into the sea. In Tel Aviv, the government dug mass graves. This was the end of us." His face sobered in the mirror.

"My battalion charged the Golan Heights. Brothers-in-arms died around me. Of my whole platoon, only I lived to tell the tale." He drew a labored breath at the memory. "We survived the war but the country was a mess. Hard to believe that now. My head was a mess. I wanted to get as far away as possible. I bought a ticket for Argentina. My mom told his dad"—he nodded at Moshe—"and the night before my flight, he came over to our house. 'Work with me,' he said. He helped me finance a taxi. Made sure I had enough clients to cover the payments and then some. A year later, I bought two more cars and hired drivers. I owe it all to David Karlin."

"Wow," Irina said. "That's quite a story."

The motor purred as they meandered through the city center. A woman in sunglasses bustled along with oversized shopping bags on her arm. A man wearing a large black skullcap bit into a slice of pizza as he stared at his phone.

Moshe asked, "Is your Mercedes in the shop?"

"Sold it."

"For a Seat?"

"Nothing beats a Mercedes, I know. But the services! And the gas! This car is not as comfortable, but that's cash in the bank. Times are not what they used to be, Moshe." Rafi sighed. Gloom settled over the eyes in the mirror. "These youngsters and their fancy mobile apps." He shook his head at the corruption of the youth. "Soon after you died, the dispatch calls dried up. I had to rely on street pickups and long-haul routes, but even those became rare. I had to let go of my drivers and sell the cars."

Moshe seemed shocked. "How many?"

"All of them. Twenty in total. Some days I get a call, some days none. But I cut my expenses. I get by. Sold the house too, moved to a two-room apartment. The boys are in the army now and the house was getting too large for Rivka anyway. She… she hasn't been very well." His eyes darkened in the mirror.

"I'm very sorry to hear that," Moshe said, but he didn't press him for details. Then, he said, "I don't understand. What about that mobile app?"

Rafi's voice filled with fire. "And turn my back on Karlin & Son? Never! I told those toddler techies to shove their stupid app you-know-where."

Moshe ran his hand through his hair and Irina understood his anguish. A good man had thrown away his business to keep faith with the dead.

"Rafi," Moshe said in a kind voice, "Karlin & Son had a good run, but times have changed."

Rafi was not convinced. "Those little squirts have no respect."

"My father wouldn't want you to suffer in his name," Moshe said. "And I sure don't want you to lose out. You've paid back our family ten times over with your loyalty. So please, my friend. Move on. For my sake. For my father."

Rafi said nothing for the rest of the trip, but in the rear-view mirror, the eyes blinked back tears.

The cab stopped at a run-down backstreet. Rafi refused to let them pay for the ride. He handed Moshe a business card through the window. "If you need anything, just call," Rafi said. "Anything." Moshe shook his hand, and the cab pulled off in search of better days.

Irina scanned the deserted street corner. Large silent buildings lined the street in varying degrees of decay. "There's nothing here."

Moshe rechecked the flier. "This is the address."

Cracked planks boarded the doors and windows of an old store. The name stenciled on the wall had faded beyond recognition.

"These guys have a very bad sense of humor."

The sound of footfalls made them turn. A man in a tweed suit jogged toward them. His hair was a mop of gray, as was his thick mustache.

"Can I help you?" Another thick Russian accent.

Moshe handed him the flier.

The man pocketed the paper without reading it. He sized them up with small, beady eyes. Irina gave him a polite smile and straightened her shoulders, as if to say, *I'm as good as any man, buster!* It seemed to work.

"This way," he said, and he trotted down the street.

They followed.

He turned a corner, then another, and waited for them outside a warehouse of corrugated fiberglass. He opened a sliding door and closed it behind them. They stood in a large airy hangar. Plastic curtains divided the grounds into cubicles that contained low steel-framed cots.

The man climbed a metal stairwell and the clank of their shoes on the steps echoed off the fiberglass walls. A narrow walkway led to a square office with large windows.

He unlocked the door and waved them inside. "Coffee? Tea?"

They declined the offer.

He took his seat behind a cheap desk and waved them to two rickety chairs. A laptop and filing cabinet lent the room an air of businesslike respectability. He leaned back in his chair and smiled.

"My name is Boris," he said. "Many people want to work but don't have the right papers. The State doesn't make life easy. Foreign workers, they call them. Infiltrators. They hunt them down. We can help."

"What kind of work?" Moshe asked.

"This and that. Manual labor. Training on the job. The pay is modest but you get two solid meals a day, and an apartment downstairs."

Irina would not have called the refugee camp of changing booths below "apartments" but she could excuse the exaggerated marketing language for a roof over her head and food in her belly, all earned by her own labor.

"Two apartments," Moshe said.

Irina nodded.

Boris made a show of deliberation. "Two apartments, then. No extra charge. Agreed?" They nodded. "First, a few technicalities." He turned to Irina. "Raise your chin." He pointed to a small mounted camera behind him. He clicked a button on his laptop. Irina and Moshe swapped seats, and he repeated the procedure. A few more clicks and a printer came to life and pushed out two sheets of paper.

The paperwork reassured her. For all its shabbiness and

dodgy advertising, Boris ran a bona fide operation.

The manager slid the pages of fine print toward them, along with two ballpoint pens. "Sign at the bottom," he said. "Good." He reclaimed the sheets and tucked them in a folder. "You start tomorrow at six AM."

Six AM! Irina had missed that in her very cursory review of the contract, but she would do whatever the job required. Moshe glanced at her, a question in his eye. Irina nodded. They had learned to read each other's thoughts.

He said, "A friend of ours needs a job too. She can stay with Irina."

Boris shrugged. "Bring her along and I'll make the arrangements. If you'll excuse me, I have other work to attend to."

He escorted them out and slid the doors of the hangar shut.

"That was simple enough," Moshe said. "Things are looking up."

"Yes," Irina said. No matter what the rabbis of the Great Council decided that night, she would stay by Moshe's side for the near future. That alone was worth the early mornings.

CHAPTER 35

Eli felt his pulse quicken in his neck when the girl appeared at the foot of his bed.

She folded her arms over her chest. "The nurse said you wanted to speak with me," she said, apprehension in her eyes and her mouth shut tight. After their last encounter, he didn't blame her. But why had his own mouth dried up?

His free arm twitched. "Yes," he said. "Eliana. Your name is Noga, right?"

She nodded. She had tied her hair up, exposing a creamy neck and her large intelligent eyes. Had the sudden vision of beauty triggered his involuntary responses, or his unease with what he was about to do? He had always kept interactions with humanity to a minimum and for good reason, but now he needed this girl.

"I owe you an apology," he said. "I had no right to talk to you like that." That much was true. The large eyes fixed on him, so he continued. "This has been very difficult for me." Another truth. "I was… not my usual self." Not strictly accurate but the words had the desired effect. Her shoulders relaxed, as did the corners of her mouth. She was starting to thaw.

"You mentioned that you were heading a research project. Could you tell me more?"

The arms loosened over her chest. "Sure," she said.

Bingo! I'm not as rusty as I thought. "Please," he said and indicated the empty visitor's chair. "Sit with me."

She did. He lifted his bandaged leg from the sling and orchestrated a soft landing on the bedsheet. Then he pressed his palms to the mattress, pushed back, and raised his body to a sitting position. He had practiced the procedure all of Saturday. The pain had subsided a little each time.

"What?" he said. She was gawking at him.

"Nothing. Just… Are you supposed to be doing that already? I thought you'd be immobile for weeks."

He shrugged. "I'm on the fast track. Now tell me about your study."

"I'm measuring gene markers across demographic groups."

"So you're a gene detective?"

She smiled. "More like a gene archaeologist. Genes mutate over time, but most pass unchanged from generation to generation. We can trace the spread of genetic markers from one ethnic group to another as populations mingled and interbred. That's how we discovered that all humans are descended from a single female."

"I could have told you that without drawing blood."

"Well, now we have scientific proof."

Scientific proof. A rationalist.

"And what genes are you tracing now?"

"The Cohen Gene."

"The Cohen Gene—as in Jews of priestly descent?" This would be easier than he thought.

"Exactly!" She leaned forward. "Priests claim to descend from one man, Aaron, brother of Moses and the first priest. If that is true, there should be genetic markers unique to priests."

"And do such markers exist?"

"We've identified a number of candidates. We call them the Cohen Modal Haplotype, a pattern of six Y-STR markers—or short tandem repeats—on the male-only Y chromosome." She paused. "Sorry, I'm boring you with the details."

"No, not at all." He suppressed a yawn. "Please go on."

"Historically, the Jewish community has been genetically aloof," she continued, her eyes flashing and her smile widening, "only marrying within the faith, and so the gene signatures are quite homogenous. That breeds genetic diseases like Tay-Sachs, but it also allows us to follow the path of specific genes, like the Cohen Gene."

Aloof. Signatures. Homogenous. Does she always hide behind long words?

"So our genes tell a story, is that it?"

"Exactly! Even if the memory of your past is forgotten, your story is embedded in your genes." She halted and her eyes glazed over, as though she had revealed too much.

What is your story, Noga? The geneticist had become more interesting by the minute.

Eliana swept into the room and they fell into an awkward silence. The nurse made a show of checking his clipboard, then winked at Noga and bustled out. Checking up on her little girl.

Time to take their relationship to the next level. "We have a lot in common," he said.

Noga flushed. "What do you mean?"

"I also find genealogy fascinating."

She raised a doubtful eyebrow. "Do you now?"

Eli had never shared this with a soul, but the circumstances warranted sacrifice. If the Day of the Lord arrived soon, as seemed likely, this revelation wouldn't matter anyway.

"In fact," he said, "I run a genealogy website."

"Really? Which one?"

"Have you heard of OpenGen?"

She cocked her head and raised both eyebrows. "You're OpenGen?"

"Not a big deal. Runs itself mostly but pays the bills. Don't worry, I won't go digging around your family tree."

She looked away and her cheeks reddened again. His attempt at humor had touched another sensitive topic. Invasive parents? Genetic deformities? He made a mental note to steer clear of her family tree in conversation.

"I'll do it," he said.

"Do what?"

"Take part in your study. Where do I sign?"

She brushed a stray lock of hair from her face, pulled a sheet from her plastic folder, and handed him a pen.

He read the printed text of the agreement. "It's anonymous?"

"Yes. We have no way of connecting individuals to their results."

"Even if the results are off the charts?"

"Mm-hmm. And our statistical analysis will ignore the outliers anyway."

Eli signed on the dotted line. A vial of his blood donated to an anonymous research project was a vial not undergoing invasive testing at the hospital. How many vials were there?

He handed her the form and pen. "There's only one problem," he said, and he produced his charming smile. "I'll need to find another excuse to see you again."

Another blush. She stood and brushed off her jeans. "I'm sure you'll think of something." She left with a satisfied smile on her lips.

He shifted his body down the mattress, returned his damaged leg to the sling, and lay flat on his back.

He needed to conserve energy. He might be home sooner than he thought.

CHAPTER 36

Sunday night, Moshe looked out the passenger window of Rabbi Yosef's Subaru and his mouth dropped open.

The giant cube of the Belz Great Synagogue blazed golden in powerful spotlights and hung over the old apartment buildings in north Jerusalem like a spaceship landing in a murky forest.

Seven narrow windows ran the length of the facade, beneath a crown of pointed merlons. The design conjured thoughts both of Herod's ancient Temple—as a boy, Moshe had viewed a model of the structure at the Holy Land museum—and, strangely, the Knesset building of the Israeli government.

"Is that it?" he asked.

The rabbi nodded. He wore a fresh black suit. He had turned off the Cyndi Lauper cassette and spoken little during the short drive. When Moshe told him about their new jobs, the rabbi had avoided his eyes and offered to drive them early the next day to their new lodgings. Did he feel guilty about their departure or was the rabbi merely nervous ahead of their meeting with the Great Council?

They plowed into the thicket of Kiryat Belz and the golden synagogue disappeared behind the bland apartment buildings. The rabbi maneuvered the car through the narrow streets, climbing upward toward the holy sanctuary. They dodged green garbage bins, men in coats and hats, and kerchief-headed women pushing strollers.

They rounded a corner and the Belz Synagogue burst overhead, a silent beacon in the night. Rabbi Yosef parked his car in the empty lot beside the synagogue. The sound of their closing car doors bounced off the walls.

Moshe placed a white velvet skullcap on his head. The great twin doors of the synagogue rose to triple his height. The ultra-Orthodox, known for their abject poverty and devotion to Torah study, must have paid a king's ransom for the extravagant synagogue. Just the monthly electricity bills must cost a small fortune. Some of the devout, apparently, had very deep pockets.

The rabbi touched the large golden knob but stopped short of opening.

"Everything all right?"

Rabbi Yosef turned to him. He seemed to wake from a trance. "I've never addressed such a gathering of great rabbis."

"You've never met them before?"

"This is the Great Council of Torah Sages. The leaders of the generation. They assemble only to discuss matters of great communal importance."

"Good thing we're on time."

The rabbi grinned. He pushed, and the door swung inward. They stood in the dim light of a wood-paneled corridor. A tall man with a long, tidy beard turned to them and smiled.

"Yosef, my friend." The rabbi, who wore a silken suit and fine black bowler, embraced Rabbi Yosef. He extended his hand to Moshe. "You must be Mr. Karlin. Pleased to meet you."

Rabbi Yosef introduced Rabbi Emden.

"Follow me, my friends," he said. "The Great Council awaits."

They followed Rabbi Emden down the corridor. The furnishers had spared no expense on the interior either. They passed carved benches and miniature crystal chandeliers but not a living soul. The synagogue must be off limits during sessions of the Great Council. A security arrangement? Moshe imagined a row of consulate-grade SUVs with tinted windows parked in a VIP garage beneath the synagogue.

Rabbi Emden halted outside another set of tall wooden double doors in a spacious foyer.

"The sages have other matters to discuss this evening," Rabbi Emden explained. "Their attendants will call when they are ready to receive us. How have you been adjusting to your new life, Moshe?"

The question caught him off guard. He had not expected small talk with a friendly, stately rabbi. "It's been challenging."

The tall rabbi gave him a good-natured smile. Moshe had not encountered a rabbi like Emden before, so suave, well groomed, and polite. Moshe had dispatched Charedi commuters for years but never chatted with any at length. Rabbi Emden was no street Charedi but a diplomat who would feel equally at home rubbing elbows in cabinet meetings as he would in the study hall.

"Oh," he said, as though just remembering an important detail. "The discussions are in Yiddish, so I'll translate where possible."

Moshe had forgotten that some people still spoke Yiddish. Although the language mixed Hebrew and German, he'd probably understand only a few scattered words.

"Rabbi Emden," Rabbi Yosef said. He shifted on his feet as though desperate for the men's room. "I tried to reach you earlier. A third survivor joined us on Friday."

"A third?" Rabbi Emden displayed rows of perfect square ivories and his eyes sparkled in the dim light. "Excellent."

"Yes, but—"

Yellow light poured from between the double doors of the main synagogue. A young bearded man in a gown of black silk and long black stockings stood in the opening and murmured a few words to Rabbi Emden.

"Our turn has arrived," said the elder rabbi. He adjusted his hat and followed the messenger inside with Rabbi Yosef and Moshe at his heels.

Moshe's heart jumped from his chest into his throat. He had never experienced a hall so enormous or so full of light. They stood at one extremity of the rectangular room. The Holy Ark towered above them, ten meters of finely sculpted wood. Nine immense chandeliers of brilliant crystal hung high overhead like funnel-shaped spaceships. The messenger moved fast, and they marched down a long aisle between rows of wooden pews, away from the Holy Ark and toward a central clearing dominated by an imposing raised platform of the same carved wood.

Bearded men in black gowns and white collared shirts filled a large block of pews beyond the platform—a few hundred men at least, but not a word between them. Some eyed the four approaching men with inquisitive expressions, but most trained their attention on the base of the platform, still hidden from view.

Moshe had entered a surreal and alien world where the laws and norms of the outside world held no sway, and he, in his new trousers, white shirtsleeves, and glossy white *kippah*, felt very out of place.

They rounded the platform. A long conference table of polished wood extended along the base, and a row of wizened old men in immaculate black attire and impressive white beards peered over the table at the seated masses.

The attendant led them to the no-man's-land between the pews and the conference table, and the three visitors faced the Great Council of Torah Sages, their backs to the many rows of silent students.

The seven sages sized them up with intelligent old eyes like judges inspecting defendants. Moshe recognized the generous white beard of Rabbi Auerbach from Simcha's soccer card.

"Reb Emden," said the sage in the center of the council.

He spoke a few more words in Yiddish. His eyes sparkled with warmth and kindness, but whether he extended those sentiments to all three of the visitors, Moshe could not tell. Rabbi Emden replied at length in Yiddish.

"Who is that?" Moshe whispered to Rabbi Yosef.

"Rabbi Alter," Rabbi Yosef whispered back, without taking his eyes from the formidable sages. "The Rebbe of Belz Chasidism. On his left is Rabbi Auerbach; Rabbi Teitelbaum on his right. Heads of Chasidic lines and leading *poskim*—authorities on Jewish law."

The Chasidic world, it seemed, had its own aristocracy, and Moshe stood before the kings of this parallel universe.

A gasp washed over the seated multitude behind them. Some of the rabbis of the council stirred as well, but not the three central figures. Emden must have gotten to the crux of their story.

Rabbi Emden concluded his address. Rabbi Alter raised his hand, and the murmurs fell silent. He turned his warm, kind eyes to Moshe and spoke in Hebrew. "Mr. Karlin," he said. "Please show us the sign."

Moshe felt all eyes train on him, and his cheeks warmed. "The sign?" He looked to Rabbi Emden for an explanation.

"Your shirt," Rabbi Emden said, with an encouraging smile. "Go on."

Moshe was not in the habit of exposing himself in synagogue, but he overcame his inhibitions. He pulled the edge of his shirt from his jeans and lifted the hem above his belly. The sages leaned forward and squinted. Eyes widened behind thick glasses.

The rabbis whispered quiet consultation, and Moshe tucked in his shirt.

Rabbi Alter raised his hand again for silence and the hall obeyed as one. He fired off a series of short questions and Rabbi Emden replied. Then Rabbi Alter spoke at length. The warmth faded from his eyes, and his tone hardened.

For the first time in his life, Moshe wished he understood Yiddish. "Is everything OK?" he whispered. Rabbi Yosef gave his shoulders a helpless shrug.

"Mr. Karlin." Rabbi Alter had switched back to Hebrew and turned his icy gaze on Moshe. "We of the Great Council long for the Redemption and the Messiah, son of David. But false hopes and deceivers litter our history. We see before us neither the mass resurrection of Ezekiel nor the return of the prophet Elijah. The Third Temple has not descended from on high with fire and wonders." The sage paused. Not a peep from the crowd.

"And yet," he continued, "here you are. A dead man walking among us. A secular Jew, who remembers nothing of the World of Souls. The sacred responsibility of this council is to safeguard the tradition of Sinai, as handed down through the ages. It is clear to us, Mr. Karlin, that you seek to undermine that tradition, to plant seeds of doubt, and to challenge our holy Torah."

A scandalized murmur rose in the ranks behind them. Moshe opened his mouth to object that he wasn't *seeking* anything, only survival, when Rabbi Alter raised his hand again for order.

"This council has reached its decision. We can find only one explanation." He spoke the next sentence in Yiddish, and banged his fist on the polished table like a judge sealing his verdict with the slam of a gavel. The murmur rose again and filled the hall. Not surprise, this time—but indignation. The murmur surged into an agitated roar. Hinges squealed behind them as seats pivoted and a hundred men got to their feet.

The robed attendant appeared beside them. "Leave," he said in Hebrew. "Now!" He waved his arm. "Out! Out!"

Rabbi Emden pointed to the door at the end of the synagogue. "Go! Go!" he said.

Moshe wasted no time. If he didn't escape now, the mob might rip him limb from limb. Rabbi Yosef seemed to fear the same outcome. At first, they walked—around the platform and down the endless aisle toward the Holy Ark. Then they ran, the footfalls of the angry mob in their ears. The roar coalesced into a chant of two strange words, over and over, the same two words Rabbi Alter had used at the end of his verdict.

"What are they saying?" Moshe asked as they rounded a block of pews and high-tailed it toward the large twin doors of the exit.

"*Sitra Achra*," Rabbi Yosef said, his voice a gasp as he sprinted. It sounded like the end of the world. "*Sitra Achra*!"

CHAPTER 37

Early Monday morning, on a derelict street in the Talpiot industrial zone, Moshe climbed out of Rabbi Yosef's white Subaru for the last time. He held his worldly possessions in one plastic grocery bag. Irina and Samira waited on the cracked sidewalk.

Moshe leaned on the open window of the passenger door. "Thank you for all you've done, Rabbi. We appreciate it."

Rabbi Yosef looked forlorn. "I'm sorry," he said, the first words he had spoken during the short journey.

"It's OK. There's nothing you can do." After the Great Council's verdict, they were lucky the rabbi had let them stay the night.

His words did not seem to console the kind-hearted rabbi. "Good luck," he said, and he drove off.

Sitra Achra. In hushed tones the previous night, the rabbi had explained the expression. The concept seemed bizarre to Moshe, but all the same, the result was "goodbye." They had found new accommodations just in time.

Moshe glanced at the gray corrugated wall of the nondescript warehouse. *Home sweet home.* He pulled at the metal handle and the corrugated wall slid sideways on a track.

They stepped inside. Nothing had prepared Moshe for the sights, sounds, and smells that greeted them. The warehouse floor teemed with men and women under the harsh white light of fluorescents that dangled in the air. Tall Nigerians in grimy overalls. Scruffy Europeans in sweat-stained undershirts. Workers of every size and shape sat on cots and peered at them with suspicious eyes. A fat bald man ladled lumpy porridge into tin cups.

A lanky Ethiopian sauntered in their direction. He looked them up and down. "Moshe and Irina?"

"Yes," Moshe said. "And this is Samira." He reached out his hand.

The Ethiopian stretched his shoulder. "Call me Damas. You work with me. Put your things in twenty-three and twenty-four, and get in line if you want to eat. We leave in ten minutes. You"—he indicated Samira with a nod of the head—"go upstairs and sign. Don't be late."

He padded off.

"He's a bundle of joy," Moshe said.

Irina forced a brave smile. Samira clambered up the metal stairwell toward the supervisor's office, and Moshe caught sight of Boris, the Russian with the bushy gray mustache, through the glass window.

The apartment was a two-meter square of tarpaulin. A tin mug. Dusty sleeping bag. Thin mattress. Rusty spring cot. Moshe kicked his plastic bag under the bed and closed the door flap.

He surveyed the hive of activity in the warehouse. Moshe had heard about the Sudanese refugees and fortune seekers who infiltrated the borders and occupied Southern Tel Aviv, but he had never given much thought to how they made their way through the country without papers or money. He was finding out firsthand. He slipped his watch into his pocket. No need to advertise his good fortune.

Irina emerged from her tent.

"Hungry?"

"Not anymore," he said.

"Yeah, I think I'll skip the line too." Good thing they had gobbled a slice of toast in the rabbi's kitchen before they left.

A loud whistle drew their attention. Damas waved at them to approach the entrance, and herded them into a white minivan that idled outside, the morning air filling with diesel fumes. A balding middle-aged man sat in the back. Moshe and Irina took the middle row. A minute later, Samira emerged from the warehouse and climbed into the van. She seemed relieved to see them and sat in the row in front.

Damas slid the door shut, climbed into the seat beside the driver, and the van pulled off.

"Thank you," Samira said, with an eager smile. "This is my first job."

"You've never had a job?"

"My husband wouldn't let me work outside the home. He made me stop going to school. I couldn't leave the house alone." Her husband. Samira still spoke of the man as though she was still under his thumb. The improvised hijab made her look far older than her twenty-one years.

"Don't thank us yet," Moshe said. "Let's see how the day goes."

"Did the rabbis of the Great Council arrange the jobs?"

"Not exactly. They said we're the *Sitra Achra*."

"The what?"

"It's Aramaic for 'the Other Side.'"

"Other side of what?"

Irina spoke up. "Demons, Samira." Irina had a way of cutting to the chase.

"Oh." Samira's smile disappeared. "Are we? I mean we were dead."

"Do you think you're a demon?"

She shook her head.

"There's your answer. But let me know if you grow horns."

Samira patted her hijab, then smiled at her own foolishness. "So that's why the rabbi…?" She trailed off, either failing to find the Hebrew words or uncomfortable about speaking against their former host.

"Threw us out? Yes."

The man in the seat behind them coughed.

"I'm sure everything will be OK," Moshe said. He should be careful about what he shared with whom.

Damas rested his arm on the backrest of the front seat and tapped the upholstery with his hand. The hand had a thumb and two fingers. The other two digits ended at the first joint.

A shiver traced his spine. Very careful indeed.

CHAPTER 38

Noga sat at the desk of the interview room at the hospital. She ran her fingers through her hair. After a half hour of fussing at the bathroom mirror that morning, she had decided to wear her hair down. She had even allowed Sharona to comb her lashes with mascara and dust her cheeks with blush.

In an hour, she would take the lift to the fourth floor and wheel Eli Katz to his first physiotherapy session. An hour seemed like an eternity. *You've fallen for him.* She giggled. The thought didn't alarm her.

Eli Katz had gone from zero to hero in a single meeting. He had apologized and volunteered to help with her research. He even shared her interest in genealogy. More importantly, he had listened attentively as she ranted about genes and haplotypes. His dark, magnetic eyes and stubbly cheek floated in her mind whenever she closed her eyes.

"Excuse me, miss," said the man across the desk. The young Arab gazed at her with concern. "You were saying?" He wore jeans and a T-shirt; his wife, a brown burka from head to toe.

Noga sat up. "I'm sorry," she said. "The study is anonymous." She recited her sales pitch by heart. Every couple undergoing genetic counseling—a euphemism for fertility treatment—passed through her interview room, regardless of their ethnicity. Most signed the consent forms. Did they really care about science or did they hope that a random act of kindness would increase their chances of success?

After a short hushed deliberation, the couple signed on the dotted line and Noga thanked them for their cooperation. She had recruited Christians, Bahai, Ethiopians, and even Swedish medical tourists in addition to the expected mass of Ashkenazi Jewish hopeful parents. She was glad that this couple had consented. She needed more Arabs to round out the control group.

She escorted the couple to the corridor, wished them luck, and made for the bathroom. Five minutes until her next interview. She washed her hands and inspected her makeup in the mirror. She rubbed her lips together to spread the fading lipstick.

Does this count as a first date? If so, her physio session with Eli would be the only date she had looked forward to in years.

She threw a paper towel in the bin and charged down the corridor. A voice called her name.

"Dr. Stern." She paused. "Is everything OK?"

The head of neurology had a distant look in his pale blue eyes. "Noga," he said. "May I consult with you?"

Consult with me? "Of course."

"The patient in room 419C," he said. "Mr. Katz. You're familiar with him, I understand?"

Rumors spread faster than viruses along the hospital corridors. "What about him?"

"He's recovering fast, wouldn't you say?" The speedy recovery seemed to worry him.

"He's making good progress, yes."

"*Very* good progress. His fractures have healed in record time. I think his case could be of great scientific interest. Now, there was a mix-up with his blood work, and, as I just discovered, the last remaining sample is marked for genetic research."

"Yes. He signed the forms." She clenched her jaw. She

was not about to give up her prized sample, or give it away without Eli's approval. Suddenly, she didn't like the idea of other doctors poking around his DNA. He belonged to her.

She said, "Have you tried obtaining another sample?" Fat chance that Eli would agree to another test. Bad with blood, he had said.

Dr. Stern frowned. "I was hoping to avoid that. He's been through enough already, don't you think? Especially after that nasty incident last week."

She could see where he was going with this.

"He's been clear since then. All the nurses agree."

"So they say." He studied her over his glasses. "But delusions are a tricky phenomenon. I think we might have to ship him off to Kfar Shaul for observation."

A hint of coercion had slithered between his words. Relocation to the Kfar Shaul Mental Health Center would mean the end of her visits with Eli and the end of his freedom for the near future. Although her gut resisted the manipulation, the fear of losing Eli won out.

She swallowed. "I'll speak with the lab," she said. "I'm sure we can split the sample."

Dr. Stern inclined his head. "Thank you."

She turned to go, eager to put a healthy distance between her and the doctor.

"And, Noga, dear," he called after her. "Take care. Delusionals can be very convincing."

CHAPTER 39

Moshe peered out the window of the van. They sped south on Hebron Road, toward Baka. Turn right and they'd land up near his old home. Near Galit and Talya.

The night they had moved into Shimshon Street, Galit had jumped for joy in the entrance hall like a little girl and wrapped him in a tight hug. She might be quick to anger but she also radiated warmth and affection. He thrived on her love. With Galit at his side, he could conquer the world.

His new job had distanced him from her.

If Galit came knocking on the rabbi's front door, she'd find an empty house. But as the van sped toward Baka, it seemed that his new job might be returning him home after all.

The van, however, gunned down Hebron Road without slowing. Soon they would cross the 1967 armistice lines and enter Arab Bethlehem. He straightened on his seat. Was Damas shuttling them into stone-throwing territory in a vehicle without shatterproof windows?

He worried in vain. The van veered right at the last moment and climbed into Gilo, Jerusalem's southernmost suburb. The van pulled up next to a new apartment block of white Jerusalem stone.

Damas turned to face his crew. "New people, listen up.

Don't speak to the customers. Not a word. Speak only to me. Understand?"

They nodded.

"Now, get out."

At the back of the van they collected tins of paint, overalls, and a wooden ladder—all streaked with white—and carried them up two flights of stairs to an empty apartment. Damas mixed cement with water in a bucket and showed them how to fill holes in the wall. While the plaster dried, they poured paint into plastic trays and whitewashed the walls with long strokes of roller brushes. Damas came in and out, leaving them to their tasks for hours at a time.

During one of those stretches, the middle-aged man rested his roller brush in the tray.

"I couldn't help overhearing," he said. He patted strands of hair over his balding pate and hope glimmered in his tired eyes.

"Overhear what?" Moshe said.

"About your new lives."

Irina looked down from the ladder. Samira stiffened. This was just the sort of attention they had hoped to avoid. This information could complicate matters with their new employers.

The man raised a conciliatory hand. "I won't cause any trouble," he said. "My name is Shmuel. I'm like you." He unbuttoned his overall and lifted his T-shirt. Shmuel was indeed like them. Moshe returned the favor. Exposing his belly in public had become a habit.

All of a sudden, Shmuel shuddered. He sank onto a closed tin of paint and bawled into his hands. "I thought I was alone," he said.

Moshe touched the older man's shoulder. "When did you return?"

"A few days ago. Woke up in the cemetery, managed to get home." He shivered at the memory. "My son has moved into my house. Wouldn't believe it's really me. The greedy little runt kicked me out."

"Welcome to the club," Moshe said.

"Yes," said Samira, her voice devoid of sarcasm. "Welcome to the afterlife." Her role of afterlife hostess gave her new confidence.

Moshe said, "Not what you expected, right?"

Shmuel gave a gruff laugh. "I wasn't expecting anything."

Moshe made the introductions.

"Tell me," Shmuel said. A sense of urgency crept into his voice. "How long do I have?"

Good question. Were they newborns or had God pre-aged their new bodies? "I don't know," Moshe admitted. "We'll have to figure things out as we go."

Shmuel's joy of discovery ebbed. He lowered his voice. "Be careful what you say here. Our employers aren't exactly philanthropists."

As if on cue, Damas sauntered into the room and scowled at them. "What is this? A summer camp? Eat your lunch." He tossed a plastic bag onto the floor. "Don't screw around. You have an hour to finish. We have another job waiting."

"What's his problem?" Moshe asked when their taskmaster had left.

Shmuel opened the plastic bag and handed out the sandwiches. "He's always like that. Do your work and keep your mouth shut and you'll be OK."

Moshe decided not to ask what would happen if he were to ignore that advice. The answer would probably not involve severance pay and no hard feelings.

His sandwich consisted of two stiff slices of white bread held together by a brown smear of chocolate spread. They munched their meal without complaint, and washed the stale bread down with tap water cupped in their hands under a kitchen faucet. Their employers did not splurge on creature comforts.

What was the company's name? The warehouse had no markings. He had not retained a copy of the contract. He had been elated to find a place to work and sleep.

They completed the paint job and boarded the minivan for

their next task: weeding the large yard of a house in Beit Zait on the wooded outskirts of West Jerusalem. Moshe and Shmuel traded afterlife stories. Shmuel, a retired journalist, had died four years ago. When Moshe asked how he had passed, however, the older man had clenched up. "Too soon," he said. Moshe didn't press the matter.

Moshe hacked at a patch of weeds with a garden hoe. He had passed the entire day in hard labor and was no closer to his family. He thought of little Talya with her bushy black curls and her mother's eyes, and acid burned in his gut.

"You OK?" Shmuel asked. He rested on his shovel. Moshe had taken out his frustrations on the undergrowth with more violence than necessary.

Moshe straightened and drew a long breath. "My daughter," he said. "She's growing up so fast and I won't see it. I'm not there for her." He listened to his own words and gave a short, ironic laugh. "I suppose nothing much has changed. When I was alive, I wasn't around much either. I spent all my time at the office."

He pulled a large wild plant from the ground and shook dirt from the roots. He had lost two years of his life and now he would miss his chance to get to know his daughter.

"You should speak with her," Shmuel said. He was still watching him.

"I tried that. She doesn't even remember me."

"When is her birthday?"

Moshe massaged the pain in his back. Black grit filled the lines of his fingers. "In a month."

"Surprise her with an early birthday present. She'll warm to you. And your wife will be more responsive if your daughter is on your side."

That was good advice. Avi's threat to his life had revolved around Galit, but not little Talya. Gifts, however, required money, and his first payday was a month away—and two weeks after the wedding date. But the idea hogged his thoughts until the sun dipped toward the horizon and the minivan drove them back to Talpiot, drained and caked in sweat.

The smells of cooking and soiled clothing filled the warehouse. Laborers limped about in small packs of Africans and Romanians. Some kept to their tents and hung damp clothing on the partition walls. A line led to the bald cook who ladled soup into tin cups. Another line led to field showers, judging by the scant dress and towels.

They waited for their soup. Moshe's stomach growled. A fight broke out further up the line. A Nigerian shoved a Romanian. Shoves turned to blows, but not for long. A giant in a gray suit marched across the warehouse floor. He swatted the brawlers to the ground with hands like boulders and dragged them away, a human King Kong, without breaking a sweat.

The line re-formed. The soup was thick with barley and beans, and after they ate, they prepared to shower.

"Go ahead," Moshe told the others. "I need to have a word with the boss."

He climbed the stairwell, crossed the metal bridge, and knocked on the door of the corner office. Hearing nothing, he tried the handle.

Boris shoved a thick wad of shekel notes in a drawer and looked up at him. King Kong stood behind his boss, his back to the wall, his arms and neck as thick as tree trunks.

"Do you have a minute?"

Boris waved him to an empty chair.

"My daughter has a birthday soon."

"Mazel tov." The lids beneath the bushy eyebrows drooped with boredom.

"I'd like to get her a gift. I was wondering: can you advance me my salary for this month? Or part of it?"

Moshe had never had to beg in his life. He felt two inches tall. He'd have to get used to that. The gray mustache wriggled like a ferret. Did Boris have children? Would he understand?

His boss drew a deep breath. "I don't do this, usually," he said. Moshe's heart did a double flip. He had expected a flat no, but Boris opened the drawer, reached in, and threw a two-hundred-shekel note on the desk.

Moshe picked up the crumpled note. He held ten percent of his monthly salary—far below minimum wage—but enough for a Barbie doll and a small cake. "Thank you."

"Don't thank me. It's your time."

"My time?"

"It'll take longer to pay back your debt."

"What debt?"

The mustache tilted. "The apartment. The food. Someone has to pay for those."

"I don't understand."

"You signed the contract. Board and lodging: eighteen hundred per month. Paid up front. Interest at ten percent."

"I didn't agree to that."

"Yes you did." Boris pushed a document on the desk toward Moshe. He had signed the same form the day before. "From the moment you signed on the dotted line, you owe us."

Moshe had not read the fine print. He didn't need to. "That's not legal."

Boris laughed. "What are you going to do?"

King Kong cracked his knuckles. Moshe was not about to make threats, but Boris read his mind. "The police don't bother us here."

"I want out."

Boris shrugged. "Walk out the door anytime you like. A few have tried. They always come back. Our associates are very persuasive. Ask Damas about that."

King Kong grinned. Moshe thought of the angry Ethiopian and his two missing fingers.

"And if you cause more trouble than you're worth, we'll call the police ourselves and give them this." His reached into the drawer and laid a card on the table like a gambler revealing the winning ace. The identity card contained Arabic writing and a photo of Moshe's face.

"Musa Ibrahim," Boris explained. "An Egyptian citizen

and an illegal alien in this country. He looks rather like you, don't you think?"

Moshe shot to his feet. The chair crashed behind him. "You can't do that!"

King Kong took a heavy step forward.

Boris kept his eyes on Moshe. "Work hard. Keep your mouth shut. If you're smart, you'll buy your way out."

"How can I buy out at ten percent?"

"There are ways. You could climb the ranks. We have other, more profitable jobs for men with the right skills and inclination."

"What skills?"

The gray mustache tilted again. "I'm glad you asked."

CHAPTER 40

That night, Moshe dreamed of his father and grandfather. He had never seen the two men together in life, but there they stood, shoulder to shoulder, in a misty twilight, on a grassy bank at the end of a long suspension bridge. Moshe shifted his feet over the rotted planks. He clutched the frayed handrails. The old ropes groaned and rocked in the chill wind over a black abyss. His forebears watched him, their faces inscrutable.

Moshe struggled to keep his balance. *Don't look down!* He urged his stiff limbs to advance. *A Karlin never quits.* But with each brave foot forward, the security of the grassy bank drifted further away.

He awoke in a dew of sweat. He felt his wrist for his watch—he had strapped it on before zipping up his sleeping bag—and relaxed when his fingers found the familiar square of cool metal.

Above his cot, black wires and rusty metal struts crisscrossed the void beneath the roof of the warehouse. The stale air smelled of dust and damp clothes. A hundred manual laborers snored in the night, like frogs trapped in a muddy swamp.

He squinted at the watch face. 4:35 AM. He reviewed his plan in his mind. All the other options he had considered would have put his friends and family in harm's way. He had no choice. He had one hope of escape, and the thought made his heart pound.

Last night, he had learned that Boris had expanded his dodgy operation beyond forced labor.

"What skills?" Moshe had asked. He should have kept his mouth shut and gone to bed, but the shock and anger over his servitude had mobilized his tongue.

Boris smiled. "Persuasion. Stores all over the city pay hard cash for our protection. Some need a little convincing from time to time."

"That's extortion," Moshe had said.

The word did not seem to bother Boris. "Racketeering, technically." He leaned forward on the desk. "You'll make an excellent salesman. I have an eye for this sort of thing. I've even selected your first customer."

Moshe tossed and turned on his cot. Springs creaked as workers shifted in their sleep and dreamed of brighter tomorrows.

At five-thirty, he rolled off his bed and dressed. He made for the bathroom, splashed cold water on his face, and peered at his unshaven visage in the cracked mirror. If his father and grandfather could see him now—a penniless, homeless slave. A dismal end to their legacy. But he could descend further still into dishonor. By the end of the day, he would hit rock bottom.

He knocked on the flap of Irina's cubicle. She pulled the curtain aside. Her platinum blond hair pushed in all directions. The fairy had just awoken, but this was no fairy tale. Samira lay on her cot, bundled in her sleeping bag.

Irina watched him with concern. "You OK?"

Moshe nodded. He had to do it. He had no choice. "I have to go somewhere this morning," he said.

Her eyes widened. "I'll come with."

"No," he said. "I have to go alone." If he told her, she might talk him out of it.

Her cheek twitched. He had told her about his conversation with Boris the previous night, and she knew the consequences of not showing up for work. He imagined the questions that flooded her mind. Where? What? Why? Thankfully, she asked none.

"Be careful," she said.

He turned away from her before he could change his mind.

He pulled the warehouse door open on the tracks and slipped out into the early morning gloom. He hurried along the dank alleys of the industrial zone. He looked over his shoulder every few steps, expecting to find King Kong or another faceless thug at his heels, but he had escaped unnoticed.

Beep-beep-beep! The high-pitched alarm of a reversing delivery van made him jump as it backed up. He hurried through the gap between the van and a loading platform, and marched on.

Sunlight spilled over Pierre Koenig Street, the two-lane backbone of Talpiot, and glinted off the trickle of commuter cars. He slackened his pace. A few blocks down, he found an empty bench, and sat like a traitor awaiting execution.

An Egged bus hissed to a stop, and a herd of cashiers and garage workers disembarked and hurried to their jobs. Did they have any idea about the forced labor camp a few streets away? Did any of them care?

Soon Damas and his minivan would set out without him. He had missed his shift. His taskmasters would deduct the workday from his salary and sink him deeper into debt. If he failed to return by lights out, their goons would seek him out. They would find him. They would make him go back. Moshe was not going back. Not as a slave.

Exhaust fumes carried in the air. His stomach groaned, but he had no desire to eat. He would not be able to keep the food down.

Across the street stood his target, a small store squeezed between a haberdashery and a hole-in-the-wall selling cheap household plastics. Moshe had driven by a thousand times and never imagined that, one day, fate would lead him to that particular store.

Soon, the store would open. He had a few minutes to contemplate what he was about to do—his last moments of innocence before he sold his soul.

CHAPTER 41

Irina boarded the minivan and sat in the middle row—the seat she had shared with Moshe the day before. Her arms hugged her chest. The idling engine made the seats vibrate and her body seemed to shiver in the morning twilight. She had never spent a day apart from Moshe, and she felt vulnerable in his absence.

Last night, Moshe had told them about his meeting with Boris.

"So we're slaves?" Shmuel cried out.

Moshe asked him to keep his voice down but said no more. He had not told them all he knew. Had he been trying to protect them?

Samira climbed into the van and claimed the seat beside her. The Arab girl turned her wide, innocent eyes on her. "Has he left us?" she whispered.

"No, of course not. Moshe would never do that." But the girl had voiced Irina's own deepest fear.

"How do you know?" The question came from Shmuel on the seat behind her.

"I know."

Their Ethiopian taskmaster leapt into the front cabin. He turned and counted them like sheep. He scowled at Irina. "Where's your friend?"

She shrugged.

"Gone fishing?" His sense of humor lasted all of one second before he slammed his fist on the backrest. "You're mine, you understand? You do as I say. Nobody runs off. OK?" Then he smiled. It was an ugly smile. "You know why they don't lock the door at night?" He let their imaginations run wild. "That's right: they don't need to. Every once in a while, a genius tries to run away. We have ways of finding lost property. We always get our property back." He held up his hand.

Samira gasped and Irina looked away. Two of his fingers ended in short stumps.

He laughed again, turned around, and tapped the driver.

As the van set out, he spoke into his mobile phone, loud and clear, for their benefit. "Boris, yes. Moshe Karlin didn't show up for work today. Good." He put away the phone.

"The dogs are out, boys and girls. Once they get a scent, nothing can stop them. Your friend will be back soon, one way or another." He glanced at the driver and they laughed.

The van accelerated toward their next job.

Shmuel leaned forward and whispered in Irina's ear. "I hope Moshe knows what he's doing."

Irina hoped so too.

CHAPTER 42

Moshe watched the store across Pierre Koenig Street. An old man wearing a flat cap rolled up the security gate and unlocked the door.

Moshe waited ten minutes. Then he crossed the street at the light. He paused outside the dusty display window. A chair of carved oak with an embroidered seat. A stuffed owl. A brass trumpet. Plates and figurines of painted China.

Bells jingled as he entered. The old man looked up from his coffee and newspaper on the glass counter. A large wisp of white hair like cotton candy had replaced the hat. He gave his customer the once-over with hungry vulture eyes.

"Let me guess," he said. "The wife's jewelry?"

Moshe had encountered yet another creature that enjoyed feasting on the unfortunate. He disliked the man already. That would make his task easier.

He drew a deep breath and unstrapped the watch on his wrist. The word "Rolex" glittered in gold leaf. He ran his fingers over the shiny silver frame for the last time, then he placed the last vestige of his family's former greatness on the counter, and imagined his forebears turning in their graves.

The vulture eyes ogled the timepiece with restrained, calculating greed. The old man snatched up the watch. He lodged a long monocle in his eye and examined the face. He turned the metal casing over and tested the black leather straps with gnarled, spotty fingers. Desire flashed in the pawnbroker's eyes.

Then he returned the watch to the glass counter, as though he had handled a dead lizard.

Moshe's heart sank. The old man had rejected his most prized possession.

"I'll give you five," he said.

Moshe's relief at the offer soon evaporated.

"Five what?"

"Five magic beans. What do you think? Five hundred shekels."

"Five hundred? You must be joking. For a Rolex Bubbleback 1948 Limited Edition? My grandfather paid a king's ransom for that watch and it has only appreciated since."

The old man shuttered his eyelids. "For all I know it was made in China."

His blood boiled. "That is no imitation. My grandfather bought it firsthand. Three generations in the family. It's worth at least forty thousand."

The old pawn dealer made a dry sound that was either a cough or a laugh. "For forty thousand I'll sell you the shop. I don't even know if I'll be able to move this trinket, never mind turn a profit."

The old man was a wily one; he had to be for his store to survive. Moshe needed to survive too. He would have to find another dealer.

Moshe made to collect the watch.

"Five thousand." The words pinned Moshe's hand like an arrow. "Five thousand. Not an *agorah* more."

Hello! The old man's bluff shattered on the dusty floor, but Moshe needed more than five thousand. Aim too high and he'd miss the deal. He needed a deal and the old man held all the cards.

"Twenty."

The old man locked his eyes on Moshe, who made a mental note never to play poker with the old vulture.

"Ten thousand. Cash."

Moshe had no bank account. No ID for cashing checks. The old man seemed to know that. Ten thousand might just be enough.

"Fifteen," he said.

A clock ticked out five seconds and then the old man nodded his head. Moshe released a sigh from deep within his chest. The pawnbroker scurried about the store, opening drawers, extracting wads of hundred-shekel notes from shoeboxes and crannies. He counted the bills on the glass counter in crumpled piles. Moshe shoved the cash into his pockets and, casting one final glance at the watch, he left the store.

Cars whizzed by on Pierre Koenig.

Phase One complete. He had the money. Phase Two also involved no small amount of risk, but he was sure Phase Two would be easier. He was wrong.

Moshe took two steps down the sidewalk and froze. A large man in a gray suit stood thirty feet away and stared at him. King Kong looked no less intimidating in public.

The towering thug stalked toward him, the threat of violence in his every step.

Moshe opened his mouth to explain, but swallowed his words. Negotiations with this Russian would be short and painful.

So he turned and ran.

CHAPTER 43

"Stand aside," Eli said. "I want to show you something."

Noga released the rubber handles of his wheelchair and stood beside the wall of the corridor.

His stamina was returning. Even after the physio session, he had strength enough to show off. He gripped the metal push rings inside the wheels, pushed with his arms, and the chair inched forward. His right leg jutted out on the footrest like a cannon. He shifted his hands back on the rim and pushed again. The chair rolled forward.

Push, roll. Push, roll.

He picked up momentum.

"Hey," she called behind him. "Wait up!"

He didn't. He careened down the hallway. A nurse entered the corridor and jumped out of his way. The wheels spun so fast, he could no longer grip the rubber tire. He pressed the plaster cast on his arm against the left wheel to adjust his course and avoid a row of chairs, and then he slammed on the brake lever. The chair stopped inches from the potted plant at the end of the corridor.

Noga reached him, panting and laughing. "Since when can you do *that*?"

"Since this morning."

"And you still let me wheel you to physio and back."

Eli winked at her. "I was enjoying your company too much."

She had no answer to that. Her flushed cheeks said it all. She said, "I'll take you back." She stepped behind the chair. "You should be more careful. Your bones still need to mend."

"Casts are coming off next week," he said.

"Next week? Are you sure?"

"Got a CT scan to prove it."

"That's… that's great."

She fell silent. He couldn't see her face. Was she impressed with his speedy recovery, or sad at the prospect of losing him?

Lose him she would, and sooner than he had thought. His body was healing and his mind would not be far behind. Once the casts came off, he would be able to complete his mission. Yet, for the first time since his arrival at Shaare Zedek, he wasn't in a mad rush to leave.

They passed a doorway and he clamped his hands on the wheels. Something had caught his eye.

Down a corridor, a man juggled colored balls. He had fuzzy orange hair.

"So there *is* a clown."

A child's voice squealed with delight and a little boy stepped into view. He reached for the flying balls. He wore a hospital gown. His head was as smooth and hairless as the plastic balls.

"That's Moti," Noga said. "The therapeutic clown. He spends most of his time in oncology."

The balls rained down on the clown's head and he fell to the floor with dramatic flair. The little boy convulsed with laughter. He coughed. He clutched his chest and doubled over. A nurse drew near and held his shoulders.

"Poor kid," said Noga.

"Yeah," Eli said. "Poor kid."

The clown inflated a blue balloon with much huffing and puffing and handed it to the boy. He pretended to fall over again and the young patient ran at him and hugged him for all he was worth.

Eli stared at the little boy and his moment of joy. The clown turned his head. He looked straight at Eli with his sad eyes and white frown.

"Let's go," Noga whispered.

They continued down the linoleum hallway. The little boy stuck in Eli's mind. Mortality sucked. How did humanity bear it? One week in the hospital had been more than enough for him.

They took the elevator to the fourth floor. Noga said hello to the nurse on duty, Nadir, a quiet Arab woman with a white headscarf that made her look like a well-tanned nun. Noga seemed to know all the doctors and nurses, and they always greeted her with smiles.

She wheeled him to his bed and supported his good arm as he rose with great effort and shifted his rear onto the edge of the bed. He stared at the small pearl buttons of her blouse. He inhaled her flowery deodorant. Her hands lingered on his arms a moment longer than was necessary. She lowered her head and took a step back.

"See you later?" she said.

He nodded and she left. He stretched out on the bed, alone with his thoughts and his racing pulse.

"*Love is in the air*," sang a man's raspy voice in English. "*Everywhere I look around*." An old man lay in the next bed.

Eli scowled at him.

The old man didn't take the hint. He smiled and his loose jowls flapped. "Oren is the name. Checked in an hour ago."

Oren had a receding hairline. He spoke with a breathy tone and effeminate lisp. "Nothing serious," he said and he threw up his hands. "My doctor thinks it's a sinus inflammation, but he sent me here just to be safe. Are you also with Dr. Mohammed?"

Eli groaned. His new roommate loved to talk, and Eli now had yet another reason to escape the hospital pronto. He decided to kill the conversation with a curt reply.

"No," he said. "Dr. Stern."

Oren frowned. "Never heard of him. I like your girlfriend, by the way. Lucky guy."

It took Eli a full three seconds to realize about whom Oren was talking. A motormouth *and* a busybody. "She's not my girlfriend."

"I don't know," Oren said in an annoying singsong. "Body language doesn't lie."

"Whatever."

"Oh, I get it!" said Oren, as though he had just discovered America. "You're married."

Eli shook his head.

Oren clung on like a bulldog. "A girlfriend? A guy friend?"

"Cut it out, OK?"

"I'd snap her up if I were you. Take some advice from an old man. Don't delay. Life is too short."

Eli gave a short sarcastic laugh.

"What?" Then Oren gasped. "Brain tumor!" He slapped his forehead. "I should have known. I am *so* sorry."

"No, nothing like that. It's just… complicated." *Why am I talking with this stranger?*

"Then what are you waiting for? She likes you. I'll tell you that for nothing."

"Just forget about her, please."

Silence settled over the room. Golden, glorious silence. He didn't have feelings for her. He was playing a part. Soon he'd flit away in a storm and a chariot of fire.

"*Love is in the air!*"

The silence had lasted five seconds. Eli wrapped his pillow over his ears. Some miracles were beyond even his powers.

Love? Please! He had moved beyond those mortal emotions long ago. What, then, was the flicker in his gut whenever he thought of the girl in the white cloak?

The sudden realization hit him harder than the truck on the Mount of Olives. Of course! The accident, the hospital—in one Divine flash, the pieces of the puzzle slid into place.

How had he not seen this before? The fracture in his skull

was probably to blame. His mind, however, was healing, and his sixth sense had transformed, a vague intuition taking the place of the Thin Voice. A new prophecy for a new era. Once he had learned to see, the message appeared crisp and clear before his inner eye. The future rolled on before him, and he knew which path he must take.

CHAPTER 44

Moshe turned a corner and sprinted down an alley in the Talpiot industrial zone. He stuffed his hands in his pockets to prevent the wads of hundred-shekel notes from fluttering to the sidewalk.

He hazarded a glance over his shoulder. King Kong lumbered after him, his face tight with concentration. Moshe, lighter and faster, might actually escape the henchman, so long as he didn't trip or wander into a dead end. He needed to put a few more feet between them before he changed direction for his next destination. King Kong would never think to look for him there.

Moshe ducked into an auto garage, running down a line of cars suspended on forklifts. Moshe had dispatched taxis to customers on every street corner in Talpiot, but he knew little of the yards and footpaths that connected them. He pushed past two greasy mechanics and out a door into a large dirt lot. Plenty of cars. A passerby or two. None would save him from the tree-trunk arms of King Kong.

He dashed to the end of the lot and took cover behind a dented fence of corrugated iron sheeting. Air burned in his throat and lungs. His heart galloped in his chest. He peeked over the fence. No sign of his pursuer.

He scampered along the fence, crouching to avoid detection. When he ran out of fence, he made sure the coast was clear and sprinted off.

Lost him. That had gone easier than he had expected. Not bad on an empty stomach. He doubled back, checking behind him every few steps and peering around each corner.

Boris was right. He could not run forever. He might escape King Kong today, but the goon would catch up with him tomorrow. Or the next day. When he least expected it. A life on the run was no life at all. Play his cards right, and Moshe would never need to run again.

He turned into a tired street dotted with litter. The slave warehouse stood across the road in dilapidated silence. Moshe scanned his surroundings a second and third time for signs of hulking thugs. He crossed the street and slid the door aside.

He had barely closed the door of the empty warehouse behind him when a brick wall crashed into him and flung him to the ground. He sprawled on the cement floor, pain throbbing in his shoulder and down his arm. King Kong stood over him. He stared down at his prey, then stepped up to finish the job.

Moshe's shoes slipped and scraped as he launched to his feet. Not fast enough. Large blunt fingers grazed his neck and clamped onto his shirt. Moshe strained against the iron grip for all he was worth. The nape pressed into his throat and threatened to choke him. He threw up his arms and slid downward, slipping out of his shirt and landing on his behind. He scrambled to his feet and ran for all he was worth.

He leaped onto the metal staircase, which trembled and twanged as King Kong followed at his heels. Moshe pulled at the handrail and bounded up the steps, three at a time. *Not far now.*

A large hand closed over his foot. Moshe kicked and wriggled until the shoe came loose and he shot upward.

He sprinted across the metal walkway and dived toward the door of the corner office. *Please be there! Please open!*

The door swung inward and Moshe fell into the room. He

thrust his hands into his pockets and dumped the stash of bills onto the desk.

King Kong filled the doorway, panting and scowling. Boris gave his head a slight shake and the thug stood down.

Boris stared at the heap of money and raised his bushy eyebrows.

"That's very generous of you."

"Not just me. My friends too: Irina, Samira, and Shmuel. Three grand each. Fifty percent more than we owe."

Boris fingered the bills.

The moment of truth. Their future lay in the slaver's hands. Moshe could only hope that self-interest would beat out spite.

His boss wiggled his mustache. "A deal is a deal," he said.

Moshe breathed again.

Boris raked in the money like a winner at a casino table. "And you," he spoke to King Kong. "You owe me a hundred shekels." The thug groaned, and Boris chuckled. "Don't be a sore loser."

Moshe waited on the street corner beside his plastic grocery bag of possessions. The sun warmed his face.

He breathed in the free air. A giddy sense of release washed over his mind. Only a slave understood the sweet thrill of freedom.

The minivan returned a few hours later. Damas jumped out and scowled at him as he charged into the warehouse.

Irina ran to him. Shmuel said, "Moshe, what's going on?"

He greeted his friends with a wide smile. "We're free to go." His eyes met Shmuel's. "You too."

Irina jumped on him. Shmuel hugged him. Samira bowed and blew kisses.

He explained, and then they collected their things and regrouped on the street.

"For a moment there," Shmuel said, "I thought you'd run off without us."

"I'm sure you would have done the same for me."

They looked to him, tears glistening in their eyes. They

would follow him anywhere. For a fleeting moment, he had returned to the helm of Karlin & Son. The feeling energized him. He wished he had more hope to dispense. A plan. A future. A promised land. He had nothing.

"Never again," Moshe said. "We must make sure this never happens again." They nodded as one, knowing that they had no power to enforce the words.

"Let's go," he said. "Before Boris changes his mind."

"Where to?" Shmuel asked.

Moshe drew a deep breath. Of their few options, only one felt right. Only one rekindled the hope for a return to his former life.

He said, "The only place we can."

CHAPTER 45

Rage drove Damas up the metal stairs inside the warehouse.

Few had left the Pit and none escaped without scars. A boiling pot of injustice brewed inside him as he launched across the walkway to the corner office. He pushed open the door without knocking.

Boris looked up. He sat at the desk, the phone to his ear, and mumbled in Russian. The Rottweiler stood at the wall and folded his thick arms. Damas didn't know his name. There was a lot he didn't know about his employers. Boris told him only what he wanted him to know. He had not even consulted with him before setting free his entire team.

Boris put the phone down and watched Damas through droopy eyelids, his face expressionless. "Have a seat."

Damas stood tall in the middle of the room. He scuffed the floor with his feet like an edgy stallion. "Why did you let them go?"

Boris considered his words, as though deciding whether to answer. He slouched back in the chair. "We made a deal. He kept his part. This is a business, Damas. The deal closed our gap for the quarter. We must keep the Big Boss happy."

"You shouldn't have let them go. It sets a bad example."

The Rottweiler took a step forward but Boris raised his hand.

"Forget about them, Damas. You'll get a new team."

Damas was not going to stand down. Moshe Karlin and his friends were laughing at him right now. Let them laugh. He would laugh last.

"We must bring them back," he said.

"Must we now?" His tone indicated that he was losing his patience. He was not used to receiving orders from a worker. Damas didn't care. For once, Damas knew something that Boris didn't, and he had saved his secret weapon for a moment like this.

"Yes," he said. "They are not ordinary people."

Boris raised a bushy gray eyebrow.

He told his boss what he had overheard and what he had seen. Every word. Every detail.

Boris stared at him for half a minute. "So these dead people just wake up in the cemetery?"

"Yes."

"Have you lost your mind?"

In his anger, Damas had not paused to think how the story would sound to a man who had not heard and seen for himself. "It's true," he said. "I swear to it by my other fingers." He held up his maimed hand for display.

Boris ground his teeth. "One good thing about dead people," he said, "is that they do not come back. They do not talk." His boss had understood right away how the discovery could complicate business.

Adrenaline burst into his arteries. "Hunt them down," he said. "Interrogate them. Tear out their secrets."

Boris put his hands together and touched them to his lips while he thought. Damas had presented his case, but would the judge rule in his favor?

"You have made a very bold claim, Damas," he said. Damas swallowed hard. His phantom fingers itched, and he hid his hands behind his back. "But a claim we can easily verify. And if you're right, this could be very profitable."

Profitable? What did he mean? He had expected fear and action, but instead, Boris smiled. Why was he smiling? When the Russian chuckled, Damas could stand the tension no longer. “I don’t understand,” he said.

“Soon you will.” His boss leaned forward and rested his elbows on the desk. “Forget about Moshe Karlin for now. Think about the possibilities. Their lives,” he added, “are our opportunity.”

CHAPTER 46

Rabbi Yosef closed the Laws of Blessings on his podium at the front of the class. Five minutes until the chime of the schoolyard bell. Time enough to atone for his sins.

"Boys," he said, "I want to discuss another topic."

Menachem raised his hand. "Rabbi," the boy said, "is it about the Resurrection?"

"No!" Yosef said, with more force than he had intended. "Something even more important."

He had their undivided attention. What could be more important than the dead rising for Judgment Day and the Final Redemption? He picked up a black marker and scrawled two words on the whiteboard.

"*Emunas Chakhomim*," he read aloud. Faith in the Sages. "Who can tell me what that means?"

Menachem's hand shot up again, but Yosef called on Dudi. "Our rabbis are always right."

"Close," Yosef said. "God gave us two things to guide our actions. He gave us our intellect"—Yosef tapped his forehead—"and He gave us the Torah. But how are we to know whether we have understood the Torah correctly?"

Menachem waved his hand so hard that Yosef feared he might dislocate his shoulder. "The rabbis tell us how to understand the Torah."

"Very good. But surely the Sages of Blessed Memory also make mistakes?"

Twenty pairs of fearful eyes stared at him. "That is *Emunas Chakhomim*. We trust that God guides the leading rabbis of the generation to the correct interpretation. The Torah tells us, 'Do not turn from what they instruct you neither to the right nor to the left.' The Midrash comments, 'Even if they seem to tell you that left is right and that right is left, obey them.' Trust their judgment, even above your own."

The bell rang. The boys collected their study materials and prepared to go home.

Yosef leaned against the wall of the empty classroom. During the meeting of the Great Council two days ago, something inside him had broken.

Sitra Achra. He shuddered. He had invited them into his home. Exposed his family. How had he not realized that his undead visitors were the agents of the unholy *Other Side*? Two secular Jews. If that had not set off alarm bells, the Arab girl certainly should have!

And yet, neither Moshe nor Irina had struck him as evil. Not even Samira. They were people struggling to survive. They were victims, not demons. They needed his help. How could that be wrong? Had his moral compass lost its bearings?

Yosef collected his bag and left the low school building. Shards of orange sunlight slipped between the apartment complexes of Jerusalem stone in Sanhedria. As Yosef climbed into his battered white Subaru, two teenagers in black hats and suits passed by, holy books in hand.

Black and white. The uniform of the *frum* world. Life was easier in black and white. Right and wrong. Nothing in between. That required faith. *Emunas Chakhomim*. To surrender his intellect and heart to the guidance of God's true representatives. *Have faith, Yosef.*

He turned the key and, defying the odds of probability, the engine started.

He negotiated the curves of the suburban streets, slowing

as hats and gowns crossed on foot. He bypassed the crowded hive of Meah Shearim, the heart of ultra-Orthodox life, and turned south onto Route 60. Traffic choked the highway, as workers returned home after a long day.

Yosef rested his elbow on the door. The world crawled on, tired and colorless. Empty. Purged of the intoxicating scent of the Redemption. Once you had a whiff, sobriety became intolerable. Yosef knew that only too well. False hope was worse than no hope at all.

Twenty minutes later, he parked on Shimshon Street. His boys had beaten him home. The scent of barley soup wafted from the kitchen, to his surprise. Rocheleh never cooked dinner on a weekday. Since Yosef had removed their unholy guests, however, she had made an extra effort. She even smiled at him.

He had not mentioned the verdict of the Great Council, and she had not asked. Best not to disturb the purity of his home with talk of the *Sitra Achra*.

Life had returned to normal. Better than normal. He poured a cup of coffee and settled at the dinner table with Uriel, his eldest, for their weekly study session.

Last time, they had completed the Chapters of the Fathers, the ethical teachings of the Mishna. Tonight they started the Eight Chapters, the introduction to those teachings penned by Maimonides. After a feverish week of Resurrection speculations, Yosef welcomed the return to timeless first principles—character building and human decency—the bread and butter of religious life.

Uriel read the text; Yosef corrected and commented as necessary. The famed philosopher kicked off with an analogy. Doctors need to understand the human body to heal illness. Similarly, we need to understand our mental faculties to correct our faulty character traits.

Yosef listened to the sound of his own breathing, the rustle of the page beneath his son's hand. In the kitchen behind them, a pot hissed on the stove. Compared to the tumult of their strange guests, the house felt empty. In time, he would forget them. *All that the Merciful One does is for the best.*

Uriel giggled.

"What?" Yosef had drifted off.

"Look, Aba." His finger marked the passage.

Yosef read the words. "'Things that make no sense or that are inconceivable.'" Nothing humorous there. He scanned the next paragraph. "The faculty of imagination," he said. "What's funny about that?"

"Aba!" Uriel said in the exasperated tone of a teenager. "Read on."

He did. "'For example, a metal boat flying in the air—'" His son giggled again. "What?"

Uriel rolled his eyes. A teenager, indeed. "A metal ship," he said. "Flying. What about airplanes?"

"Ha. You're right." Yosef had missed the glaring error.

"Aba, didn't he know about airplanes?"

"Maimonides lived a very long time ago," he explained. "In the twelfth century, a flying boat was unimaginable. But today…"

He gazed at the turbaned rabbi in the framed picture. Maimonides had erred—black on white. Not by any fault of his own. According to the physics of his day, a flying metal ship was, indeed, inconceivable. But still, the passage gave him pause.

For three seconds.

There came a knocking at the door.

"Expecting anyone?"

Uriel shrugged. Yosef rose to his feet and crossed the living room. He opened the front door.

Moshe Karlin stood on his doorstep. Behind him stood Irina, Samira, and an older stranger. "Sorry, Rabbi," Moshe said. He gave him an apologetic smile. "We had nowhere else to go."

CHAPTER 47

Irina awoke Wednesday morning to the sound of angry voices. The rabbi and his wife were arguing again, or, more precisely, she was shouting and he was emitting meek consoling noises.

Irina lifted her head from the armrest of the couch and rubbed the pain in her neck. How had Moshe slept there five nights in a row? Samira lay huddled in a blanket on the other couch. Moshe and Shmuel made the most of the living room carpet.

In the kitchen, spoons clinked in cereal bowls and mouths slurped chocolate milk.

The voices grew louder. She lowered her head and pretended to sleep.

"Boys," the rabbanit called with forced restraint. "Time to go. Wait for me outside. Now!"

Chair legs scraped the kitchen tiles and little feet pattered out the front door.

"Get rid of them today," she continued in the harsh tone she reserved for her husband, "or I will. Do you understand? Think of our children!"

The front door slammed shut.

Silence reigned for a few seconds.

Rabbi Yosef was a good man. A kind man. He didn't deserve this. None of them did. But what were they supposed to do?

The rabbi cleared his throat. "Moshe?" he whispered. Moshe raised his head from the floor. The rabbi stepped into view. "I have to go to work. Help yourself to food and drink—whatever you need."

Moshe nodded. "Thank you."

The rabbi gave him a brave smile and left the house.

Moshe sat up, rubbed his eyes, and yawned.

Irina said, "Sleep OK?" She had slept fitfully herself, waking at every creak of a door, gripped by the sudden fear that Boris and his henchmen had come to drag them back to slavery. *You don't have to worry about that anymore. You're free.*

Moshe smiled. "Better than last night. And probably better than I will tonight."

Humor, even in desperate situations. That was Moshe. His attitude made their predicament seem less hopeless.

She swung her legs off the couch. "I'll make breakfast."

She freshened up and got to work in the kitchen. They had raided the fridge the previous night, wolfing down frozen dinners as fast as the rabbi could heat them. Irina toasted the last four slices of bread and fried the last three eggs.

She served Moshe, Samira, and Shmuel at the kitchen table. They chewed their last foreseeable cooked meal.

"How many of us are out there?" Moshe asked.

"How many resurrected people?" Irina said.

He nodded

Shmuel said, "More than the four of us, that's for sure. And good luck finding them. I hadn't told a soul until you lot showed up."

They pondered the fate of their fellow resurrectees as they ate.

"What do we do now?" Samira asked.

Moshe washed down his egg with a glass of tap water. "I'll make some calls. Let's shoot in all directions: anyone who might take us in for a night."

He withdrew a wad of shekel notes from his pocket and

divided them into four equal mounds on the table. "We have seven hundred shekels each. That won't get us very far."

Irina stared at the money. The crumpled bills were all that remained of Moshe's treasured family heirloom. He had bought their freedom and now he was treating them to the rest of his cash. He did it without fanfare, as though it was the most natural thing to do. The others shared her sense of awe and gratitude. They would do anything for Moshe Karlin.

"I have a nephew in Hadera," Shmuel said. "It's a long shot but I'll see what he can do."

Irina had nobody to call. "I'll clean up," she said.

"And I'll wash their clothes," Samira added. "Maybe the rabbi's wife will grow to like us."

They laughed.

Irina got to work on the dishes. Galit Karlin was a very poor judge of character. She didn't know her husband at all. Over the past week, Moshe had passed up many opportunities to make advances on her. Lately, she had been inclined to accept. But Moshe still loved his wife. Were all good men stupid?

She hung the dishcloths to dry.

Moshe sat on the couch with a notepad in one hand and the house phone in the other. The rabbi's battered laptop lay open on the dining room table.

Irina sat at the computer and nudged it awake. She opened an Internet browser and searched for two words.

Moshe had sacrificed so much for her. She could at least return the favor. As a woman and an unknown, she could go where Moshe could not.

The results for "Galit Karlin" returned a Facebook profile—friends only—a genealogy site, and a Ynet listing. She clicked the link and arrived at the schedule for a club in Emek Refaim.

Well, well, well. Now who's been leading a double life?

Irina knew exactly when and where to find her. She would have to dress for the occasion.

"Galit Karlin," she whispered, "tonight is our first date."

CHAPTER 48

Wednesday noon, Rabbi Yosef returned home from school. He had made his decision and it tore him up inside.

When Moshe and his fellow resurrectees had shown up on his doorstep the previous night, he had acted on instinct. His visitors were no demons, just desperate people in dire need of help. How could he turn them away?

That morning, however, away from the eyes of his guests, Rocheleh's words had simmered in his mind. She was right. He could lose his job. His well-intentioned generosity might get his children expelled and ruin their marriage prospects. If he had told Rocheleh about the *Sitra Achra*, she would have thrown him out along with his evil guests.

"*Ve'chai bahem*," the Torah wrote. Live by these teachings. From this verse, the rabbis of the Talmud inferred that "your life takes priority over another's." Those who pity the cruel will, in the end, act with cruelty against those deserving of mercy. By pitying these strangers, he had endangered his innocent, young boys.

He piled on the quotations to strengthen his resolve, but the sharp talons of conscience still clawed at his heart.

He opened his front door quietly, like a thief. The living room had never looked tidier. Samira smiled at him from beneath her hijab. She folded a boy's T-shirt and placed it on a pile of freshly laundered clothes on the couch. Moshe and Irina emerged from the kitchen.

"Welcome home, Rabbi Yosef," Moshe said. Behind them, white grocery bags sat on the kitchen counter.

They were not making this easy for him. "My friends," he said. *Don't cry, Yosef. Hold it together.* "We need to talk." The smiles waned.

Shmuel entered from the corridor. "Come here, Rabbi, I want to show you something."

"Shmuel, I was just telling the others—"

"In a moment. Come on."

He gave in. He followed Shmuel down the corridor. The older man pushed open the glass-paned door that led to the yard. "What do you think?"

Yosef stepped into his yard. The weeds and wild grasses were gone. In their place, tidy rows of turned soil bordered the enclosure walls, with parallel lines of little circular ditches.

"Surprise!" said Irina.

"Gerberas on the sides," Shmuel explained. "Sunflowers in the middle. In a few weeks you'll have a lovely flower garden."

Yosef could hold back no longer. His shoulders trembled. He felt a gentle hand on his shoulder. "It's all right," Moshe said.

Yosef wiped his eyes. They stood before him, hands at their sides. Unarmed men and women facing the firing squad.

"You are good people," Yosef said. "I'm sure there's been a mistake and that, once they get to know you, the rabbis will change their minds. But you have to understand, I have a family. They need me and I need them. There's only so much I can do."

They listened in silence and studied the dirt. He had rehearsed the speech in the car on his way home. He had imagined a firm delivery and an amount of angry resistance. Reality had disappointed on both counts.

His next words would seal their fate. He had no choice. "And so," he said, "with much regret and a heavy heart—"

The doorbell rang. They looked at each other. Yosef was not expecting any visitors and Rocheleh had a key.

Oh, no! The boys had opened their mouths at school. Or messengers of the Great Council had arrived to ensure that he had complied with their decision.

"Wait here," he said. "Please." They nodded.

Yosef went indoors. "Just a moment," he called. He hurried down the corridor and brushed lint from his suit jacket. He peered through the peephole but saw neither Rabbanit Schiff nor men in Chasidic uniform.

He opened the door. A little old lady peered up at him. Her eyes filled her glasses. The aromas of tasty hot food rose from the tall stack of large tinfoil trays in her arms.

A middle-aged man with creased olive skin stood behind her. He carried a similar stack of trays, and yet more piles of trays waited on the backseat of the white taxicab that idled in the street.

"Rabbi Yosef?" the old lady said.

"Yes?"

"Here." She offloaded the trays onto his arms and stepped into the living room. "Where are the others?" she said. "It's time to eat."

CHAPTER 49

Noga strode into room 419C on a gust of anticipation, but when she rounded the divider curtain, she found Eli's bed empty.

The good feeling fled. They had arranged to meet that afternoon. Had he tried to walk and slipped? She had warned him not to push his luck. Or was he avoiding her? He had seemed edgy that morning. Had she crowded him?

"Oren," she said. "Where is he?"

The older man in the next bed peered over his *Yediot Acharonot* and shook his wobbly jowls. "Have a closer look." He nodded toward the empty bed and winked. "Romeo might have left you something."

She approached the bed and sure enough, a folded note of lined paper lay on the pillow. She read the spidery handwritten message and smiled. Every day she discovered a shiny new facet of Eli Katz.

She pocketed the note and marched down the corridor. She took the elevator to the first floor, walked past the Steimatzky bookstore and flower shop, and pushed through a glass door that led to a small green courtyard. She had pointed out the hidden garden to Eli on one of their wheelchair tours. He had remembered. What could Eli possibly want to say to her—or do with her—in the privacy of the courtyard?

Her cheeks warmed.

Eli had parked his chair beside the wooden bench. He had combed his hair and shaved. He hid his arms behind the chair. A gift? His lips trembled as he smiled. Eli Katz—nervous? She sat on the bench beside him.

"For you," he said. He revealed one arm. It held a single long-stemmed rose.

"Thank you." She accepted the flower, breathed in its scent, and savored its meaning. She was more than a friend. That explained the nerves.

"And there's this." He revealed his other hand. It held a small box in black velvet. Her heart skipped a beat. They had met barely a week ago. A rose was one thing, but a jewelry box…

Her concern must have displayed on her face. "Don't worry," he said. "It's not a ring."

She exhaled audibly, and he gave a short, nervous laugh. She placed the rose on the bench, accepted the box, and flipped the lid open. On a bed of black velvet sat a strip of white paper. He had printed four digits on the slip.

"I had to bribe a nurse to get the box," he said.

"I don't understand," she said.

"It's the code to my apartment. 103 Jaffa Road."

"Your apartment?" Was he asking her to move in with him? And what apartment had a code and not a key? None of this was making any sense. She would have preferred a ring.

He looked at the myrtle sapling in the corner. "I haven't been fully honest with you, Noga."

Her mouth went numb. She remembered the feverish intensity of his eyes when he had grabbed her arm that first time. *Oh, no, Eli. Please. Don't.*

"When we met," he continued, "I felt… a sudden connection. I had never experienced that before."

Her lungs inflated. This wasn't so bad. In fact, this was excellent. "Me too," she said, then she held back. *Don't be too eager.*

"What I'm going to tell you will seem absurd, even crazy."

Love at first sight, she thought, as crazy as it gets. *Spit it out already!*

"That's why I've given you the code. The proof is in my apartment. I wish I could show you some other way, but I can't… I can't…"

He seemed to teeter on the verge of tears. She reached out and touched his hand on the armrest of the wheelchair. "You don't have to prove anything," she said. "I feel the same way."

Finally. That intimate connection. The man she had longed for.

He shook his head. "Please," he said. "Promise you'll hear me out."

"Of course."

Then he spoke. As he spoke, the numbness returned to her face. His name was Elijah. He was three thousand years old. The Day of the Lord had arrived. And Noga had a special role to play in the unfolding Divine drama.

"That's why I had the accident," he said, his dark eyes flashing. "That's why I landed up here, in the hospital. To meet you!"

A breeze ruffled the leaves of the trees. The world shimmered around them.

She had said that she would hear him out. "So I'm part of this End of Days?"

"Yes!"

"What exactly is my role?" Her voice had an edge of impatience, sharpened on the rubble of her broken heart.

"I don't know yet," he said. "But we'll figure it out. Together."

Together. That would have sounded romantic—if he wasn't raving mad.

She hid her face in her hands. *You idiot. You simple, trusting fool.* Tears poured from her eyes. Dr. Stern had tried to warn her. Self-pity boiled over into rage. She shot to her feet. She wanted to slap him across his handsome face. Instead, she hurled the object in her hand. The jewelry box hit him right between the eyes and bounced on the dirt floor.

"Please, Noga. It's true."

She turned on her heels and stormed off, back to the hospital and out of his life.

CHAPTER 50

Moshe crammed trays of surplus food into the freezer. Rafi helped him rearrange the containers so the door would agree to close. Pity to waste good food. Their charm offensive had not changed reality and when the rabbanit arrived home, they'd be out on the street.

"Thanks," Moshe said to Rafi. "I really appreciate this."

"Anything for the Karlins."

And thank you, Dad. His father's kindness to a traumatized soldier forty years ago had returned to help Moshe in his time of need. Perhaps Rafi would let them crash on the floor of his apartment tonight. He hoped it wouldn't come to that. Moshe's loyal friend had lost enough in the name of the Karlins, and a band of homeless intruders would not help his wife's failing health either. Besides that, Moshe longed to stay on Shimshon Street.

"What's the matter?" Rafi asked.

"Nothing. Let's have lunch."

Trays of drool-worthy food covered every inch of the dining room table. Stuffed cabbage. Beef goulash. Baked chicken. Pullet on a bed of fried onion. Boiled ox tongue. White rice. *Nokedli.* Savta Sarah shoveled the steaming delicacies onto the plates. Moshe waited his turn and dug in.

The music of busy cutlery and contented eating filled the

air.

Savta sat back in her chair, her plate empty. A veil of melancholy fell over her features.

"The cattle train arrived at Auschwitz very early in the morning," she said.

Moshe knew the story by heart. At the death camp, SS men sorted the new arrivals: the able-bodied to the left, the young and old to the right. Sarah, her mother, and her younger siblings had stood in a long line that led to the showers.

"My baby sister cried for food," she continued, "so my mother asked me to run back for the bread in the bag we had left on the train."

The sounds of eating ceased.

"I ran back right away and grabbed the bag. But on the way back to my mother and the children, an SS officer stopped me. 'How old are you?' he said. I was fifteen. 'From now on, you are eighteen," he said. 'Stay here.'"

Savta stared into thin air and shook her head. "I never saw them again. They were killed in the gas chambers that day."

Moshe glanced at Savta Sarah. She had prepared food all her life: wedding banquets and bar mitzvahs for Jerusalem's well-to-do, and pro-bono meals for the sick and needy. Generations of Jerusalem Jews had grown strong on her stuffed cabbage and meatballs. With each of those meals, a lost and lonely little girl tried to deliver a bag of bread to her beloved mother and siblings on a cold morning in Auschwitz.

A chill wave washed over Moshe. Was he any different? He had spent his new life paddling backward against the flow of time. Would he struggle forever? Or had the time come to raise his oars and follow the current of a new life?

Samira placed her fork on her plate. "My name is Samira," she said, and glanced at Rafi. Moshe had forgotten to make the introductions. Savta Sarah's confession seemed to have given her courage.

"I grew up in Deir Al Ghusun, near Tulkarem. I married when I was sixteen. At seventeen, I gave birth to a baby boy." She smiled at the memory. Then her beautiful smile faltered.

"My husband was a jealous man. He would lock me in the house when he went to work. He said he'd set me free and divorce me if I gave him full custody of our baby." Her lips trembled. Moshe thought she would cry but she steeled herself.

"He sent me back to my parents. He spread rumors that I had been unfaithful. He posted a petition on the doors of the mosques demanding that my father restore the honor of his family. Everyone signed it, even the elders and our cousins."

A lone tear rolled down her cheek. "My mother sent me to her sister in Ramallah for a few weeks, to wait until the pressure subsided. Then my parents brought me home. Everything would be all right, my mother told me. The next afternoon, however, my father came into my room. No one else was home. He had a cold look in his eyes. He hugged me, and I thought, 'At last the storm has passed.' Then he put his hand over my mouth and nose, and I couldn't breathe."

Irina touched her arm. Rabbi Yosef offered her a tissue and she wiped her eyes.

"I woke up in a garbage dump a few days ago, naked and alone. I don't think I even had a proper burial."

A reverent silence filled the room.

Moshe cleared his throat. Samira's intimate revelation demanded that he reciprocate. "I'm Moshe," he said, following her lead. "I don't remember dying but I did. I died." An unexpected knot of emotion lodged in his throat. Saying the words aloud in the company of friends had made his status more real and final. "I had a wife and daughter. A family business. But I think I've lost them all."

He paused. If he said another word, he'd collapse and weep.

Irina saved him. "Hi everyone," she said, upbeat. "I'm Irina. At least I think I am. I don't remember a thing about my life, so I'm done."

Chuckles all round. After three depressing life stories, they welcomed the comic relief.

"How about you, Shmuel?" Yosef asked.

The older man's eyes widened. He folded his arms. "I can't…" he said. "Not yet. And I don't want my old life back. I'm not wanted there."

"That's OK," Rabbi Yosef said.

A magical sense of unity, warmth, and acceptance hung in the air like pixie dust.

"This is wonderful," Moshe said. "We should do this again."

Rafi said, "Like a club?"

"Exactly. A weekly meeting. Like that group for people with drinking problems, what are they called?"

Rabbi Yosef coughed. "Alcoholics Anonymous?"

"That's it. There are bound to be more of us out there. Shmuel, you said as much last night. We can help each other. We should start an organization. A non-profit."

"We can't even work legal jobs," Shmuel said. "Now we're going to start a company? You need two signatories to start a non-profit."

Moshe felt his shoulders sag. "You're right. We'll need identity cards to do anything official." He was still dead in the eyes of the state bureaucracy. The trickle of inspiration dried up.

"I have an identity card," said Savta Sarah. "Will that help?"

"Me too," said Rafi. "Where do I sign?"

New life flowed in Moshe's veins. "Excellent!" he said. "We have our two signatories."

"We'll need five more," said Shmuel. His voice had softened as the idea gained support. "To get tax benefits." All eyes turned to him and he shrugged. "I was a journalist. You learn a thing or two over the years."

A plan grew flesh and bone in Moshe's head. "We can collect donations," he said, "and rent a place to live."

"What should we call ourselves?" asked Samira.

They shot down a flock of early suggestions: The Hope. Second Life. The Undead. The Living Dead. The Resurrection Club. They made good titles for zombie movies or computer games, but not a satisfying name for their fledgling social movement.

"Reborn?" said Shmuel.

"Too Christian," said Rabbi Yosef.

Inspiration flashed again. Moshe said, "The Dry Bones."

Rabbi Yosef smiled. Moshe knew the rabbi would like that one.

"Sounds like a comic strip," Shmuel said. "Or a rock band from the seventies."

"The Dry Bones *Society*," Rabbi Yosef said.

Heads nodded as they warmed to the idea.

Moshe said, "Let's vote on it. All those in favor raise your hand."

The front door opened behind him, and the enthusiasm drained from their faces. Moshe turned around. The rabbanit stared at the party in her living room, her mouth open. The four boys stood behind her like nervous ducklings.

Her face turned red and a vein throbbed on her forehead. "Yosef! What is going on here?"

Savta Sarah ambled up to her and offered her hand. "Rabbanit Lev?" she said, her voice radiating royal charm. "Sarah Weiss. Of Weiss Catering. How good it is to finally meet you!"

The rabbanit lowered her confused gaze to the friendly old lady. "Weiss Catering?" The name seemed to ring a bell. "*The* Weiss Catering?"

"The one and only. *Glatt* kosher. Strictly *glatt* kosher. Do I have a surprise for you!"

The aging chef snatched her hand and led her to the table. She introduced each dish as though announcing heads of state at a palatial ball. She sat the rabbanit at the table and the tasting began.

"This is *good*!" The rabbanit had tasted the ox tongue.

"There's more of everything in the freezer. You won't have to cook all week."

"How do you get the meat so soft?"

"The recipe is yours, my dear." Savta winked at Moshe.

"But not today. I'll be back tomorrow for a private demonstration. Moshe dear, please let me know how I can help with your promising new venture. Rafi, let's go. It's time for my nap."

The granny and her driver bid them farewell.

The rabbanit chewed another mouthful and closed her eyes. Then she opened her eyes and woke from Savta's trance. Annoyance and desire battled on her forehead. "One more night," she said to Yosef. "One more."

Shmuel punched the air. Samira jumped for joy.

One more day of borrowed time. They had better move fast. They cleaned the living room and kitchen, and huddled to assign tasks. Moshe would download the registration papers and coordinate with Savta and Rafi. Shmuel would contact a journalist friend to scrounge free publicity and search for a rental apartment. There were bank accounts to open and phones to order.

The rabbi helped his children with their homework and fed them an early dinner.

Moshe browsed government websites on the rabbi's laptop. He was speed-reading the legal requirements for non-profits when he noticed Irina slip out the front door.

Strange. She usually told him where she was going, so he wouldn't worry. They had no mobile phones yet.

"Samira," Moshe said. "Did Irina say where she was going?"

Samira folded a second load of washing on the couch. "No. Maybe she just needed some fresh air."

"Yeah," he said. "I suppose you're right."

CHAPTER 51

The skyscraper on Jaffa Road towered over Noga, blocking the late afternoon sun and casting a cool shadow over her. She had walked past the shiny new apartment building of polished white marble countless times but never considered that people actually lived there. Not anyone she knew firsthand. The tall glass façade of the lobby and the chrome banister whispered of private jets and luxury yachts, not of deranged invalids in the Shaare Zedek neurology ward.

That morning she had stormed down the hospital corridors, cursing Eli under her breath, and cursing herself for falling for him. Proof lay in his apartment, so he had claimed. Proof she would find, but not the kind he had intended. His fantasies would fade away in the harsh light of hard evidence for the existence of Eli Katz, mortal of flesh and blood.

She steeled herself before the tall doors of expensive tinted glass. She had never dared to enter the building, never mind sneak into one of the apartments. *Don't worry, Noga. You probably won't even need to.* His claim to an apartment at the exclusive location was most likely yet another delusion. This would be a very short visit.

She crossed the forecourt of white stone. The glass double doors snapped open with an audible whoosh and a blast of air-conditioning blew in her face. The expansive lobby stood two floors high. A security guard sat behind a long counter of black wood and studied a hidden book or screen. The doors snapped shut behind her. The rubber soles of her old walking shoes squeaked over the large slabs of white marble. The guard looked up, a question in his eyes.

"Mr. Eli Katz," she said.

His eyes moved from her old T-shirt to the frayed strap of her shoulder bag.

He did not throw her out, and the name Eli Katz did not seem to surprise him. "First time?" he said.

She nodded.

"The cleaning equipment is in the closet on the right as you walk in." Two degrees and a doctoral grant, and she still passed for the maid. The wonders of higher education.

"Which floor?" she asked.

"Penthouse."

She swallowed hard. "Thanks."

She made for the corridor of elevators at the far end. Eli Katz lived in the penthouse. What were the chances that another Eli Katz lived in the building? Or had he stolen the identity of a wealthy stranger? What did she know for sure about the mystery patient in room 419C?

A roman letter appeared above each elevator. Instead of the familiar round buttons for Up and Down, she found a golden keypad. She pressed the key for "Penthouse" and the letter A pulsated on a digital display. The doors of elevator A shot open with another elegant whoosh.

She stepped inside. Mirrors lined the walls. The letter P projected in black on the golden lintel, while another ephemeral digit climbed upward.

1. 2. 3.

P came after 21.

Time to see who you really are.

The doors whooshed open, and she almost walked into a mahogany door. Another golden keypad appeared above the handle. She punched in the four-digit code Eli had placed in the jewelry box and the door clicked open.

She entered a large dark expanse. She touched the wall and fumbled for a light switch, when hidden motors purred. Blinds swiveled and shifted along tracks, and sunlight flooded the room through large continuous windows. Her breath caught in her throat. A set of low couches in cream leather faced a one-hundred-eighty-degree view of the Jerusalem skyline. Eli had the entire top floor to himself!

She stepped onto the shiny marble tiles and avoided trampling the carpet of cream-colored fur with her street shoes—she could not afford that dry cleaning bill. She reached the French windows and her breath clouded the glass. A forest of downtown offices and hotels gleamed white in the afternoon sun. The city sprawl traced the hills and valleys that led to the thick ancient walls of the Old City, with its domes and minarets. Beyond the Old City rose the Mount of Olives, bristling with gravestones and tombs. It was like looking back over history.

As the awe of the view faded, she noticed the smell. The acrid stench of decomposition came from the open-plan kitchen in stylish chrome and dark wood paneling. She blocked her nose as she drew closer.

Leave now. Jump into that elevator and go! But—serial killer or sloppy housekeeper—she had to know. She pulled at the door of the closet beneath the sink and stepped back. No severed heads or limbs, only a pile of putrid olives.

Sloppy housekeeper. With a thing for olives.

She tied the strings of the garbage bag, pulled it out of the bin, and leaned the olive graveyard against the front door. She'd take the bag down on her way out. She had become his cleaner after all.

She washed her hands in the sink and dried them on a soft kitchen towel. *OK. So you're rich and you have a great interior decorator. That does not make you an immortal prophet.*

She ran her fingertips along the dining table—a thick glass plate on marble pillars—and leather, high-backed chairs.

A passageway opened onto a bedroom the size of her entire apartment in tasteful creams and dark paneling. She parted the blinds of another set of tall French windows. She sat down on the soft, unmade bed. The owner had woken up one morning and left in a hurry. He had not bothered to empty the trash. He had not expected to spend the next week in hospital.

No photos of family or friends. No mementos or collectibles. The man who lived here had loads of cash but no life.

A spacious walk-in closet. Piles of T-shirts, blue jeans, and a set of leather biker jackets. A spacious bathroom and Jacuzzi tub.

On the way back, she tried the door of a closet in the hall. Her fingers found a light switch on the wall and, with a satisfying click, she found herself in different world.

Five carpeted steps led downward, creating a square, sunken den in the center of the room. Objects hung on the outer walls. A shaggy fur cloak. A leather shield. A sword in a leather scabbard. A rounded clay urn. An oriental rug. A clunky pistol with a rounded handle. She had wandered into a private museum. Or a shrine. A shrine to what?

She scanned the walls, but touched nothing, sensing that her fingers would violate something very personal and secret. But Eli had sent her here.

She descended the steps into the central den. A padded bench lined the inner walls. A meditation chamber? A meditation chamber with bookshelves and a flat-screen television. She ran her fingers along the spines of the worn volumes. *The Jewish War* by Flavius Josephus. *The Innocents Abroad* by Mark Twain. A Hebrew Bible.

A universal remote lay on the padded bench. She sat down and pressed a button. The lights dimmed, and the television flickered to life.

Within minutes, everything made sense.

CHAPTER 52

As the shadows lengthened on Emek Refaim, Irina lurked beside a streetlight, wondering whether she had arrived at the wrong address. Pedestrians of all shapes and sizes flowed around her. They spoke English, French, and Hebrew and bustled toward coffee shops and boutique stores. Only a handful of the passersby, however, had entered the building across the street, all middle-aged women in ankle-length skirts and head coverings.

Irina assumed that Moshe's wife had not yet hit fifty.

The streetlight flickered on. *Time to go undercover.* Irina waited for a white taxi to pass and she crossed the street. At a thrift shop on the way, she had bought a pair of black leggings and a sports top, and the outfit had won her more glances than usual on the Jerusalem sidewalks.

She entered the office building and took the stairs to the second floor.

She assumed her role as a spy with ease. For all she knew, her current persona might be her true self. Or perhaps she had been a spy to begin with? She liked that idea best.

The pulse of club music carried down the stairwell. She entered a corridor on the second floor and stopped at the sign that read "Emek Refaim Fitness Club."

She opened a door and walked in. A dozen middle-aged

women in gym togs hopped on a wood-paneled floor, doing their best to mimic their instructor.

Her long ponytail of black hair swished as her body moved. Slim black leotard. Curves in all the right places. The face reflected in the mirror on the far wall had high cheekbones, large bright eyes, and full lips. Good skin, too. The girl from the wedding portrait on Savta Sarah's wall.

Irina's stomach tied in a knot. The thrill of espionage fled. *Am I jealous?* Her legs made to leave when Galit Karlin spun around, sent her a broad smile, and beckoned her to join in the fun. *No escape now.*

She dumped her plastic bag of clothes among the other gym bags in the corner and joined the back line. Hidden speakers blared an edgy pop tune worthy of a seedy dance club. A saxophone melody swirled as young women chanted, "I'm worth it," amid the grunts of a male rapper.

She did her best to match Galit's movements. She gyrated her hips and waggled her bum. She raised her arms above her head and shook her bust. Her thighs burned as she performed provocative squats.

The song segued to another fast-paced dance hit.

A competitive urge made her push her boundaries, but, according to the mirror, she had trouble keeping up even with the grannies. As they turned and contorted, she recognized the faces of the skirted and capped women she had observed on the street. In the safe and secluded environment of the studio, the religious wives and grandmothers pole danced like MTV pros to the chorus of "All the Single Ladies." Underneath their clothes, people were not very different after all.

The forty-minute class left her drenched in sweat and out of breath. She had cut corners toward the end, not bending as low or jumping as high when she thought no one was looking. The older women chattered and pulled skirts over their leggings and hats over their hair.

Galit Karlin walked up to Irina, radiant and energized, hands akimbo. "You're good," she said. "Have you danced

Zumba before?"

Irina understood how Moshe had fallen under the spell of those large, smiling eyes. "First time," she replied. "As far as I can remember."

Galit waved goodbye as the other dancers filed out the door. "How did you hear about us?"

"On the Internet."

Galit nodded.

The two women smiled at each other in silence. What had she planned to say to her? Had she wanted to bring them together or had she come here to check out the competition?

"Great workout, right?" Galit said to ease the silence that had grown between them.

"Yeah. You're in great shape."

Galit made a self-effacing grimace. "Thanks. I've been instructing for a year, so that helps."

Irina liked this Galit Karlin, despite herself. What had gone wrong between this lively, earthy woman and her kind-hearted husband?

For you, Moshe. As long as you want her, I'll do what I can.

She said, "Your husband is a lucky guy."

The smile dropped. The bright eyes narrowed with suspicion, then relaxed. "I knew you looked familiar," she said. "You're his new girl, aren't you?"

"His new girl? What's the matter with you?"

"I saw you walking together on our street. You have some nerve, you slut! Get out!"

"He doesn't have another girl. He loves you. Why won't you believe that?"

Galit picked up a gym bag and hugged it to her chest. She turned back, one foot out the door. "Ask his good friend Sivan," she said, her eyes dripping venom. "You'll have a lot to talk about."

CHAPTER 53

Ahmed opened his eyes.

Dark blue skies above. Raw earth below. A chill breeze. And a burst of intense heat as his body exploded.

He cried out and writhed in the dirt. Then he paused, panting hard. He patted his chest, his belly, his thighs. He was alive. Naked and filthy, but whole. The vision of fire was but a dream. No. Not a dream. A memory.

He rolled onto his side and looked about. An empty field. Leafy trees peered over a perimeter wall of rock. A mountain wind whistled through the cracks.

He laughed. He laughed long and hard, until tears collected in the corners of his eyes.

He had done it! He had fulfilled his mission, and now he had entered Paradise. Hasan had spoken the truth. *Eternal life. Eternal pleasure.*

The images of heat and flame flickered again in his mind. The sway of the bus as it pulled off. The wary eyes of the other passengers as he staggered down the aisle. The sting of sweat in his eyes. His final meal—a double Mac and fries, a poor choice on so many levels—threatened to surge up his throat. Cold electric wires snaked along the inner lining of his jacket sleeve and pressed against the flesh of his arm. His thumb hovered over the smooth curve of the detonator button. And then, that split-second of Hellfire and excruciating pain.

Hasan had been wrong about that—he had felt every nail and ball bearing as they ripped through his flesh.

He staggered to his feet. Pain flared in his head and he doubled over with a whimper. He caressed his temples. Hasan had not mentioned any headaches either.

In truth, to the last moment, he had not fully believed that he would wake from death. He had not wanted to press the button. He had not wanted to die or to drag tens of strangers with him.

Sons of pigs and monkeys, Hasan had said. *Killers of prophets.*

But the man at the back of bus number eighteen had reminded him of Yigal, his boss at the Rami Levi supermarket in Talpiot, where he unpacked crates, mopped floors, and laid out fresh vegetables for the Jewish customers to buy. Yigal had joked around with him in Arabic. He had asked after his family. He let him take Fridays off. How many Yigals had he killed that day?

He shivered. This was Hasan's doing. His cousin from Ramallah had visited for a few days. His mother had made Ahmed share his room with the guest. *He'll be a good influence, make a man of you.* She was always saying that, ever since his father had moved out with his new wife five years ago.

But Hasan had discovered the copies of Penthouse he had stashed inside his mattress. Ahmed had found the pile of shameful Israeli magazines in the supermarket's garbage enclosure and smuggled them home.

A disgrace, Hasan had said. To defile himself with infidel women. *Shame on his family name.* His father would hate him if he found out. There was only one way to cleanse the blemish on his family honor, only one way to purify his Jew-loving soul.

He stumbled forward, one hand at his head, the other over his privates.

Was his mother proud of her martyr son? Had the bulldozers destroyed their house? Perhaps now his father would think of him with pride. Perhaps now he would return home.

That's weird. The stony hillsides reminded him of East Jerusalem. He hobbled toward a tarred road—were there cars in Paradise?—and a folding table. The white cloth billowed in the breeze. A man slouched on a chair behind the table. He wore a gray suit. He had the pale skin of a Westerner, fluffy gray hair, and a bushy mustache. He tinkered with his mobile phone but looked up as Ahmed approached, his hands covering his privates.

The scene reminded Ahmed of the registration desk at the voting station. He had turned eighteen six months ago and exercised his right to vote only once.

"Welcome," the man said in Hebrew with a strong Russian accent. He handed Ahmed a folded square of white fabric. A thin cloak.

Ahmed put it on and tied the paper-thin belt.

Roads. Phones. Hebrew. Not what he had expected of the Afterlife. The man did not even appear to be a Muslim. He offered Ahmed a plastic glass of water and two white pills.

"What is this?"

"Acamol," the man said. "For your head."

"Oh. Thanks." The man seemed to know how things worked. Ahmed washed the pills down with the water. At least the Afterlife was organized.

The Russian pulled a sheet of paper from a transparent folder. "Name?"

Ahmed told him.

He held out a ballpoint pen.

"Sign here."

"What's this?"

"A technicality. For your housing and food."

That's more like it. Infinite reward awaited martyrs. A palace. A seat at the Heavenly banquet. Despite his misgivings and half-hearted faith, Ahmed had done the deed. He had left his miserable, old life behind and stepped up for *istishhad.* As a *shaheed*, he would collect his due.

Ahmed signed on the line.

"Wait in the van."

He waved to a white minivan that idled down the road.

Ahmed hesitated. "About the girls…"

The man looked up from the paperwork and grinned a wide amused grin. "Your seventy virgins?" The man barked a laugh. He had fielded that question before.

Ahmed's spirits plummeted. "Sixty?"

The man coughed. "You'll find"—he read his name off the signed form—"Ahmed, that Heaven is a bit different from what you were promised."

Ahmed hid his disappointment. He could settle for fifty virgins. Or ten. Five would be sufficient. He would be happy with one pretty girl, if it came to that.

He limped down the road on bare feet and climbed into the white minivan. Strangers in the same flimsy cloaks filled two of the three rows of seats. They stared at him. Young and old. Dark-skinned and light. Some of their faces looked strangely familiar. An Ethiopian glared at him from his seat beside the driver.

Ahmed stared out the window as the engine purred and the seat quivered. His headache was subsiding. He hoped the Heavenly banquet would start soon. He had the mother of all appetites.

CHAPTER 54

Thursday afternoon, Eli lay on the hospital bed and stared out the window.

How could I have been so stupid?

The sunbeam had crept down the wall and slunk from the room. Half the day had passed and still no Noga.

He had opened his heart to her. She was the key to his mission, the reason for his injury and pain. The Boss had sent him to her. He had felt that in his bones. Together they would trigger the Final Redemption. He could not leave her in the dark.

"Aren't you going to eat your food?" said a soft, sympathetic voice.

Eli didn't shift his gaze from the window. His lunch tray sat on the side table, untouched. He was not in the mood for a chat with his nosy roommate. Every morning and evening, Oren's wife, children, and grandchildren filled their room with their chatter and the smells of their food and flowers. Their presence made him feel all the more alone. Why, after all these years, should that bother him?

"You can get her back," Oren said. He had put two and two together.

Eli turned his head. "What makes you say that?"

Oren smirked. "Experience."

Eli had to laugh. "You have no idea, Oren."

"You had a fight. You said something careless—it doesn't matter. Go get her back."

Eli closed his eyes and focused on the rise and fall of his chest. "She's gone. Trust me."

"Send her flowers. A card. Anything. But don't delay. Never delay. Or you *will* lose her."

"Thanks for the free advice."

"Well, what do you know," Oren said.

Eli opened his eyes. Noga stood at the foot of his bed. A T-shirt and jeans. No white cloak. Her mouth sealed tight. She wore her hair back, the way she had the first time they had met. He sat up on his elbows. Had she gone to his apartment? Did she believe him now?

Oren swung his legs over the side of the bed. "I'm going to go for a stroll," he said. He winked at Eli. "Stretch these old legs." He closed the door behind him. Eli was starting to like the old man.

Noga drew near, reached into her shoulder bag, and with the stiffness of a court messenger delivering a summons, she handed him a thick manila folder.

"What is this?"

"Facts," she said. "Newspaper articles. Official documents. All you'd ever want to know about Eli Katz."

"Where did you get this?"

"The Internet. The university library." She spoke with an even, restrained tone. "Your parents died in a car crash when you were sixteen months old. You attended the Miriam kindergarten in Katamon, then Chorev Primary. You enrolled for a first degree in Computer Science at the Open University then dropped out in your second year, the year you started OpenGen."

"Noga, wait—"

"You're a real person, Eli. You were born. You grew up. You had a life. And then, somewhere along the line, you became Elijah."

The girl was good. But not good enough. Eli accepted the

folder and placed it on top of his untouched meal. "I know all this," he said. "All the details. You know why?"

"Because they happened."

"Because I planted them."

"Give me a break! You can't plant public records."

"You can if you know how."

"And newspaper reports?"

"The parents died in a car crash. That much is true. Their little boy died later. But his identity number lives on."

Her chest heaved. "Like in the movie."

"What movie?"

She pulled a DVD jacket from her bag. A Scottish warrior in a sheepskin cloak stood on a hilltop, beneath stormy Highland skies. He leaned on the hilt of his Claymore.

He groaned. He knew how this must look. "That's just a movie."

She read the back copy. "'A group of immortals battling to the death....'"

"That's got nothing to do with it."

"I watched it," she said. "He leaves his wealth to a dead infant and takes over his identity. Sound familiar?" She had him on that. The screenwriters had copied a page out of his life.

"What about my collection?"

"Bought at antique stores. Or on eBay."

"But I know the story behind each piece. How do you explain that away?"

She looked both sad and frustrated. "False memories," she said. "The product of childhood trauma and movies like this." She eyed the manila folder. "There's a paper on reconstructive memory and confabulation in there too. You should read it."

She had him cornered. There wasn't an argument she couldn't cut down with that theory. It was like a self-reinforcing delusion. "No," he said. "That's not true."

"And then there's this." She held up another exhibit for the jury: a book. "101 Magic Tricks. I'm sure that came in handy for your 'miracles.'"

The Earth shuddered beneath him. Was she right? Was his entire life a comforting fiction for a lonely little orphan?

"No," he said. "That isn't true."

She reached for his shoulder, and he flinched. He had hurt her with the truth and she had avenged her pride with lies.

She sat down on the edge of the bed. "I never knew my parents either," she said. "My adoptive parents are good people, sure, but they weren't my real parents." She exhaled a long, deep breath. "They couldn't have just given me away, right? One day they'd sweep back into my life. I was so sure of it. They had made a mistake. They wanted me back."

She sniffed. "The years passed, and I grew up. No one came to claim me. My parents were stupid teenagers, or addicts. Who else abandons a newborn baby, right?"

She wiped her eyes with her fingers. "You were right. We have a lot in common. I guess that explains our interest in genealogy…" She gave a short ironic laugh and looked him in the eye. "There's no magic, Eli. No miracles."

Eli shook his head and avoided her eyes.

She gave him a long, hard stare. Then she stood up. "Keep that up and you'll never go home," she said. "Dr. Stern is itching to throw you in the madhouse."

He said nothing.

She exhaled another deep breath. She didn't seem angry anymore, only tired. "OK," she said, after another long silence. "I guess this is goodbye."

CHAPTER 55

Thursday morning passed in a flurry of activity.

First, Moshe printed the online forms he had completed on the Israeli Corporations Authority website. Rafi picked him up at 8 AM. They collected Savta Sarah and met with a lawyer friend of Rafi's at his downtown office on Shamai Street. In his presence, they signed a declaration that the non-profit did not involve any funny business. Then they rushed to the Corporation Authority offices to hand in the application and received an invoice to pay at the post office. After that, the waiting game began. Small wonder anyone accomplished anything in this country with so much red tápe.

They raced Savta back to the rabbi's house, where the rabbanit awaited her first cooking lesson. Sitting in the passenger seat with the window open, a summer breeze in his hair, the white buildings ablaze with sunlight, Moshe felt alive for the first time in his second life.

The car jumped a speed bump and his stomach lurched.

"Sorry," Rafi said.

The vertigo transported Moshe to the rickety bridge over the black chasm. The dream had returned last night, except this time on the grassy bank stood Galit. Her hand rested on Talya's shoulder. He stepped onto the next cracked plank and shifted his weight forward. As before, with each step, the bank drifted further away. *No!* He called to them, but their stony faces disappeared in the misty gloom.

Afternoon sunlight warmed his arm on the windowsill of the passenger door. He should follow through on Shmuel's advice and buy that Barbie doll and cake. With one week until the wedding, he had no time to lose. But a numbing inertia had set in. Over the last few days, he had poured his energy into escaping slavery and finding shelter, leaving little bandwidth for Galit. All his attempts at reaching her had hit the same brick wall. Would today be any different? His thoughts drifted to the growing checklist of tasks for the new nonprofit.

They reached Shimshon Street at 1 PM. Moshe scarfed down his lunch of reheated Hungarian treats.

"How long can I keep up this diet," he said at the table, "before I have another heart attack?"

Rafi laughed. Rabbi Yosef smiled. Irina didn't respond. They hadn't spoken since she had skipped out of the house yesterday afternoon.

Before he could ask what was on her mind, the doorbell rang.

"I'll get it," he said.

He checked the peephole for angry best friends, murderous Arabs, and slave drivers. The stranger at the door belonged to none of the above.

"Moshe Karlin?" the old man asked when the door opened. He wore a pinstriped shirt, baggy gray trousers, thinning white hair, and a lost expression. He peered past Moshe and his face brightened. "Shmuel!" he exclaimed, and he hurried past Moshe.

Shmuel wiped his mouth and embraced the visitor.

"Back from the dead, you old bastard."

"Everyone," Shmuel announced. "This is Eran. A friend from the old days at Yediot."

"Channel Ten, now," Eran said. "Producer. Documentaries, mostly."

Moshe shook his hand. "Pull up a seat and have some

lunch."

"Don't mind if I do. Is that *nokedli*?"

Eran sat between Shmuel and Moshe and piled food on his plate. With Moshe's permission, he pressed Record on his iPhone. He asked questions between mouthfuls and listened while he chewed. Moshe described all that had happened since he had awoken last Tuesday morning on the Mount of Olives. Rabbi Yosef added the scriptural references and religious dogma.

"Incredible," the reporter said. He had wiped his plate clean. "This changes everything. Had I not known Shmuel here, I would never have believed it. Channel Ten hasn't had a groundbreaking report like this in… well, I don't think anything comes close. This is historic. Epic."

"When will the story air?"

"I'll need to come back with a camera crew. Interview a few more people. Dig around. You know—more perspectives to round the piece off. Then there's editing and scheduling. On the fast track, I'd say a week or two."

"Perfect." Moshe should have things ready by then. He pulled out the sheet of paper with his checklist.

Rafi leaned in to get a better look. "What's our next stop?"

"Bank account." Moshe glanced at his watch, then remembered again that he had pawned the Rolex on Pierre Koenig Street. He found the time on Eran's iPhone. "Two PM. Banks are closing already. We'll continue tomorrow. Not bad for our first day."

Savta Sarah entered from the kitchen, undoing an apron and trailing a pensive rabbanit, with pen and notepad at the ready. "When it boils," Savta said, "put it on low and mix in salt, pepper, and paprika. Lots of paprika."

"How much?"

Savta shrugged. "As much as it needs. I never measure anything. Rafi, let's go. Time to rest. I'm not as young as I look."

She embraced Moshe. "I'll see you tomorrow." She sent a meaningful glance at the rabbanit, who tensed as she prepared to object, then relented. The list of recipes ran very long and Savta had started with the slow-cooking dishes. The rabbanit would require a long internship to learn Savta's culinary expertise. Moshe and his crew had won another night under the rabbi's roof.

Moshe escorted Savta and Rafi to the taxi and then cleaned up the dining room table. He stacked the dishes in the meat sink and soaped the sponge, his mind afloat with strategies for the week ahead. Their campaign should highlight their plight to create sympathy. They needed contacts in the Ministry of the Interior and National Health Insurance. Other resurrectees might have connections. How many wandered undiscovered on the streets? He stacked the last dish on the drying rack. They should buy the rabbi a dishwasher, too.

Irina huddled on the couch in the living room, her knees pressed to her chest.

"Where is everyone?"

She avoided his eyes. Was she crying?

He sat beside her. "What's going on?"

She wiped her eyes and forced a smile. "Who is Sivan?"

The name caught him off guard. "She works at Karlin & Son. Or used to. Why?"

Irina looked him in the eyes. "Did you sleep with her?"

"No. Of course not. She was my employee."

Irina emitted a nervous laugh. "I didn't think so. But Galit does."

"Galit?"

"I spoke with her last night. She teaches Zumba on Emek Refaim."

Zumba. Galit had signed up years ago but missed every class. Moshe had always returned home too late from work. With him out of the way, she had trained as an instructor. *Good for you, Galit.* He turned his attention from his past failings to the first part of Irina's revelation. *Sivan.*

"Dear God," he said. He leaned forward on the couch. The facts clicked together like falling dominoes. "She must have thought… Or Avi must have told her that…"

Zohar the Hairdresser's voice rang in his mind. *I know your type.*

The room pitched and tilted around him. Everything made sense. Galit's refusal to speak to him. Avi's threats. Even her choice of Avi.

"I have to tell Galit."

Irina sniffed. "She won't believe you. She even thinks that we're together now." Her red eyes held his, searching for an answer to her own silent questions.

"Then I'll have to convince her."

CHAPTER 56

Eli rolled down the polished corridor of the hospital. He slapped the wheels with unnecessary force. Tomorrow morning, come what may, he was out of here. He had mapped the route to the exit—fifty meters from his room to the elevator, seventy meters to the exit of Emergency Care on the first floor, and fifty more uphill to the taxi rank.

He had managed to go to the bathroom without assistance; they couldn't hold him against his will. He'd hire a private nurse if he had to. With Noga out of the picture, what was keeping him there?

Stupid, stupid, stupid. Stupid to open up to her. Stupid to think she would believe. They never believed. You could rain down fire from heaven, but the moment the embers cooled, their faith fled.

He pressed the button for the elevator. The doors of the large metal box opened at the speed of the continental drift. Eli rolled inside and parked beside a large wheeled bed and a male nurse in blue fatigues. He pressed the button for the fourth floor.

He had no time to twiddle his thumbs while his muscles strengthened. He had places to go, people to anoint. A Final Redemption to announce.

Or did he?

As the doors closed, one millimeter at a time, another explanation for his miserable situation rose in his mind, like a distant ripple on the ocean: The Boss had deemed this generation, like all earlier generations, unworthy. In the last minute, the balance of merit had shifted, and He had aborted the nascent redemption.

The Boss had pulled the plug before. King Hezekiah had come close. Bar Kokhba had crashed and burned. A handful of saintly souls throughout history had shown promise but fizzled out. But each time, the Thin Voice had whispered the verdict in Eli's third ear. Why the accident? Why the torment of human pain and helplessness?

If the Divine Will had postponed the End, surely Eli would have known?

A third explanation arose. This one accounted for all the facts. His accident. The lengthy recovery and missing powers. His wonky intuition.

This theory was no ripple on the horizon—it was a tidal wave! Ominous. Inescapable.

There would be no Redemption. Not today. Not ever. The Boss had heeded his advice, finally, and given up on humankind.

And with no hope of Redemption, there was no longer any need for a harbinger. The Boss had abandoned him to the whim of Nature. He would never regain his former strength and powers. He would remain trapped in this mortal coil to live out the rest of his, now numbered, days.

No. No!

The elevator doors opened on the fourth floor. Cold drops of sweat dripped down his forehead. The walls of the corridor swayed before his eyes.

He made for the kitchenette, pulled a plastic cup from the dispenser, and poured water from the cooler. He gulped the clear liquid and gasped for air. *Take it easy. Relax. That's it.* He poured another glass.

A familiar voice giggled in the corridor. One of the younger nurses. Liora.

Eli placed his cup between his legs and inched his wheelchair toward the doorway. Liora leaned against a wall, paper cup in hand. She smiled up at a man. Eli saw only the back of his head but knew him at once by his wild, carrot-colored hair and baggy, motley clothes.

The nurse giggled again.

Love is in the air. Oren had not been wrong about body language. He rolled to the edge of the doorway.

Liora sipped her drink and grew serious. "Don't you get depressed? All those poor kids?"

Moti the Clown gave his head a shake. "The kids are brave. Resilient. Distract them a little and they'll have fun like any healthy kid."

The bastard could speak after all. His voice was deeper than Eli had imagined.

"What really gets me down," the clown continued, "are the adults. They won't let go. Not for a second." He lowered his voice. "Like him." He nodded toward the end of the corridor.

"Who?"

"The nut case. The Messiah."

Liora tittered. "You mean Elijah the Prophet."

News traveled fast.

"Whatever. How do you help someone like that? He's trapped in his own world."

Eli rolled back an inch. So that's how they saw him. *Nut case. Trapped.* Let them jeer. They were the pitiful ones. Or were they?

A week in the hospital. A week as a cripple. A week without The Magic. Would he even recognize the Thin Voice if it spoke again? Had it ever truly spoken?

He waited for them to leave. He rolled down the corridor. Nadir glanced up from the nurses' desk as he passed. He avoided her eyes. Would he ever be able to look any of them in the eye again?

In his room, Eliana stripped the sheets off his neighbor's bed and made to leave.

Eli paused halfway to his bed. "Eliana," he said, "has he checked out already?"

She paused at the door. "Who?"

"You know. Oren. Older guy. Nosy. Many progeny. That was his bed." Oren would surely have said goodbye. Any excuse to talk.

Eliana straightened. "No one told you?"

"What?"

"He passed away. This morning, during surgery."

The world swayed again. Oren was dead.

Never delay, Oren had said. Wise words. They seemed all the wiser now that he was gone.

The touch of a hand on his arm jolted him from his reverie.

"I'm sorry," Eliana said. "Life is short." The beefy nurse gave him a long, compassionate glance and left.

He wheeled the chair around the empty bed, put his hands on the armrests, and heaved his body onto the edge of his own mattress. He lay down. He turned his head toward the naked, empty bed. Then he stared, long and hard, at the thick manila folder on the table.

CHAPTER 57

The hostess ushered Moshe and Irina to a corner table in Kaffit, a coffee shop on Emek Refaim. The pockets of teatime patrons didn't give them a second glance.

"Wouldn't it be easier to meet at the house?" Irina asked, when they settled at their table.

Moshe had wondered the same thing. "Maybe she's more comfortable meeting in a public place," he said. "Fair enough. Until a week ago, I was dead." Sivan had not sounded surprised to hear his voice on the phone, but had hesitated at his request for an urgent meeting.

A waiter in a black T-shirt and matching apron approached and Moshe ordered a jar of water while they waited. If Sivan stood him up, at least he wouldn't waste precious shekels.

Irina bit her nails and sent glances over her shoulder at the street traffic. She avoided his glance. A silent storm seemed to rage within her. Did she believe his innocence? Had he lost her trust? He didn't ask. Soon he'd clear his name—again—and open a back door to Galit.

Would his wife ever welcome him back? He had always thought his marriage strong and good. The past was not what it used to be. He had neglected her, pouring his energies into Karlin & Son, while the void he created at home had filled with suspicion and distrust. In the last few days, the void had widened. Was Zohar the Hairdresser right? Did she deserve better?

Moshe and Irina didn't wait long. Sivan walked in at a brisk pace, clutching a handbag. He almost didn't recognize her. The feisty young girl had traded her trademark torn jeans and T-shirt for a business suit and Louis Vuitton. She spotted their table. Her eyes flitted to Irina and her hand loosened on the bag.

Moshe stood. "Sivan, thanks for coming." His arm hesitated at his side. She didn't offer her hand either. A friendly kiss on the cheek would be a bad idea. Best not to feed the rumormongers.

The awkward moment passed. She sat in the empty chair and brushed a strand of blow-dried hair from her face. "I got your message Saturday night," she said. "I'm sorry I didn't return your call."

He had wondered about that, and now her apology gave him pause. Should he be offended? "Did you know—?" he began.

"Mathew told me," she said, interrupting him. "After all that had happened, I thought you hated me."

Moshe felt he had stepped into the middle of a conversation. "What do you mean? Why would I hate you?"

She looked him straight in the eyes. "After you passed, Avi called. He said you had wanted to fire me."

Just when Moshe thought he had a handle on things, everything he knew flew out the window. Avi had conspired to take over his life before his dead body had cooled. "I didn't know that," he said. "I thought you were laid off a few months ago, when the company ran out of money."

She studied the tabletop. "I was depressed for months. Then I pulled myself together. Got a job in customer service at a hi-tech company in Malcha. Got promoted a few times. Now I'm VP Marketing."

"No kidding? I mean, congratulations. That's fantastic." She smiled and flicked her hair behind a shoulder. *Don't lay it on too thick. But lay it on.* He was about to ask a lot of her.

"A VP in under two years," he added. Leaving Karlin & Son had been a wise career move for two of his employees. The fact made his ego twinge a little. "I didn't want to fire you at all," he continued. "And you're not the only one Avi lied to. I think he told Galit that we'd had an affair."

"You and me?" Her eyes widened.

He nodded. "He moved in with her—into my house. They're getting married next week."

"But now that you're back…?"

"She won't speak to me. I tried. Avi attacked me in the street and threatened my life. And on top of it all, we've both been struggling to survive with no home, no job, and no money."

Sivan looked to Irina. "So you're also… like Moshe?"

Irina nodded.

Moshe breathed in deep. "I'm really, really grateful that you came to see me today. We don't have many friends." His chest tightened. He'd been fighting every step of the way since the day he was resurrected. He'd been deceived and cheated and beaten up; slandered and enslaved. He could really do with a hand up.

Sivan glanced from Moshe to Irina and back. She said, "How can I help?"

CHAPTER 58

Dusk settled over the German Colony as Moshe, Irina, and Sivan walked down Emek Refaim. They crossed the defunct train tracks to Shimshon Street and paused a few houses down from the Karlin residence. The slatted shutters sealed the windows but Galit's white Kia Sportage hugged the curb outside.

"You should go alone," he told Sivan.

"What do I tell her?"

"The truth. There was nothing between us. Nothing romantic. If she responds well, I'll be right here."

She nodded and set out down the street, her heels echoing off the stone houses. Moshe's stomach churned. After all the failed attempts, he had almost despaired of ever breaking through the barriers to Galit's heart. Finally, he understood why she had locked him out. Finally, he held the key. But would the door open?

And if it did, would he come face-to-face with his deepest, darkest fear—that Galit simply did not want him back? He felt his cheeks drain of blood. In the next few seconds, one way or another, he'd find out.

Sivan climbed the three steps and knocked on the front door. She waited and cast a smile in Moshe's direction. After a few moments, she pressed the buzzer.

The shadows deepened as the light faded.

Any moment now, the door would open. Galit would appear at the threshold. From her reaction, Moshe would know his fate. Sivan shifted on her feet and jabbed the buzzer again.

She put her ear to the door. Then she turned and abandoned her post.

"Nobody's home."

"Her car's outside. It's seven o'clock."

Sivan shrugged. "Do you have her number?"

Moshe knew that one by heart. Sivan dialed the number on her phone. "Voicemail. Maybe they went out to eat?"

"And turned off her phone?"

That didn't make sense. Had Avi flown her overseas to escape his advances? A deep pit of dread opened at the base of his stomach. The ground had disappeared beneath his feet. Any moment, he'd fall.

Sivan scratched her neck. She had somewhere else to be. There was no sense in detaining her any longer. "I guess we'll call it a day," he said. "Thanks anyway."

She asked him to let her know if she could help further, and then walked away toward Emek Refaim.

Moshe and Irina made for the rabbi's house in gloomy silence. So close and yet so far. The darkest moment of night is right before the break of dawn. He had read that in one of the rabbi's books. They could try again tomorrow.

Rabbi Yosef answered the door to their knock. "Where have you been? Savta Sarah's called twenty times."

"What happened? Is she OK?"

"She didn't say."

Moshe dashed to the rabbi's phone and dialed Savta's number. Ambulances blared in his imagination. The four boys ate Savta's goulash at the dinner table and eyed him with concern. He gave them a brave grin. The number rang and rang. *Oh, no. Poor Savta.* He tried her mobile. This time, she answered.

"Moshe," Savta cried, breathless. "Where have you been?"

"Are you OK, Savta?"

"Get yourself over to Ramat Rachel now!"

"Ramat Rachel?" The neighborhood in South Jerusalem had a hotel and an event hall, but no hospitals.

"The wedding is starting."

"What wedding?" Again, the universe slipped from under his feet.

"Galit and Avi's. They brought it forward. They only told me half an hour ago. They must have figured out that we're in cahoots. I'm on my way in a cab. I'll see what I can do to hold things off."

Moshe put down the phone. Irina and Rabbi Yosef stared at him. He stared back at them, like a stunned fish.

"Rabbi Yosef," he said, his voice strangely calm. "Can you give me a ride?"

"Where to?"

"Ramat Rachel," he said. "I have to stop a wedding."

CHAPTER 59

Irina fastened her seatbelt. She watched, alone in the back seat, as events hurtled out of her control.

Rabbi Yosef started his car, and they pulled off into the night. Moshe sat in the passenger seat, silent and tense.

She should never have looked for Galit. Ever since their meeting last night, conflicting emotions had been colliding inside her. She had not believed the accusation of infidelity, not for a moment. She knew Moshe better than that. The one person she had not known well enough, though, was herself. The ticket to his reconciliation with Galit had dropped into her hands, and her first impulse had been to shred that ticket.

Fortunately—for Moshe, at least—she had been unable to keep the secret for long. She simply could not lie to him. Destroying his dream in order to fulfill her own—what would that make her? By the afternoon, she had confessed, and now she tagged along as Moshe tried to use that ticket to hurry back into his old life and out of hers forever. The wedding was her only hope.

"What are you going to do?" she asked. The engine gurgled and groaned as gears changed within the rusty beast.

"I don't know. Tell her the truth, I suppose, before it's too late."

Part of her cheered him on; the rest hoped that he would

fail.

"Ramat Rachel," Moshe said. "That's where we got married. That bastard Avi is trying to rewrite the past."

Irina and Avi shared an enemy: the past. The mound of memories that stood between her and Moshe.

Streetlights flew by. Rabbi Yosef changed lanes, weaving between cars, racing against time. Moshe turned the radio on and a cassette played. A soothing bassline of synthesizer chords. A drumbeat like a fast ticking clock. An electric guitar jangled to the rhythm of a young, breaking heart, and Cyndi Lauper sang of love, separation, and devotion.

The song seemed to speak for Irina. If Moshe fell, she'd catch him; she'd be waiting. Time after time.

Life had given her this tumultuous week with Moshe. Life might grant her more. Either way, Moshe would be a part of her forever.

The groaning of the engine had become a scream. Smoke billowed from the hood. "Oh, no!" Rabbi Yosef said, and he pulled over to the side of the busy two-lane boulevard.

They got out. Moshe walked around the ruined car. He tried to flag down a passing car or a taxi. None stopped.

"I'm sorry, Moshe," the rabbi said.

Moshe put his hands on his head. He had tried so hard. He didn't deserve this.

"How far is it?" Irina asked.

"Not far."

"Then run."

He stared at her. Hesitation flickered in his eyes. He didn't want to abandon them on the side of the road.

"Go on," she said. "We'll be fine. Go and get her."

He inclined his head in thanks. Then he sprinted down the street. He turned left and disappeared behind a wall.

"Good luck, my friend," she whispered. "And goodbye."

CHAPTER 60

The lab technician at Shaare Zedek had to work fast.

Her colleague was on maternity leave. A week of blood work had accumulated in the laboratory fridge and, in half an hour, she had to collect her daughter from ballet class.

She pulled a set of vials from the batch holder, scanned the bar codes, and slipped them into the microcentrifuge. Her fingernails clicked on the counter as the machine hummed and cells separated from the serum. She stopped the machine, added a drop of Laemmli buffer to each tube, and placed them in the slots of the heater. Then she pipetted the stained proteins into an acrylamide gel, which she placed in the electrophoresis apparatus. While the gels ran, she scanned the next batch of tubes and loaded them into the centrifuge.

Multitask or die—her motto at work and at home. In her kitchen on Friday mornings, a tray of chicken would brown in the oven while onions sautéed on the stove and schnitzels bubbled in a frying pan for her children's lunch. She used timers in both arenas to great effect. She could do with bar codes in the kitchen too.

She retrieved the gel sheets from the apparatus and moved them to the computer monitor. Each transparent strip displayed the characteristic blue smudges of protein electrophoresis that resembled a child's tie-dyeing experiment. She scanned a bar code and recorded the result on the keyboard of the lab computer.

Scan. Record. Click.

Scan. Record. Click.

Scan. Record. *Hello!*

The blue patterns on the sheet—the spread of proteins and enzymes—were unlike anything she had ever seen. She double-clicked for more details on the sample and found the referring doctor. She picked up the phone and dialed his number. Her fingernails clicked on the desk yet again as the phone rang on the other side.

Pick up, Dr. Stern. I don't have all day.

CHAPTER 61

Galit smoothed the fabric of the wedding dress over her hips in the mirror of the dressing room while her mother fussed with the lace of the veil.

She had worn the same dress at her first wedding. She had floated down the aisle on a cloud of joy to join Moshe under the *chuppah.* She had never imagined that, eight years later, she'd wear that dress again. This time around, a very different kind of butterfly upset her stomach.

Am I doing the right thing?

After tonight, there was no turning back.

"There," said her mother, her eyelids puffy from lack of sleep. "You're good to go."

"Thanks, *Ima.* Sorry about the short notice." Her parents had changed clothes on the eleven-hour flight from Newark and rushed straight from Ben Gurion Airport to the wedding hall in Ramat Rachel.

A crack appeared in her mother's smile. "I still think you should have waited for the appointed day. You've been dating for two years. What's another week?"

Her mother was right. Galit could have married Avi any day during those two years. Why had she held out? Avi loved her. He worshipped her. But he was no Moshe. Despite everything, a corner of her heart still belonged to Moshe.

When he had returned from the grave, those dormant emotions had erupted.

Avi had brought the wedding date forward. Had he sensed her doubts?

"It's complicated," she said. The sight of Moshe had raised her memories of the good times too. His dreams and drive had inspired her and given her hope. Together, they would conquer the world.

Her mother knew her only too well. "Who cares," she said, "if that cheating good-for-nothing is back? Who does he think he is?"

Right again. Galit detested liars and cheaters. When Avi had told her about Moshe and Sivan, her love had turned to hate. Moshe had betrayed their shared dream of conquering the world and turned to conquering other women. He would tread that path alone. God might have given him a second chance, but she would not. Cheaters didn't deserve second chances.

"I'm sorry," her mother said. She dabbed at Galit's eyes with a tissue.

"It's OK," she said.

Outside, a trumpet played a jaunty wedding song. Time to face the crowd. Time to put Moshe behind her. She sucked in a deep, brave breath.

"Let's go," she said. "I'm ready."

CHAPTER 62

As Moshe reached the hilly parking lot of the Ramat Rachel Hotel, he heard the festive sound of a trumpet and his heart fell. *Am I too late?* The hotel sprawled upward over the tiered hillside. He had no time to catch his breath from the climb; he pushed on.

He raced between rows of parked cars and launched up a stone staircase to the grassy knoll between the hotel building and the event hall. The *chuppah* stood at the edge of the green patch, overlooking the Judean hills, now shrouded in twilight. A white carpet ran between the rows of empty chairs dressed in white. White sheets and pastel nosegays adorned the wedding canopy. No sign of bride or groom. Had he missed the ceremony?

A wave of déjà vu disorientated him. Memories of his own wedding ceremony. Galit floated in his mind like a beautiful ghost in a white dress. Her ecstatic smile and adoring eyes through the diaphanous veil.

"It's a disgrace," said a voice. Moshe spun around. Savta Sarah wore a beige suit and matching hat covered in lace. She scowled through thick layers of makeup, like war paint. "No chopped liver," she said. "Or smoked salmon. And they call themselves caterers!"

"Where is Galit?"

Savta pointed to the tiered garden behind her. "Up there. The bridal chair."

Moshe sprinted along a path of irregular rock slabs. He dodged manicured bushes and colorful flowerbeds. A clarinet played "Pretty Woman."

He entered a green patch lined with food stations. He cut through the press of mingling guests in collared shirts and evening dresses. A woman with nebulous brown curls gasped and pointed at him—Galit's cousin. He dodged the waiters with their trays of Riesling and finger food.

No bridal chair. No Galit.

He continued up another set of steps to the next tier. A clump of women hovered around a wicker couch draped in white sheets and cushions. He parted the crowd of women and stopped dead. The bridal chair was empty.

He scanned his surroundings for a white dress and panted while the clarinet rose an octave for the chorus.

"The bride," Moshe asked the women. "Where is she?"

Blank stares and shaking heads. He had to find her!

"You!" said a familiar, whiny voice. Zohar Raphael sauntered over, a wineglass in hand. The celebrity hairdresser had not changed out of his low jeans and tank top. He jabbed a finger at Moshe. "What are you doing here?"

Moshe wished he'd keep his voice down. "Where is Galit?" he hissed.

"Come to cause trouble, have you?" The finger waved from side to side. "Oh, no you don't. Girls!" he yelled. "Meet Moshe, Galit's cheating ex-husband. He doesn't belong here."

A small army of petulant women mobilized behind their megalomaniac commander, brandishing miniature kebabs and heavy designer handbags and eying Moshe with extreme prejudice.

Moshe retreated to the reception tier, hoping to lose Zohar in the crowd. He ducked sideways and took cover behind a uniformed chef, slicing slivers of entrecote for a line of hungry guests. Moshe surveyed the enemy territory. Zohar led his platoon of angry women through the crowd to the other side.

The delicious scent of roast meat reached his nose, but he had no time for distractions.

His gaze shifted and his breath caught in his throat. Beyond the leaves of a shaggy bush, a man in a tuxedo engaged in a hushed conversation with a rabbi.

Moshe stepped through the foliage, squeezed between the bushes, trampled a patch of yellow gerberas, and emerged on the stone pathway. He marched over to the groom. "Where is she?"

Avi turned to him. His eyes widened, and his lips parted. His face drained of color. "Get away," he croaked. "Get out of here."

Moshe turned to the rabbi and offered his hand. "Moshe Karlin, Galit's husband. Yes—she's already married. You can't let this—"

"OK, OK," Avi said. He stepped between Moshe and the rabbi. "You win. I'll take you to her."

Avi led the way, leaving the befuddled rabbi on the rocky path. He stomped through the hotel lobby, the lapels of his tuxedo flapping. He opened a door labeled "Bridal Room" and closed it behind them. Gift-wrapped boxes, stacked chairs, and wheeled partitions littered the chamber.

"Where is she?"

Avi stuck out his chest. "Did you think you could just waltz in here and ruin my life?"

"You rotten liar. You told her I cheated with Sivan!"

Avi's face softened. He hadn't expected Moshe to know that.

"What if I did?"

"You knew that wasn't true. I love Galit. Always have, always will. You stole her from me."

"Can't steal from a thief."

The Hebrew proverb made no sense in the argument. "What are you talking about?"

"You're the thief," Avi yelled. "You stole her from me!"

"You've gone mad."

"Hangar 17. The night you met her. Newsflash—I spoke with her before you even laid eyes on her. The beers I bought—they weren't for you and me. You just took them from me, the way you took her too." His chest heaved.

The information threw Moshe off balance.

"All I could do was watch," Avi continued, his voice breaking, "while you charmed her and danced with her. At your wedding. Your daughter's birthday parties. I kept thinking, 'What if I hadn't saved his life? All this would be mine.'"

Moshe had not known about any of this suffering. But the call to pity would not make him give up all he held dear.

"You saw her first—is that what are you're saying? Are we in kindergarten?" Avi had no answer for that, so Moshe plunged on. "Stop feeling sorry for yourself. Stop blaming others. Get your own life. Stop turning Galit against me with your lies."

"I didn't have to turn her against you."

"What are you going on about now?" Moshe had no patience for another sob story.

"You turned her against yourself."

"Oh, please."

"You were never home. You worked late for months on end. You only cared about your precious company. You had no time for Galit. You were never around for Talya either."

The nerve! "Why do you think I worked so hard? It was all for them."

"No. Not for them. Face it, Moshe. You did it to prove yourself, to please those old photos on the wall. You cheated on her, all right. Just not with Sivan."

Moshe opened his mouth to speak but found no defense. Zohar had told the same story. Moshe the neglectful husband. Moshe the absentee father.

"She doesn't want you," Avi continued, smelling blood in the water. "She told me. I didn't think you needed to hear that, but you've given me no choice. Whatever love she felt for you died with you."

The words winded Moshe like a lightning punch to the solar plexus. His deepest, darkest fear had been realized. Galit had fallen out of love. She was better off without him.

Moshe had accused Avi of blaming others for his own problems, but he himself was no different. The fault lay in his own actions, all along. Far in the past. Beyond fixing.

"You're dead," Avi said. Not a threat; a diagnosis. "Now, for Galit's sake, stay dead."

Avi straightened the lapels of his jacket. He turned his back on Moshe and left the room.

Moshe stared at the cracked tiles of the floor. His breath came in short, halting wheezes. He had no right to be there. He didn't belong. He staggered through the hotel lobby, his head down, his mouth dry. He passed the gardens and the buffet. He hobbled down the steps of the slope, through the parking lot, and into the dark night.

In the distance, the trumpet played a new song.

CHAPTER 63

Moshe strolled along Hebron Road. Cars whizzed by in the night and blew exhaust fumes in his face.

He had failed in his old life. Failed at home. Failed at work. He had failed in this new life too. *A Karlin never quits*, his father had said. This Karlin had. Who said he was still a Karlin, anyway? Had he shed his heritage along with his body? The thought did not console him.

The cracks of the sidewalk pressed through the soles of his shoes. Television screens reflected off apartment windows. Stars glittered in the heavens above.

He was a single dust mote lost in an infinite cosmos. If he lived a thousand lives, would he grasp even one iota of that mystery?

An emptiness filled him. Not hunger, although he had skipped dinner. An emptiness of the soul—the desolation of a man who has nothing left to lose.

The past had always been a safe shore, a haven in stormy seas. Now the ropes had severed, and he drifted out to sea. He floated on the formless ocean. Unfathomable deep below, unreachable stars above. He might perish on that wet desert. He might sail off the edge of the world. Then again, he might discover a new horizon.

So this is how Irina felt. A clean slate, at once terrifying and liberating.

The dark hulk of the rabbi's white Subaru lay abandoned on the side of the road. Moshe laid his hand on the hood. The billowing smoke had dissipated. The metal had cooled.

The car had reached the end of the line. Salvage what you can, then move on. He left the dead chassis behind.

He placed one foot in front of the other. In his dreams, the faster he crossed the bridge, the further the grassy bank had fled. Had fate played a cruel trick on him, or had he simply been facing in the wrong direction?

By the time he reached Shimshon Street, the empty feeling had settled into an inner calm.

Irina opened the door. She wore a loose pajama T-shirt and shorts. She studied his eyes for answers to unspoken questions. He stepped into the soft lamplight of the living room. Samira and Shmuel turned hopeful glances toward him. He plopped down on the couch, and their hope subsided into disappointment.

Irina joined him on the couch. "We're sorry about your family," she whispered. The rabbi's children were probably asleep in their beds. She smelled of soap and the rabbanit's sweet deodorant. The T-shirt fell below one pale shoulder. The large fairy eyes drank him in.

"We're all family now," he said.

A loud knock on the door startled him. Who came calling at the rabbi's house at this hour? The knocking came again—*bang-bang-bang*—and threatened to wake the household. Irina gripped his arm. The specter of his former slave drivers loomed in his mind too.

Moshe approached the door, peered through the peephole, and opened.

Avi stood in the doorway, his hair a mess, his tie loose, the dress shirt creased. He shot Moshe an angry look and barged inside.

"Where is she?"

"Keep your voice down. The rabbi's kids are asleep. Where is who?"

The intruder prowled the living room, his forehead glistening. He sent fiery glances at Irina, Shmuel, and Samira on the couches, and circled back to Moshe. "Where are you hiding her?"

"Hiding who? What are you talking about?" Moshe dared not hope.

Avi seemed to age ten years in an instant. He held his head in his hands. "Galit," he muttered. "She didn't show up at the *chuppah*. Nobody knows where she is." He drew near again. "Swear to me you don't know where she is."

"I swear it."

Avi clenched his jaw. Moshe thought that his ex-friend was going to hit him again, but he just skulked out the door and into the night.

Oh. My. God. Galit had backed out of the wedding. Had she finally come around? There was only one way to find out. He made for the door.

"Moshe," Irina said. "You said you didn't know where she is."

"I don't," he said. "But I have a hunch."

CHAPTER 64

Dr. Stern launched up the stairs to the fifth floor. In another ten seconds, the Medical Genetics Institute would close for the evening.

The vague message on his phone had confirmed his suspicions: Mr. Eli Katz was no ordinary man. His genome held the secret Dr. Stern had chased for decades. Soon he would hold in his hands irrefutable proof for his suspicions.

Academic papers. Clinical trials. FDA approval. The future rolled ahead with clarity. A Nobel Prize would be nice, but he didn't care for fame or fortune. The discovery was its own reward—a milestone in human progress that would change humanity forever.

He burst through the door of the stairwell and onto the hospital corridor, collided with a cloaked nurse, and dashed toward the doors of the Institute. Lights still burned inside. He opened the door and charged toward the lab, stopping only when he reached a long, rectangular office. Computer screens, microscopes, and other specialized machinery covered the counters. He caught his breath.

A podgy technician wearing a blue sanitary shower cap folded a white lab cloak. "I was about to leave," she said.

"Dr. Stern," he said, by way of introduction. "I got your message."

"Never mind," she said. "False alarm. I should have let you know."

His heart dropped into his shoes. She had seemed so certain in her voice message. "What do you mean?"

"The protein spread was bizarre."

"Yes?"

"Unlike any known human protein. The sample was contaminated. Bacteria, probably."

"Is your equipment sterile?"

She removed the cap and reached for her bag. "Yes. Of course. The contamination must have occurred at collection. You'll have to retest the subject."

"Retest? No, that won't be possible." He did not elaborate about his complex relationship with Mr. Eli Katz. He glanced at the white strips with the waves of blue suspended by clips on the shelves. "Let me have the results. I'll double check myself."

"Sorry," she said. "I destroyed the sheet. Standard procedure for contamination."

"And the remains of the sample?"

She gave him an apologetic grin. "Destroyed too."

"Don't tell me: standard procedure."

She nodded. "I have to go fetch my daughter. Turn off the lights on your way out."

She shuffled past and left him in the empty lab.

Dr. Stern exhaled his frustration. Back to square one. The director of the Institute was an old friend. He'd have a word with him about changing procedures.

"This isn't over, Mr. Katz," he swore to the empty room. "Not even close."

CHAPTER 65

The Old City of Jerusalem looked like a shiny gold ring in a box of black satin. Moshe walked along the edge of the Haas Promenade, a bouquet of red roses on his arm. He had picked the flowers in Liberty Bell Park on his way.

Pairs of lovers, young and old, sat on the steps and benches in the soft glow of distant streetlights, enjoying the romantic night skyline. None noticed him as he passed.

On the barrier wall, toward the end of the Tayelet, a lone woman dangled her legs over the edge. She wore an elegant white dress.

Moshe sat down beside her and swung his legs over the wall.

They stared at the mighty timeless walls of the Old City, ablaze in spotlight.

"You're late," she said, a tear in her voice.

Tears of regret or joy?

"I got here as fast as I could."

He held out the flowers.

She accepted his gift and breathed in their scent.

"Did Savta Sarah get to you?" he asked.

She gave a short, sad laugh. "I was hiding in the Bridal Room," she said. "Wedding night jitters."

"Oh." She had overheard his argument with Avi. She

knew the truth.

"I didn't mind the late nights," she said. "Your dreams were mine. We were one person. I would have followed you to the ends of the earth." She wiped her eyes. "Until the day before your birthday party. Avi came by the house. He said he couldn't keep silent any longer. He told me about you and Sivan. I never imagined that he could have made that up. I was in shock. Then I was furious." A short, bitter laugh. "You know me. I had already invited everyone we knew. Cancelling was not an option. But afterwards, you were going to pay. It would be your farewell party and good riddance." She shuddered, as though reliving the anger and hurt of that time.

"A farewell party it was," he said, trying to lighten the mood.

She turned to him, her eyes damp. "Can you forgive me?"

"Hmm." He made a show of thinking it over, then smiled. "There's nothing to forgive. It wasn't your fault."

She gulped air and wiped her eyes again.

"Although," he added, his voice brimming with incredulity, "Avi—of all the men in the world?"

She took her time answering. "He was around when I needed him," she said. "And I knew that you never really liked him."

Moshe nodded. "Got it." She had let Avi move in to get back at her dead, cheating husband. The female heart—yet another mystery that he would never comprehend.

She gazed at the ancient golden city. "When you showed up again, I thought I was going crazy. I couldn't believe that it was really you."

Moshe chuckled. "Sometimes I'm not so sure myself."

She shot him a quick glance loaded with suspicion.

Time to put her doubts to rest. "Listen to me," he said. "It's me. And it's always been you. Only you. I don't care if we're apart for two years or two thousand years, I will always love you. And I will do anything to get back to you—so long as you still want me—even if I have to rise from the grave."

She searched his eyes for the truth. He reached out and wiped the tears from her face.

"No more crying, OK? This is a new life. A fresh start."

She leaned her head on his shoulder. Her hair rose in the breeze and caressed his cheek. He inhaled the sweet scent of jasmine. He was getting his old life back but nothing would be quite the same.

"We'll figure it out," he said, and he stroked her hair. "One day at a time."

CHAPTER 66

Two weeks later, Eli placed a crutch under his shoulder, slid off the hospital bed for the last time, and prepared to face the world.

His palms were clammy and his stomach ached. He had wanted to escape the hospital from the moment he had awoken from his coma. Now that the day had arrived, he hesitated.

The casts had come off. He hardly felt any pain. That morning, he had tied his own shoelaces for the first time. Dressing was easy—the real challenges lay outside. The world had changed since his accident. Or, more accurately, he had changed.

He took a step forward, leaning on the crutch. Then he took another.

Dr. Stern looked him over and frowned. "What's your name?" he said.

Eli laughed. "Still Eli Katz."

"Are you sure?"

"Doctor!" said Eliana, the busty, energetic nurse.

"Just asking."

"We got you a little something." Eliana presented him with a white box tied with a red ribbon.

"Thanks. You shouldn't have." Eli felt his eyes moisten.

The hospital team had become his friends—no, his family—over the past few weeks. He accepted the box clumsily, his one arm clamped over the crutch. He placed the box on the bed and undid the ribbon. A tray of Ferrero Rocher and a paperback: The Man who Mistook His Wife for a Hat. That would be from Dr. Stern.

A chain of motorcycle keys and a folded wad of black leather. Eli shook out the jacket. Long gashes marred the sleeve and bisected the flaming chariot emblem on the back. *Did I actually wear this?* No wonder they thought him insane.

He tried on the jacket.

"Thank you all. Really. You've been wonderful."

He limped forward on the crutch and shook hands with the line of well-wishers. The nurses, Liora and Nadir. His physiotherapist. Moti the Clown hugged him.

Dr. Stern handed Eli his card. "Call if you need anything."

"See you around."

"Oh, I'm sure you will."

Eli wasn't sure he liked the sound of that.

At the end of the line waited a girl in a white cloak.

"I'll carry those," Noga said. He handed her the chocolates and book.

She locked his free arm in hers and escorted him down the corridor.

After Oren's passing, Eli had studied the papers in the manila folder. According to the documents, he was a regular guy in the prime of his life, not a broken prophet on a god-forsaken planet. Life is short, Eliana had said. Oren's death had demonstrated that only too well. But he didn't have to live out his days alone. With luck, he might share them with the girl in the white cloak.

As he read and re-read the papers in the folder, he became increasingly convinced that they told the truth. For the first time in his life, he felt compassion for the sad little boy who had constructed a fantasy world from the fragments of his shattered life. When that world came crashing down, he called Noga on the phone. After a lot of convincing—and three bouquets of roses delivered to her door—she had appeared at his hospital bed, a hesitant smile on her lips.

"You take care of each other," Eliana called after them.

"We will," they answered as one.

Noga squeezed his arm and smiled. She pressed the button for the elevator.

Eli put his hand in the pocket of his jacket and his fingers brushed against a piece of paper. He unfolded the yellow square.

A telephone number and a name. *Yosef Lev.*

The name pulled him back in time. *The Mount of Olives. The bearded man by the white car.* He had called the ambulance and must have left his details with the paramedics. Eli had been on his way to meet him. *The Thin Voice. The End of Days.*

Or had he? Delusions stuck to his mind like gum to the sole of a shoe. He had scraped as best he could, but his mind was not yet spotless.

"What is it?" Noga asked.

He crumpled the note and tossed it in the waste bin.

"Nothing," he said. "Nothing at all."

CHAPTER 67

A happy thought woke Dr. Sandler from her slumber.

Today her oldest daughter, Ester, would step under the *chuppah*. When she looked at her, she still saw the bubbly toddler who had insisted on boarding the El Al flight from New Jersey to Tel Aviv on her own two feet. She had adjusted well to their new lives in the Holy Land. A week ago, the medical school of the Hebrew University had accepted her application, and she would follow in her mommy's footsteps.

She yawned and listened to the chatter of morning birds.

She had met her for coffee last night at Café Aroma on Jaffa Road—their last heart-to-heart before the big day. Ester had shared her hopes and dreams for the new chapter in her life. Her eyes grew large when she talked of her betrothed, Lior, a quiet, kind-hearted Israeli. She had chosen well. Dr. Sandler's heart warmed to see her so happy.

Her recollection darkened. A disturbance had interrupted their get-together. What was it? Oh, yes. The Arab youth at the door of the coffee shop.

Dr. Sandler treated Arab patients every day at the Emergency Unit of the Hadassah Medical Center in Ein Kerem. Over the years, she had picked up enough Arabic phrases to manage a basic conversation and help her patients feel at ease.

The Arab boy at Café Aroma was definitely not at ease. His forehead sweaty, his eyes glazed over, and the straps of a blue backpack tight over his shoulders, he struggled with the uniformed guard. She had thought to get up and intervene when…

Oh, no. No, no, no!

She opened her eyes.

Clear azure skies. She lay supine on a gravelly bed.

She clambered to her feet. A small patchy field of dirt. A low wall of rough-hewn stones. *Where am I? And where are my clothes?*

A savage migraine pounded at the back of her eyeballs. She covered her nakedness with her arms. She stumbled forward over stones and pebbles.

She had to get to the hospital. Ambulances were on their way. She needed to oversee triage and direct the interns. She had sat with Ester right at the door. She might be in one of those ambulances, or even…

She froze. Leafy trees whispered in the morning breeze. The rounded ends of Jewish tombstones poked over the wall. She panted. Her heart raced. Tears burned down her cheeks. *My Ester.* There would be no wedding today. Or ever.

The urgency of the hospital faded. Her hand moved to her head by force of habit but found no head covering. A road of black asphalt passed nearby. *Is this real?*

She staggered forward. A table stood at the side of the road, surreal and out of place, like a painting by Magritte. A white tablecloth flapped in the breeze. A gray-haired man in a tweed suit slouched on a chair. The doctor approached with as much dignity as possible under the circumstances.

"Ester," she cried. "Where is Ester?"

The man yawned. "My name is Boris," he said in Hebrew with a heavy Russian accent. He handed her a square of fabric that unfolded into a gauzy white cloak like a disposable hospital gown. Dr. Sandler turned aside and donned the gown. She accepted a disposable plastic cup of water and two white Acamol tablets.

"Thank you."

"Name?"

Dr. Sandler told him. The man filled out a form.

"Where is my daughter?"

The man said nothing.

As an observant Jewess, she believed in life after death, but in a vague and general way. Bright light. Long tunnel. A welcoming committee of dear departed souls. Pearly gates. She had never imagined the afterlife to be so, well, like life, complete with Russian bureaucrats and ballpoint pens.

"Sign here." The Russian pushed the sheet of paper toward her and held out the pen.

"What is this?"

"For your food and shelter."

Food and shelter. That didn't seem right, but she was in no position to argue.

She took hold of the pen and leaned over the table.

"No!" a distant voice yelled. A man ran toward her. "Don't sign that!"

Boris watched him without expression.

Running Man had dark hair, kind eyes, and an earnest smile. "Come with us. We'll help you, and you don't have to sign anything."

"Us?"

Running Man pointed down the road. "Around the corner. The others came out on the other side." *The others?* Hope quickened in her heart. He stuck out his hand. "I'm Moshe," he said. "Welcome to the Afterlife."

"You," Boris barked at him. "Stay out of this!"

Moshe ignored the Russian. He handed Dr. Sandler a thick white robe of soft cotton, the kind she had enjoyed at the Bellagio spa after a convention in Vegas.

Dr. Sandler chose the spa option and donned her new robe.

Moshe walked her down the road and a second table came into view, decked in blue and white, with Stars of David and matching helium balloons. A tall woman with short blond hair waved and smiled.

"I was in your shoes a month ago," Moshe said. "You probably have a lot of questions, and we'll answer them as best we can. But first, have some breakfast."

The tall blond gave her a warm smile and shook her hand, then handed her a pair of spa slippers and a paper cup of sweet mint tea.

Dr. Sandler cupped the tea in her hands and picked a *rugalah* from a platter of the chocolate pastries. Questions queued in her mind. She licked her fingers and dropped the empty cup in a small garbage bin.

"This afterlife," she asked Moshe, "will I like it?"

Moshe thought for a while. "I'm sure you will. In time. The main thing, they say, is not to be afraid." He brightened. "Irina will escort you to your ride." He pointed to a minibus taxi that idled further down the road. The driver, a balding Yemenite, waved.

Dr. Sandler turned to Moshe. She opened her mouth to ask her question but froze, afraid of the answer she might receive. Moshe seemed to have read her thoughts.

"The others boarded earlier," he said. "They'll be happy to meet you. One of them in particular." He smiled and added, "She'll be very happy indeed."

CHAPTER 68

Moshe joined in the chorus of voices. "Hi, Avner."

Galit sat beside him in the circle of a dozen chairs. He rested his hand on her knee and then retracted it. He had returned home two weeks ago, but he still slept on the couch downstairs. Galit was still adjusting to his presence. He shouldn't push his luck. Talya, on the other hand, had showered him with hugs and requests for bedtime stories, although that was probably thanks to his ready supply of her favorite candy: Elite strawberry-flavored toffee in a pink wrapper.

Avner, a gaunt young man in a black T-shirt, cleared his throat and told his story.

Night had fallen on Jaffa Street outside the window. The office space of Karlin & Son had not seen this much activity in months. At its current rate of growth, the Dry Bones Society would need to expand into the neighboring offices. Expansion required money, and that depended on tonight.

So far that evening, they had met an accountant (suicide), a Romanian construction worker (fall from scaffolding), and a doctor and her grown daughter.

Shmuel folded his arms over his chest and listened. He had still refused to discuss his own death, and it seemed he never would.

Across the circle, Rabbi Yosef smiled and nodded, encouraging the stranger who had joined their ranks.

The meeting concluded with the singing of "*HaTikva*"—the national anthem—and Rabbi Nachman's "Narrow Bridge," followed by mingling at the refreshments tables. Savta Sarah wore her apron and pushed stuffed cabbage and meatballs on her grateful clientele.

Rabbi Yosef remained in his seat. His shoulders slumped and a haze of sadness hung over him. Moshe knew what tonight meant for him. His life would never be the same.

"One moment," Moshe told Galit. He was walking over to the rabbi when Samira called for their attention. "Everyone!" she said from the edge of a cubicle. "It's starting!"

The legs of a dozen plastic chairs squeaked and Moshe retook his seat beside Galit. Irina aimed a remote at the large mounted television and switched to Channel Ten.

The stony hillside of Jerusalem panned across the screen. The camera cut to the cemetery in East Jerusalem. A man walked among the rows of tombstones. He wore a blue polo shirt.

"One summer's morning," said the voice of Eran, Shmuel's reporter friend, "Rami Alon awoke in the Mount of Olives Cemetery, naked and alone. He found his way home and made a shocking discovery: he had died three years earlier in a car crash."

On screen, Rami knocked on the door of a house and fell into the embrace of his beautiful wife and two teenage children. A close-up showed the happy family on a living room couch.

"We thought we had lost Rami forever," said the beautiful wife, holding his hand. "But God gave us a second chance."

The narrator continued. "Others have received a second chance as well, but not all were as fortunate as Rami."

The camera showed Moshe walking down Shimshon Street. The offices of Karlin & Son erupted in cheers and applause, and a smile stole onto Moshe's face. He had never appeared on television before.

"Moshe Karlin awoke two years after a fatal heart attack

and found himself on the street."

Galit gave him an apologetic pout. He had asked Eran to tone down the story for the sake of his wife and the reporter had kept his word.

The television framed Moshe as he sat at his desk. "My daughter didn't recognize me," he told the camera. "I had lost everything I held dear. I needed help."

"One man," the reporter continued, "came to Moshe's aid: Yosef Lev, the rabbi of Moshe's neighborhood synagogue." Rabbi Yosef filled the screen with his dreamy smile. More cheers from the group.

"We are witnessing the fulfillment of biblical prophecies," said the rabbi. "The Resurrection is one stage of the Final Redemption."

The real-world Rabbi Yosef watched the screen but did not smile. This was it. He had sided—on national television—with the dreaded demons of the Other Side.

"How does the Resurrection process work?" Eran the reporter asked.

"It is a great miracle," the smiling rabbi said. "Our ancient writings talk of the Dew of Resurrection, which recreates the physical body from the Luz, a small, indestructible bone in the spine."

The camera shifted to the tiered campus of the Hebrew University on Mount Scopus. "Others," the narrator said, "have provided less miraculous explanations. We spoke with Professor Yakov Malkovich of the Hebrew University."

A bespectacled man with tufts of white cotton candy hair sat behind a large desk. Certificates and awards graced the walls behind him. He was not a happy old man.

"Nonsense," he said. "Utter garbage. People do not spontaneously regenerate."

"Then how do you explain the people who have returned from the grave?"

The professor shrugged. "An elaborate hoax."

Eran the reporter appeared on the screen. He walked between rows of gravestones. "Ezekiel's Resurrection or a clever prank? One thing is for sure: the number of the self-proclaimed resurrected has grown. They come from all segments of Israeli society, and they claim to share a peculiar physical irregularity." He patted his paunch. "No belly button. Some of them have formed a non-profit to provide social and economic aid to their fellow new arrivals."

Moshe appeared again, sitting at his desk. "Rejection by family and friends. Exploitation. Bureaucratic difficulties. That is why we started the Dry Bones Society."

The shot cut to a circle of men and women sitting on plastic chairs in the office space where Moshe now sat. A balding man stood and spoke from the heart while the others listened.

Moshe's voice continued in the background. "We depend entirely on donations. If you're resurrected and have the means, or if you'd just like to help, please call our toll-free number." Then Moshe's face filled the screen. "Who knows?" he said, his expression earnest. "Your dear departed loved ones might need our help right now."

Moshe stood up in the middle of the room and clapped his hands together. "That's our cue, friends. Battle stations!"

As the toll-free number displayed on the screen, men and women—Jews and Arabs, established Israelis and new immigrants—ran to cubicles and donned headsets. Irina switched the television to the display Moshe had set up ahead of time.

The counter of incoming calls remained a large, round zero on the screen.

Moshe rested his arm on the cubicle divider. He heard the sound of his own breathing. He felt every pair of eyes on him. The office lease ended in two weeks. Their fledgling organization had burned through the little cash they had scrabbled together. The Dry Bones Society needed an urgent infusion of money. Every person in the room knew that.

A telephone rang. The incoming call counter rose by one. Shmuel raised his hand above the cubicle wall. "I got it." He clicked a button on his terminal. "Dry Bones Society," he said, as Moshe had scripted. "Shmuel speaking. How can I help you?"

Moshe heard the sound of his own heart beating. The entire room soaked up every word and inflection.

"Yes. Yes? Thank you. Thank you very much!" He put his hand over the microphone. "A hundred shekels!" A cheer and a short burst of applause. "Let me take your credit card details."

A hundred shekels. Not much but a start.

The Total Sales counter jumped from zero to one hundred. A sober silence descended on the waiting army of phone reps.

Then the phone bell rang again. And again. The incoming call counter moved from one to two to seven.

Irina punched the air. "One thousand shekels!" she cried. No cheers this time. The others were too busy fielding calls with donors.

Total Sales now covered three months' rent and change. Reporters called in, picking up the story and verifying facts. A few cynics and pranksters too.

From the corner of his eye, he saw Rabbi Yosef head for the door, his head low. "I'll call you back," Moshe told a correspondent from Israel Today. He caught the rabbi in the quiet of the corridor.

"Rabbi Yosef." The rabbi turned and managed a brief smile. "Thank you. For everything."

He left the details unspoken. The rabbi would lose his job, for sure. Moshe had realized this too late. He had overheard the rabbi talking on the phone with the rabbanit. A contingent of rabbis had visited the Lev household on Shimshon Street last week to deliver the ultimatum.

"And," Moshe continued, "I'm glad to offer you our first full-time position."

The rabbi lifted his head. "Full-time?"

"Or as full-time as you'd like. Our members need guidance and counseling. Who better to help them than you?"

The rabbi's lips parted. His back straightened, and the sparkle returned to his eyes. "I... I don't know what to say."

"Say yes. And, just between you and me, you're the only candidate. You're the only non-founder with a valid identity card."

The rabbi laughed in earnest for the first time in days.

He shook Moshe's hand and continued down the corridor, a new spring in his step.

Moshe studied the door of frosted glass. Someone had taped a white page with the words "Dry Bones Society" over "Karlin & Son."

"There you are!" Galit peered around the door. She followed his line of sight. "They'd be proud of you," she said. "Very proud."

Moshe inflated his lungs. Mending broken lives probably trumped taxi dispatch on the cosmic scales of merit. "I think so too."

"Working late tonight?" There was no hint of reproach in her voice.

Moshe visualized his checklist. He had grand plans for the Dry Bones Society: fundraising, lobbying, expansion, medical drives, and education. He didn't know where to begin.

"Nope," he said. "Strictly office hours from now on. Besides, one late night won't scratch the surface. We're only getting started."

"All right then," she said, with a mischievous glint in her eye. She took his arm in hers and led him to the elevator. "Let's go home."

ALSO BY DAN SOFER

An Accidental Messiah
The Dry Bones Society, Book II

A Premature Apocalypse
The Dry Bones Society, Book III

A Love and Beyond
Gold Medal Winner
(Religious Fiction)
American Book Fest 2016 Awards

ABOUT THE AUTHOR

DAN SOFER writes tales of romantic misadventure and magical realism, many of which take place in Jerusalem. His multi-layered stories mix emotion and action, humor and pathos, myth and legend—entertainment for the heart and soul. Dan lives in Israel with his family.

Visit **dansofer.com/list-dbs1** for a free story and updates on new releases.

Made in the USA
Monee, IL
01 July 2020